THE DARK WITCH CHRONICLES

CHRONICLES

BOOK ONE

THE DARK WITCH CHRONICLES

BOOK ONE

The Curse of the Cymmerien Dragon

AARNA N. WILLEM

PARTRIDGE

A Penguin Random House Company

To order additional copies of this book, contact
Partridge India
000 800 10062 62
orders.india@partridgepublishing.com

www.partridgepublishing.com/india

Contents

ACKNOWLEDGEMENTS

First and foremost, I convey my thanks to the Almighty for His blessing. I am grateful to my father for being the first person to have had faith in this book. This dream wouldn't have been a reality if not for him. Mom, for the endless support that she's given with my writing and always appreciated all kinds of things that I wrote, no matter how silly they were. The rest of my family, for assuring me that I was taking a good step by publishing this book.

Aisha, for having faith in me and this story since the start, and being one of the first readers. Vishnu, another initial reader whose support I'd like to acknowledge. My other friends, who encouraged me all along.

My editor, Komal Shah, for bearing with my idiosyncrasies associated with this story and coming up with all sorts of ideas that proved to be really helpful. She might as well be a co-writer.

Lastly, Partridge India for turning my dream into this beautiful book.

DEDICATED TO

Dad, for the unfailing faith you have in me.

∞ ∞ ∞ ∞

PART I

∞ ∞ ∞ ∞

CHAPTER ONE

∞∞∞∞∞

BLOODLUST

∞∞∞∞∞

Year 1801

Verain.

*A*n old decadent, now dilapidated castle stands in the fore. *The ramparts of this old decadent castle make way for innumerable hutments, which line an already dusty and rocky road. All the houses are a dusty beige with large and intricate lattice windows. It seems as though the dust from the streets is what makes the houses. Back in the distance, a draught of wind draws up a moody sandstorm. Women hide their faces in their flowing gowns as the sand threatens to enter their eyes and nostrils and their feet move faster in an attempt to enter into the safety of their little homes. A few old men sit at their doors chewing on* Hul Gil[1] *and shouting across the street to talk to one another. A few stray children run amok as the* peganos[2] *with beady eyes makes his*

---

1   Hul Gil – *old term for opium leaves*
2   Peganos - *Local word for ice-cream vendor*

way around the impossibly narrow streets screaming hoarsely "ice sticks! Ice sticks! Blue, yellow, red, pink, take your pick". An angry mother slams the window of the hut he is standing in front of in order to shun the peganos. *Unperturbed, he continues to scream and walks away along the street dragging his feet, unsettling the settled sand as he pulls his cart along.*

At the end of the same street, in a nondescript corner, two gaunt boys sit snickering, heads together as though plotting something. The wind makes the window above them creak open and they duck and saunter into the next street. A muffled voice is heard from the window that is now ajar.

"Mother! Have you seen Arion?" Amara shouted as she searched the entire house, her gown scrunched up messily in her hands so she would not trip due to the wetness.

Her brother, Arion, had once again poured a bucket full of water on her while she was stitching. The scarf that she had been working on was now soaking wet and she feared her mother's reaction. She wanted to find Arion so she could reprimand him but as usual, the boy had disappeared.

"Why are you drenched?" her mother, Maia – who had just entered the room – asked furiously as she looked at Amara who was drenched from head to toe.

Wonderful, *thought Amara.*

"Arion poured water over me," she said, pushing a stubborn wet strand of hair away from her cheek.

"But he's been out with Leopold since this morning!" Maia snapped, annoyed at how clumsy her daughter was.

"I'm not lying, mother. I was in the lawn, stitching the scarf as you had asked me to and…and he poured water on top of me from the window of my room," Amara replied in protest.

"I would have heard him if he were back from Leopold's. You know what a ruckus he creates upon entering the house," Maia said.

"But, mother! Do you think I fancy getting drenched on purpose?" Amara retorted, now livid.

"You do remember how many times I have asked you to behave like a graceful woman. You are far too clumsy..." Maia said resignedly.

Amara could not believe how dense her mother was behaving. She was tired of hearing that she should behave like a graceful girl; carry herself off better and this and that. But hard as she tried, nobody seemed to be impressed. Is it my fault that I cannot walk elegantly? She would wonder.

Amara opened her mouth to reply to her mother when she heard someone sniggering behind her. Arion and Leo were standing in the corner, trying to hide their laughter but failing miserably to do so. Amara flushed upon spotting Leo as she was obviously not in a state she would want to be seen, especially by him. Her face flamed more in anger when her eyes fell on Arion, whom she had vowed to give a dressing-down to when their mother was not around. She huffed in annoyance and deciding to deal with her brother later, stomped away to get cleaned up.

Maia shook her head at her son who seemed to find the situation hysterical while Leo stood there straightening his shirt. He had stopped laughing when he saw that Maia was present and walked over to her.

"Good evening, m'Lady," he said, bowing slightly.

"Good evening, Leopold. Would you like some tea? I'll have Amara make some," she said as she smiled benignly at him and began to call Amara when Leo stopped her.

"No, I've just had early supper with Arion, but thank you for the offer. I wonder, would it be okay if I took Amara out for a walk?" He asked as Arion sauntered off, cackling to himself.

"Of course! I'll just-"

"I am not going anywhere with you," said Amara as she walked down the stairs, bone dry and her thick black hair down on her shoulder in a loose braid. Leo looked up at her and she shifted her eyes away from him in anger. He had laughed at her because of Arion, and that annoyed her.

"Amara! You will not be so rude to your betrothed," Maia said, glaring at Amara who pursed her lips and began walking towards the kitchen. Maia was about to shoot another remark when Leo shook his head and gestured to her to stay quiet. He smiled to himself and began following Amara.

"Come now, don't be angry," he said as sweetly as possible and Amara tried her hardest to ignore him. She was about to grab something to eat when Leo caught her arm and she swiftly turned to face him with her eyes wide.

"Mother is right outside!" She hissed and he chuckled before letting go of her arm.

"Let's go and take a walk. Come," he pleaded with a smile that made Amara melt. She resisted the urge to grin back at him and rolled her eyes.

"Alright," she whispered, looking down and he turned around to leave. She followed him and looked for her mother to inform her that she was leaving with Leo. She knew mother would not mind.

Maia adored Leo more than anyone else. He was the son of one of Maia's close friends, Marzya. The moment Leo had met Maia, she had wanted to get Amara married to him. Amara had not protested either. Leo was really sweet and handsome, which had Amara smitten instantly. She was only seventeen after all. She was young and all of her friends were to be married. Amara felt rather lonely not having anyone for her. But when Leo had come along, all her worries had gone. She was happy, very happy.

As the both of them left the house after bidding Maia goodbye, Leo escorted her towards a rocky and immensely barren enclosure nearby. He then held her hand as they entered a secluded area. It was quite peaceful where they were. Amara's face flamed at the contact.

"It's only a few weeks to our marriage. Father said that we shouldn't be meeting until then," said Amara as they took steps ahead together.

"Your mother seemed quite happy to let us go. I think it's alright," he replied with a smile.

~ ~ ~

It was around eight in the evening when Leo walked her back home. Amara turned to him at the door and gave a smile.

"Will I see you soon?" he asked her.

"Maybe if mother allows me to," she replied shyly.

"Come meet me in the forest of Majoricka, a week later. I have something to show you," he said to her and she nodded in response.

"I'll have to speak to father," she said.

"I shall ask his permission. Don't you worry," he responded and took off. Amara watched him walk away and then turned to go into the house. She was excited for the day that she would get married to Leo. Amara imagined a small house with him, where she would live happily and they would have a beautiful family. Grinning at the thought, Amara entered the house.

* * *

The night was dark; rain splattered on her head as it fell hard on the ground. . . silvery beams of the moonlight lighted her path as she treaded purposefully along a winding path. The moist grass under her feet felt like soft cotton caressing her bare ankles gently and the wintry sensation gave her a sense of calmness. Her black gown cascaded around her ankles making a swishing sound as she walked. As the moonlight shone upon her, her ivory skin stood out in the blackness, with her defined jaw, and deep-set eyes that were a cold black, threatening, frightening and dark; she had a beautiful appearance that was terrorizing and serene at the same time. The wind running through her long tresses: the black hair that fell so elegantly around her shoulders, reaching right up to her narrow waist. Her hands; soft, yet strong enough to be able to grip a throat tight. She paused slightly to breathe in the rustic smells of the rainfed earth, and rested her slender figure onto a large oak tree.

She stood tall, the other hand holding a silver dagger, that which had an eagle engraved intricately on its handle fell on top of the grass, making a soft sound as it touched the surface next to her feet. She pushed the fabric of her gown aside – one that was coming in the way of her hand – and stepped away from the tree she was resting herself on. Her face – that was concealed by the darkness of the night – appearing as she leaned close to the dead body that lay on the ground a few feet away. She crouched next to the corpse that lay there, whose throat was slit effortlessly. Blood trickled out of the slit throat and the dead woman's eyes, now glassy and lifeless, lay wide open. With a snap of her fingers, the body elevated in mid-air as she stood up picking the dagger that she had dropped on the ground. Pushing her feet into the brown, knee-high boots, she strode ahead in the direction of her destination as the levitated body followed her.

A few moments later, she reached the woods that were surrounding the castle. The woods dry, as though rain never had come there at all. As she entered, passing the big trees and imposing shrubs that covered the area the intricately lattice carved iron gates that stood before her, opened noiselessly to allow her inside. In front of her was a graveyard, that covered the ground as one had to walk past the graves to reach the doors of the castle. Sculpted goblins and fairies lined the narrow path that led to castle. She walked further and the gates shut behind her. One of the sculpted goblins bent in welcome. Ravens flew off the graves, the wind swished past the dusty floors, leaves scrunched below her feet as she walked ahead and arrived at a large imposing pair of double wooden doors with intricate designs of the elements. They heaved open to let her in. Behind the graveyard, the castle was surrounded with trees, making it look like there was nothing there but dense woods behind it. To a human, they would look like the deadliest woods ever.

In the land of Acanthus, humans were rarely found. But the ones who dared to enter were terrified by the appearance of the daunting mountains that traversed the land, and the violent blue-green sea that bordered Acanthus was terrifying as well. Surrounded by the great mountains of *Carvelli* and *Lunaire*, Acanthus was a beautiful land. Woods protected the covens of the greatest Conjurers that ruled Acanthus; caves of great sorcerers and lakes of valiant waters enhanced the beauty of the land. Ruled by the great King Orcus, descendant of the magnificent kings that had ruled before, the land was protected by guards and goblins that made sure no human or enemy entered without permission. Two covens resided here, surviving on the unspoken alliance of the coven rulers. An invisible and intangible uneasiness lingered around.

As custom followed, the dead body that she was carrying had now reached into the largest chamber of the castle where everyone sat along with the ruler of their coven. She entered the great hall and the body followed closely behind. The great hall was a circular chamber with a few flaming torches resting on the pillars. Chairs circled around the sides, covering the large chamber and leaving space in the middle. They created a passage from the door to the throne situated at the far end of the hall, in the centre, with a figure upon it.

Lord Lucifer sat with his slender fingers resting on the arms of the throne, his shoulders stiff and the towering body that he had, propelled unyieldingly on his seat. He wore a black robe, a blood red cloak above it that rested on his shoulders and covered his whole being. His silver hair, illuminated by the moonlight, reached up to his shoulders. His green eyes and long beard stood out in his features. His hands that sat on the armrests, appeared strong and the veins that stood out from his skin distinctly manifested his warrior skills. The Conjurers of Acanthus were aware of how many wars Lord Lucifer had been the victor of and how his merciless killings had rendered them all speechless. His power that spread around the land was well known and the coven that he had created, consisted of the strongest Conjurers. Lucifer was the most intimidating Lord one could have ever come across. His presence gave off a stilling aura, ultimately restoring discipline wherever he went.

"Amara."

His voice was deep and husky, and when he spoke, eyes drowsily surveying the surroundings, it was almost to himself, as though he was speaking to someone sitting right next to him. Yet, she heard him and so did the others. Out of all his apprentices, Lord Lucifer trusted her the most. The coven consisted of almost thirty other Conjurers that Lord Lucifer had gathered in the two hundred years of his existence. All his apprentices had proved their worth of belonging in his coven but Amara was the most loyal. She was faithful and had the greatest amount of respect and admiration for him. He was the power that she worshipped and gave the utmost importance to.

She walked towards the throne, snapping her fingers to let the body on to the floor. The body gently dropped down and Amara knelt before her Lord with her head facing downwards, eyes fixed on the dead body beside her. She looked away, her gaze now resting on nothing in particular as she began to talk to Lord Lucifer.

"My Lord," she replied, bowing her head.

"Is this her?" He asked, lazily gesturing to the body that lay lifeless on the floor.

"Yes." She nodded.

"Ambrosius," he drawled and another one of them stood up from his seat.

"My Lord?" said Ambrosius, eyes cast on the floor, head tilting slightly.

"You know what to do."

Ambrosius nodded once before looking at the body and it rose in the air, following him out of the chamber through another door in a corner. Amara stood up and Lord Lucifer's gaze lifted itself from the floor to look at her; it softened with the assurance that she had done the job well. Amara never defied him, and he knew that. She kept her stature at the highest point, not letting her Lord down and completing all the tasks better than he expected. The body that she had just slain was of another witch-hunter that had come to attack her. To kill threats like those was a job given to her most of the time.

Silence continued to reign and when their Lord was addressing Amara, it was their duty not to speak since they were the two most powerful people in Acanthus. Amara was known for being the most brilliant witch that they had all ever come across. Her beauty, power and incredible strength was well known and no one ever tried to cross her. For as brilliant as she was, there was a danger that lurked around whenever she was present. They all respected her most after the Lord.

As she stood up to leave the great hall, she began to say something to Lord Lucifer when a loud, shattering scream interrupted her. It was so painful that it pierced the ears of everyone around. Amara snapped her head in the direction the sound came from, and so did everyone else. Lord Lucifer, however, did not have to look there to know what was happening. It was something he would see every few years. A new apprentice of his coven was in pain.

"My Lord?" Amara turned, looking at him questioningly.

"Go. You know what has to be done," he said to her and she nodded before making her way to the girl who was screaming in a corner, with her knees pulled into her chest as tears ran down her face.

Had she witnessed this a hundred years ago, Amara would have felt immense displeasure, but now, it did not matter at all. She was used to watching people in pain. The torture that she inflicted on them was worse than what she was seeing right now. Every new witch had that experience upon entering *this* world. It was more of a mental trauma that gave them such pain. The sudden grave surroundings induced terror in them. Akin to that, their own mind caused them the physical pain. To a witch who had come from the human world without any knowledge, it was new and troublesome.

Amara presumed that the screaming girl had probably just left the human world. With a grasp on her hand, Amara pulled the girl to her feet and she showed no resistance at all. She wanted to leave this place, and if a beautiful lady who looked like she had just come out of a beauty pageant of evil people was helping her, she would be all for it.

"What is your name?" Amara said when they reached a room lit with a single torch of fire.

There was a round table in the middle; a dead dove lay on top of it with blood surrounding its wings. The girl cringed at the sight and looked away. She found a man seated on the floor with his head hung low and a hood covering his face. For a moment, she thought that it was the man that she had seen outside in the huge chamber - the one that everyone called, 'my Lord'. Then she realized that this man looked rather different from the way he was sitting on the floor. She wondered how someone could sit on that cold surface, which, whenever she stepped on, made chills run down her spine. It was cold, frightening cold. She turned to look at the woman who spoke, her voice so soft and elegant; she felt like smiling, but it was also cold and intimidating, which confused her.

"Iris," she answered.

"Do you know what you're here for, Iris?" Amara asked.

"No. Do you mind telling me who you are?"

"My name is Amara," she replied, stroking the dead dove on the table. Iris scrunched up her face in disgust. This place was the most disturbing one she had ever seen.

"What are you?" Iris asked.

The question slipped out of her involuntarily. She immediately wanted to take it back even though she was curious to know what these people were capable of and why the place looked like it had all kinds of dead around.

"Didn't you notice? I'm a witch," said Amara, turning to look at her.

And a second later, Iris was screaming again as pain shot up from her toes right up to her head, and she dropped onto the floor with her eyes rolling upwards.

CHAPTER TWO

∞∞∞∞∞

THE DARK WITCH

∞∞∞∞∞

"*F*ather! How did you do that?" Amara watched in amazement as her father, Azar, stared at the earth for a long moment and there appeared a tiny crack. Azar always did unusual things that took Amara by surprise. She had never seen anybody else do that. Not her mother, not Arion, not Leo. But Amara loved watching those graceful movements of Azar's slender fingers and how he produced Fire out of thin air. She had talked to her mother about it, but she always seemed to avoid the topic. Amara had then mentioned it to Leo once, who had seemed extremely interested and had also asked her to help him see what her father did, someday.

Azar was never up for it. He always denied it whenever Amara mentioned his unusual skills in front of Leo. Azar had also told her not to talk about it in front of anybody. But she could not resist gushing about how wonderful those skills were. She wanted to be like her father. She wanted to learn those things. Azar had told her that she was too young to learn all of that. It would always make her sad but she would make up for it by watching her father.

"Come and see," said Azar and Amara grinned before skipping over to him. They were out in the lawn. It was early morning and the gentle sunrays bathed the lawns in a luscious golden light that ensured an iridescent glow around the patio. Nobody was awake. Amara was told by her mother to wake up at sunrise because she was about to be married and needed to learn to wake up early. She did not have anything against that idea because her father would show her those magical things in the morning. He would leave for work then and she would see him only at dinner.

Amara walked over to her father. "Look closely. You'll see water," he said to her and once again, stared at the ground. Sure enough, a tiny jet of water sprung from the tiny crack and retreated. Amara fell to the ground and watched with a wide grin on her face. It always amazed her how easily her father could do such things. It was astonishing.

Azar looked down at his daughter and smiled in contentment. She was so bright, so interested in his abilities that it gave him an assurance that she would be just as good someday. His daughter had inherited the boon of being a witch. But she was young and joyful, and did not need to be acquainted in the darkness for now. He knew that she was going to become a brilliant witch, but that would come at a cost. He was aware of everything that was going to happen in her future. Hard as he tried to avoid her being with Leo, he knew that the Gods had planned this for his daughter. It was her fate and nothing could change that. To keep her aloof from what destiny had in store would be devastating for the world of Conjurers. She had to enter that world, and she had to enter it after facing some things that would scar her permanently. He hoped that it would not be too painful for her to endure. But the truth was something entirely different.

"Can you bring the Fire again?" she asked and Azar blinked.

Amara loved watching the Fire come and go out of nowhere. It was the most intriguing part of her father's magical skills. The others interested her, but Fire was something she loved to see. It was beautiful to her. Azar clicked his fingers and a little flame appeared. Amara squealed in delight like a little girl.

"I wish I could do that," she mumbled and a sad expression took over her features.

Azar placed a hand on her head and patted it lightly before adding, "Someday, you will." She smiled again.

"Really?" she beamed. Azar nodded in response and the flame that he had produced, vanished just as it had appeared. Amara blinked and wondered when she would be able to do something of that sort.

* * *

Visions flooded through her mind as she lay on the ground, motionless. Her eyes were dark, dried tears stuck to her skin. A normal person would have attempted to help her up but Iris knew this place was far from normal. It was everything she wanted to avoid. Moments ago, she had started screaming in agony and then realization struck her like a bolt of lightning. She had seen that place, she had been there, dreams of that place had haunted her nights since the day that she opened her eyes. Her mind filled with numerous visions of how her parents had thought she was silly to think that she had nightmares that made her want to scream in pain. However, she knew it was far from silly. It did not seem normal. Others did not have such dreams. They never saw a room full of people dressed in black robes with hoods covering their faces, and killings happening inside that same room.

It was illusory. She wanted to stop those things from happening inside her head but she could barely wrap her mind around it all. Every day she saw a new vision. Sometimes it was of a woman killing a bird, other times it would be a man scraping a staff across a graveyard and sometimes she would see dark woods only to hear an alarming scream. *Frightened would be an understatement*, she thought. Whenever she saw those dreams, something changed inside her and she became more and more familiar with those visions. At times, she would see herself in those places, she would be killing someone and she would hear herself screaming. Every time the pain felt real, the surroundings seemed real. She thought that she was not dreaming at all. Nevertheless, this time she knew it was not a dream, because this time the pain was real, all too real. It was killing her on the inside and she could not bear it.

"Who am I?" She asked, her eyes fluttering up to Amara who stood there looking down at her impassively. Iris wondered whether or not she had any feelings at all. She seemed so inhuman, so different yet familiar. *This is not going to be easy*, Iris thought.

Amara knelt down beside Iris; her eyes fixed upon the timid looking girl who had no idea what she was doing there. Amara was confused herself, because unlike other witches that were brought there, Iris did not know anything about herself. The others at least had an idea of who they were and what their job was. Iris was different, she seemed fragile, almost insubstantial, and for a moment, Amara flinched at the pain Iris was going through. She immediately pushed that feeling away. She was not supposed to feel anything. Her heart was void of emotions. It was blank.

"You're a witch."

Iris widened her eyes. *A witch*, she wondered. A day ago, she had been in her house, wondering about what food she was going to eat and suddenly a new reality dawned upon her. She thought that she was having the worst nightmare ever. Besides, *are witches not supposed to know their identity?* Iris thought and sat up, pushing her body off the ground and Amara settled herself with her back resting on a wall and her legs stretched in front of her. Iris wondered whether or not this witch had a working heart.

"And why am I here?" She asked again, questions flooding her mind.

"Because you're part of our coven and you will learn to do everything that we do. That is in short, witchcraft. Do you not know anything about yourself?" Amara asked, furrowing her eyebrows.

"I just found out that my parents are dead. I don't how. I haven't seen their bodies either, and then this huge man comes along and says something that makes me faint and when I wake up I'm inside this huge chamber filled with the most terrifying people I've ever seen, and a moment later I'm screaming in pain, which is caused how, I have no idea. The only thing running through my mind is utter confusion and you ask me if I know anything about myself? I'm not even sure if I'm alive right now! It feels weird. I mean, look at this place, there is a dead dove on the table and you touch it as though it is your long lost lover. There is blood all around. Out of nowhere someone tells me I'm a witch and I, for the life of me," she looked to her left, "don't know how this man sitting in that corner of the room is halfway in the air. Don't you people know there's something called gravity?"

Amara stared at Iris blankly. She was lost, clearly, and she had no clue what she was doing there. She tried to ignore the outburst and be completely calm in the situation. The Lord was surely trying to test her patience by sending a complete knob-head to her. She had dealt with new witches but this one was turning out to be a clueless one.

Amara hated clueless people. Letting out a sigh, she shifted her eyes back to the dead dove that lay on the table for the ritual that was supposed to be performed later that night. Iris surely had no clue what that had to do with her being a witch. She was demanding answers and Amara was the worst person one could ever go to demanding answers from.

"Okay, Iris, you don't know anything about yourself and there is no way I'm going to be aware of who you are. So if you want answers, you talk to him," Amara said, pointing to the hooded figure that was halfway in the air. Iris looked at the man.

"Who is that?"

He had not moved an inch since she had entered the chamber. The only time there was some difference was when she suddenly saw him in the air instead of on the floor.

Is he even alive? She wondered.

"Erasmus. When new witches need answers, they go to him. He knows everything," Amara replied.

"He doesn't seem like the one to talk." Iris frowned to herself.

"He will. Go to him." Amara stood up to leave the chamber.

She had other things to do and Iris did not seem so important now. Erasmus could handle her. He was not as intimidating as new witches thought he was. In fact, he was more cheerful than the others were. The new ones felt rather comfortable around him.

"This is a bad idea," Iris muttered under her breath while Amara walked out of the chamber.

Iris approached Erasmus. His face was invisible. Clearing her throat, she half-expected him to acknowledge her but he made no effort. He merely hovered in the air for a few moments before dropping back to the floor. His eyes were shut but Iris noticed his face that was now clear in the light of the torch between the darkness. He had a set jaw, light brown hair and a slight hint of stubble. His face was mature yet childishly handsome and he certainly did not give off the vibe as the others she had seen. His presence was somewhat calming and not as dangerous as she thought it would be. He wore similar kind of black-grey robes that the others did, yet looked quite different.

"Iris, isn't it?" He said with his eyes still shut. "You're sixteen years old, almost seventeen. Strawberry blonde hair, blue eyes, average height. Lived in the city of London since birth, adopted by James and Caroline George. Your mother was a well-known witch and your father a sorcerer, but they were killed in a battle against witch hunters. You were taken by humans. Brought back to the world of Conjurers when mature enough to reveal true identity. You've always had strange dreams about people of our kind, but unknown to it all. You like the colour red, don't you?" Erasmus opened his eyes when he finished.

Iris stared at him with her jaw dropped. She wondered how easily he predicted everything about her without even looking at her once. Everything he had said was true, even the part of her liking the colour red, but she did not understand the part about her parents. *My parents were part of this world?* She wondered.

"You don't know about your real parents at all, do you?" He asked, raising his eyebrows.

Iris noticed that his eyes were a bright hazel, almost complimenting his curly brown hair. She just shook her head in answer. The fact that she was adopted was something she already knew; but she was not aware about her parents having anything to do with witchcraft. The family that she lived with had told her that her parents were dead. How, when, where, they didn't know.

"Your parents died while fighting a battle against witch-hunters. Then you were taken by humans and they didn't tell you about your true identity. You are a witch by birth. The only difference is that you need to be familiar with this concept. Your abilities have been showing up from time to time during your life in the human world, haven't they?" He said, now standing up towering over Iris's tiny frame.

Iris thought about how she had sometimes managed to do things that she never thought she was capable of. There were many incidents where things happened all by themselves and she never even realized that she was the cause of it all. Her foster parents always told her there was something wrong with her and that she was imagining things, yet she never believed them. A part of her said that it was real. She felt it in every ounce of her.

"Don't worry, we'll make you aware of what you truly are capable of," he told her while she stood there, perplexed.

As Erasmus began telling her about the world that she had just entered, she listened to every word carefully, not wanting to miss anything. They stood next to the window overlooking the dark woods behind that covered a huge graveyard ahead. The trees stood tall, gleaming in the moonlight that shone upon them, the darkness nearly unseen yet relevant enough to the eyes. Iris spotted a figure walking deep into the woods until it vanished out of her sight.

* * *

Amara walked further in, passing the trees to reach the lake that was located in the deeper parts where she would sit all night and watch the lost souls wander around across the huge woods. She spent most of her time there when she did not have much to do. No one would go there at this time of the night. She spotted someone standing in the middle of her path and stopped walking.

Lord Lucifer turned around to face her, holding his gaze onto her for a long moment. Her eyes shifted to look down at the ground. With her head facing downwards, she waited for him to address her.

"Where is Iris?" He spoke, breaking the silence.

"She's with Erasmus, m'Lord."

"Does she know anything about herself?" Amara shook her head in response.

"I thought as much. You will help her out once she gets answers from Erasmus," said Lord Lucifer, taking a step forward.

"I understand, m'Lord. I will help her," Amara said, keeping her eyes fixed on the ground.

"She is capable of becoming a great witch and no one better than you can train her."

"I would be honoured, m'Lord," she replied, bending her head in agreement. A moment later, he was gone.

Letting out a sigh, Amara walked further into the woods and sat herself upon the branch of an old tree, gazing at the moonlight. She shut her eyes, inhaling a deep breath as the cold air created a peaceful atmosphere around. She liked being in the woods, it was calm. It was dead. The idea of a dead place always made her feel close to herself, it was comforting. There were whispers of the souls communicating to one another. The woods were a haven for the wandering souls that travelled around aimlessly. Amara had a silent connection to them. They never had a way of communicating, yet her presence made them feel serene.

Her mind wandered around like those souls with various thoughts running across her mind. She kept trying to find herself, but could not put a finger on the missing piece. Maybe that was why she understood what those lost souls felt like. She felt lost, stranded and aloof from everything else. There was a slight sense of loneliness that she tried to fill up by spending most of her time with the woods that had creatures like her lurking around in search of something they were not aware.

The visions she saw when her eyes were closed made her want to run away from the woods and stay in there at the same time.

There were so many questions that she needed the answers to and each time she tried, she met with nothing. At times when she would sit in the woods with her eyes closed, she would see herself walk a long abandoned road that probably had no end. Then her eyes would open suddenly, and she would stop herself from going back there. Even though she needed the answers, she was afraid of what might happen once she got them. The visions never stopped though, most nights she would have her past flashing in front of her closed eyes that refused to open even when she tried hard enough.

That night as she sat on the branch of the tree with her eyes shut, she restrained herself from getting those visions again. Yet they crept into her mind the way they always had, and she began to get lost inside the world of her past memories. They never left her, even though a hundred-and-twenty-years had already passed.

* * *

They were sitting outside in the balcony of Amara's room. She was trying to suppress her laughter as he cracked silly jokes. They spoke in hushed whispers so as not to wake the others. God only knew how her mother would react if she saw Leo there with her at midnight. He had come to meet Amara. He said that he missed her. Amara could only blush at that. Initially she had protested but then gave in as she saw that he had brought her a beautiful red rose. She held it in her hands as they talked.

"Has your father performed any of his magical tricks yet?" Leo suddenly asked and Amara looked at him with gleaming eyes. She loved talking about her father's abilities and Leo was the only one

that seemed interested. In fact, he seemed more interested than her. The moment that she had first mentioned it to him, he had asked her so many questions that she lost the will to answer them all. At times, he only seemed interested in the magical abilities her father possessed, instead of paying attention to her. But those complaints faded away in her mind as soon as she began talking about her father.

"He does them every morning! I would love it if you watched those with me. They are so beautiful!" She gushed, her mind going back to the incident.

"Really? What did he perform today?" He asked.

"He made a crack in the earth and water sprung out of it. It leaped out and went back in again. Father made that happen a few times before producing a little flame."

"A crack in the earth, you say?" He enquired with his eyebrows raised.

"Yes! It was brilliant."

"I have to leave now." He said abruptly. "Will I see you next week?" He asked eagerly.

"But father would-"

"I spoke to him," he cut her off. "He said yes."

"Really?" Amara asked, surprised. Azar never seemed to agree on having Leo and Amara meet weeks before their marriage was to take place. She wondered what made him agree.

"Yes. Don't forget," he told her before giving her a heart-warming smile and jumping down the balcony. Amara watched as he walked away, waving goodbye to her and she then turned to go back into her room.

She had a nightmare that night; of someone hurting her and she was crying in pain. It was unbearable and Amara felt as though it was real. Leo was the one hurting her and she could not begin to bear it. She woke up with a scream, her heart hammering inside her chest. The door of her room opened and Maia walked in worriedly before she saw Amara shivering in fright. Maia rushed towards her daughter and pulled her into an embrace. Amara clutched onto her mother and squeezed her eyes shut as her eyes went moist.

"It's alright, darling. I'm here," Maia whispered and stroked Amara's head.

Amara drifted off into a deep sleep in her mother's arms.

* * *

Something had her opening her eyes. Amara realized that she was about to fall off the branch that she was sitting on. Letting out a breath, she jumped down onto the ground softly. The visions of her past life refused to leave her mind even after a hundred years had gone by. Some or the other way, she would see parts of her past life that she wanted to bury somewhere deep. She was not sure when those thoughts were going to leave her.

Her feet carried her forward and she looked for the one being that could give her the peace she was looking for. She heard the sound, the calming voice that made her insides relax. Craning her neck she looked up to find her owl, Sceiron, seated elegantly on the highest branch, ruffling his feathers as he hooted gently, out of sight, yet prominent enough. She closed her eyes, lifting herself from the ground and rose up to the branch Sceiron was perched up on. He hooted in acceptance when she sat beside him. Amara gently grazed her fingers along Sceiron's head and he shifted closer to her side. For the longest time, she sat there with Sceiron, letting all her memories drift off once again, wishing they would never come back and haunt her.

* * *

"*What is father doing?*" *Arion whispered into his sister's ear as they sat in the kitchen, gazing outside in the sunlight. Azar was sat outside on the lawn with his eyes closed and breathing deep breaths.*

"*Meditating,*" *Amara answered blankly. She had seen her father do that so many times that it was not a surprise. It was early morning as usual and Arion had somehow decided to wake up. Amara wondered why.*

"*What-*" *Arion began to ask when Maia walked in.*

"*Be quiet, Arion. You don't speak when your father is meditating,*" *she said and Arion immediately shut up without asking what meditation was.*

Amara was busy stitching another scarf that her mother had given and a smile was across her lips. She was going to meet Leo in the forest of Majoricka today. She wondered what it was that he wanted to show her. Maybe it was going to be a boat-ride in the lake, maybe he would teach her how to climb a tree. She had always wanted to learn that. Or maybe they would again talk about those unusual things that her father did. That would be interesting as always.

"*Amara,*" *Maia called out.*

Amara's eyes were elsewhere. She paid no attention.

"*Amara,*" *Maia said again. Amara did not reply and was still busy grinning and stitching.*

"*Amara!*" *Maia hissed in a whisper so as not to disturb her husband.*

Amara looked up and her grin vanished at the furious expression on her mother's face. She gulped and took in a breath.

"*Yes, mother?*" *She asked, starry-eyed.*

"*Can't blame her. She's young and in love,*" *Maia mused and Amara frowned, for she could barely hear what her mother had said.*

"Go and call your father," Maia said and Amara glanced at Azar once before nodding at her mother and getting up.

"Why are you disturbing father if he is meditating? Mother said you should not be speaking," Arion said and Amara looked at Maia with her eyebrows raised. He had a point.

"Just go," Maia said and sighed. Amara shrugged and began walking outside to call her father.

When she reached outside, she heard her father chanting something. She took a few hasty steps forward so as not to disturb him and strained her ears to listen. He was chanting too softly.

"Lord of winds and nymphs of water, great kings of flames and of spirits, goddess of the earth. Give her the vigour to outlast the evil. Her strength lies in thee, thy power so valiant, give her the command to battle those that torment. Lords of winds and nymphs of water, great kings of flames and of spirits, goddess of the earth, my prayer in thy sacrament. Her doom so near, pray give her the power, give her the strength to triumph over the evil. . .my prayer in thy sacrament. . .gods of the realm. . . ."

Amara heard as her father chanted those words over and over again. She frowned and a perplexed expression covered her features. What was father doing? Why was he praying to some gods that she never knew existed? Why was he crying? Those questions kept running across her mind when Azar opened his eyes and looked at his daughter. He beckoned her to go towards him and she did so quietly.

"Come to call me for breakfast?" He asked and Amara nodded blankly.

"Go inside and wait for me," he said to her and placed a soft kiss on her forehead. Amara stood up and left with the questions flooding her mind. She made it a point to ask her father why he was chanting those words. She did so when he entered the kitchen.

"Just a prayer, sweet one," he said and Amara opened her mouth to question again when Maia shot her a look. Amara quieted down and they all ate breakfast in silence before it was time for Azar to leave. He gave Amara a short hug and kissed the top of her head again before walking out of the door. Amara wondered why her father was being so affectionate towards her today. He was affectionate – that was for sure – but not at this rate. Nevertheless, she liked it.

CHAPTER THREE

∞∞∞∞∞∞

BROKEN SOULS

∞∞∞∞∞∞

*T*he forest of Majoricka was beautiful. It had tiny bushes and large shady trees that were beginning to shed their yellowing leaves as autumn approached. She was walking through the woods, grinning as she thought about meeting him when her ears were struck with the most horrific scream she had ever heard. She stopped walking and cringed at the shrill sound. The ear-splitting cry was making her shiver. Whomever the sound came from was in a lot of pain and obviously needed help. She started running in the direction the scream came from. It was getting louder with each passing second. She neared a lake where a girl sat under a tree, pulling on her hair. Her dress in shambles, her body covered in deep scratches. It seemed like she was in excruciating pain. Amara approached the girl whose face was covered in scars along with her hands that were extremely white. Flinching at her appearance, she nearly took a step back. She wanted to help her, if there was any way she could.

The sun was starting to set in the horizon and it was becoming darker around. Tiny stars were appearing in the now inky blue sky. She had to get out of the woods soon, or there were chances of her getting lost. Besides, she was alone apart from the petrified girl in front of her. Looking around to see if she could get anyone to help her, she knelt down beside the girl. She had her eyes tightly shut as tears rolled down her cheeks; but Amara noticed that those were no tears. What flowed out of her eyes was blood. She hesitantly placed a shaking hand onto the girl's shoulder, who showed no reaction apart from screaming again. Amara bit her lower lip in nervousness. Why has no one else heard the cries of this girl?

"What happened to you?" Amara gathered her courage to ask.

Suddenly, the girl stopped screaming and opened her eyes to look at Amara. She flinched away upon looking at the eyes of the girl. They were covered in blood. It was frightening. The girl clutched Amara's wrist, the long nails piercing her skin.

"Help me," the girl croaked while Amara tried to get out of her grasp.

"I-how do I help you?" She asked timidly.

"They'll kill me. They will torture me," she whimpered.

"Who will kill you?"

The girl did not reply, but her eyes flickered away from Amara and she stared ahead blankly. Then she raised a hand and pointed her index finger to where she was looking. Amara turned her head around slowly to see where the girl was pointing. What she saw was not something she was expecting. It was Leo, her Leo, who stood there with a torch of fire in his hands and a fierce look on his face. He was staring straight at the girl as though he had no idea that Amara was present.

"Leo?" She whispered and he looked at her but his expression did not change.

A moment later, he was looking at the girl again. She had started to tremble where she was. Amara was getting scared of everything that was going on. She was confused as to how Leo had anything to do with the tortured girl next to her.

"You can't run away anymore," Leo snarled at the girl, taking a step forward.

Suddenly Amara saw a few other men joining Leo from behind some trees. The girl's grip on her hand loosened and Amara turned to look at her.

"Run," she whispered.

Amara stared at her dumbfounded. She had no clue what was going on.

"Run," the girl said again.

Before she could do anything, Leo was grabbing her arm from behind and pulling her up to her feet. Amara struggled in his grip trying to break free.

"Stop moving or I'll have to kill you as well," he scowled into her ear and she felt as though it was not her Leo that was talking, but someone entirely different from the man she had fallen in love with.

"What are you doing?" She shrieked when the men snatched the girl from the ground forcefully. Amara felt that they would rip her apart into two.

The men started chanting something she was unable to understand. Leo loosened his grip on her, pushing her away. He walked over to where the girl stood limp in control of those men. The chanting did not stop. It was making her furious. The noise, deafening, made her want to cover her ears and not listen to it anymore, ever. Amara started screaming. It was beginning to make her nerves rattle. She was sure that she heard the girl screaming as well and felt like someone was setting her on Fire, as though the flames were engulfing her into the pain that she was now starting to feel from her toes. Her whole body was shaking, while the men circled around with their weapons clanking together, making noises that made her feel like her head was about to explode. She screamed louder when she felt a hand grab her from the waist and pull her somewhere. Her eyes shut, and she let out another scream as the pain increased with the sound of the chants.

Then everything was silent. Amara opened her eyes to find the girl gone with a pile of ash on the ground in front of her. She looked at the men standing there who were strangers to her. She could not recognize Leo as well; he stood right in front of her smirking evilly as he held a torch in his hands. That was the only light in the otherwise darkened forest. She felt as though she was the girl whose ashes were before her. Those strange looking men surrounded her with deathly weapons; weapons to kill her in one go.

"Holy spirit, I pray to thee; to end the realm of witches, wizards, warlocks and sorcerers of great power. I pray to thee for solace, I pray to thee for destruction. I pray to thee for the demolition of all the rituals and the spells, of all the crafts of witches, the end to immortals and end to the carnal. I pray to thee for destruction of them all," *their chant began, first a whisper, but now gaining strength, volume and momentum.*

The burning sensation began once again, trickling up through her toes and slowly encompassing her whole body. She let out another scream as she stood there shivering with the pain that chant was inflicting upon her. Her eyes began to burn as the men circled around her and started to chant the same words again which infuriated her beyond measure. Her knuckles were turning white as she dug her nails into her palms.

A moment later, she was running, unaware of where she was going. Her feet scraped the ground wildly as she ran to save herself from those men who were making her so agitated that she wanted to kill them all. Her dress entangled in the fallen branches of the trees, making her escapes a real struggle. She could hear them following her and it would not be long until one of them caught hold of her and ended her life just like the girl before her.

* * *

Killing was easy. It was calming, peaceful even. Sometimes she felt more alive after a kill. She closed her eyes, inhaling the soothing scent of blood and Death that lingered around her, surrounding all her senses. Death was something she looked forward to, because every time she killed someone, a part of her died inside and that made her feel closer to herself; the pieces of her soul scattered inside her that she tried to assemble every single time she killed. The coldness of the blood, the colour of it, the free-falling rain, everything was her way of finding solace. She did not have to think at all. It came so naturally that her fingers danced as she killed. Bloodlust travelled inside every vein, every particle of her body and she rested herself in front of the dead, the three corpses that lay before her, covered in blood. *Training a new witch has never been better*, she thought.

Iris was standing there wide-eyed with her hands wilted at her sides. The effortlessness that Amara had while killing in front of her was beyond the limits of imagination. Never in her wildest dreams had she thought that she would be witnessing a killing, let alone three. She could only stare with a blank expression, unable to move an inch or utter a single word. She was surprised as to how she was breathing. There were three dead people in front of her and Amara had killed them so easily that Iris could not even comprehend what was happening. It had happened that fast. It seemed like someone or something had meddled with her brain so badly that she was afraid it would make her go insane. Not every day she saw three people killed mercilessly.

Moreover, there was no doubt that Amara was used to what she was doing. It seemed like second nature to her when she fearlessly stared at one man with blood-red eyes and he had started to tremble in her gaze. Then she had merely used one hand to slit the man's throat and he had collapsed in one go. She had raced after another man who began running as soon as his companion was killed but she caught him in a swift motion of flying halfway above the ground. With just one hold on his clothing, she had brought him down to the ground and plunged the dagger deep into his throat, sliding downward in one go and stopping at his ribcage. The third was a woman already on the verge of fainting as she started taking steps backwards, until she had her back pressed against the bark of a tree. Amara walked further in the woman's direction, carrying the blood-covered dagger in her hand, clenching her fingers around it tightly.

A moment later, Iris saw the dagger fly fast in the woman's direction and she almost thought it vanished somewhere, but when her eyes shot up, the dagger was right between the woman's forehead, her eyes wide open as she stood there limp, head stuck to the bark of the tree. If this was not traumatizing, Iris did not know what was. She fell to the ground, drenched in the rain that had begun a few moments ago. She stared blankly at Amara, who stood there with a content expression as she closed her eyes and pulled the dagger out of the woman's head and the body fell to the ground. Amara turned to look at Iris who sat there with her eyes stuck onto the dead bodies, her mind completely blank with no thoughts clouding inside. She did not know what to think or what to do. Amara crouched in front of Iris. She looked at her incomprehensibly.

"Is this really necessary?" Iris whimpered, tears blinding her vision and mingling with the rain.

"You're going to be killing those who go against our kind, Iris. You have no choice. This is your life now," Amara replied, standing up.

Iris followed her movements, gathering her courage to stand up after everything that she had just witnessed. She walked behind Amara who had started going back to the castle where they had come from. Two nights ago, Iris had no idea she would have to witness killings and get informed that she was supposed to do the same throughout her existence. *If only suicide was an option here*, she thought. However, hours before she came here to watch people die, she was given a potion that made sure she lived longer than humans ever did. They called it the *Elixir of Immortality*. Why she had agreed to take it was something she could not put a finger on. The moment Amara said that she had to drink it, Iris had asked no questions because the way that witch was looking at her, it made her feel as though she was not supposed to act smart or she would be subjected to torture again.

One thing she had experienced after joining this world was that whenever she felt like she did not belong here, she would be inflicted with torturous amounts of pain, whose origin she was unaware of. It was blinding, burning, and its sheer force broke every piece of her soul. It was killing, yet it kept her eyes open to the pain and awakened her senses. She shuddered every time the thought occurred.

"How was it?"

Iris snapped her head to find Erasmus standing in front of her with his eyes wide with excitement as he looked at her. She had not even realized that they had reached the castle and Amara had already gone, leaving her in Erasmus's chamber. He expectantly waited for her to reply but she could not – for the life of her – utter a word. Erasmus was not surprised. When he had first met this timid girl, she had been so scared of everything around her that he felt like consoling her and giving her a hug but everyone knew the rules: new witches were not supposed to be given any kind of affection.

It would be meddling with their strength to cope with things. Therefore, Erasmus had ignored his will to comfort her. When he had told her everything about the world of

Conjurers that she was completely unaware of, she had not reacted the way he expected her to. Normally a new witch would have been shocked and terrified of the harsh realities but Iris remained quiet and nodded every time he said anything to her. She was calm and even though it looked like she would explode, she never did. Her mind seemed like it was filled with thoughts that she could not collect and decipher.

Her reaction to the killings that she saw was something Erasmus was expecting. He knew that it would catch her off guard and make her feel extremely uncomfortable. When she stood there in front of him with no words coming out of her mouth, he made her sit on a chair and sat on the other side of the mahogany table resting between them. She had not taken her eyes off the floor all the time, not after he spoke to her, and not when he moved her to sit on the chair.

"Iris, what did you see?" He asked, even though he was perfectly aware of what Amara had shown to her.

She was the darkest, most brutal witch that Lord Lucifer had ever created and everyone was afraid of her. She spoke to no one but the Lord and only did what he asked of her. She liked to be alone. Nobody wanted to interfere with her loneliness. Erasmus had tried his hardest to figure her out but he could never do it. One moment he thought he knew her, the second she would become something else and he would be confused again, going back to start. There was no one as mysterious, as dark and potentially interesting as Amara was. Nevertheless, now, Iris was his job and he had to know what she had seen in the mountains.

"She killed three people," her murmur, almost inaudible, "Effortlessly!" her voice getting clearer, louder. "I honestly don't know what made her do that and how she can remain so calm after murdering someone," she said, a look of shock and disbelief had spread on her visage now.

"They were supposed to die," Erasmus added.

"Nobody deserves to die like that. It was pure, cold-blooded murder." She countered.

Iris kept her gaze locked to the floor blankly as though trying to understand what the reason for such brutal killings was. Erasmus began telling her the reason that made them commit those murders.

"This is the job we all have to do. We do not kill humans unless we have a reason. They are witch-hunters, a threat to our existence, and we kill them because that is the only way we protect our kind. Humans have never really appreciated us. They have always thought we are dangerous and ruthless. Those who dare to challenge and go against us are to meet with this fate. Witchcraft is something humans fail to understand and that is why some of them want to end us. The result is that they become witch-hunters," he said.

Iris listened to him attentively, trying to understand whatever he had told her. She was still unable to wrap her mind around the fact that this was going to be her job. She had to fight with the ones that were a threat to her existence. Those visions she saw in her dreams seemed so much more real now that she saw them happening while she was wide-awake with all her senses alert. It all made the dreams seem easier to understand. Earlier she had been avoiding those dreams and she was succeeding at that, but now that this was her life, she did not know how she would avoid any of it.

"Maybe they go against us because people think witches are evil?" She said, now looking at Erasmus.

He gave her a small smile, leaning forward and resting his elbows on the table between them.

"We're only evil when they are. The difference is that we're stronger and more powerful than fifty of them combined," he shrugged, standing up. Giving Iris one last thoughtful look he strode out of the chamber.

Some of the things she had to ponder upon all by herself. Erasmus was there to help her, but the answers to some of the questions could only be answered on her own. Her journey now was with herself. Iris sat still in her spot contemplating to what Erasmus had just told her. Her mind wandered back to the time when her parents recited bedtime stories about witches and how people had killed them and made them suffer because they did bad things. Never in her wildest dreams had she imagined that she would turn out to be one. When she had talked to Erasmus two nights ago, it had been awfully easy for him to know nearly everything about her, starting from when she was born up until now. He knew everything. She was surprised at the amount of things that his brain could hold. But then again, he did say they were more powerful than humans were, so their minds would obviously be sharper.

"All the things that you were capable of, while in your human surroundings, including the dreams; it was all because you are not a usual mortal. You were always a witch. You were always different. That is why they stayed away from you. Humans only accept those who are sane enough like them; one tiny difference and you become the outcast. The qualities of being a witch that were born with you never left you. They kept you away from everything that reminded you of who you were. If only you could have deciphered your dreams, you would have known who you actually are. Now you can learn everything. You will learn to invade minds, manipulate them, and you will make people do whatever you wish. You will control their very existence once we train you. Every witch has one quality that becomes their identity and your quality is controlling minds. The dreams you had were just a reflection of what was going to happen in future. You can

control those dreams now," Erasmus had told her the night she asked him all the things that she was unaware of.

His answers confused her; in some way, she did not know what he meant by them, yet she knew what he was trying to say. The more questions she asked, the more he put her mind in a mess. He never gave her a simple answer. If the questions were confusing enough, so were his answers. However, she was aware that he helped. Had he not, she would have been clueless. With Amara training her by killing people all the time, she would have ended up going insane.

Iris stood up and looked at the dove on another table in a corner. Every dove symbolized a human that was killed, Erasmus had told her. They used doves for those souls to reside in before sacrificing them in a ritual that happened almost every two months in the largest chamber of the castle. He had advised Iris not to go there. They kept the doves in a chamber for a night and then escorted them away for the ritual. Apart from the Lord and Amara, no one went in the chamber where they sacrificed doves as a symbol for those human souls.

Iris realized now that even after their Death, the world did not leave those souls alone. Every soul was destroyed and it only increased the power of the one that killed them. She understood how Amara seemed powerful and enigmatic every time she ended a life. The euphoria that she felt while killing those humans was so strong, that Iris could feel it around her.

She stared out the window as cold air flooded in and chills ran down her spine. She could clearly see dead souls of the witches roaming around but never getting out of the graveyard. Iris saw a figure lying on the branch of a tree, one hand hanging at the side, long hair flowing like waves in the air, and a black gown torn from a few places, sashaying as the wind blew past, yet it all looked elegant. Iris was always surprised how calm Amara could be with no trace of any emotion on her face. *She truly is magnificent,* Iris thought.

Amara closed her eyes, a slight smile on her face, of which one would question the existence. She breathed in the cold air as it calmed her from head to toe, creating a series of silent rhythms playing in her ears. That was what she always felt after a kill: calmness and peace. For her, killing those humans was like killing Leo – the one that had ended her family, her friends and everyone that belonged to her kind, thinking that they practiced black magic. Hard as she tried, the vision flashed into her mind repeatedly whenever she killed.

* * *

He chased after her along with the other men that had killed the girl in those woods while she somehow tried to make her legs move faster. She knew they were close and would catch up to her any moment. She was not wrong, a few more steps later, despite all her efforts, Leo had grabbed her leg from behind and she fell to the ground; tears streamed down her face. She tried not to make a sound as he pulled her hair and made her sit up. Her back was knocked onto the bark of a tree. Blood trickled out from the back of her head, as she felt it drip onto her gown, making her queasy as she winced in pain. Leo got on his knees before her and she looked away not wanting to see his face. He grabbed her chin, forcing her to look in his direction as he gave her a murderous look, the same one that he had when he killed that girl.

"Where is your family?" He probed, as she struggled to turn her face away.

Infuriated, at her non responsiveness, he took her by her hair and pulled on it hard so her head was now twisted backwards, making her cry out her pain but she tried not to scream.

"*What do you want from me?*" She managed, aside all the pain, her eyes shut at the excruciating pain she was experiencing.

She was unable to believe that it was her Leo; she wanted to know what made him behave in this manner all of sudden. How could he be this cruel, and merciless? He was not the man she had fallen for a year ago. This man was someone she failed to recognize at all.

"*Tell me where they are!*" He snarled, jerking at her hair again.

She groaned in pain, blood flowing faster out of the wound and the burning sensation increasing. She was finding it hard to breathe.

"*R-R-ose cl-iff,*" she stammered and he let go of her with such force that she fell back down to the ground. Her vision blurred, her senses almost concussed.

"*Take her to the dungeons. We need her to know the locations of the others. Don't let her die.*" She heard Leo say and moments later, they tied ropes around her wrists and lifted her up to standing. The ropes slashed across her skin and she squeezed her eyes shut at the stinging pain. Her head felt heavier than ever and she struggled to stand in place.

"*Follow me,*" ordered one of the men and she silently obeyed, not wanting to go through any more pain.

She limped behind the man, trying to keep track of where he was going but she could barely walk straight; her vision was foggy and she felt like she was about to faint. Somehow she kept her gaze locked on to the man and followed him, tripping on stones every now and then. He led her to a huge cave-like structure, and wide doors opened to allow them inside. Amara stopped walking as her legs became weaker and weaker. She dropped to the floor, struggling to get rid of the pain. The man turned around, and grabbing her by the elbow, he forcefully pulled her up to standing. He dragged her further in and she heard a few noises from around *her that sounded like wails and cries, similar to the ones that she had heard from the girl in the woods. She wondered why they were there; she wondered why she was there. The burning sensation began once again from the wound on her head as blood dripped out faster. She was sure she would faint soon enough.*

The man pulled at her arm and pushed her into a cell, closing the gates and locking her in. Not being able to keep her eyes open any longer, she let them shut by themselves as she collapsed on the floor.

It seemed as though years had passed when she woke up and found herself on a blanket with her head wrapped in a bandage and her hands still tied in the ropes. The blood was visible on her wrists as the ropes cut through her skin. Ignoring the pain, she tried standing up but there was no strength left inside her. She wondered if Leo had tended to the wound on her head but thought otherwise when she realized that he was the one that gave it to her.

"They killed your parents," said a voice from her side and she turned to look at the source.

It was a young boy. He sat in a corner of the cell with his legs bound in chains. She gave him a confused look with a frown covering her forehead.

"I saw it. They burned your parents alive. They tied their hands by ropes onto a pole and let them hang in the air when the chants started. The ritual began and they killed your mother first, the Fire finished her in one go. Then they killed your father the same way. Then they found your brother, he-"

"STOP!" She screamed.

* * *

Her eyes flew open as she jerked herself to an upright position, breathing heavily. Tiny beads of sweat glistened on her forehead as she bit her lower lip. A slight fear crept up into her veins but she pushed it away quickly, telling herself she did not have to feel anything. Everything was over. It was past. It was gone and it had been more than a hundred years she lost it all. She was not supposed to be thinking about it. Letting herself fall gently onto the ground she made her way towards the lake, placed her foot into the cold, chilly water, and then proceeded to walk further. Wind caressed her face and she dipped her head into the water, pulling herself out again after a few moments. Closing her eyes, she tilted her head upwards and let out a loud scream. The water gushed around her in waves as the wind became faster upon hearing the sound. She let herself scream as loud as she could and all of the pain went off once again. Then she dipped her head below into the water one last time.

At a distance, Iris watched everything with her eyes focussed on Amara, who was now deep into the water. She realized right then that she had just seen what Amara had seen. That vision had made Amara seem vulnerable for a few moments. Iris now understood what Erasmus had meant when he said that she could invade minds. She had just entered into Amara's mind and seen what she had seen, felt every bit of what Amara had felt. Iris felt Amara's pain; she felt the agony and she felt the loss.

CHAPTER FOUR

∞∞∞∞∞

THE MIND READER

∞∞∞∞∞

E rasmus looked at Iris disbelievingly. He was aware that her powers were not refined and went haywire more often than one would like; but he did not think she would invade someone's mind so easily. Maybe her powers were too strong for her to handle which ended in her doing silly things without noticing. "You invaded Amara's mind?" He asked, raising his eyebrows.

Out of all the people that she could have entered the minds of, she chose Amara. After knowing that Iris could read minds, he had thought it would take time for her to develop into that habit and would need training. Because invading a complex and intimidating mind like Amara's was not easy. Iris's ability to do the same was astounding enough, yet there were flaws since she was new to it and certainly wasn't used to walking into minds like that. To learn the control and to shield herself from being recognized, she was yet to discover. A sixteen-year-old witch obviously did not have the ability of being so focussed to control it all on her own. She had a lot to learn.

"I don't know how it happened," Iris replied, shrugging.

She was aware of the fact that reading Amara's mind and seeing things that she saw, was not something she should have done. Even though she was new to this, Iris could conclude that Amara's mind was a haven for many thoughts that were unlimited, complicated, and extremely difficult to put a finger on. They were also highly disturbed. Of that, she was sure. Erasmus was not helping at all; he made it look like she had just committed a crime. However, she could not be blamed entirely for what happened; she had no control over it. It just came and went all by itself, without letting her realize what she had accidentally done.

"Iris, listen. You cannot control someone else's mind when you're not sure you can control your own," he said, emphasizing every word.

"But I-" she began.

"I'll tell you something about Amara." He cut her off. "She is the most convoluted witch you can ever come across. Her life before she came here wasn't easy, and that has made her harsh and inconsiderate. While some of us are caring and human enough in many ways, she is not. Her behaviour, the way she talks, and the way she keeps to herself, how she does not appreciate anyone interfering in what she does, is different. We can all be cruel when we want to and when the need arises, but she is the same every single moment of the day. She does not care about anyone apart from the Lord; most of the time she does not care about herself either." He concluded.

"She is reckless." He continued. "And someone I have failed to understand how ever hard I've tried. We all have friends, acquaintances, we even have our mates. We have human emotions that she evidently lacks. She likes no one – and when I say no one – I mean absolutely no one. The only person she would ever come close to liking or admiring would be the Lord. She speaks to no one unless needed. Besides, she tortures. She tortures infernally and I am sure you have experienced it yourself. If she finds out you invaded her mind, believe me, Iris, it's not going to be a wonderful sight."

When he finished talking, Iris stared at Erasmus blankly. She could not digest everything that he had said at once. The image that he had created about Amara in her head was terrifying. She was not someone with whom one would like to meddle. Dangerous was the perfect word for Amara. Iris wondered how in a hundred years none of the sorcerers had fallen for her.

"Believe me, a lot of us have," Erasmus chuckled.

Iris frowned at him.

"Did I say that out loud?" she asked quizzically.

"No, I can read minds to an extent." He smirked. "But I'm not as strong as you," he added, nodding his head.

"So you mean to say that if she finds out that I invaded her mind, she'd kill me?" Iris asked, furrowing her forehead.

Erasmus shook his head. "Killing is an easy job for her. Amara believes in torturing and then killing. You saw how she killed those men; she didn't end their lives straightforward. It was torture for them, correct?" He raised an eyebrow.

Iris's mind went back to how Amara had slit throats and made two of the remaining victims see how the other one died. She not only tortured them physically but mentally as well. Also, taking their souls away and trapping them inside a dead dove's body was not the end of torture. It was only the beginning of how the souls were going to be sacrificed in a ritual. One does not come across that every day.

"So you must realize that there is a possibility that she finds out and tortures you as well," Erasmus said, breaking her train of thought.

Panic was starting to build up inside Iris and she held her breath for a long moment, thinking of what Amara would do to her once she finds out. A thought flashed across her head to enter into Amara's mind again and see if she had found out or not; but she knew it would be a foolish idea. She could not do that. If she did, then the possibilities of Amara finding out about it would be higher than what they already were.

"What do I do?" Iris whispered almost to herself.

"Wait and watch. That's all you can do and besides-" a loud screeching noise cut him off mid-sentence.

Erasmus snapped his head in the direction of the sound as did Iris. Squeezing her eyes shut at the shrill sound, she got up along with Erasmus who was now starting to walk to the door of the chamber as the sound continued to vibrate the walls. For a human it would have been deafening but it did not make much of a difference to Erasmus. Iris, on the other hand, felt a little pain in her ears but it was not her topic of concern. All that was on her mind was Amara torturing her to the point of insanity. As the sound began once again, Iris pushed Amara's thoughts out of her head and started walking further.

They followed the trail of the sound and reached the castle hall where Iris had first met Amara and the others. She blinked as a vision flashed in front of her eyes and blinded her for a long moment. Iris caught hold of a windowsill on the side to steady herself. She had thought that getting visions similar to her dreams would stop, since she was now where she was supposed to be, yet the flashes continued. Although, this time it was different, it was unfamiliar; not something that she had seen before and in a second, it was gone. As soon as she stopped seeing those visions, Iris followed Erasmus further in until they were standing along with others who had come to see what the noise was. A man stood right in the middle of the room, a hood covering his face like most and a huge staff in his hand. *So that was where the noise came from*, Iris thought. The man had possibly dragged the staff on the stone floors that made the screeching sound.

"Who is he?" Iris whispered to Erasmus who stood there confused.

A moment later, his expression changed into that of shock and he stared at the man wide-eyed, while Iris stood there, her head tilted to the side curiously. Why did this man look like he had just come out of her dream? Her doubts were cleared when Lord Lucifer entered the hall and the man took off his hood. Even though she had not seen his face clearly in the dreams, she knew it was the same man; her intuitions prominent in her head.

"Who is he?" Iris persisted, stressing each word as she did so, nudging her elbow in Erasmus's rib.

He turned and glared at her warningly. Getting the message, she looked down to the floor and decided it was better not to become enemies with Erasmus – her only saving grace in this otherwise daunting surrounding, where people seemed like they were ready to torture anybody who came along. Erasmus concentrated on what was about to happen. He was fairly aware of why the man was here.

"May I ask as to why you decided to grace us with your presence, this evening?" said Lord Lucifer, taking his seat.

"Where is she?" The man asked, dropping his staff to the floor loudly.

Iris winced at the shrill sound echoing through the walls. Whoever this man was, he did not seem too glad to be there. *Amara*, Iris thought; *he's talking about Amara*. Something was wrong, and Amara had everything to do with it. The man was only thinking about her name.

"Who are you talking about?" Lord Lucifer replied uninterestingly with his eyes examining his slender fingers.

"You know who I am talking about. You know what she has done."

The man took a step forward threateningly, but Lord Lucifer did not seem the least bit affected.

"That was her job," he said calmly.

"A *job*? She killed three innocent humans; I don't reckon that would be a simple *job*."

The man was now fuming. Iris could feel it. Numerous visions flashed across her eyes, ranging from a woman's child crying to a dead man's wife weeping, to another man's family destroyed. Iris blinked to clear it all away. She stared blankly at the man standing there. *Were those humans innocent?* She wondered. Why had Amara lied to her saying those humans had been witch-hunters?

"What imbecile told you those humans were innocent?" Lord Lucifer scowled softly.

Iris was surprised as to how easily he was handling the situation when the man was now on the verge of burning their place down.

"Of course they were. What had they ever done to her?" The man shouted throwing his arms in the air in frustration.

"If she killed some humans, then she must have had a reason. She does not kill people for fun and frolic, Lord Mikhail."

"They were following my orders. And as far as I know, that is not a crime," Lord Mikhail shot back, anger evident in his tone.

Iris's mind was pushed into another vision where Lord Mikhail was addressing the two men and the woman Amara had killed a night ago. She could not hear the voices, but she could see Mikhail giving them an important message. A moment later, she was brought back to the present and shook her head to clear the fog in her mind.

"Were those not the orders of stealing my powers, Lord Mikhail?" Amara glided in through a door, proceeding towards Lord Mikhail slowly, her voice as calm and cool as that of Lord Lucifer's. She did not seem affected by Lord Mikhail's outburst either; but of course, she could be just as brutal as she was calm.

"You" hissed Lord Mikhail, pointing his index finger that was shaking with anger, "Had no right to kill my servants," he completed glaring at Amara.

Amara threw her head back and let out a malicious laugh, to everyone's surprise. She sounded so devilish in that moment; it was frightening. Iris shuddered at the sound, as chills ran down her spine, drawing on every nerve inside. She was still not used to this extent of evil lingering around her in every part.

"Lord Mikhail, surely you know who you are speaking to, don't you?" She retorted menacingly, taking a step forward in his direction.

"You have broken the law. Do you want me to remind you of that?" Lord Mikhail barked, his eyebrows raised.

"It is forbidden to kill innocent humans; I'm aware of that," said Amara disinterestedly. "Although, may I remind you that the humans were certainly not innocent?" she growled, crossing her arms across her chest as she stood there proudly.

"For the last time, they were carrying out my orders." Spat Lord Mikhail.

Lord Mikhail was getting impatient with every passing moment and that was not a surprise to everyone else around. His face showed it clearly; it was evident that he was not happy about what Amara had done. Amara, on the other hand, looked like she had done a great deed and that Lord Mikhail was a fool to come and argue with her about nothing so much close to a valid point.

"Lord Mikhail, your servants were trying to diminish my powers. Do you think I would let them do that?" Amara asked, raising an eyebrow questioningly.

"You are a threat to our kind," he spat, taking a step back. His voice was confident, yet he looked a bit off; intimidating as Amara was.

"You make me laugh, Minister," she scoffed. "Have you no knowledge that I am the one who has always followed the laws and stuck to doing what was right? I was the one that helped you kill the witch-hunters that were close to ending your existence. *You* call me a threat. If that isn't you being dim-witted, then I don't know what is."

Amara shook her head disappointedly, a menacing smirk across her face as though she was ready to kill Lord Mikhail using his own staff. She could not believe the fact that he thought she was a threat to their kind, when everyone was aware of how helpful she had always been.

Lord Mikhail sighed, picking up his staff. There seemed to be no way he could fight back. She was not wrong; his orders were to diminish some of her powers since her rise was turning out to be a huge problem for some of his loyal and exceptional apprentices. He also had another motive that was not to be discussed in Lord Lucifer's castle; for it was dangerous to do so. That she had saved him was not a lie either, but if that was going to create rifts between his ardent apprentices and him, then sure enough, she was a threat. Getting rid of some of her powers would not make her any less of a great witch. It would just make her a little weaker, so he could let himself get what he needed. He wanted her out of his way. If that came with a price to pay, he was ready to do it. Nevertheless, arguing with a witch like Amara and trying to prove her wrong was one of the most foolish ideas he could ever have come up with and he knew that. Yet he wanted to fight. Losing it was another matter entirely.

Seeing he had no hope left, he decided to leave without having any more indignant words thrown at him. Pulling his hood up, Lord Mikhail turned to look at Lord Lucifer who sat there, smiling proudly. Amara always seemed to surprise him with her answers and the way she fought back, giving him a sense of satisfaction knowing that he had created her, made her this powerful, yet it was her own will that had added to all the skills he had taught her. She was a brilliant witch and the best one he could ever have had.

"Shall I escort you out, Lord Mikhail?" Amara asked silkily.

Without a word, Lord Mikhail turned around and swiftly on his heel and walked out of the great and resplendent hall. Amara rolled her eyes and glanced at Iris for a moment who was staring after him blankly. Again, she had invaded someone's mind without having any control over it. *If only I had not been able to do that,* thought Iris, *I could have avoided watching families cry for the Death of their loved ones.* However, the word 'love' did not exist as long as Amara was around.

"Amara," Lord Lucifer said.

"My Lord," she replied, bowing her head.

"He might send someone again. Be careful."

"Always am, m'Lord." She nodded her head and a moment later, Lord Lucifer vanished from the hall.

Erasmus grabbed Iris's hand, pulled her out of the hall and dragged her back into the chamber that they had come from. They failed to notice that Amara was still watching Iris. She had observed how Iris had flinched every now and then, as she kept her eyes fixed on Lord Mikhail, and her doubts about Iris invading her own mind were confirmed. From the corner of her eye, she saw Erasmus dragging her back into the chamber and stealthily enough, Amara crept up behind them, making her way all the way up to the ceiling inside the chamber; settling herself in a corner where they could not spot her. Erasmus shut the door behind him without noticing that Amara had followed them. They sat on opposite chairs while Amara stood there suspended in mid-air waiting for them to begin talking.

"Wh-wh-what was th-that?" Iris stuttered, assured that Erasmus would answer her now and not brush her off.

"Lord Mikhail works for the King who makes the laws for us and controls everything that we do. Apparently, the humans that Amara killed were out on Lord Mikhail's orders and he certainly did not approve of what she had done. So he was here to give her some punishment but we all know how cunning Amara is," Erasmus told her.

Up from where she had positioned herself Amara raised her eyebrows in amusement at, and smirked at his description of her.

"I might have entered his mind," Iris managed sheepishly.

Erasmus's eyes shot up to look at her.

"You invaded Lord Mikhail's mind, as well?" He asked disbelief clearly visible in his voice.

"I couldn't help it." She shrugged.

"You already got yourself into trouble by invading Amara's mind, and now you went into a powerful sorcerer's head." Erasmus slapped his palm on his forehead.

She needs some serious training, he thought.

"I don't know how I'm supposed to control it." She said, worried. Before Erasmus could reply, the door of the chamber opened and someone stepped inside.

"Erasmus, the Lord want to see you," said the man who stood at the door.

"Alright," Erasmus replied and stood up without waiting for Iris to ask him any more questions. The door shut by itself and Iris sighed. She slumped in defeat.

"Tell me, Iris. Is it easy to set foot in someone's mind?"

Iris's head snapped up to find Amara floating in mid-air above her. *She has heard everything,* Iris thought in dread. Petrified, she held her gaze onto Amara as she landed on the floor without a sound. She looked spine-chilling and Iris was at a loss of words and movements. Amara's eyes were infiltrating her insides, making her feel like every part of her was being torn apart, yet she felt absolutely no pain. Her gaze scrutinized her, piercing into her veins that Iris was surprised as to how she managed to stand on her feet. She took a step back, stumbling a bit in the process.

"Reading thoughts is such an interesting power, isn't it?" Amara drawled, tilting her head to the side, while Iris kept moving backwards.

Before Iris could justify herself, or even utter a single word, her body went rigid as Amara fixated her eyes on her. Iris opened her mouth to scream, expecting the same pain that she went through before, but it never came. Moments later, something burned inside of her, prickling through every part of her skin, consuming her and her eyes went still; her breath caught in her throat. At that moment, the only thought that crossed Iris's mind, was that of Death.

CHAPTER FIVE

∞∞∞∞∞

THE WITCH-HUNTER

∞∞∞∞∞

Iris's mind was a little more complicated than Amara had thought. She was finding it irritating to train this new witch. It gave her headaches and she often had to use potions to get rid of them. *If only there was a potion to get rid of her,* she thought. Iris was not a simple job, but of course, Amara had never dealt with simple things. Her jobs were always difficult and challenging. Iris did not seem any different and she took it as a challenge, but at times, it would get very maddening. She was still a child, nevertheless, and Amara had no way to help it.

"How long is this going to take?" Iris asked, hopelessly.

She was exhausted, that was for sure. Trying to control her mind and keeping it secure in one place was a strenuous task. Amara was being quite patient about it, and Iris was surprised as to how she had not gotten infuriated. Her thoughts went back to how displeased Amara was a few hours ago when she had found out Iris had read her mind. She almost thought she would torture and kill her as she had done with those humans; but she did nothing of that sort. It came as a shock to Iris when Amara blocked everything around and pushed her thoughts into Iris's mind. She saw a mess of things. The strength that Amara had in deflecting everything else and just making Iris concentrate on what she was showing was appalling. The burning sensation inside of her came and went soon and was replaced with Amara letting her into her mind, allowing her to read everything that was there. Yet, Iris could not compete with the dominance of Amara; she saw nothing but a million visions without having the control to make any sense out of them. She felt lost.

A while later when Amara had stopped the visions from flooding into her mind, Iris immediately fell to the floor. Her breathing was ragged. She blinked, tears in her eyes from all the stress, to clear it away and when she stood up again, Amara was looking out of the window.

"You need to learn to control your mind and be careful that the victim doesn't find out you are invading into his," she had said and then the training had begun.

After that, Amara had made her concentrate on no more than one object at a time for a long time, which she could not do without being distracted every few moments. Now it was Amara's turn to be exhausted.

"You have absolutely no control over your mind, Iris. This is not going to help you," she said, letting out a long, tired sigh.

"Can you read minds as well, like me?" Iris said, ignoring Amara's comment.

"No, I can let someone read my mind if I want to and once I know someone is doing it, I can control my mind accordingly. Every witch has a distinct gift."

"What is yours?" ventured Iris, frightened at the prospect of being shot down for her over curiosity.

"Some witches have many powers; some are strong and some are weak. While you have one distinct quality, I have many powers. And those were achieved in the hundred years that I've existed."

"Why can't I control my mind?" Iris grimaced.

Iris was getting impatient. She wanted to learn control over her mind but it just would not come to her. She felt as though her head was going to explode with so much pressure. Keeping her mind fixed on one thing was something she had always found difficult and she did not like it one bit. She liked thinking about various things at once since it had always been that way, but concentrating on one thing and controlling it was turning out to be a very tedious task.

"You're too young right now. Controlling minds is not a simple task. It is complicated and hard to adapt. Moreover, this is only the start. You have to learn the basics. Since you don't know what exactly you are capable of, you need to begin at the beginning. For that, you need to learn the art of meditation, which isn't so easy either. But you'll learn," Amara answered, standing up, brushing the uneven sleeves of her gown.

She told Iris to follow her into another chamber and she stood up, walking behind Amara to where she was leading her. She made her way into the deeper parts of the castle and Iris followed suit. As they approached the inner parts, they passed a series of chambers along the many passageways they crossed, where Iris heard chants of hymns from inside a few chambers, which made her feel as though she should never think of entering those. Smoke was coming out from one of the chambers and she assumed it was from potion-brewing. Amara stopped swiftly at the end of the passageway in front of a tiny wooden door with a bronze dove carved immaculately in the centre; that she opened shortly; making Iris bump into her as she was so lost trying to figure out what secret was being brewed behind each door.

A strange aroma greeted Iris as she walked in after Amara, easing Iris's worked up senses instantly. Fog surrounded the room and chimes hung on walls, creating a sweet melody. The room was dimly lit, and the soft melodies echoed off the walls. Iris realized the room was enchanted. This was the only place that did not seem horrid and potentially threatening to her. There were tiny doors inside the chamber that looked like small cabins from the outside. Amara opened one door in a corner and stood waiting for Iris to follow.

"This is the meditation chamber. You sit here for as long as you want," said Amara softly when Iris reached to where she was standing.

"So I close my eyes and sit here, right? But I don't sleep," Iris replied, just as softly.

"Yes, don't fall asleep at all. Focus your mind on one thing; any abstract thing and you will be able to meditate. It's not easy so you have to try hard."

Iris was not too sure about this, but the atmosphere around was welcoming enough. Therefore, she made her way into the small chamber and Amara closed the door before making her way out. She started walking in the direction of her chamber. Stepping down the stone staircase, she reached the lowest chamber that had been allotted to her when she had first arrived. The door opened to let her in and shut by itself when she walked inside. Her chamber was lit with three torches of fire on the walls. It gave just about enough light whilst letting ample amount of darkness stay; the way she always liked it. A round table rested in a corner with one chair beside it and a few books upon it. A huge chair sat in front of the now damp and dead Fireplace where she sat and read her books. A trunk of weapons lay in a corner and Amara pulled a dagger out before making her way to the Fireplace, in front of which stood a dove. It stared at her as she looked down at it emotionlessly. Killing doves was an easy task for her.

Amara sat in front of it, legs folded behind. She closed her eyes and took a deep breath. With a slight touch of the tip of the dagger on the dove, it started to flutter it's wings as though realizing something wrong was about to happen. The dove twirled around, frightened as the dagger started approaching it even closer. A moment later, Amara slit the dove's throat swiftly and the white bird dropped to the floor, whimpering in pain. Its eyes lay open as it shivered for a while before it went completely still. Eyes closed, she dropped the dagger and raised her arms in the air to summon the souls of the dead that were to be trapped inside the dove's body. Wind gushed inside the chamber through a window, and quiet sounds were heard as the souls dragged themselves inside.

Amara started chanting the hymns and the souls entered faster, trying to set themselves free but she held them as though putting a barrier around and keeping them hostage. Invisible chains tied themselves around the souls as her chants continued to echo through the walls and became louder by the minute. A clock ticked away in a corner and a bell sounded from it as the clock struck twelve. A wolf howled from a mountain as the wind kept rushing inside and the curtains on the window flew in the air furiously. Amara's chanting continued and the souls began to descend. They surrounded her, running in circles as she raised her head and spread out her arms to the sides. Her gown swished around her ankles as she stood up and hair flew with the wind as the souls finally entered into the dove, and calmness settled around. Slowly, the wind lowered its pace and the curtains no longer made the horrible sounds. Amara's hands returned to her side again and everything went silent.

She let out a sigh, opening her eyes and rested her back on the wall next to her. Summoning souls and trapping them inside the body of a dove was not comfortable for her even though she had done it numerous times. It made her feel like a part of her soul was fragmented every time she imprisoned the souls. With every soul that went inside, the dove's soul would be trapped in as well, with no fault of the latter. A pang of guilt stabbed Amara whenever she killed the innocent bird, yet she pushed it away, for it was her job and she was not supposed to feel anything. She would never allow herself to feel anything. The moment she felt a little emotion inside of her, she would push it away and try not to think about it.

She stood up, cleaning the dagger before grabbing a goblet of water placed on the table. She gulped it down in one go and let it fall to the floor, making a cluttering sound as she started to walk out of her chamber. The door opened and she walked out, making her way up the stairs again. As she reached the hall, a fellow sorcerer who was pacing around the passageway greeted her.

"Amara," he said, spotting her standing there.

"Fabian," she responded, a tiny frown covering her face.

"I have a message for you." Fabian took a step forward and so did Amara.

"What is it?"

"Lord Mikhail has been sending out orders to kill you."

Amara raised her eyebrows, "Kill me?" She repeated.

"Yes, I've heard that he wants to destroy our coven as well."

Fabian's face was covered in a worried frown. Though he was well aware that there was absolutely no one that could beat Amara and end her existence; he was also familiar with the amount of power Lord Mikhail possessed. If he wished, he could use tricks to kill Amara. Being the incomparable witch of her time, Amara was not someone the coven could afford to lose. If she died, so would their coven. Naturally, Fabian was bound to be afraid of what might happen if Lord Mikhail decided to strike.

"Don't worry, Fabian; nothing will happen as long as the Lord is here. And I can assure you I will protect our coven with every part of my body and soul," she said, giving him a nod.

Fabian examined her with an uncertainty before nodding back. Amara was like the lifeline of the coven. If a single damage occurred to her, they would all be doomed. She was their strength, and everyone had their hopes on her in times of a calamity. Even their Lord depended on her, despite the fact that he was the one who trained her to become such an exceptional witch.

Fabian watched Amara walk away with the signature gracefulness that she had. She managed to be the most beautiful and evil witch at the same time. One could not decipher what she was actually like. Every single time he met her; there would be some sort of difference from the last time. She could leave everyone confused and awestruck by her presence alone.

Amara made her way to the woods, wondering whether Iris was adjusting to the meditation process or not. With the shake of her head, she ignored other thoughts and walked further into the woods, inhaling the scent of wet grass as it had rained during the day. She walked past the old tree where Scerion sat on the high branch, hooting softly. Glancing at it once, she started walking to the lake where she rested her back on the bark of a tree and let her hand dip itself into the water, as the waves slowly gushed around it. Closing her eyes, she let herself fall into a slumber while the cold water continued to flow in waves around her hand.

* * *

In the meditation chamber, Iris sat with her eyes shut, her back straight and her head held high in place as she concentrated on the sound of the lake just behind. She could hear the soft waves along with a few other sounds. Hard as she tried, her concentration would not stay on the sound of the waves, yet after a long time she was able to focus her attention on the water when she heard a new sound. Someone was near the lake. She realized that whoever it was had not gone back or further ahead but stayed in place at the lake. Iris forced her mind to concentrate on who it was. Her mind blocked out everything else and she concentrated on hearing the sound of the person. In her curiosity and impatience to know who it was, she stretched her vision far enough that by the time she realized that she had invaded a mind, it was too late to get out.

* * *

She heard a scream. Amara shut her ears to stop the sound but realized it was no one else but her. With tears streaming down her face, she opened her eyes and looked at the boy seated opposite to her in the corner. His description of how they killed her family made her see it all as though it was happening right in front of her. She tried to block those visions from her mind, but could not manage to do that as the thoughts kept coming back to her; making her realize she had no one to go back to and no one to find shelter with.

The boy stared at her vacantly, holding his gaze onto her as though he had something more to tell her. Amara did not want to hear anything else. All she wanted was to get out of that prison cell and run away somewhere, or maybe just die and not face the reality that was the loss of her family. After hearing how her parents died, she did not want to know how they killed her brother. If that was not torturing, then she did not know.

The boy kept looking at her as though waiting for her approval to tell her everything. She was lost. Her mind refused to function and she did not know what to do, as blank stupor engulfed her now fraught senses. She was unaware of what would happen once Leo came back and start asking her things; she did not want to know what he would be like. She wanted to die, that was the only thing going through her mind. Blocking the boy's image away, she turned her head to the side and rested it on the cold wall beside her, pulling her knees up to her chest, as tears kept running down her cheeks. She bit her lower lip hard until it drew blood and started hurting. However, that pain was nothing compared to the one that she felt emotionally. She wanted to tear her head apart and end all the agony, but her whole body was chained.

"They won't kill you," said the boy, snapping Amara's attention back to him.

She stared at him silently.

"They want to know about the others. They will kill everyone but you," he said again.

"Why would they not kill me?" She asked out of curiosity, but more out of the will to die rather than suffer here.

"Because you are the key to them. Once they find the other witches, they will kill you. But it will take years to end everyone."

It felt like he was psychic, or he just knew everything. Amara wanted to know more, yet not at the same time.

"Who are the others? Why does Leo want to kill them?" She asked, letting her eyes focus on the boy.

"Witches. Leo is a witch-hunter and so are his other apprentices. He came into your life because you are a witch and you could help him find the others so he could kill them. He will kill me too, now that he knows where my Lord is," said the boy, a sad look settling on his face.

"I'm a witch?" Amara widened her eyes and stared at the ground with a horrified expression.

It was all a lot to take in. The reason I can make things happen with just the blink of an eye is that I am a witch, *she thought. She used to think it was because she had some magical abilities as her father did, but did that mean he was a witch too? Did that mean her whole family was of that sort? Out of all the things that struck her, the most shocking one was about Leo. He came into her life just so he could find others like her and kill them, just so he could kill her parents, her brother. She wanted to scream and demand answers but her helplessness was making her weaker and weaker.*

Before she could ask the boy any more questions, the door of the cell was unlocked and opened as Leo stormed inside followed by another man. He bent down to her level and grabbed her by the scruff of her neck, pulling her up onto her feet. Her legs lifted into the air as he held her by the neck and she squirmed to get out of his grip.

"Where are the others?" He snarled, his eyes blazing with anger.

Amara shivered at his tone, his grip tightening around her neck as she winced in pain. Not a sound came out of her mouth.

"I don't know," she croaked.

"Tell me!" He yelled, and she squeezed her eyes shut.

"She doesn't know," said the boy, and Leo let go off Amara, and she fell onto the floor as Leo turned on his heel and walked over to the boy sitting in front of him.

"And you know everything, don't you, little Thomas?" Leo asked silkily, a menacing undertone in his voice.

"Yes," the boy replied, softly.

"Then tell me why I should not kill you now that I've found your Lord."

"Because I know who is going to kill you."

* * *

Iris jerked back into reality as the door of her chamber burst open. Amara stood there with a scrutinizing gaze over Iris. With a dark look covering her face, she grabbed Iris's arm and pulled her outside where she was sure that nobody else would be disturbed.

"You invaded my mind again," she barked, staring hard at Iris.

"I'm sorry I-"

"I asked you to concentrate on one thing, *not me*. Do you not get it?" She screamed threateningly.

Amara tried to remain as calm as she could, but it just would not work when it came to Iris. She was capable of blocking Iris out of her mind, but when it came to having visions of her past inside the woods, all her control seemed to vanish.

"I *was* concentrating, but then I don't know what happened," Iris said, panicked. This time she knew she was going to be in trouble.

"What did you see?" Amara asked, looking away.

"I. . ."

"What did you see?" She repeated fiercely.

"The prison, the boy. . .Leo and-I don't understand anything." Iris shook her head, tears blurring her vision.

"You saw almost everything," Amara sighed. "Iris, you will help me with something."

CHAPTER SIX

∞∞∞∞∞

DAWN OF THE FIGHT

∞∞∞∞∞

I ris stared blankly at the tree in front of her. Her mind was still, calm, unclear and distraught, all at the same time. She felt like all her strength was draining out, starting from her head right to her toes. She had no idea how she was supposed to control her mind, let alone that of others'. Apart from that, she didn't know what task Amara wanted her to help with. It was as though she left her hanging by a loose thread and she had to hold on until the time she was told what had to be done.

Moreover, reading minds now felt like the worst thing that could ever happen to her. As much as she wished she could have a normal life and not have powers like reading minds – with the addition of controlling them – she had no choice anymore. She was stuck here, and she had to accept that fact.

"What's wrong?" Erasmus asked, as he stood in front of Iris. She was sitting next to a grave as the sun shone brilliantly down at her. It was early evening, and the sun was about to set. She realized she had been at this very place for more than three hours. How she had plucked the courage to sit in a graveyard was something she failed to understand. Yet, there she was and she didn't wish to go anywhere else. Horrid as this place was, she was now starting to get immune to it, even though she had to try hard for that.

"What's wrong is that I'm a witch and very bad at it," replied Iris, resting her chin on her knees.

Erasmus sat down beside her.

"It's only been a week. You have a long way to go. Don't give up so soon," he said, gently.

"You're right, it's only been a week and I've been asked to help a brilliant witch with some task that I nearly have no idea about," she let out a frustrated sigh.

"Amara asked you for help?" Erasmus raised his eyebrows, clearly shocked.

"Yes and she hasn't told me what it is. She wants me to prepare myself for it. Apparently it's a very complicated task," she responded.

Iris held her breath for a moment, thinking about what it would be that Amara needed help with. *Couldn't a great witch, especially the likes of her, do everything herself?* Iris wondered. Why would she need help of a new witch who until a week ago didn't even know she was one?

"Amara never asks anyone for help, Iris. But if she has asked you for something then it surely is going to be important."

"That is *precisely,* what scares me. A witch of her stature asking for me to help her is like a lion asking a mouse to go hunt for food," Iris said.

Erasmus looked at her for a moment before letting out a slight chuckle. Out of all the witches around, Iris was the only one who could match his humour and he liked helping her out. He had dealt with all kinds of witches but Iris was better than most new witches he had trained. Lending a hand her out was some sort of an entertaining task for him, and he surely didn't mind that.

"Take this as a challenge, something you have to achieve."
Erasmus gave her a small smile.

"The problem is that I don't know what I have to achieve.
She hasn't told me what she needs help with." Iris shrugged.

Her mind wandered everywhere, to the most random
possibilities of what Amara wanted but she ended up nowhere.
There were so many things she could need help with, but so
less an amount of things that Iris could actually do. A witch,
who had lived a hundred years, was asking a new witch for
help wasn't only surprising but confusing as well. When she
had asked what it was that Amara wanted, she had just shaken
her head and said, *"I'll tell you when the time comes. Right now,
I just want you to prepare yourself for it. And it's not an easy task,
keep that in mind."*

That was all it took for Iris to be scared out of her wits.
What could she possibly want?

A sound of gushing water had her snapping her mind
back to reality. In the distance, she could see a huge wave
approaching out of nowhere. Erasmus stood up immediately,
along with Iris whose jaw dropped in shock. The wave
was coming closer and closer, creating an array of sounds,
which, in moments became deafening. Wind blew her hair
backwards and she struggled to stand in place when Erasmus
said something that she could not hear. He shook his head and
grabbed Iris's arm before dragging her away.

They were running back towards the castle at what Iris
thought was lightning speed, as the wave started approaching
closer and closer. Once they reached the castle, Erasmus
pushed the door open and they entered inside. Arriving at the
great hall, Erasmus spotted Lord Lucifer seated in the centre
with others surrounding them.

"M'Lord, there is something you need to see, now," he
said, still huffing from his escape, pointing somewhere behind

him in the distance, to Lord Lucifer who frowned and seeing the urgency on Erasmus's face, he stood up.

Erasmus opened a window and they could see the wave approaching, which was now almost at the graveyard. Dust flew inside the castle through the window and everyone else that had gathered around to witness what was happening, hastily covered their eyes and faces. Lord Lucifer turned swiftly to find Amara and asked Ambrosius to call her immediately. Ambrosius ran to her chamber and hesitated for a moment thinking that he should not disturb her, but the Lord needed her and he had to obey. Thus, he knocked on the door urgently, and it opened in a few moments. Amara stood there with an angry frown covering her face, not wanting to be disturbed at the time of her reading.

"The Lord needs you. It's important," he said and in a moment, Amara's frown disappeared as she pushed past him, hastily making her way to the hall.

The wave was approaching closer and Lord Lucifer stood outside the castle along with a few other witches who were trying to do something that could push the wave back but their efforts were not enough to stop it. Amara rushed outside the castle and stood before the wave, as it had now reached past the graveyard. Everyone behind struggled to hold themselves in place as the wind grew stronger and stronger along with the water approaching.

Raising both her hands to the sides, Amara shut her eyes tight and hummed numerous chants that made the wave rise up in the air while she wrestled with the amount of wind that was surrounding her to hold the wave above.

Moments later, she disappeared into the air and dust, while everyone watched as the lifted the wave above and kept ascending; until it was high up, that they had to crane their necks to see what was happening. Iris stared in awe and held a tree to stand in place with the wind threatening to knock her off. The wave was now circling above and Iris blinked for the fraction of a second. When she opened her eyes, it was raining. Her mouth opened as she stared upwards, the water falling on her, drenching her completely in moments. Amara slowly but steadily dropped her hands to the sides but her spells continued. The wind calmed after a while and they could all spot Amara standing there in the middle of the graveyard, reciting the chants. She had calmed the angry wave into drizzling rain.

After a while, everyone started walking back into the castle while Iris stood there silently, watching Amara as she proceeded towards Lord Lucifer who offered her a smile and a nod, placing his hand on her shoulder for a second before he left to go back into the castle. For an hour and a half, Amara stood there chanting as it continued to rain. Iris didn't have the ability to leave. She held her place next to the tree, not moving an inch as she watched this extraordinary witch perform her magic. The rain subsided and Iris observed as it ended a while later. Then, it was completely calm. The wind became normal, and there was no huge wave threatening to kill her. Yet, Iris waited there.

Amara turned to go back into the castle and raised her left hand, pointing to where Iris stood and waved her fingers, muttering a spell and a slight gush of wind dried Iris's clothes and her hair. Not a drop of water rested on her and she let go of the tree while Amara opened the castle door and walked inside. Iris sighed before following her back into the castle. She wanted to ask her questions but by the time she stepped in through the door, Amara was already gone.

"Bloody brilliant witches," she muttered to herself and started walking to Erasmus's chamber.

She raised her hand to knock on the door when it opened and a witch stood there disinterestedly. She gave Iris a dirty look before pushing past her and walking away. Iris stared after her with a frown. *Why are all the witches so good looking here?* She thought and shook her head before making her way into the chamber. Erasmus was sitting on a chair, flipping through a book when he looked up to find Iris walking towards him. Assuming she was here to ask him more questions, he shut the book and kept it aside as she sat on the chair opposite to him.

"Who was that?" She asked.

Erasmus raised his eyebrows in amusement. He wasn't expecting that question.

"I thought you wanted to ask about what happened," he said.

"I do, but that lady looked at me as though I just killed her cat." Iris said rolling her eyes.

Erasmus chuckled and said, "Her name is Sienna. She came here to ask me about her mate who left her and never came back."

"*Oh,*" she said disinterestedly, "Well, it's none of my business." She completed apathetically. "What in the devil's name happened just now?" She asked abruptly coming to the point.

"Lord Mikhail made that happen, a threat to tell us that he is going to destroy the coven soon," Erasmus replied.

"*A threat?* But that would have destroyed the castle anyway."

"Yes but he knew that Amara would definitely stop it from happening. All he wanted to do was give a message." He explained.

Iris nodded her head in understanding. She didn't know much about Lord Mikhail but she was now aware of what he could do. If he could send a huge wave to drown them all just to convey a message, he could do anything.

"But why couldn't anyone else stop that wave? *Why Amara?*" She asked curiously.

More than twenty of them standing there and none of them had the power to battle the wave but when Amara was called, nothing else was required. *Obviously since there were others, they should have some powers,* she thought.

As though reading her mind, Erasmus replied, "Amara's distinct ability when she was a new witch was to tackle two elements: Fire and Water. In all these years, she has developed many powers, but her dominant ones are controlling the two elements. Every witch has to have the power of command over elements, if not all of them then a few, but elements are what make the world, it is what makes the living beings on earth. So being able to influence elements is what a witch is supposed to learn in witchcraft. It is one of the most important things. All us others do know how to control elements, but Amara has the upper hand in Fire and Water, yet she couldn't gain much control over the Air that was surrounding her, which proves that her control over the element of Air isn't that good."

"So I have to learn that too?" Iris raised her eyebrows.

Erasmus nodded in response.

As interesting as this was, it didn't appear to be easy. She had seen how hard it was for Amara even though she had the power. Being a new witch, Iris wasn't sure how she was going to master this art. The amount of things that a witch was expected to know kept on increasing day by day and she only felt more pressured. To top that, there was some help Amara needed, which she had no idea how she was supposed to handle on her own.

* * *

Amara sat on the windowsill of her chamber, her head resting behind with her eyes scanning the woods that lay out there. She wasn't bothered about anything else but the fact that she had asked an inexperienced witch to help her with something so crucial. There were many things that Iris was capable of, if she succeeded in learning the art of controlling minds; but it would be a long way to go until she truly became capable of it. That needed a lot of determination and Iris hardly had any. She was childish and just a week old in this world. For her to help Amara with what she was desperate to know, seemed miles away from where she was standing right now. She could not lose hope, this was the only way she could find out what she wanted to, and there were things that needed to end, if not in reality, then in her head. Iris was the only one that could help her and she had to assist the little girl with it. She would not be able to do it alone.

Amara stood up, deciding to help Iris go through with this as soon as she could, and started walking outside, making her way to find Iris in her chamber. When she opened the door, she found an empty chamber. Frowning, she started looking for Iris when she bumped into Erasmus who was walking along with Iris to the great hall.

"Erasmus, I need Iris for a while," she said to him.

Erasmus looked back and forth between the two witches and then nodded, giving them way. Amara gestured to Iris to follow her and she glanced at Erasmus once before following behind. Amara walked towards the potions chamber and Iris walked in with her. There were a variety of potions being brewed in the chamber. Cauldrons that contained brewing potions, smoke gently bellowing out of them, freshly brewed potions that had distinct odours, dusty old bottles filled with pint-sized amounts of some potions. The whole chamber had numerous bottles of various shapes and sizes containing different coloured potions. There was a mixed smell, but the stench did not overpower her senses as she thought it would. Surprisingly so, it was tolerable. Iris thought it had something to do with bewitching the chamber.

Amara stopped at a table, where a pot rested upon a flame, a black coloured liquid boiling inside it. Iris cringed at the smell and looked away.

"Do you know what this potion is, Iris?" Amara said, holding a tiny bottle of glass, which had a glittering red and orange-tint liquid inside. For a moment, Iris stared at the potion in awe. It looked beautiful on the outside. Then again, this place had all kinds of things that looked beautiful, but were pure evil inside.

Iris shook her head in denial.

"This is *Phoenix Blood*. It has the power to grant life to a dead; but the effects of it are so strong that people cannot contain it. Whoever drinks this potion has to be extremely powerful to take it in and hold it for as long as they wish to live. Once it has been consumed, it is so difficult to get rid of, that one has no option but to kill one-self. If this potion grants a life, it has the power to take it away as well. There was a witch who had the power to drink *Phoenix Blood* and live again for a day before she could not contain it anymore and had to set herself on Fire. It is known to have caused insanity and torture. *Yet*, if you are strong enough, it gives you what you want, it lets you control it," said Amara.

Iris listened to her silently. She could not understand why Amara was telling her all this. *She's right,* she thought, *as beautiful as it looks on the outside, it is worse inside.* Amara didn't wait for Iris to answer and continued,

"The human mind is just the same. If it allows you to invade itself, it will give you the power to control it, it will let you do anything and everything, yet if it is not in your power to endure it, if you do not have enough strength to manipulate it, it can make you go insane. It can make you end your own life. You have the power to read minds, Iris, you also have the power to control them, but if you don't have enough skill to do the same, it can cause you enough traumas."

Iris realized just how complex yet important it was to put her powers to good use. Now she understood what could happen if she wasn't careful and compelling enough in using her powers. It was the most interesting and amazing power any witch could ever have, but it had its share of darkness as well. If she didn't learn to control her own mind, she could never control the minds of others. It was challenging enough, and it was frightening; but she had to do it, because she was born with it, she was supposed to do this. And at that moment, Iris realized that whatever Amara wanted help with, was going to involve extremities of her power and all the loose ends had to be tied together to get what had to be done. She didn't know what she was supposed to do, but she had a clue and she had a chance to prepare herself for it.

"I want you to know that your existence now, has to be devoted to what you are meant to do. There are great things you can do, but if you are not capable enough to handle everything, it will not only make you go insane, Iris, but it will also make you do wrong. You have to realize the seriousness of what this is and work accordingly. You have the potential of being a great witch, but you have to strive for it. And one day, you could be the greatest witch the world has ever witnessed."

Amara set the bottle of *Phoenix Blood* back on the table, and walked outside the chamber, letting out a deep breath as she did so. Visions of her parents being burnt alive flashed across her eyes once again and she shook her head to get rid of those thoughts. A tear threatened to slip out of her eye when she scraped her nails across the wall behind forcefully, producing a shrill sound that sent chills down her spine. Her toes curled up as she struggled to stand and the pushed the tears back, changing her expression back to how it was supposed to be, blank.

She started walking towards the woods while Iris stood inside, closing her eyes for a while, contemplating everything that Amara had said to her. She opened her eyes and made her way to the meditation room, with a new determination to prevail the challenge that was set forth. Iris shut the door of the chamber she was in and began the quest to achieve what she had to. She concentrated on her mind, everything that flashed and captured one thought, keeping her mind focussed on it, even if it was an unimportant thought like drinking water when she felt thirsty. Those tiny things would make way to the bigger things that she was supposed to confront.

Outside in the woods, flames of Fire danced gracefully upon the water, creating different designs. Amara's owl settled itself beside her while she waved her fingers in the air, creating different illusions with the Fire. One flame went right up to the highest branch of a tree and came swishing back in, just close to touch the water, yet far. Amara's eyes swung back and forth from one flame to another as her hands made innumerable patterns in front of her. She gathered all the flames together and created two birds that touched each other and then flew into opposite directions, scattering into tiny pieces before assembling back again into a circle of Fire.

Sceiron hooted from beside Amara when she held one hand in the air, as though holding the flames in position while her other hand, dipped below, raising some water above to the level of the Fire. She crossed her arms in the shape of an X and the flame of Fire danced along with that one wave of the water. It created a beautiful symphony with the sound of the wave and a moment later, the Fire morphed into the image of a flaming fairy, before diving inside the water. It was calm, the wave fell back to where it evolved from and Amara raised herself in the air, flying up to one high branch of a tree and stood upon it, gazing up into the moonlight.

CHAPTER SEVEN

∞∞∞∞∞

UNHEARD CRIES

∞∞∞∞∞

*S*he shuddered as she drew in deep gasps of breath. Eyes rolling upwards and head throbbing with pain, Amara struggled to let out a scream. Blood trickled down her forehead, the chilly night making wisps of wind as it echoed softly in her ears. Her heart was beating faster with every passing minute and the rain splattering across the bars of the broken window pane made it even worse. She struggled to keep sitting, her hands bound to the chains and her legs still in place. The numbness that surrounded her entire body made her want to cry, but no one would hear her screams. She knew that.

Her eyes travelled to the young boy, Thomas, sitting across from her, curled up in a ball. He was crying, sobbing to himself so softly that she had to strain her ears to know the sounds. She wanted to ask him what was wrong, to try to know why he was crying. He looked so vulnerable that she felt like pulling him into a hug. He reminded her of Arion, her little brother, her little eleven-year-old brother. They had killed her innocent brother.

They had killed everyone, and she could not understand what their fault was. Is it my fault that I am a witch? She wondered. She had the ability to make things happen without even trying. She could make a flying bird descend to the ground, she could make people cry if she was angry, she could move things around, yet she could not understand how that happened. She didn't think that those abilities had anything to do with her being a witch and that Azar too was like her. She had never told anyone about what unusual things happened without any effort from her side. She felt a bit scared to discuss it with her father as well, even though she presumed that he might understand. Now that she knew she was a witch.....

Her eyes widened at the thought as realization struck her like a bolt of lightning. The raindrops fell onto her face from the window above and she looked down at her hands, at the chains that were controlling her limbs. If it was true that she was a witch and she could make things happen, surely she could set herself free as well. The moment that thought crossed her mind, the chains loosened and she sat there staring at her hands, which were no longer bound by chains, but were bleeding from the wrists. The sensation of the chains still lingered on her feet and wrists. She looked up to find Thomas sitting opposite to her, now appearing as though he had not shed a single tear from his eyes. He gave her a tiny smile and she returned it while looking at his chains. They left his limbs as well.

He shook his head to which Amara frowned. His expression suddenly became horrified and eyes went wide. Shaking his head again, he stood up, a trembling body along. She looked at him in confusion.

"You shouldn't have done this," he said shakily. Amara got up to her feet and stumbled as she wobbled along the floor. She placed one palm on the wall to steady herself. Her legs were threatening to give away any moment.

"What are you talking about, Thomas?" She asked, confusion etching on her features.

The way he was looking at her, the disconcerted expression told her something bad was going to happen. He kept shaking his *head rapidly and she could only stare at him, unaware of what he was trying to convey. He opened his mouth as if to say something but not a sound escaped and he stopped shaking his head as his eyes widened with shock. Amara tried to understand and listen to him, when she felt a pull as a strong arm stealthily slithered around her waist. She jerked her head around and disbelief encompassed her eyes as she saw Leo's face inches away from hers, eyes mere slits, highlighting his hollow, high cheekbones, a wicked smile playing on his lips, as he hummed an innocuous tune. Her breath hitched as she tried vehemently to push him away, but he began dragging her out of the cell, as she kicked and flailed helplessly. Pools of tears flooded down her eyes as she bit down on her lip. Her toes curled inwards, nails dug into her palms and pain wrenched on her insides.*

"RUN!" bellowed Thomas as Amara struggled to get out of Leo's grip.

But it was too strong. She screamed, her voice cracked, the deathly echo bouncing back, it was as though the whole chamber shook with the trembling sounds she made but no one came to her rescue. She did not know what was going to happen to her, she did not know what Leo was doing and where he was taking her. All she wanted to do was to get out of his grasp.

"Come now, princess," he said silkily.

They passed through a few cells where behind the bars, she saw people crying and wailing and some bodies like mere corpses floating above the floors, some of them looked at her and gave her silent apologies while she screamed her lungs out as Leo's nails dug into her flesh. Her head throbbed with pain, the blood now flowing free.

As they crossed the cells and walked towards an unknown destination, she could feel biting cold wind enter from somewhere. And suddenly, she was thrown onto a cold, hard floor inside a chamber. Leo locked the door carefully before turning to her with a menacing expression across his face and carelessly started strutting towards her.

Chills ran down her spine, she was unsure whether it was from the cold or his foul expression as he began walking towards her. Somehow, she managed to gather all her strength and slithered a few inches behind trying to get herself in an upright position, her heart pounding. Her wrists hurt as though someone was meticulously driving a blade across her skin and the unbearable stinging sensation made her unable to move her hands. Her feet throbbed with pain from where the chains had trapped her and her head was oozing out blood that covered the right side of her face and shoulder. The pain was becoming stronger, and her body more rigid than it had ever been. She was unsure if she would even be able to move beyond this. Her strength was giving up and the harder she tried to get away from Leo, the closer he got.

Leo continued to hum as he approached her and crouched beside her on the floor where her back was now pressed against a wall as she lay there in an uncomfortable position, unable to move. His hand rose up to her cheek, and his fingers slid slowly along her temple as he pushed a strand of hair, dampened by blood, behind her ear.

Amara shuddered as his touch made her cringe inwardly in disgust and she let out an inaudible cry. She did not want him to touch her. She did not want him anywhere close to her.

As happy as his presence and closeness had made her feel just a week ago, now it made her want to push him away and not let him get anywhere near her. She realized that she couldn't bear to be in the same room with this man anymore, and hated his guts. She detested the way he was looking at her as though she was some prey.

"Such a pretty girl," he drawled. "But with a brick for a brain." He spat. Chuckling he added, "How silly of you to trust a man so easily," he said, his hand had moved from caressing her face to a Deathly grip around her throat, while the other was stealthily running up from her knee along to her inner thigh. She choked, gasping for breath and trying desperately to let loose his grip, her jaw fell open, and she made gasping sounds as she struggled to breathe.

"Isn't it funny, the way you believed my claims of love, only to land yourself here? The place where you might get tortured, or worse, killed," he whispered, his lips close to her ear.

She shivered as his breath hit her ear, wanting to get away from him; she forced her eyes shut as he chuckled maliciously. His voice rang in her ears, piercing through her every nerve and she tried in vain raising her hands to push him away, but his grip on her throat tightened.

"Tell me, little princess, where is everyone? Or do you wish to go through more?" he said, as his other hand gripped the waistline of her gown. With one swift movement, he had ripped her flimsy gown apart and he threw the cloth away his nails scratching across her abdomen, drawing blood. A bloodcurdling scream left her mouth as he released her neck, her voice cracked. Tears streamed down her eyes as his fingers curled themselves in her hair behind her neck, pulling at her hair threateningly.

"TELL ME!" he bellowed.

Amara cringed and felt disgusted. His touch was unbearable, more unbearable than the pain that she felt. The little clothing that covered her was threatening to fall away from her chest making her vulnerable. God only knew what he would do once the rest of it was off. Something began to break inside of her and she fought to get away from him. She was frightened even thinking about what he was going to do to her. How would she fight him?

She was already weak. Before she could retort, the rest of her clothes were off in one go. There were scratches on her body. Scars covered her skin as his fingers pierced right into her flesh. She writhed in pain. Her eyes rolled upwards as she let out a breathless shriek of agony.

"NO!" she screeched.

Her body shivered uncontrollably as Leo forced himself onto her. His very action of tearing the remnant skirts off her made her want the earth to open up right there and swallow her. Tears streamed down her face as she cried out. Her body shook with the immeasurable pain he was inflicting upon her.

Leo's hands mercilessly dragged across her skin, burning wherever they travelled. His touch sent waves of disgust down her body as she screamed out loud. Amara wept at the pain coursing through her and her eyes squeezed shut as her skin stung at the cold air. The numbness in her body did not help either. Even though she knew what she was capable of, right now, her strength seemed to have disappeared; hollow cries left her, her eyes now drawing pools of tears, her cheeks stained in blood mixed with the tears.

The man she had fallen in love with was vile, cruel and indignant, and she realized what a huge mistake she had made. Her whole body was in flames. It was as though she was being shattered into a million pieces. The screams came out from every part of her soul as Leo mercilessly defiled her. To silence her screams, Leo placed a hand on her mouth. With trembling fingers, she raised her hands above the floor in an attempt to push him off but her hands were unable to leave the cold surface. Her eyes blinded and heart throbbed inside as his breath fanned her face. She couldn't bear it. His presence, his touch, his smell, his skin....

Gathering her strength, Amara raised her hands and started to push Leo away when he gripped her wrists tightly and slammed them back onto the floor. Yet, her muffled cries shook the walls, but her efforts to set herself free were failing. His assault continued; nails pierced the skin at her wrists as she lay there writhing beneath him, bloodcurdling screams escaping her mouth every time the pain increased. She struggled under his weight, shaking her head from right to left and left to right, not being able to contain it any longer. Tears stung her skin as they effortlessly fell out of her eyes. She wanted to crawl away somewhere so she could wash his touch off every part of her body but the more she struggled, the more pain she felt. Her neck twisted backwards and she shook her legs violently to set herself free somehow...anyhow but nothing was going to help.

Disgust coursed through her from head to toe at the feel of his skin against hers and she could no longer struggle; for he had taken what he wished to. She had lost herself. He had exercised his power on her and she had no control over it anymore. Her eyes opened as the pain shattered her very core and she saw his face mere inches from hers. She wanted to scream and fight but Leo's smirk of satisfaction made her go still in place. Her legs stopped shaking, hands stopped trembling, neck in place, and she stared up at the ceiling with her eyes wide open. Her fingers loosened their hold and palms turned upwards. She gave up when his weight shifted off of her but the sensation of him was still as present, still as prominent.

Shrieks of agony refused to leave her lips as she felt Leo shuffling around and then taking steps towards her again. He began to say something to her but Amara's eyes were stuck at the ceiling, she heard nothing as the remnant teardrops slipped down. Her chest heaved as she breathed pants of breath. The door of the chamber opened and Leo strode out while Amara lay there in place, letting out a deep breath before blinking a few times. Pulling her knees slowly towards her, she cringed at the pain as her limbs shifted closer to her chest. Wrapping her arms around her sore legs, Amara turned to her side and stared at the wall before her. Cold air swished inside through the open window and hit her bare skin, searing right through her as she shivered every now and then.

She lay there for what seemed like hours, unmoving, with her arms protecting her curled up body. When the sun began to rise and light streamed in through the window, Amara blinked once again before tears started to slide down her eyes once again as her mind went back to what had happened mere hours ago. The walls shook with her cries, the violent screams that she let out as pain engulfed her with every passing moment. Her body trembled but arms stayed in place, head buried in them as she wept. Tears slowly slid down her bloodshot eyes, landing on the floor. Her breath struggled to get even, as her body shivered every once in a while, reminding her of what had just happened, making her weaker by the moment.

And then her heart grew slower, her breathing shallow as she faded into unconsciousness.

* * *

Iris sat in a corner, her knees close up to her chest as she stared at the floor silently. She had never felt this much pain. Never had she experienced what Amara had. Her eyes started to water as she looked up at Amara who was standing with her back facing Iris, her gaze focussed out the window. Biting her lip, Iris opened her mouth to say something but no words left her mouth. She shut her eyes for a moment, trying to block away the visions of what she had seen after Amara had let her into her mind. Even though she was not the one experiencing it, Iris felt every bit of pain that Amara did when she was being tortured. If this was not the reason for Amara to be so ruthless, then Iris did not know. There was so much agony; so many infuriated thoughts inside of Amara's head, that Iris could no longer feel the dislike she felt towards her when she first arrived. *Why would a woman not inflict pain on others when she had been subjected to extreme torture at such a young age?* She questioned herself. *How could a man even think of assaulting a woman like that? Was it justified? Was it, in any way, righteous to take a woman's innocence without her will, so forcefully? Did he gain information of the other witches that Amara had no idea about? Did he achieve the innocence of a seventeen-year-old who was unaware about what her fault was?* Iris' head was overflowing with questions that she decided were best left unanswered for the moment.

It wasn't the victims' fault when she gave pain to them, but it wasn't Amara's fault either. She was young, she was childish and she trusted a man who assured her happiness, but did she know where that would lead her? Iris wiped her tears and stood up, pushing her hair behind her ears. The amount of pain that Amara had gone through was beyond her imagination. She could never envision herself in a situation like hers. Now, her mind flooded with thoughts of what she would have done if she were in place of Amara. Iris shivered at the mere thought of it.

"It wasn't easy, of course, but I don't know what made me stay awake through it all," Amara said just as Iris started to approach her. She wanted to give her a hug but she knew better than that. Emotionless, that is what Amara was. She had a valid reason for that.

"The worst part is; I don't even remember how many times he came back after that. Maybe I was just too numb to notice," she said again, her voice void of all emotion and Iris remained silent.

This was the first time Amara was being honest and open without letting Iris invade her mind. She was actually telling her everything rather than showing it to her. However, Amara felt nothing, not one emotion crossed her mind when she thought back to what had happened. It had been years, and it did make her disgusted with herself but she was so far away from it all by this point, that she could hold a straight face and not wince as Iris did when she found out. Amara had grown accustomed to the incident that made her stronger and weaker all at the same time. She stared out the window; thinking about how she would make Iris trained enough to help her.

The cold vibes that she gave off to everyone was something she had adapted over time. Never letting her emotions come in way of what she wanted to achieve, and never letting herself grow any weaker after being vulnerable at one point. Her heart had gone cold, her mind had gone cold and her soul was under the cover of a stone. It was as though no part of her felt human, as though she had caged her soul inside. She felt no pain, no sorrow, nothing. Her heart and mind were trapped inside of her, and she held herself strong to keep it that way.

"Iris, I know this is hard for you to take. It has only been about two months since your training began. You are doing incredibly well and I know I didn't make the wrong decision in taking your help; but you still need to get stronger. You see these episodes of my past life so that I can make it easier for you to help me. I want you to be stronger from now on," said Amara as she turned around to face Iris.

"I understand, but can't you tell me what it is that you need help with? I need to know," she responded, stepping further.

Amara sighed, "I cannot tell you that at the moment, but I will when the time is right. I just want you to concentrate on your training for now. And when the time comes, I will tell you everything."

Iris nodded her head slightly as Amara walked past her out of the chamber. Letting out the breath she was holding, Iris walked to a chair and grabbed a decrepit volume of *Ancient Witchcraft* from the table on the side. Flipping through the pages, she pulled her feet up on the chair, and settled herself comfortably. It wasn't until the page of her book had a few drops of water on it that she realized she was crying. Her heart felt as though it was aching inside as she squeezed her eyes shut and let the tears fall.

* * *

Outside, Amara flew up to the highest tower of the castle and circled it before placing herself inside. She rested her fingers on the railing, inhaling the fresh morning air as the sun shone down at her.

"Pleasant morning, isn't it?" a voice said from behind her startling Amara slightly, as she turned around to find Nicholas, Lord Lucifer's nephew, standing there with his hands behind his back, grinning

Amara nodded in acknowledgement and turned back around to the scene in front of her. Nicholas was the hundred and fifty-year-old sorcerer, who still looked as though he was of twenty and known to be a charming one. He usually travelled a lot and occasionally visited Lord Lucifer. He was famous for being bright with the element of wind and had helped Lord Lucifer in training Amara. Known for his good looks and exceptional skills, he had witches falling at his feet. Amara was least affected. She had long eliminated the chance of any sorcerers being anywhere close to five feet of her. Nicholas, on the other hand, seemed just friendly, but not overly, because he was perfectly aware of how Amara was. His interest lay in other witches who were easily available. The coven knew how cold Amara was towards all the males and Amara knew why she was that way. She didn't have to explain herself to anyone.

"I heard that Lord Mikhail sent threats," he said, as he came to stand next to her.

"Mm, yes," she replied softly, giving a nod. Her eyes were scanning the woods surrounding the castle, and how it was illuminated by the sunlight. The castle gleamed in the brilliant rays of the sun. The woods in the distance, ominous, looked just as beautiful as they did at night.

"I have requested for protection from the King. But I'm sure he is under Lord Mikhail's influence," Nicholas said, looking out at the woods.

"I do not trust the King or his servants. Although, I don't reckon we need protection either. All of us are perfectly capable of protecting the castle."

"I am aware of that, but-"

"Nicholas, the King will only send people who are Lord Mikhail's servants. We can't take that risk." Amara shook her head, now looking at him.

"Then what do you suggest we do?" He asked, raising his eyebrows.

"Wait and see what our dear High Minister wants." She shrugged.

"Or send spies," Nicholas suggested.

"Spies? Who would want to spy on Lord Mikhail and put their lives in danger?" Amara said, raising an eyebrow.

"My messenger, of course." He smiled, as though stating the obvious. Amara frowned in confusion while Nicholas raised his hands in front of him and flicked his fingers when appeared a majestic, tawny eagle, flapping its wings and then coming to rest on his extended arm, as it gently nudged Nicholas on the cheek in a gesture that was an expression of pure and unadulterated love.

Amara stared at the beautiful bird in awe. Eagles, being magnificent creatures, she had always admired them. They were elegant and fierce at the same time. As a child, they fascinated her. They intrigued her and she wished to be around them. Eagles made her feel closer to herself but she had no idea how.

"Gather your kind and get us all the useful information about Lord Mikhail and what he is doing. I shall wait for you to return," he whispered to the bird who bowed its head, obeying what Nicholas said and looked at Amara once before flying away into the sky.

"I don't think their lives are going to be in danger. I suppose Lord Mikhail needs to be careful of these malevolent creatures," Nicholas said, smiling at his eagle.

"Well then, that is settled. If there isn't anything else, I think I should go back into the castle," said Amara and started walking to the staircase that led down into the castle.

"Wait, there is something I think you should know," Nicholas said and Amara stopped in her tracks, and waited for him to continue.

Nicholas walked over to her and looked at her seriously to which she focussed her attention. She sensed something important.

"Iris is being trained by Erasmus, am I correct?" He asked.

"Not particularly, he is just around to answer her questions. Mostly I am training her," Amara replied.

"Erasmus is Lord Mikhail's first target," he said.

"Erasmus? But he's harmless," Amara responded, giving a confused expression.

"Precisely, but he is very friendly with Iris. And she surely is a potential threat."

Amara nodded her head in understanding, a worried expression etching across her face. Erasmus was the link to Iris who had the capability of becoming a great witch. If Amara was a threat to Lord Mikhail, so was Iris one of the contenders who could stand in front of him in a war and defeat him. She had the potential to become a brilliant witch if properly trained. Erasmus was acting as a connection to her and the world of Conjurers. He was helping her adapt to everything that was new around her and he was the only person with whom she felt comfortable in the castle. If anything were to happen to him, there were chances that Iris would get weaker. Her motivation to deal with the surroundings of the darkness that she was about to face would go down a few levels and it would be difficult to help her reach her goal.

With Erasmus gone, Iris would be the next target. There was no doubt about his strength. He had been in the coven for more than two hundred years. He was strong enough to face the battles that were put forth. Iris was capable of being strong in every other thing, but the one weakness that she had, was Erasmus.

CHAPTER EIGHT

∞∞∞∞∞

THE KEEPER OF SECRETS

∞∞∞∞∞

L ord Mikhail strolled along the court, hands clasped behind his back and a perplexed expression across his face. King Orcus sat on the throne with his chin resting over his palm, in deep thought. The clock ticked by on the wall, the only sound heard in the otherwise silent court. All the Ministers and knights sat in grave silence, their thoughts lingering about in their heads for some way to solve Lord Mikhail's dilemma. Since the day Lord Mikhail had expressed his desire to take away Amara's powers, everyone had been trying to find some way of doing it so it would stay hidden. However, the results were all against them. For a long time, everyone tried to know why Lord Mikhail wanted to end the great witch, but he refused to divulge the information. Yet they all were given orders to find ways to do the task.

"Your highness, being a King, it is your duty to help us all. I ask for a little help, for taking away the powers of a weak witch and you can do absolutely nothing about it! Should you even be King?" complained Lord Mikhail in an angry voice.

The King looked up from the ground and stared at Lord Mikhail silently. He had no answer, he kept telling himself that he should be a good King but he never wanted to be one.

He wished for a simple life, away from all of this, where he could live peacefully with his wife. *If only my brother, King Salmoneus, had not abdicated*, he thought, *I wouldn't have been the heir*. His mind went back to a day several moons ago.

* * *

"*I apologize, your highness. But I won't be able to serve you as High Minister,*" *said Lord Lucifer, bowing down in grace to King Orcus.*

They were in the court of the king's palace, Lord Lucifer and the other Ministers sat there on their thrones, to appoint Lord Lucifer as the High Minister.

"*Lord Lucifer, your ancestors have been our High Ministers for centuries now, why must you deny such an honour? It would only be breaking the tradition,*" *argued the King.*

"*Your highness,*" *Lord Lucifer began.* "*Acanthus is in threat. The attacks by witch-hunters have increased and there is absolutely no protection for the land. I wish to create a coven of the strongest Conjurers to keep Acanthus safe.*"

"*Lord Lucifer,*" *said Lord Mikhail, standing up from his throne.* "*I believe that you can gather your Conjurers even while serving His Grace. As far as protection of the land is concerned, I believe that is being taken care of by our guards and goblins at every corner of Acanthus. Why then, do you wish to break a tradition?*" *Lord Mikhail strolled up to Lord Lucifer to where he was standing before the king.* "*In all honesty, Lord Lucifer, there are plenty of us Ministers who can take your post but none of us wish to break a century old custom. We strive to maintain traditions in our land, and we would appreciate it if you did the same.*"

"*I am sorry, Lord Mikhail, but I cannot accept the post. My only concern is to protect our land and that can't be done while* serving as High Minister. There are responsibilities that I will not be able to fulfil if I were to serve the realm," said Lord Lucifer.

"You can-" Lord Mikhail began when King Orcus raised a palm to silence him.

"My lords, do not trouble yourselves over a trivial matter such as this. If Lord Lucifer wants to resign from the post then he is allowed to do so. We can always have another High Minister. All of you are capable enough and it does not matter who takes the post," the King said and Lord Mikhail began to protest, when he continued. "Lord Mikhail, you are welcome to take the post of High Minister and serve the realm. Lord Lucifer is free to go."

"Your highness." Lord Lucifer bowed in grace before taking a few steps backwards and leaving the courtroom.

"Your magnificence!" Lord Mikhail exclaimed. "Lord Lucifer is merely trying to create a empire of his own this way. We cannot seem to agree to let that happen. I am sure we can appoint more guards for Acanthus to be protected from the attacks of witch-hunters. This is not the way to-"

"Lord Mikhail, let us not ponder upon this anymore. Let Lord Lucifer protect the land. I give him my consent. It will take time for him to create a strong coven. There is nothing he can possibly do to harm us. I would appreciate it if you agreed to take the post as High Minister so the proceedings of the court can continue peacefully," the King said and Lord Mikhail let out a breath before nodding his head.

"I would be honoured, your highness," he said. After all, there was only so much you could protest in front of a King, how much ever feeble and incompetent he may be.

* * *

"Forgive me, Lord Mikhail," he said in a meek voice, waking the king from his reverie, "But I believe this is not the way you speak to the King. *However* unsatisfied you are with him. It does not give you the right to talk to him this way," concluded Samael, the youngest Minister, a bit more confidently.

"And who are you to talk, *Lord* Samael? You *dare* address me? An inexperienced sorcerer who has next to no knowledge," Lord Mikhail replied, a menacing look on his face. Samael looked down, ashamed.

"Lord Mikhail, I have always tried to be of help to you but we all know that she isn't a weak witch. That is the reason we cannot compete with her. For a witch like Amara we need someone who is as brilliant and as brave as her, who can finish her off using wit above strength." the King sighed.

Lord Mikhail looked at the King for a while. *Well, he is right for once*, he mused to himself. As much as he wanted to deny it, he knew Amara was nowhere close to being a weak witch. To defeat her, they needed someone as strong or stronger. It wasn't an easy task, finding someone who could stand forth her and fight. What she was protecting, needed incredible strength that, which she possessed. To achieve that, to gain that, a fight was essential. Her powers were to be taken away; her greatness had to be brought down to get what he wanted; but who would be capable of standing against her?

"We need a trained, powerful witch or sorcerer to defeat her. All those who have enough power are in Lord Lucifer's coven. We require a skilled warrior," Lord Zachariah said, looking with a hopeful expression at Lord Mikhail.

Lord Zachariah, the eldest sorcerer in the land of Acanthus knew everything about Lord Mikhail. From his birth to his training, he knew all the little details. Being the only person that Lord Mikhail respected, Lord Zachariah had knowledge that knew no bounds. He was learned in witchcraft, had performed various rituals in his life, created spells, potions, trained Conjurers of all kinds. He was seven-hundred-years old, and was getting weaker since he stopped taking the *Elixir of Immortality*. Lord Mikhail regarded Lord Zachariah silently, trying to understand his message. When he nodded, the great Lord smiled knowingly. He had gotten the message.

"If his highness permits, we could declare war," Lord Mikhail offered, looking at the King and the Ministers hopefully.

"A war?" The King raised his eyebrows.

"Yes, your highness. Our Ministers seem to agree upon the fact that Lord Lucifer is creating a coven this strong so he can become the next King. If a war is declared, we can destroy his entire coven."

"I believe Lord Mikhail is right," said Lord Gabriel.

The King paused for a few moments and then said, "All said and done, Lord Mikhail, you should allow the Ministers and me a fortnight, to ponder over the matter and come to a conclusion." He concluded sighing.

"A fortnight would be too long, I believe, your highness, but if you insist," said Lord Mikhail. Lord Mikhail bowed curtly, with one last lingering look in the direction of Lord Zachariah, he stalked out of the court, his black robes swishing behind him along the marble floor. Letting out a sigh, the King glanced around and left the court as well to find some fresh air.

The thought of having to face war again was daunting. The King would rather not think about it and decided to shun it aside. He always knew that war was impending since the day Lord Lucifer walked out of his castle to commence his own coven. The years of mutual animosity between his coven and that of Lord Lucifer's was kept at bay due to his, the King's, disinterest in such matters. But, that fateful day was now dawning. And hard as he tried to avoid it, it was bound to dawn.

* * *

Back in his seat, Lord Zachariah closed his eyes and connected immediately with Lord Mikhail's mind. *You will find Lady Calypsa in the deep waters of Cypress. Meet with Lord Perseus. He will be your guide to the one who will vanquish Amara.*

As soon as the message entered Lord Mikhail's mind, he began his journey to the Sea of Cypress.

* * *

Inside her chamber, Iris sat on a chair with Erasmus opposite to her. She wanted so much to tell him what Amara had made her see, but she had sworn not to tell anyone. It was Amara's past, her secret to tell and Iris had no right to reveal it to another person. It was better that Erasmus didn't know, he was already privy to lots of other things. Nevertheless, he could help her with meditation that she had been trying to master for the past month. After a while, she had started to get very impatient and wanted to give up, but Erasmus urged her on and helped her in any way he could.

"Imagine a ferocious dragon," said Erasmus, trying to cheer up an unresponsive Iris. For the past two days, she had been quite down and moody. She barely spoke at all, which was beginning to bother him.

"Why?" She retorted apathetically, her eyes fixed on the rug below her feet. Erasmus rolled his eyes, letting out a sigh.

"Iris, what is it that's bothering you so? You have been acting really strange," he finally said, unable to control his curiosity.

"I just can't do this, you know! I mean, I have been reading books about witchcraft and witches and everything, but I don't know what I am supposed to do. There are so many skills witches have, and I am sitting here with absolutely nothing! What am I doing?" She let out a frustrated sigh.

Erasmus sealed his lips, running a hand through his hair. *This girl is extremely impatient*, he thought to himself. She refuses to understand the concept of time. It wasn't easy to be a good witch even though she possessed the skills. She was unaware of putting them into action, which needed training. Training took a lot of time. Witches spent more than ten years to master the arts and here Iris was getting impatient in just a couple months.

"I told you this before, it takes time. This is not easy. You have the skills but you need to be good at them, and you need to give yourself some time. Calm down," he said, placing a hand on her shoulder in an attempt to assure her. Iris glanced at him once before standing up and pulling on her hair in frustration. Erasmus had not seen a more infuriated witch. She was going mad.

He opened his mouth to say something when a knock sounded on the door. "Am I interrupting something?" Nicholas poked his head in through the door, a little smile across his face.

Erasmus straightened up and smiled back at his old friend. Nicholas and Erasmus had been friends from the day they had joined the coven, but since Nicholas travelled a lot, they hardly got to spend time with each other. "Good evening, Nicholas," he said, and Nicholas stepped inside before giving a warm, brotherly hug to Erasmus.

Iris turned around only to have her eyes widened at the sight of the beautiful creature standing in front of her. Erasmus hid a chuckle at her reaction. She stood there agape, a surprised look etched upon her face. It seemed as though she was at a loss of words. Nicholas glanced down, hiding a smile and shot a mischievous look at Erasmus before turning back to Iris who was still staring at him, motionless.

"It's a pleasure to be in the company of such a delightful witch. I'm Nicholas, by the way, and you are?" He asked, extending his arm in front of her even though he was perfectly aware of her identity. He always did background research on the new witches that joined the coven, despite of the fact that he was barely ever in Acanthus. For a moment, Iris looked lost but gained her senses and blinked, noticing the outstretched hand of the Adonis standing in front of her. *Well, I'm only a sixteen-year-old human,* she mused to herself. She was allowed to admire good-looking men, regardless of the fact that they were sorcerers and she knew nothing about them.

"Iris," she finally replied, a little out of breath albeit, placing her hand in his. Nicholas smiled at her, bending a bit and bringing her hand up to his lips as he gently placed a kiss on it. Iris resisted the blush that was creeping along her cheeks. Erasmus cleared his throat, biting back an amused laugh and looked at Iris, "Would you like to have some tea, Iris? You need to clear your head," he said.

Iris snapped her attention back to Erasmus when Nicholas let go of her hand.

"Oh I-no… I think I'm, I'm, I am okay," she stammered, giving a slight shrug of her shoulders. Erasmus sent a silent message to Nicholas who nodded and stepped closer to Iris. She attentively looked at him when he did so. Her eyes were still wide enough and Nicholas resisted the urge to snigger at her innocence.

"It would break my heart if you didn't come have tea with us, Iris, it really would," he said, dramatically placing a hand on his chest, with a sad expression on his face. Keeping his eyes focussed on hers, he gave her the daunting stare that could make people give into his charm.

Not surprisingly enough, Iris nodded her head with her eyes still stuck on his face as he stepped away smiling. He gestured to Erasmus to follow him. Iris blinked, dazed and then frowned for a moment before sauntering out of the chamber behind Erasmus. She felt as though she didn't know what had happened a few moments ago. Shaking her head, she walked behind the two men as they led her to the kitchen.

Pots rested above the stoves, the spoons stirring themselves inside as light smoke wafted out of a few cauldrons, creating the fragrance of different sorts of food in there. Iris suddenly missed the normal food she had had back in her home. The food here was definitely different but the same as what humans ate. Everyone was a vegetarian and herbs were the main ingredients. In the month that she had been here, Iris had become quite accustomed to the eating patterns that she took a little time to adapt.

In the morning, everyone had tea and fruits, which was followed by a lunch at noon that consisted of salads and herb juices. For five hours, they were allowed to have water and then some juices. Dinner never happened, and if anyone got hungry, which they barely did apart from Iris, they were allowed to have a salad of herbs. Everything tasted very good, but she got hungry quite a lot of times during the day. *They all have such appalling physiques and beautiful faces only because they all are generally on every fat-free substance*, Iris thought.

"Have a seat," Erasmus said pointing at an old and rickety three-legged stool to Iris who now held a cup of steaming herb infused raspberry tea in her hands, staring at it blankly. She could still not get the image of Amara being tortured by Leo out of her head. It haunted her every now and then and she could barely forget about it. The worst part was that she could not tell anyone. Nicholas tugged at Iris as he gestured for her to sit. She glanced at him once and then sat on the rickety stool, next to Erasmus and Nicholas who sat opposite to her. Nicholas rested his hands on the walnut panelled table in between. They talked in the kitchen for a while, sipping the tea as Iris tried her best to take part in the conversations but every now and then, her mind would wander back to Amara. *How could she experience all that and be calm about it?* She thought. *Did she not feel like screaming in frustration? How could a woman build up so much strength?*

More questions ran through her mind, the answers to which were never found. She kept thinking upon what it could be that she was capable of helping Amara with. How could she be of any help to such a great witch? To a woman who had gone through so much and yet emerged out this strong. Just at the thought of her parents being dead, Iris would shudder in pain while Amara had watched her family being burnt alive, in front of her along with the additional pain of being the victim of Leo. Her reverence for Amara kept on growing the more she thought about it, and the nagging stabs of pain thinking of how she went through it also increased.

Nicholas observed Iris calmly after Erasmus had left to go for some work and Iris had not even noticed him walk away. Her face was expressive, Nicholas could understand that there was something bothering her and she wanted to get rid of it. He could sense that she had the potential of being a great witch. The only thing coming in her way was her childishness and impatience. If that was gone, she would realize her true capabilities. Erasmus and Amara were doing a good job but they needed assistance, and Iris needed motivation. *She needs lots of motivation*, he said to himself and took it upon him to help Erasmus and Amara with the job.

* * *

Miles away, the waves of the Sea of Cypress crashed upon the shore, the waters black and terrifying. Under the moonlight and the darkening sky, the wild waves could have petrified a human. A tall figure stood upon the rocks at the shore. Arms spread to the sides, it rose in the air before diving graciously into the water, vanishing immediately. The water roared as though trying to fight something and the clouds thundered with lightening.

Lord Lucifer stood at a distance, watching the grave waters as the lightning illuminated the sky. Raising his foot, he placed it on the water for a long moment and the waves suddenly went still. Calmness surrounded the shore, and the wind – now colder than ever – stung his skin but he could barely feel it.

Closing his eyes, Lord Lucifer pulled his foot away to find a wave rising up from the middle of the sea, swirling around ferociously and morphing into the hooded figure of a woman. She stood there, her head low and hands bendy at the sides. Moments later, she lifted her head to look at Lord Lucifer. Gliding across the water, she approached him and stood before him over the water. Her face was hidden, her body covered in a huge mouldy green cloak. Only her wrists were visible. Her fingers were thin and wrinkled with long dirty nails. She had a frightening appearance, almost ghastly. She had no feet and dangled in the air, centimetres above the water, her robes so long, she seemed to be coming out from the waves behind her.

"What does the Lord seek? What is your concern, great Lord? Does he need weapons, or strength, or does he wish to sacrifice a human to me?" She spoke, her voice a mere whisper, husky and deep. It was horrible in the most subtle way.

"I'm here to have you take an oath for me," began Lord Lucifer, "You have always been of great help, oh Empress of the Seas, and I do not question your loyalty. Although I must make sure that your duty remains solely to me," Lord Lucifer concluded, in a calm but serious tone.

Lady Calypsa remained silent for a while as though pondering upon something. Then she spoke, "I owe my existence to nothing, oh great Lord. I have created myself, hidden myself in these waters and safeguarded the greatest treasures that your ancestors have possessed. They trust me to protect everything and I swore to it. You ask me to take an oath, which implies your wavering trust on me, m'Lord. I have my duty to all the sorcerers and all the witches that seek my help. I swore to be of assistance to all those who need me and not be caged to one. My freedom is of no concern to you, great sorcerer. Although, I must assure you, the secrets that you tell, the help that you need will remain with me for as long as I exist and to eternity. An oath, however, I have never taken, and never will. Express your need, m'Lord and I shall seek the solution." She circled around him in the air and stood in position again, her gaze focussed on Lord Lucifer who seemed in deep thought.

"The treasure that you and my most loyal apprentice guard is to be kept safe for as long as I am here. Some seek that treasure, some desire it, and some need it. The threat is increasing, Great Lady. Your strength will be questioned, the prophecy will be known to all when the dark forces try to steal the treasure away. Swear to protect it, swear to protect my loyal apprentice, swear to never divulge it to those who ask for it," he said gravely.

"Oh glorious Lord, I have my duty to you, unfailing faith is what I desire from you. Your apprentice, your trusted will be protected. The treasure will be safe. The prophecy is bound to be known, and no one can stop it. The truth will be told, but Lord of mine, I swear to protect the treasure forever, for as long as you wish for it to be safeguarded. And she will be safe, do not perturb yourself, oh Lord, she will live to tell the tale."

With that, Lady Calypsa swirled back into the water and disappeared, the waves starting to get wild once again. Lord Lucifer held himself back from summoning her once more. As loyal as she was, she could also be vile when she wished to. With one last lingering glance in the direction of the sea, he started taking steps back to the way he came from. If Lady Calypsa swore to protect Amara and the treasure, he had nothing to worry about. He had no choice but to trust her, for she was loyal, faithful and devoted. Lord Lucifer took hold of his robes and sauntered away into the valley of the huge mountains, starting his journey to gather more apprentices for his coven. For if it was true, what Lord Mikhail sought, he was going to need as many Conjurers as he could.

The waves crashed at the shore behind him again and a light rose up from the middle of the water, in a moment it reached the skies, trembling as it did so. Deep inside the sea at the bed, Lady Calypsa shut the door of the passage that led to the possession of Lord Lucifer's ancestors that was kept hidden inside a cave millions of miles below at the bed of the sea. The light descended from the sky back into the water and chains bound themselves on the door, sealing the passage completely. The Lady swam around in the sea, shooting up wild waves upon the shore wherever she went past.

* * *

In the castle, Amara sat perched upon the railing of the highest tower, the lake about thirty feet below her. Her legs dangled in the air. She stood up, spreading her arms to her sides and turning her back to the water. Lifting herself off the railing, she twirled around and dropped herself into the water, the waves rising up for a moment as she dove in. Iris sat in her chamber, watching the scene unfold in front of her and she could not help but think about the dream that she had when she was in the human world. In her dream, she had seen a figure diving into a vast terrifying sea, the same way that Amara did.

∞∞∞∞∞

CHAPTER NINE

THE GUARDIAN

∞∞∞∞∞

A mara looked at Iris, puzzled. She was standing outside her chamber, holding a book in her hands and a tiny vial of *Phoenix Blood*.

"Yes?" Amara asked, raising her eyebrows.

"I have a few questions. May I come in?" Iris asked with a hopeful smile.

Amara contemplated whether to let Iris in the chamber. No one had ever entered her chamber and she didn't want to change that. Although, now, Iris was on the verge of forcing herself inside so Amara reluctantly nodded and gave her way. Her grin widened and she stepped inside, glancing around the chamber in awe. Iris admired the dark atmosphere, the deep blue curtains sashaying playfully as a chilly wind entered from the slightly ajar window, the side table with two rickety chairs, a little bed in the corner, a Fireplace with a huge sunken chair and a dead bearskin for a mat at its feet, lamps glowing gently, resting on the walls at a few places and a bookshelf that contained many interesting old books.

Ignoring her, Amara walked up to the side table and took a seat on a chair. Iris followed, settling on the chair opposite to her. She placed the book of *Ancient Witchcraft* on the table along with the vial of *Phoenix Blood* before turning to look at Amara. She was lost watching the flames dance in the Fireplace.

"Amara?" Iris said, hoping she would look at her. Amara snapped her attention to Iris.

"You told me about *Phoenix Blood*. That it grants life, but whoever drinks it cannot contain it for long; and you told me about a witch who drank the blood. Who was she?" She asked with a curious expression on her face.

"Did you not find anything in the books?" Amara retorted, raising an eyebrow.

"Not exactly, it only says that the witch was a great one and her name was Lilith. There is no mention of the story behind her taking the blood. I mean, given the consequences and that she was a great witch, she must have had a good reason to do what she did. Can you tell me anything about her?"

"It's a very long story, Iris. I think you would get bored," Amara replied, unsure of whether or not she should reveal the story. Iris seemed adamant.

"I won't get bored. Please do tell me," she said with a curious glint in her eyes. Impressed by the determination the new witch had, Amara began telling her the tale of the great witch.

"Lilith Angelique Juniperus was born in the year 1538. Coming from a great sorcerer's family, she had no parents. Lilith lived with her dying grandmother. Once, while looking for potential mentors, she came across a book at the age of sixteen. The book belonged to the then King of Acanthus, King Abraham Baltheir who had bewitched it for protection from the enemy land. The book was about the darkest witchcraft and he was looking for a solution to destroy it or save it from getting into wrong hands. One day, when he was travelling to meet learned sorcerers, he met with some witch-hunters. After fighting bravely to save himself, he was abducted, but using his powers, he hid the book so only the virtuous and the deserving find it and destroy it.

"When Lilith came across that book in the great woods of *Aughmor*, she realized that it contained dark witchcraft. After consulting her grandmother, who died few days later, Lilith went in search of finding a mentor. Reaching Acanthus, she met with a great sorcerer by the name of Hermys. He trained her in witchcraft and Lilith became an exceptional witch who had vast knowledge and did great deeds during her existence. She lived for two-hundred-years but could never find a way to destroy the book so it would not get into wrong hands. Her quest never rested.

"Years later, exhausted, she lay at the shore of the Sea of Cypress where a lady emerged from the dark waters and addressed her saying the book wasn't to be destroyed, but hidden somewhere no one would find it. The Sea of Cypress was known to have saved great treasures and Lady Calypsa, being the guardian, had been protecting everything. Lilith agreed to hide the book in the bed of the great Sea, but she was heard by King Abraham's enemy, who had been keeping track of her for a long time. When she was about to hide the book, the enemy attacked a now weak Lilith. Yet, she used all her strength to fight but was on the verge of dying. Lady Calypsa could only help by offering her *Phoenix Blood*, with the consequences told. Because the enemy had taken away the book from her, leaving her to die, Lilith agreed to take the blood.

"It was very difficult for her to control it but she tried her hardest and fought with the enemy again while Lady Calypsa snatched the book away after he was distracted. The book was hidden in the Sea soon after, and Lilith, in the end, lost herself to her pride on saving the book. Her haughtiness of being the only one to endure *Phoenix Blood* and contain it inside of her drove her to the point of insanity, until she was begging for Death. Unable to control herself any longer, she set herself on Fire. From that day on, nobody dared to drink *Phoenix Blood*. Lady Calypsa, in the Sea of Cypress is known to have hidden grave treasures and possessions of witches and she still continues to do so."

Iris's mouth was agape when Amara finished telling her the story. She told herself there was no way she would ever take *Phoenix Blood*. She would rather die.

Letting out a sigh, she said, "Okay, um, and the book is still hidden in the sea? Did nobody ever try to take it?" Iris asked.

"People did try to find out what the book was about. Nobody knows what all it held because Lilith never told anyone. And Lady Calypsa has been protecting it until now," answered Amara.

"What all things are there in the Sea of Cypress?" Iris asked again, the curiosity bubbling inside of her. A tad bit impatient, Amara did answer her questions.

"As far as I know, there are possessions of great witches who had no capable heirs so they handed them over to Lady Calypsa. Things like swords, ancient books, the gifts granted by goddesses, powerful weapons, and-" she hesitated.

"And?" Iris urged.

There was one other thing that could not be revealed to Iris or anybody else apart from Amara, Lord Lucifer and Lady Calypsa.

"And other things that I am not particularly aware of," she said, dropping the subject.

Iris's face fell. Her curiosity was unsatisfied and for a moment, she considered invading Amara's mind to know what she was hiding. The way she hesitated, Iris was sure there was something she had not talked about; but she knew that there was no way Amara would let her know if she didn't want it to be known. She was capable enough of hiding it even if Iris invaded her mind.

"How do you know all this? The books didn't give me so much information," Iris enquired.

"The Lord is a descendant of the Lord Hermys, who was a great sorcerer and the one that trained Lilith. His valour was well known. Legend has it that he extracted the blood of the last Cymmerien dragon, which is known to be the deadliest poison there is. It's supposed to be one of the things that Lady Calypsa protects in the Sea of Cypress," Amara said. "But it could only be a story. There is no proof of it being true. Cymmerien dragons went extinct centuries ago," she paused. "I want you to keep this information to yourself, Iris. Enough people know about it and we do not need more. You are not to discuss this with anyone else. Do you understand?" Amara said in all seriousness.

Looking at her face, Iris realized the intensity of the situation and nodded her head quickly. "I won't talk about this again," she said.

"Good. Now is there anything else you want to ask?"

"No. I'm done," replied Iris as she stood up to leave, since she understood she wasn't supposed to linger around in Amara's private chamber after her work was done.

Although, she did like the ambience. Her chamber wasn't this lavish. Shaking that thought out of her head, Iris proceeded towards the door and walked outside with the bottle of *Phoenix Blood* in her hand. It looked much more dangerous now that she knew the whole story. Shuddering at the mere thought of it, she replaced it in the potions chamber before retreating to her own.

* * *

Inside her chamber, Amara let out a sigh as the piece of parchment trembled in her hands. She read the words again:

To possess it, a loved one must be killed.

Placing it back inside the book, she shut it and kept it in the bookshelf again. Amara shut her eyes for a moment, forgetting about the Sea of Cypress and jumped out of her window to go into the woods. It was a new moon night and as custom, she had to meditate.

* * *

Iris sat in her chamber going through the book of *Ancient Witchcraft* when the sound of swirling winds came from outside her window. Frowning, she stood up and walked to the window to find Nicholas standing outside rotating his arms in the air.

"What is he doing?" She whispered to herself.

Nicholas raised his arms higher in the air and wind rose above carrying stray leaves from the ground that circled around him for a while then fell back down and the whirling sound vanished.

"Wish to join me, Iris?" He asked, turning bemusedly to face her. She looked at him quietly before stepping out the back door of the chamber. When she stood next to Nicholas, he gave her a smile and raised his arms in front of him again.

"Try to copy me," he said to her and she followed his movements, raising her arms above.

Nicholas closed his eyes and twisted his arms so the wind again made a whirling noise and the leaves rose along. Iris bit her lower lip and copied what he was doing, but nothing happened. She tried once again, but the leaves remained on the ground and the wind made no sounds around her. Dejected, she let her arms fall to the sides, thinking that Nicholas had invited her outside just to make fun of her. She began retreating when he opened his eyes and looked at her with his eyebrows raised.

"It's not that easy," he said.

"Of course it isn't. How do you expect me to do it? I'm new and I'm not a trained witch," she replied with remorse.

"Well, you will only be trained when someone helps you; and all new witches started from the scratch."

"At least they knew who they were from the start." She shrugged, looking away.

"Not all of them. Some were like you, curious, impatient, childlike." Nicholas winked at her. Iris dropped her jaw, narrowing her eyes. *Was it necessary for all good looking men to be so mean and arrogant? Were witches not different from humans?*

"I'm not a child," she said, offended.

"Obviously not, but your mind refuses to grow up," he whispered in her ear, circling around her and coming to stand in front of her. Iris looked at him with her forehead furrowed. She didn't like the way he was talking, but what could she possibly reply to that?

"My mind is fine," she managed finally and turned around to go back in her chamber when Nicholas appeared in front of her and she stepped back, startled. Folding her arms across her chest, she stood there with an annoyed expression, not wanting to hear what he had to say if he was only going to shoot insults.

"Learning to handle elements is the first step to becoming a great witch. You have to start from the beginning. A short temper isn't going to help, though," he said, smirking.

Iris wanted to punch him for being so arrogant but he had a point. Her impatience was acting up. For a while, she had thought she was going back to normal after forgetting about Amara's past but this man had to come along to remind her that she had lot of things to do.

"Fine but I'd rather learn from Erasmus." Iris turned back around and Nicholas let out a slight chuckle.

"He isn't so good at tackling the element of Air. I am," he said, shrugging.

She didn't reply, but Nicholas got the message and turned to face her completely.

"Close your eyes," he said and Iris did so, but as soon as her eyes went blind, the sensation of a vision entering her mind began to work its way. She wanted to open her eyes immediately when she realized she was invading someone's mind. There was no one's mind she had been able to invade apart from Amara's, when she was thinking of her past. Nicholas's voice was now just a foggy whisper that she was unable to decipher. She tried hard to pull herself out of Amara's mind, but flashes of a few scenes continued.

* * *

"The prophecy is hidden yet known to many. . ."

"I swore to protect her and I will do so!"

Lord Lucifer pulled his sword out and slashed his neck, grabbing Amara by the arm and dragging her away from the dungeons.

"He will save you," Thomas said and jumped out of the window, running away. Amara screamed in agony, "LEAVE ME! LET ME GO!" Her leg caught in his grasp and she struggled to get away.

"She has to protect the treasures. . ."

"NO!" she screamed.

* * *

Iris opened her eyes to someone shaking her gently. She was breathing heavily, half-lying on the ground, her head cradled in Erasmus's arms. He helped her up and kept an arm wrapped around her shoulder to support her tiny frame. Nicholas held out a glass of water and Iris took it from him, gulping it down in one go.

"Are you okay?" Erasmus asked. Iris nodded, unable to say anything. She blinked a few times to register her surroundings.

"Here, get up," Nicholas said and held out a hand, pulling her up to standing.

"Let's get her inside. Give her the *Fire and Ice potion*," Nicholas said to Erasmus and he nodded, taking Iris inside the castle with him.

Nicholas turned around and started walking towards the woods where he knew Amara would be present. From what he observed, Iris's condition had something to do with Amara since she called out her name twice before collapsing. Whatever it was, things were getting seriously complicated and he had to find out before he left to travel again.

Once he reached the woods, he made his way into the deeper parts upon hearing a chanting sound; the prayers for the Goddess Luna. Approaching the sound he set his feet in position when he found Amara seated on the ground, her eyes closed and back straight, she recited the prayer and the words literally ascended to the sky, which was now starting to thunder. Nicholas stood there for a while, thinking of whether or not he should disturb Amara. The ritual of the new moon night went on until dawn and it was nowhere close to daybreak now. She would not like it if she were disturbed. Retracing his steps, Nicholas started to go back when a spirit appeared in front of him, circling around to block his path.

"She is in grave danger. Save her, save her!" the spirit whispered before vanishing away from sight. Nicholas stood there perplexed for a moment and then swiftly walked out of the woods and back into the castle. Iris was in danger.

* * *

The rock broke into crystals and shattered around as Lord Mikhail stood outside the cave, now rid of the huge rock blocking his path. Pushing the crystals away, he ventured inside the dark cave that was only lit by the torch Lord Mikhail was carrying in one hand. He walked further in a long passage, which went up and down as his feet moved forward. A while later, he was met with a figure seated over a big stone, candles burning around him. Lord Mikhail observed the man. With a long beard that reached his chest, he wore a red robe around his shoulders that cascaded down to the ground after overlapping the stone, white hair as long as his beard, and a wrinkled face. The old man sat in clear concentration, his body rigid and the only movement seen was his chest rising and falling slightly as he breathed.

Lord Mikhail approached further in and stood in front of the man, unable to go ahead because of the candles in the path.

"Lord Perseus, I come here to seek help," said Lord Mikhail, bowing his head in respect.

The great sorcerer, Lord Perseus, was five-hundred-years old and known for defeating dark witches. After years of bravery and fighting wars, he had taken to rest in the caves of Darald where he meditated for years and helped lost travellers find their way. He was known to have an answer for everything. Lord Mikhail waited for the great sorcerer to open his eyes.

After a while, Lord Perseus looked at Lord Mikhail who was standing there in position patiently.

"Lord Mikhail, High Minister of King Orcus," he said, his voice deep and clear.

"Yes, m'Lord." Lord Mikhail nodded.

"What do you desire?"

"You are aware about Lady Calypsa in the Sea of Cypress. It is said that she only appears to those who have either known her for centuries, or those who have prayed to her for years. I wish to meet her, but I do not know her and I don't have the time to pray to her. I seek help, m'Lord. How do I get her to speak to me?" asked Lord Mikhail, placing his torch in a corner.

"Lady Calypsa is a spirit of greatness. If one cannot pray to her for gaining her approval, one has to have the eminent desire to see her. Your mind should be that strong and unmoving. She should be the only concern for whatever reason you wish to meet her. If your desire and your faith are that strong, she will appear without the years of praying," answered Lord Perseus.

Lord Mikhail sighed in contempt. He didn't know whether he could have the strong will that the Lord had just described. His only concern was what she was protecting. He was unsure if he could make her his only concern or desire. Lord Perseus closed his eyes again and resumed his meditation, leaving Lord Mikhail with the answer, which was his job to put into work. He stood there for a longer time, thinking about what he would do. Lady Calypsa surely didn't seem an easy goal to achieve. But then again, what he wanted from her wasn't something easy either. There had to be some sacrifice if he wished to gain what he desired.

A while later, Lord Mikhail picked up his torch from the corner and began walking out of the cave to find his way to the Sea of Cypress thinking that somehow he would eventually find a solution even though Lord Perseus had just given him the answer to his queries. But it was said that whatever answer the great Lord gave was always difficult to work upon. His answers were confusing but correct at the same time. It was up to the seeker to get to the right way of solving problems. When Lord Mikhail was about to walk deeper into the passage to get out of the cave, a voice stopped him. "There is but another answer to your question, Minister," said Lord Perseus.

Lord Mikhail turned around and walked back to where Lord Perseus was sitting. His eyes were still closed, but he said, "Lady Calypsa is not the only one guarding the treasures that you so dearly seek. There is a witch who protects the treasure and does not need to be prayed to."

CHAPTER TEN

∞∞∞∞∞∞

SPIRIT OF DEATH

∞∞∞∞∞∞

There was a knocking sound. At first Amara ignored it. When it persisted, she sat up from the bed that she was halfway asleep on, to look at the time. It was 3 am and the knocking had not stopped, it was getting louder. Frowning, she stood up and walked to the door, resting a palm on it and staying silent as to wait for the sound to come again. As soon as it sounded again, she said, "Who is it?"

"Fabian, Amara open the door it's urgent," came the voice from the other side and Amara immediately opened the door, coming to face Fabian. He stood there panic-stricken, breathing heavily as though he had run a few miles.

"What's wrong, Fabian?" Amara asked, stepping out of her room.

"Nicholas, he's injured. You have to come," he said and turned around, expecting her to follow him and she did as they began rushing to where Fabian was leading. Moments later, he stopped outside the great hall, where everyone sat in a circle. Some were standing while others were crouched on the floor. Amara pushed through them and reached the middle where Nicholas was lying on the floor, trembling every now and then as blood splurged out of his abdomen, a gash across his forehead and his left leg twisted in a painful way. In a corner, Iris was shivering next to Erasmus who was trying hard to comfort her. Beside Nicholas was seated the coven's healer and two-hundred-year old sorcerer, Soter. He pressed one of his palms on Nicholas's abdomen, which had been injured. It was a deep wound.

"Amara, the *Healing Potion* is over. I cannot find it anywhere. Apart from me, only you know how to formulate it. I need you to go and prepare it, now," said Soter, looking up from Nicholas to Amara.

"But it takes three days to get it properly prepared," Amara said, worriedly as she bent down to sit on the floor.

"I know, but you can prepare it in three hours using one drop of the *Spirit of Death*. I can hold him until then with *Dove's Blood*," replied Soter.

"*Spirit of Death* is dangerous. It could kill him!" Sienna, another cloaked witch protested from the side.

"One drop wouldn't. Amara, you know what to do. Go, we don't have much time," Soter said and Amara stood up immediately, rushing to the potions chamber. Iris watched her walk away while Nicholas screamed when Soter let a few drops of dove's blood onto the injured part of his abdomen. Gathering her strength, Iris pushed herself away from Erasmus and proceeded to go to the potions chamber. When she entered the chamber, she spotted Amara rushing from one corner to another, gathering the ingredients for the potion. Iris approached her and stood at the side, saying, "Do you need any help?"

Amara glanced at Iris once before shifting back to the work at hand. "Fetch me the box of herbs and some water from the lake in the woods. Run," she replied hastily as Iris grabbed the box of herbs, handing it to Amara before rushing out to the woods as fast as her legs could take her.

In the goblet she was holding, she filled the fresh water and ran back to the chamber, making sure the water does not fall out of the goblet. Panting, she placed the goblet on the table next to the pot that Amara was stirring the herbs into. She added the water and other ingredients before letting it stir itself while she mixed a few other ingredients in a cauldron. Iris silently watched, taking in mind all the ingredients.

"Do you know what happened?" Amara asked, not looking away from the work she was doing.

"Nicholas was teaching me the power of the element of Air in the mountains of Carvelli, as you know, since the last three days. Everything was good until midnight when I was meditating and Nicholas was lighting the Fire. I am not aware of what exactly happened, but I heard him arguing with someone. Since I had only just started, I left the meditation and began looking for him. When I found him, Nicholas was battling with another man. Blinding lights were shooting from their fingers and I didn't know what to do. Then suddenly I saw that man turn to me and a red coloured light rushed in my direction, when Nicholas jumped in front of me and took the blow, while throwing a curse at him. The man collapsed. The curse that the man had cast hit Nicholas's abdomen and injured him." She paused to take a breath. "Because he jumped in front of me too fast, he twisted his ankle in the process. Then I somehow managed to get him back here. The fact that the Carvelli Mountains are not very far was a good thing." Iris revealed, a tear slipping down her eye and she wiped it away immediately.

Amara stared at the cauldron in front of her. "Why would anyone try to attack you?" She whispered to herself when realization struck her and she dropped the spoon onto the table, using which, she was going to mix the ingredients.

"Of course, how could I forget?" She said to herself.

She had forgotten about the threat that Lord Mikhail had sent, along with everyone else. Six months had passed and nobody had thought about it. She had also forgotten what Nicholas had told her about Iris and Erasmus being in danger. Of course, Lord Mikhail had sent this attacker, thinking that since Erasmus wasn't present; they could battle Nicholas and then harm Iris. Amara immediately turned to look at her.

"Keep an eye on the pot that is being heated. After the water boils along with the herbs, add these other ingredients in it. Pay proper attention while I am gone. I will be back in a few minutes," Amara said to her as she sprinted out of the chamber to find Erasmus.

Reaching the hall, she looked around to find him when she spotted him sitting beside Nicholas who was now resting on a cot in the side. Everyone else had gone, leaving Soter and Erasmus with Nicholas who lay there unconscious.

"Erasmus, I need to speak with you," she said and he turned his head to look at her.

"Yes?" he replied and followed her to the passageway.

"Did Nicholas say anything about the attacker?" She asked.

"He just said Lord Mikhail's name," replied Erasmus, running a hand through his hair and shaking his head.

"I need you to listen to me carefully, Erasmus. Iris is in danger. Nicholas had warned me about it and surely, Lord Mikhail sent the attacker. Iris needs to be protected along with you. We need to take special care that nothing happens to either of you. I am not warning Iris since she is under trauma. I want you to take care that she never goes anywhere without at least two people around her. Clearly, Nicholas wasn't enough. We need more protection," she said.

"Lord Mikhail wants to harm Iris, but why? She's a new witch. . ." Erasmus replied, perplexed.

". . .With the potential to be a powerful one. She is a threat to him." Amara shrugged.

"Alright, I'll take care of her. Meanwhile, I need someone else to be with her since I'm busy with Nicholas."

"I'll stay with her for the time being," she replied.

Erasmus nodded his head, before taking a step back and retreating to where Nicholas was. Amara sighed, and walked back to the potions chamber where Iris was stirring the potion in the pot.

"Has it boiled yet?" She asked, standing beside her.

"Almost," Iris replied, stepping away so Amara could take over.

"Amara," Iris said, after a long moment of silence.

"Yes?" She asked, glancing at Iris once.

"I've been meditating for a long time now. I-I think I am capable of handling it. I can concentrate on one thing for as long as I want to," she said, biting her lip in nervousness. She was unsure whether this was the right time to say things like these, but she wanted to let Amara know how far she had come in all this time. It had been six months and she was curious to know what task Amara had for her. She was still waiting for Iris's meditation stage to get over. *Maybe I am already past that stage,* Iris thought.

"Well, we'll just have to test it to know if you are good enough," Amara replied, giving Iris a nod of acknowledgement.

"May I ask you something?" Iris said again after they got busy with the potion for a while. Amara said nothing but nodded, her eyes focussed on the beans she was crushing.

"You said this potion takes three days to get prepared, then how can one drop of *Spirit of Death* get it done in three hours?" She raised her eyebrows in question. Iris was confused. The name itself said it had something to do with Death. *How could it be of help in a Healing Potion?* She wondered.

"*Spirit of Death* is a highly confusing potion, yet simple," Amara began. "It does not kill one's body or destroy the physical being. A very deadly potion, it actually aims on destroying the soul. By destroying, it really means wiping off all the wrong substances inside a soul, the impurities within. It enters the soul through the body and destroys all the bad things, making the soul pure. Usually, it is given to those who have done great deeds in their existence. To perform good deeds, one must go through a bad phase. To purify them of all evil, this potion is given right at the time of Death so their soul remains pure, and peacefully rests after Death. The name *spirit* doesn't just mean the liquid but it is another word for soul. Since it directly aims at the soul, it is known as *Spirit of Death.*

"But one has to be very careful, for it can also destroy the soul itself. This potion has the power to finish off the soul along with the evil inside. The quantity matters. Four drops of the *spirit* end all bad things, but a tiny drop more and it destroys everything. The ingredients used in the *Healing Potion* are mostly herbs. When these herbs are plucked out from the earth, they do not remain as pure as they were when they lived within the earth. There are impurities, which settle deep inside the herbs and need to be killed to make the potion pure again.

"Therefore, we boil it and three days are needed. At the time of such emergencies, if one drop of *Spirit of Death* is added, it goes on to kill the impurities, rendering the potion pure enough to be used. Note, just one drop for the herbs and it does not take much time. Mostly, just three hours. It is not recommended to be used all the time, just when it is needed the most at times like these, to save a life."

Iris stared amazed at the vial of *Spirit of Death*, which rested on a stand upon the table. Amara picked it up and examined the black liquid inside the vial. A dull looking liquid on the outside, it gave off the aura of a magnificent one. It had a smoky appearance. When Amara was sure the potion was beginning to boil, she pulled the cork out and tilted the vial over the heating potion, slowly and very gently, letting one drop of the liquid fall into the pot. The colour of the *spirit*, although black, appeared crystal clear when it touched the potion in the pot. The brewing potion that was a brownish hue now had a clear, water-like appearance for a split second before turning to its original colour again. Iris watched the process with her eyes wide and Amara let out a sigh, replacing the vial of *Spirit of Death* back to its spot.

"We'll come back and check it in about two and a half hours," Amara said and started to walk out of the chamber followed closely by Iris. Since she was supposed to stay with Iris, Amara asked her to follow her out to the hall where Nicholas was. Iris wanted some time alone, but obeyed and proceeded to the great hall. Nicholas was laying on the cot, still unconscious, the bruise on his forehead covered with a paste of herbs. Soter was chanting some spells, moving his hands over Nicholas's body in the air, a few white lights falling out of his hands wherever they moved. His ankle was now in a proper position as Soter, with a click of his fingers, mended it.

Iris shifted to the floor and sat down, resting her back on a pillar behind. She pulled her legs up to her chest and placed her chin over her arms. She looked at Nicholas and a tear slipped out of her eye, thinking about what he had done for her. If something happened to him, she would never be able to forgive herself. He put his life in danger for her. All this time he had been teaching her witchcraft and handling elements, leaving Erasmus in charge whenever he had to go somewhere. Iris felt indebted to him for saving her life. He was helping her in so many ways and then he had to go and put him-self before her. How was she going to pay him back for that?

The two people here whom she had gotten close to, who made her feel home, were Erasmus and Nicholas. If she didn't have Erasmus, she wasn't sure how she would have survived. With Nicholas added to the game, it was better; him teaching her everything that she needed to know, helping her with meditation, handling elements, and some ways to deal with Amara, who was also becoming a better version of herself. She wasn't as rude to her anymore or uninterested like she seemed before. *Maybe because she needs my help*, Iris thought. Then again, what did she even have to do anyway? She had made this task her sole motive until she achieved it. If she had to do it, then she was going to do it the right way and make efforts for it.

"Nicholas taught you how to tame the element of air, correct?" Amara asked, settling beside Iris on the floor while Soter was busy in conversation with Erasmus.

"Yes, there was still a lot left to teach. He told me so," she replied.

"How good are you at it, as of now?"

Amara wanted to know more about what Nicholas had been helping her with. Since she was busy with taking care of other things as Lord Lucifer was travelling, Amara had not gotten a chance to know what Iris had been doing. Although she would observe Iris at times and notice her dedication to learn new things, she would be relieved thinking about the fact that she had chosen the right person to help her with what she wanted to do.

"I can hardly make the leaves go two inches above the ground," Iris said, letting out a nervous chuckle. She felt strange to show any kind of happy emotion around Amara, she was always so blank and devoid of feelings. Iris would sometimes feel as though Amara's heart was plainly made of stone, but then she would think about what she had gone through and would tell herself that Amara was now *built* of stone. It wasn't just her heart.

"It's alright, you'll come along," Amara assured her with a nod. Yet her expression was static. Iris wondered how she could hide and stop any single emotion from showing. It seemed like a hard task.

"How long until the potion will be ready, Amara?" Erasmus asked, when Soter left to get something for Nicholas.

"At least two hours," Amara replied.

Erasmus nodded, looking at Nicholas again. He was feeling sad after a long period. His old friend, who had risked himself to save Iris, was fighting for his life while Erasmus had not a single harm done to him. For the first time, he felt empty, because even though Nicholas wasn't around as much, he was still a very important part of his life. He sadly smiled thinking of how much fun they had when they were both new in the coven. Erasmus dreaded losing Nicholas.

"I haven't gotten into your mind in a while," Iris said suddenly, startling Amara.

She raised her eyebrows in amusement, "That's because I haven't allowed you to. Your training was more important. I'll let you in with more information when I'm sure you'll be able to handle it," she said. After that incident when Iris saw flashes of Amara's past, she had not gotten a chance to know more. When Amara had found out what had happened, she decided it would be better to delay it all for a while since it was getting hard for Iris to handle. She was still amateur and didn't have enough strength to take in such grave information together.

They sat in the hall in silence until daybreak, and as the sun rose, Amara stood up to go and check if the potion was ready. Iris had fallen asleep somewhere between the two witches talking about how difficult it is to tame the element of Fire. As Amara was talking about it, Iris had dozed off, her head now resting on a pillow that Amara had conjured after she fell asleep on the floor. Nicholas was still unconscious and Erasmus had not left his position from beside him.

Amara walked into the potions chamber and looked at the brewed potion heating on the table. She lifted the pot from the stove and placed it over the table on top of a thin cloth to sustain the heat. She waved the smoke away with her hand and grabbed a spoon to stir it. When she was sure it was prepared, she poured the required amount into a goblet and took it out to the great hall where Soter was waiting. As soon as Amara brought the *Healing Potion* out, Soter let a few drops fall into Nicholas's mouth. He waited for a few moments before Nicholas started coughing and then drank the rest of the potion. The wound on his abdomen healed almost instantly, making it look as though nothing had happened. He still had some pain when he tried to sit up properly.

Iris was now awake, next to Nicholas immediately when she found out he was okay. She sat beside Erasmus who was grinning along with a cheerful Iris. She felt content, and more so, relieved that he was safe and not dead – like she had thought – because of her. Nicholas groaned, holding his head as pain shot up there, stinging his bruise even though it had healed on the outside. Just the pain was there for a while. When he was comfortably sitting, he opened his eyes. Iris was eagerly waiting to hear from him that he was okay.

"Well, this hurts," he croaked, earning chuckles from Soter, Iris and Erasmus. Amara stood at the side, looking out the window. She didn't exactly know how she was supposed to react.

"How are you feeling?" Soter asked, placing a hand on his shoulder.

"Like a mountain fell on me, but other than that I feel okay. It just pains a lot," he said, his voice a bit cracked.

"That is natural. You will be alright in a few days," Soter said, with an assuring smile.

"Iris, are you okay?" He asked, looking over at her.

"I'm completely fine," she replied, "I'm sorry you had to-" she began when he cut her off.

"Don't worry about it, love. I'm still as striking as I was before and you're still going to have dreams about me," Nicholas said and winked. As much as she wanted to roll her eyes, she just laughed at it lightly.

"Nicholas, who was the attacker?" Erasmus asked.

"Oh yes, I had an argument with that fool. It was Samael, one of the King's Ministers. He came to tell me that Lord Mikhail had sent another warning and that he was going to declare an attack soon. The message was to be given to the Lord. I asked him why Lord Mikhail was sending silly threats instead of attacking already. That led to a few other argumentative words and then he started cursing. Subsequently, Iris entered."

Erasmus began saying something when the sound of wind entering forcefully inside the hall was heard, and everyone turned to look at the source. Amara pushed herself away from the window and approached the door from where the sound came. A moment later, the door was banged open, vibrating the walls. A black dove flew inside, treading upwards and then shattering into pieces, only to assemble again and form a message. The words hung in the air, as though dripping blood from them.

> **'Bloodshed awaits,**
> **Destruction awaits, and when it strikes,**
> **Will nothing remain.**
> **I declare war.'**

The message then vanished, leaving the aura of black smoke in the hall, silencing everyone around. Lord Mikhail had officially declared war.

CHAPTER ELEVEN

∞∞∞∞∞∞
THE SAVIOUR
∞∞∞∞∞∞

I ris sat on the branch of the sprawling, aged banyan tree, her gown playing softly along her ankles as her gaze fixed on something far in the distance. She listened to the beautiful melody of a flute coming from somewhere inside the woods, Iris didn't know where, but her guess was those were the nimble fingers of Sienna working their charm. Erasmus had once told her that Sienna was flawless at playing the flute. The calming sounds that the flute created made her want to close her eyes and concentrate on nothing else but that. It was beautiful, and after all the mind numbing incidents that had taken place over the past two days, the music was gently healing her soul.

Nicholas didn't cry in pain anymore as it had begun to subside. Erasmus was bustling around the room taking care of him, helping him around and getting him back to how he was. So Iris was mostly left on her own. Although Amara was being co-operative and helping her meditate, she was left by herself most of the times with nothing much to do.

The wind was blowing gently around her, making her shoulder length hair move in the blustery weather. As she rested her head on the tree, closing her eyes, her mind began to wander, settling in the strangest of places. She saw a mass of water break out from under huge rocks, the figure of a brawny man sliding down with the flood. Flames of Fire danced upon a castle that was being burnt down. Then she saw a storm approaching and taking a few humans away in its cruel grasp. Iris cringed to herself and distracted her thoughts, focussing on the sound of the flute. But her mind continued to remain a muddle of things that she could not decipher. As she was about to open her eyes and leave, a vision rushed into her mind.

* * *

"LET ME GO!" she screeched, pain immediately travelling up to her head. The burning sensation ran up through her feet to her skull, stinging every bit of her soul inside. She struggled within the chains tied around her, her leg savagely glued to the floor. Tears streamed down her eyes, her heartbeat going wild as he placed a nail over her ankle, holding the hammer right above it. She screamed louder and louder, the sound rang through the walls making them shudder. But he didn't stop even though her screams were ear splitting. He didn't stop himself from hammering the nail into her ankle.

"I don't know! I don't know anything – LET ME GO! LEAVE ME!" She bellowed yet again, tears falling furiously down her eyes as she sobbed and pleaded in pain.

"Where is the boy?" Zeidan asked with a murderous look. His voice was calm as still water. Zeidan was one of Leo's servants, who had also been a part of torturing her.

"I don't know. I d-do-don't kn-know," she whimpered.

Amara struggled harder to get rid of the chains. He started hitting the hammer on the nail, piercing the skin below her ankle. As he hit it harder, she screamed again, the cry creating trembles in the chamber.

"He will save you," *Thomas had said to her hours ago, before he had escaped. He possessed the power of invisibility and could set himself free. In all the time that he had been in the dungeons, he had gathered up his powers. They were not too strong, but enough to help him escape. Amara had wanted to stop him, or go with him but he refused. Thomas had told her that there was someone that would save her, and that going with him would only bring her more sufferings.*

"My journey is difficult, Amara. I have to go alone," *he had said. In the end, she had let him go, hoping that at least the fifteen-year-old boy would find a way out for himself. And maybe someone would come and save her. Someone would help her.*

Her screams never went silent as the tears slipped down her eyes effortlessly. She was dying. Her will to survive and to save herself was all fading away. She had no strength, no way of rescuing herself. The only thing that she wanted now, was Death. She wanted to embrace Death. The pain shooting up from her ankle was unbearable, but less agonizing than what Leo had done to her for three long weeks. He had gotten no information out of her, yet he kept tormenting her, damaging the very soul inside her that longed to set itself free. She needed Death. That was all she was capable of hoping for.

As Zeidan began to hammer the nail deeper into her ankle, a strong current of air slammed the window of the chamber open, and the shadow of the storm that was gradually building on the outside entered in. Rain splattered across the room and drenched the floors. The shadow wildly began to approach where Amara and Zeidan were. Zeidan's hands stopped, and Amara's eyes – blinded by her tears – searched for clear vision. She blinked as the shadowed figure coolly made its way inside and Zeidan was suddenly thrown onto a wall, his body crashing on it and collapsing on the floor. The blurred figure of a man standing in front of Zeidan appeared. Amara quickly blinked the tears away.

Her vision got clearer and a hooded figure dressed in dull red robes stood tall with his back to Amara. He grabbed Zeidan by his collar and pulled him up to standing. Taking a step back, the man dragged him forward, holding him by the throat in a tight grip. They were talking about something, but Amara heard nothing due to the sound of the storm. The man slammed Zeidan's head into the wall, blood spluttering out of his head as he fell to the floor. Amara stared at the scene in front of her with her eyes wide. Not a single thought crossed her mind as the walls shook with the force Zeidan was hit by. The man retreated, still not facing Amara as he raised his arms in the air and Zeidan ascended along rising up to the ceiling, his body limp and unresponsive.

The storm around refused to calm down and continued blinding her vision. She saw Zeidan being lifted higher and then suspended in midair, his face covered in blood and it beheld a horrid sight. Amara wanted to shut her eyes but before she could, a dagger flew out of the man's robes and with great force, ascended towards Zeidan's body. Before her mind could gauge what was happening, the dagger had slammed into his throat, travelling straight through and fixing him to the wall behind, just below the ceiling. Amara stared in horror, her eyes wide and jaw dropped open. The man turned around, his face still covered in a hood and started walking towards Amara. She was glued to her spot, her mind too disturbed to react in any way.

The man crouched down before her, tracing his hand towards her ankle, the nail halfway in. Amara felt nothing as her senses were numb and he gently pulled the nail out without even touching it. Blood dripped out of the wound and spilled onto the floor. The raging storm continued to drench the chamber. Amara was covered in blood and rain. The man raised his head and glanced at the chains that were around Amara's wrists. A moment later, she was free of those. Yet her mind refused to react, even when he offered her a hand, and without a question, she placed her bleeding fingers onto his extended palm. The man stood up, helping her to her feet and Amara trembled, and fell back onto the floor. Before she could try to stand up again, her vision blurred and she collapsed on the floor.

Her strength had vanished somehow and she could only feel that the man had now picked her up and was approaching the door. She heard voices and through clouded eyes she saw the doors of the prison being opened, letting many other prisoners out. Clashes of weapons were heard for a long time as she felt the movement of the man who was holding her. A few moments later when she was able to open her eyes, she felt herself being dropped to the floor, her head hitting a hard surface. The man was now pulling a sword out and slashing it across someone's neck before dragging Amara away with him.

Once again, her eyes heavy from the fall, her head in a near state of concussion, she became semi-conscious and the sounds faded away. The only thing she felt now was the realization that she was free. She was out of the dungeons. As the cold wind and rainwater fell upon her half-conscious being, she silently faded into nothingness.

* * *

When Iris opened her eyes, she was lying on the ground. Amara stood before her, offering a hand. Iris blinked, grabbing Amara's wrist and stood up. She stared at the wrist she was holding, which, moments ago in her head, was bound in chains. Iris shuddered inside, thinking of how Amara might have felt with the chains and the nail ruthlessly being hammered into her leg. *How can one person endure such an amount of pain?* She asked herself again.

"Are you alright?" Amara asked, raising her eyebrows.

Iris's head shot up to look at her. She wanted to ask if Amara was okay, but it had been over a hundred years that this had happened. Iris was new to it, Amara was not.

"I'm fine," Iris replied, looking down, unable to meet Amara's gaze.

"I didn't want to let you in today. I was going to wait but your meditation skills were very good. Usually new witches take at least a year to be satisfactory but you did it in six months. Even then, I was stopping myself from giving you permission, without you asking for it. But somehow I felt it was time for you to know the whole story," Amara said, turning to walk towards the woods. Focussed, Iris blindly followed behind.

"Who was it that saved you?" Iris attempted as they walked deeper into the woods.

"It was the Lord. After he saved me, he took me to the mountains of Carvelli. That's where all the new witches were trained before being brought to the castle. Of course, now it has changed, but training does take place in those mountains in the beginning. The castle had not been built properly enough then. The Lord made Soter heal all my injuries, but physical harm wasn't the only barrier. I was emotionally broken. I had no will to try to become the witch that the Lord wanted me to. When my injuries were gone, Nicholas trained me in combat. I learned archery, sword fighting and other war strategies. It took years for me to be perfect in the physical training.

"Meanwhile I read books on witchcraft and everything that was essential to be a good witch. When they were sure my physical strength was sufficient, the Lord began with the spiritual one. To purify my soul and heal it from the damage that had been done. At that time, after ten years of physical training, meditation began. I don't remember how much time I took in that but soon enough I was taught the nature of all the elements and how witches are supposed to tame them. Three years later, I became what they made me. I turned into the witch that they needed, the one that they had created out of the broken shards that I was. I owe my existence to the Lord, I'm indebted to him for saving me and making me what I am today," said Amara.

They were now seated on the ground, the lake below their feet. Iris sat there listening to Amara silently, her eyes focussed on the water below. Now, she realized why the Lord was so important to Amara and why she had this amount of respect for him. He surely deserved it. And as Amara relayed the story to her, Iris could see the narration happening right in front of her in the calm water. She saw Amara being healed, her physical training, her meditation, the familiar spots of the mountains of Carvelli and the vulnerable, weak girl turning into a strong and beautiful witch, who had the stoic expression across her face that was always there since Iris had first seen her. She didn't know what to say. Whether to express the immense respect she felt for this great witch, or tell her that she was over-whelmed. She didn't quite put her emotions to use. Maybe her expressiveness would not go down well with the blank witch next to her, who had lost all kinds of emotions making her void of every feeling.

Then again, had Iris gone through all of that, she would never have had the will to get trained in being a witch. She would have wanted to kill herself somehow even after being saved. Going through all that pain and then coming out strong, Iris could never imagine herself doing that. Amara was different, she was exceptional, extremely strong willed and brilliant in every way. Iris could only wish to be like her, but never attain that goal. Because Amara wasn't someone anybody could be like. It required strength more than one could ever imagine. Amara was in herself, the most astonishing being Iris had ever come across.

Yet, all of that didn't answer the question of the task that Amara wanted Iris to help her with. She was still in the dark, and she didn't know when and how Amara was going to tell her what it was. But she decided not to ask her since she had always said that she would reveal it to her when the time was right. Iris would wait for the right time and be patient. Meanwhile, she could keep her concentration on other things that were important.

"But how were you so strong? Didn't it haunt you every now and then?" She asked, unable to contain her questions.

"For a while it did, but then I became immune to it. I used to have a lot of nightmares. I even tried to drown myself once, and tried setting myself on Fire because the memories of the pain stabbed me inside every moment. But the Lord didn't let me fail and after a while I became used to it. The pain began to subside and I started forgetting about it. It's the power of the mind, you learn to face it," she replied. Iris's heart shattered thinking of everything that Amara had been through and come out stronger than ever.

"How difficult was it? The spiritual training, I mean. Did it take much time?"

"Well, it wasn't easy. I had to keep my mind focussed on one thing, which was difficult given my condition at that time. Then as I started to think about how important all of it was over the past, I began to learn to control the emotions getting in my way. That helped me to become stronger and I learned to sustain the pain. After I learnt to meditate properly, I could focus on things easily and it all started to become what I wanted to achieve. I made it the only goal I wished to reach." She paused for a few moments, her palms joining at the tips as she surveyed Iris and then said, "You know, Iris, the pace at which you are adapting to this world and learning everything, it amazes me. I have not seen a witch so determined and focussed to achieve a goal. I'm sure you might make a great witch someday. Your determination reminds me of someone."

"Who would that be?" Iris asked, perplexed.

Amara tilted her head to look at Iris and a tiny smile grazed her lips, before she said, "Me."

Iris looked at her with wide eyes silently, blinking once to digest the fact that Amara was actually smiling. It made her want to squeal in joy thinking that she was the one that brought that smile onto her face. Although the smile was so little and almost non-existent, Iris was delighted at the mere notion of it. In all the time that she had known her, Amara had never once genuinely smiled, not even a hint of it. For a witch who was devoid of all feelings, who could not express any emotion apart from anger and coldness, a smile as tiny as this was something extremely joyful for Iris. But, once again, her expression went back to how it was before, the smile vanishing. That didn't change the fact that Iris had made Amara smile. It would stay with her for the rest of her life as a happy memory.

"Was everyone set free that night? All the prisoners," Iris asked curiously, wondering what exactly had happened since Amara was unconscious and didn't know much.

"The Lord told me some of them died fighting, but most managed to escape," she replied.

"And that boy Thomas, ho-how did he escape?"

"He had the power of invisibility. During the eight months that he was in the dungeons, he had learnt to invoke all his powers. Being the son of a powerful sorcerer, he possessed a few powers since birth but he didn't have proper control over them due to lack of training. He also had the power of premonition, because of which he told me that someone was going to save me. His powers were not that good, and the invisibility could last only for a few minutes. He didn't need much time to escape out of the prison but once he was out, the invisibility would stop working. Then he would have to save himself some other way. He managed to escape in time while the powers were working. It was a day before I was set free," said Amara, her mind going back to how vulnerable she was when he left. Thomas was her only hope but he had promised her that she would be rescued. She had believed him.

"But what happened to him?"

"I don't know. I tried to find out but they said he was captured by witch-hunters and was probably dead. But some said he went into hiding and no one was able to find him." Amara shrugged.

Iris wanted to know more about the boy. He possessed similar powers to hers and she wanted to know if he was still out there. Maybe if he were alive and if he belonged to the same coven, he could have helped her. His powers, in a way matched hers and maybe he could have understood. *But, thinking about that is not going to be of any use*, she thought. Pushing the thoughts out of her mind, she concentrated on the other question that she wanted to ask.

"How difficult is it to handle the element of Fire? Erasmus told me you're very skilled at it," Iris asked, now sticking to the numerous questions that she had. She didn't want the conversation to end. If this was the way Amara was going to open up to her then be it. There were so many things that she could find out. And Iris was in no mood to pass up on that chance.

"Very difficult indeed!" Amara answered with a glint in her eyes. "The element of Fire is extremely tricky to tackle. All the elements are, but Fire holds a different place, altogether. Given the fact that it is the most dangerous one of them all and if you lose focus for just a second, it can become highly destructive. I was given a choice to pick the two elements that I wished to handle. They suggested Water and Air but I was interested in Fire. It was challenging and I wanted to tame it. The reason Fire is difficult to handle is because the other elements: Earth and Wind are at your beck and call when you want. To conjure up Water, it does not take as much patience. But if it is Fire, one has to be cautious enough and focussed to conjure it with proper strength of mind. Because even while you are summoning it, you cannot lose focus.

"If you do, it can get extremely destructive. It is dangerous. It took a lot of time for me to learn the nature of that element. Focus is the key and that is where your meditation comes in. The concentration that you practiced can be used here to tackle Fire. In the beginning, it was hard to deal with and I almost burned down a forest once, but after a lot of practice, I could handle it and keep control over it. The secret is that the element of Fire is like the human mind, complex and wildly unstable. You know the phoenix bird is born out of Fire, and that is why *Phoenix Blood* is said to be as confusing as Fire itself. It is dangerous and if you cannot contain it, it can make you go insane. The way *Phoenix Blood* is in connection to the mind, Fire is also directly related the same way. Yet if you learn control; it serves you the way you wish."

Iris let out a sigh as though she was holding her breath awhile, as Amara had been speaking to her. The amount of complexity the world of Conjurers had would make her think that she was actually going mad. But the world was like that, if you had control over yourself you could survive. If not, destruction would occur. It was how the universe maintained its balance. However, witchcraft had its own different perquisites to offer. In addition to being interesting and challenging, it was also the most intriguing world one would come across. Iris was beginning to like it despite all the disadvantages.

They sat in silence for what seemed like hours before another question started nagging Iris's mind. She was confused whether to ask it. Maybe it was a bad idea and it would infuriate Amara. *If I am supposed to know her story, I should know everything, right?* She pondered. Yet, something stopped her from asking that question and she held herself back while Amara playfully moved her feet in the water, gently splashing it around. She was careful not to get them drenched.

"We should go back into the castle. It's getting late," Amara spoke suddenly, starting to get up.

The feeling of asking the question refused to leave her and Iris wanted to know the answer. Maybe Amara would tell her and not get angry like she was thinking. There were a lot of things she already knew and knowing the answer to that little question wouldn't kill her. So gathering up all her courage, Iris stood up to follow Amara as she had begun walking back in the direction of the castle.

"Amara, wait," she called out, running a little to catch up with her.

Amara turned around, her eyebrows raised in question and waited for Iris to catch up with her.

"Yes?" She questioned, as Iris remained dead silent.

"I have one last question to ask you," she said slowly, choosing the words wisely in her mind so as not to make it sound like she was being nosy.

"Go on," Amara urged.

"Um…What happened to Leo?" She finally managed after a long moment of silence.

Amara went silent for a while, she surveyed Iris, and Iris realized that she had asked the wrong question at the wrong time. She wanted to run back into the castle for she was sure that Amara was going to get angry and probably torture her. But what Amara said next made Iris stop dead in her tracks, and her jaw fell open.

"*That* is exactly what you are going to help me find out."

CHAPTER TWELVE

∞∞∞∞∞

VEHEMENT DREAMS

∞∞∞∞∞

L ord Mikhail stared perplexedly at the huge waves crashing on the shore. The air refused to slow its pace and continued to sway around him as he stood below the tree thinking about how he was going to summon Lady Calypsa. If only, there was some way to get her to meet him instead of spending years in praying to her or having enough dedication for the same. It didn't seem like an easy task as such.

If there is some way that she would appear without having enough will to meet her, thought Lord Mikhail. *How could Lady Calypsa possibly know that someone wished to summon her? How was it that someone could let her know they wished to be in her presence?* Lord Mikhail realized that Lord Perseus had just given him an idea, planted a message inside of him, which he had to figure out on his own.

He was aware that there was no way he could get to meet Amara and ask her to reveal what Lady Calypsa was hiding, since she was the only one who knew the entire story. After sending Death threats to her and now declaring war against Lord Lucifer's coven, thinking of getting help from her would be the silliest idea ever. It would be completely ridiculous to think of something like that. Then what could he possibly do to achieve what he wanted? Fight her or forcefully summon her? Lord Mikhail didn't know how he was supposed to fight or force her. He needed a solution out of the answers that Lord Perseus had given.

Resting his back on the bark of the tree behind, he closed his eyes and concentrated on what the Lord was trying to convey.

"If you have enough will and dedication. . .

"There is someone who does not need to be prayed to. . .

"Your mind should be strong and unmoving. . .

"She should be the only concern. . .

"A witch who guards the treasures. . ."

Lord Mikhail repeated whatever the Lord Perseus had said to him and hoped that he would arrive at a conclusion. There was always a hidden message in his answers. Being such a great sorcerer, he was aware about the rivalry between Lord Mikhail and Lord Lucifer's covens. Surely, he would not suggest seeking help from Amara. There was something else that he meant, there had to be something hidden in what he was saying. And as Lord Mikhail focussed on deciphering what the message was, the wind began to slow down and an unfaltering calmness settled around. His mind set itself on one track, concentrating on the hidden meaning of what Lord Perseus had said.

The wind echoed the sound of the waves on the shore, hitting the rocks forcefully yet gracefully and Lord Mikhail opened his eyes, the corners of his lips twitching with a small smile. Setting the staff he was holding back on the ground, he pushed himself away from the tree he was resting on and with a lingering glance in the direction of the sea, he proceeded to journey his way. The message was deciphered and he now knew where he was going to go and whom he was going to need for the task.

* * *

Lady Calypsa swam her way back into the water from where she was observing her visitor, a little confused as to how he didn't wish to summon her. With a glance at the sky, she descended back into the sea, vanishing away as Lord Mikhail strode out of sight.

* * *

Lord Mikhail walked further ahead, now aware of where he was going to journey for the one he was supposed to meet. Lord Perseus had subtly enough, planted the message inside his head, that there existed someone who didn't need to be prayed to for summoning Lady Calypsa, apart from Amara.

Whomever he was going to meet had the power of weakening his enemy, as a result, rendering enough strength to his side. Once that person got the enemy under control, everything would be in Lord Mikhail's hands. That person didn't need to be prayed to; and he would get the key to his dilemmas. Lord Perseus was invariably intelligent and had helped him quite simply. That was the most redeeming factor of great sorcerers; they were highly reasoning and could offer any sort of help through clues.

* * *

Inside the castle, Iris sat still, her eyes wide in worry. She did not know what to do. The task that Amara had given was making her want to rip her head out and tear it into shreds. It was the most confusing and impossible task one could ever hope to do. Amara had gone to read in the vast and sprawling library of the castle, which was located in the farthermost corner situated levels below the surface she was. The lowest level of the castle consisted of the sacrificial chambers where most of the rituals of sacrificing souls were performed along with torturing them. Iris didn't wish to go anywhere near that just to meet Amara and ask her the questions that she already had asked, for half an hour.

Back when they were in the woods and Amara had said that she needed Iris to help with finding out what happened to Leo, she had stared at her confusedly, unable to figure out what exactly she had meant by that.

"How can I be of any help in that?" She had asked.

"Well, the task is difficult and extremely complex but I'm sure you can do it," Amara had replied confidently, despite the clear bewilderment that Iris showed.

Iris had thought to herself how Amara could have so much of confidence in her when she herself wasn't aware of what was going to happen.

"Are you going to tell me what it is?" She had asked, hoping to get the answer this time. Now after hearing the gist of it, she was unable to wait any longer.

"As a matter of fact, I will." With that, Amara began explaining what Iris was supposed to do.

"You have now learnt control over your mind, which means you are capable of learning control over that of others'. Reading someone's mind and manipulating it are two very different things. But all you have to do here is read a mind; there is no manipulation needed. So the task becomes relatively easy. You see, I have no clue of what happened to Leo, as much as I wanted to find out all those years ago. I didn't dare ask the Lord because the mere mention of that incident would get him enraged. So I decided I would ask Nicholas as he was friendly to me. But, he refused to divulge any information apart from the fact that the Lord wasn't the one that killed Leo even though he was the one that captured him. What I wish to know is, after he got captured, why the Lord didn't wish to kill him. I want to know who did, and whether he died at that point of time or not.

"A hundred years have passed yet I am unaware of that little piece of information and the feeling has not left me since. I have not found anyone remotely close to venturing into someone's mind as easily as you do. Hence, the long wait. I am completely sure that *you* can perform the task I am about to tell you," she said, pausing to take a breath. "The Lord has inconsiderable amount of control over his mind. No one else does to the limit that he does. Entering his mind and finding out what happened years ago from his memory is not going to be possible now. Also, he isn't here at the moment-"

"You want me to read the Lord's mind?" Iris cut her off mid-sentence, her eyes wider than ever. *How in the devil's name could I invade the Lord's mind?* That was the silliest thing one could ever imagine.

"Let me complete," Amara said, giving her an intimidating glare which shut Iris's mouth. "Like I said, invading his mind now will be of no use because he would easily be able to find out and you will be punished for that. But you can invade *my* mind. You can see what happened all those years ago if I allow you to. Through my mind, my thoughts and my memories, you will get inside the Lord's mind, a hundred years back. That way there is no chance he would find out you invaded his mind."

Iris stared at Amara quietly, not a single thought crossing her mind as she listened to what she was saying.

"Wait a minute. You mean to tell me that I have to invade the Lord's mind through yours when I metaphorically go back a hundred years ago in time?" She said, hoping that this was all a silly joke that Amara was playing.

"I mean *exactly* that." Amara nodded a slight smile on her lips.

"You're joking," Iris remarked, chuckling nervously to herself but deep down she was sure that Amara wasn't joking at all.

"Have you ever heard me joke, Iris?" Amara replied, the smile disappearing and a grim look replacing her features.

"How is that even possible in the simplest of ways? Invading an entirely different person's mind through yours; how is that going to work?" Iris said, baffled.

"Everything is possible in our world. The events that happened when I wasn't there and when I was unconscious are in the Lord's memory. Those events can only be found if you invade his mind. Since it is not possible at the moment, the only chance you have is to get inside his mind through the connection in mine. The visions that you see, basically, take you back in time when all of that happened. If from the time I lost consciousness, you get into the Lord's mind, there is a chance you will be able to find out what all happened and tell me everything. It's not easy, I know, but that is the only way."

"Why can't I just invade Nicholas's mind?" Iris's head was boggled, her thoughts were everywhere and she had absolutely no way to contain them.

"Because he is going to be travelling from tomorrow and wouldn't let you invade his mind. He is skilled enough to manipulate you without entering your mind." Amara said, rolling her eyes.

"This is not possible. It's not humanly possible in any way." Iris shook her head.

"And you forget the fact that you are not a mere human. Maybe it is impossible for mortals but not for you. The complexity of the task is unnerving, I agree, but we can make it simple. The mind has innumerable powers if you know how to put them to use. The mind is capable of doing impossible things with a simple control technique. Of course, that needs enough strength but you have it. It is a power you were born with and it is being polished in the best ways. As far as I know, meditation has helped you control your mind entirely. If you can manipulate your mind into doing something, you can do the same with others. You have the power. Put it to use. Your mind is capable of doing this and I know it. The mind is a notorious thing, Iris. It is in fact, insane. As long as you can control your mind, you survive, once the mind begins to control you, it leads you to insanity. You are capable of holding your mind in the right place and making it do whatever you wish. You have the power to do this. The mind can perform all the things that one assumes cannot be done. I believe in you, you can do this. Think about it," she said, trying her best to make Iris understand her point.

And after that, the both of them had gone back to the castle, where Amara left to go to the library and Iris was now sat inside her chamber, trying to configure a way to do what she had been asked to. The first thought that Iris had, was that Amara had gone entirely mad for suggesting something as silly and impossible as this. Invading the Lord's mind through hers, how completely daft did that sound? She was lost, and she could not tell anyone about it. Not even Erasmus; and talking to Amara again would do her no good. *I could back out from doing this*, she thought, *or maybe that would be unfair*. Amara had the right to know what had happened to Leo. She had all the right in the world after going through what she had. If it were Iris, she would have wanted to know, or probably kill the man herself if she could.

For a witch as great as Amara, Iris had to do this. Where else would she put her powers to use? The world that she had entered had made her a better person. It had made her realize what her true worth was. And it showed her what pain was. What going through real problems was, and if she wasn't capable enough to accept that and live her life, she didn't deserve anything that this world gave to her. Letting out a deep breath, she left the chamber and started walking down to the lowest level, gathering up all her strength to do so. As frightening as that part of the castle looked, Iris was always curious to know how it would feel like if she was there. Making her way across the passage, she passed the ritual chamber, the sacrificial chamber and then Lord Lucifer's chamber.

As far as she had heard about it, Lord Lucifer's chamber was the largest after the library and the most dangerous one you would ever come across inside the castle. But of course, no one was allowed to enter apart from Ambrosius and whoever he would give permission to. Ambrosius had forever been his servant, his companion who would do anything and everything for him. Not even Amara was allowed inside his chamber even though she was his utmost favourite. Iris stopped outside the doors of his chamber, observing the carvings. Two big doors were guarding the chamber, a huge lock around it since he was travelling for now.

Letting out a sigh, Iris retraced her steps and began walking towards the library, which was at the end of the passage. The doors were open and as she stepped inside, she was greeted by millions of books stacked upon the shelves. Iris titled her head upwards to see how tall the stands were. They almost touched the ceiling. Bringing her eyes back to level, she started walking further to find Amara. After looking around for a while and finding a few witches seated in corners with books clumsily stacked around them, some open, some hovering at a little height with the witches furtively scribbling down notes, she spotted Amara flipping through some stray parchments. She was standing between the passages of the stands, replacing the parchment from her hands into a book. Her attention was focussed on what she was doing, and she hardly noticed Iris walking towards her.

"Amara," Iris called out without realizing how loud her voice was. All the witches looked at her with scowls and she mouthed a 'sorry' to them with a sheepish grin. Amara gave her a flat look before turning to her book again.

"Have you never been to a library before, Iris?" hissed Amara.

"Actually, no. I'm not really fond of books. I could barely read the school books and I-"

"What are you here for?" Amara cut her off as she looked up at her with the book now sitting close to her chest.

"Oh yes. I had to talk to you about the task that you have given to me," she whispered, careful to keep her voice low this time.

"What about it?"

"When do you want me to do it?" Iris followed Amara to where she was going and sat down opposite to her on a chair.

"Whenever you think you're ready," she replied, her attention now on Iris.

Iris had no idea how thankful Amara was that she was doing this for her. The amount of years that she had spent thinking about what happened to the man that betrayed her and destroyed her world made her all the more aggravated. She wanted to know why it was hidden from her. She wanted to know what had happened to him. Her mind had not rested even once after that incident. It didn't matter that over a hundred years had passed. If there was one way to get those visions of her past out of her mind, it was to know what happened to Leo.

"I don't know how I'm going to understand whether I'm ready. Do you think I am?" Iris said. She felt extremely confused.

"You will realize it when you are. So come to me when you get the idea. Without that we cannot proceed. It is a dangerous task. As simple as entering someone's mind is, it is more difficult to get out of it. And once you enter a mind through another one's, there are chances you get lost in that place and that time, which will make you go insane to no limit. Therefore, your control should be incredible. It has to be. Or else you will end up in the asylum. I don't want you to lose control over yourself and I surely do not want you to go insane. You have to be very careful. So when you have enough confidence over yourself, only then will I give you permission to do this."

Iris nodded her head in understanding. Of course, there were going to be the pros and cons of the powers that she possessed. If she lost control by any chance, it would result in disastrous consequences. And she didn't want to go mad if it was going to be that way. She wanted to give Amara the truth that she deserved to know, but also protect herself from any harm.

"I told you, the mind is like Fire. One moment you lose focus and it will destroy you," she said again when Iris remained silent, her mind going to various possibilities of what could happen if she wasn't confident about what she was going to do.

"Okay. I will let you know when I think I am ready," she said and stood up to leave.

"Iris," Amara called out, when she was about to leave the library.

"Yes?" She said, turning around.

Amara's eyes were fixed elsewhere for a moment, before she shifted them to look at Iris and said,

"Thank you."

Iris smiled, pushing a stray strand of hair behind her ear and gave a slight nod before walking out of the library, making her way to the upper levels.

"This is going to be interesting," she muttered to herself and proceeded to go into her chamber to get some sleep. The night was about to end and she had not gotten even a blink of sleep all night. With her mind travelling across the visions of Amara's past, she faded into a deep slumber, unaware of what her mind was about to show her. Unconsciously, the delusional dream pulled her away to the shore of a dark sea where sat the hooded figure of a man, his head hung low. His black robes surrounded the place he was sitting on, flowing with the wind. The hood covered his face, his shoulders broad and strong as he sat there with his back straight.

The wind around him moved in a pattern, creating illusions of varied designs that vanished in the fraction of a second. He sat still. The only movement was of his fingers resting on his knees, going up and down, which showed that he was managing the wind around him just with a swish of his fingers. They didn't have to leave the surface they were resting on. As he sat there with his eyes closed, the waves pushed themselves away from him, not daring to get close to him in any way. The birds that were arriving anywhere close to the shore took different turns. The darkness that had been created around the sea was blinding and every single creature was scared.

The aura surrounding him made any human want to hide. There was a Deathly vibe coming off him. The night made his powers younger and stronger. His hands were like stone: clear, hard and rough. His eyes were darker than the night, crystalline and a pellucid black, whenever he had the Deathly aura around him. As he stopped controlling the wind, his hood fell and he lifted his face up towards the sky and let out an earth shattering spell that created thunders, blackening it completely and rain began to fall viciously all over, the droplets were pure black but they dare not drench him. He stood up, pulling the hood over his head again and approached the sea, stepping into it before walking in further and vanishing into the water.

Iris's eyes shot open and she immediately sat up, the image of the dream vanishing out of her memory. She turned her head to look outside the window. It was raining.

CHAPTER THIRTEEN

∞∞∞∞∞

THE RETREAT

∞∞∞∞∞

Nicholas stood next to the railing of the tower, staring off into space as his eagle flew over and settled itself beside him. He turned to look at it and stroked its head gently with a smile on his face. "Pelagi," said Nicholas, acknowledging the great big tawny eagle. Pelagi bowed his head and accepted the gesture graciously before lifting himself upwards and settling onto Nicholas's extended arm. Leaning close to his ear, Pelagi whispered something that only his master could understand and when it was done, shifted away. Nodding his head, Nicholas placed his arm back on the railing and the majestic eagle bowed his head before flying away. Amara stood behind him, just entering the tower and began walking towards him. She was aware of the fact that his eagle would arrive today after spying on Lord Mikhail. And she was hoping Nicholas would be at the tower at this time in the evening, before he left to travel that night.

"He's gathering an army," Nicholas said, noticing her presence behind him.

"He did announce a war." Amara shrugged as she stood next to him alongside the railing. Leaning along the railing, she looked down at the lake beneath them, stretching to boundaries afar.

"He is also going to meet someone. Pelagi spotted him near the Sea of Cypress. Why do you think he would go there?" He asked, looking at the trees in front of him.

At the mere mention of the Sea of Cypress, Amara's heart skipped a beat and she blinked a few times, stopping herself from telling Nicholas as to why Lord Mikhail would go to the Sea of Cypress. Apart from the Lord and herself, no one was aware of what Lady Calypsa was protecting. And no one needed to know either. She could not let Nicholas know even though he was trustworthy. She had sworn to keep it a secret. Her mind still recalled the day, almost eighty years ago when the Lord had come to talk to her about it. But she could not reveal anything to anyone even if her life depended on it. She had sacrificed her own blood to promise that she would guard the treasure with every part of her soul.

"I'm not sure about it but he wouldn't go there to gather an army of course," she said, pushing away the obvious thoughts of what Lord Mikhail had gone there for. *Of course, he wanted to gain access to what Lady Calypsa was protecting. Why else would he want to go to the horrible sea that could terrify the living daylights out of a normal powerful witch?*

"We need to be careful. I've sent Pelagi to get more information. I shall send you the messages when I receive them," Nicholas replied, turning around to go back to the castle to prepare for his leave.

"Alright. I shall wait for your message," she said and gave a small nod before following him down to the castle and going her own way.

She walked towards her chamber and shut the door behind her after entering inside. On the table in the corner was the book that had the piece of parchment kept inside it, which held the little part of the prophecy that Lady Calypsa and Amara were guarding. There were a few things that were inside the sea, one of which was a prophecy. Part of it was given to Amara by Lord Lucifer to understand what it meant. Once again, she pulled it out of the book and read it to herself.

To possess it, a loved one must be killed

It was only a piece of parchment on which Lady Calypsa had designed the words, but it held utmost importance. This part of the prophecy was extracted from the whole and given to Lord Lucifer to guard. His forefathers, in a bid to protect it, had performed the task so as to save it from being taken by the undeserving. It was about the treasure that was sealed in the Sea of Cypress. Amara didn't know the complete prophecy, but she was well aware that the words she held in her hands were as important. To anyone who was unaware of the complete prophecy, this broken part would always be hidden and even if they acquired the other part from the sea, they would not be able to achieve what they wanted, since they could only fulfil the part that was known to them.

Amara observed the writing carefully. If a person had to possess the treasure, a loved one had to be slain. *Maybe*, she thought, *the blood of a loved one is required*. If this part of the prophecy wasn't fulfilled, the one seeking the treasure would never achieve it. She remembered the time when the Lord had made her swear to protect the part that was given to her. The only reason Lord Mikhail had found out was because he had been a companion of Lord Lucifer when they were being trained together. By some means he became the worst enemy Lord Lucifer could ever have. Amara didn't know what the reasons were.

Letting out a sigh, Amara replaced the parchment back into the book. She had to inform Lady Calypsa that the treasures were under threat. She knew now that Lord Mikhail was looking for a way to summon Lady Calypsa. His powers were well known, he was as strong and as trained as the Lord, and if he wished to, he could always summon her to get what he wanted. Although Lady Calypsa was assigned to protect the treasures and not let someone like Lord Mikhail acquire them, she surely was unaware of what he was capable. There were a lot of ways he could get what he wanted, which might involve destroying Lady Calypsa even though she was invincible. The only ones who had the power to end her were Lord Lucifer and Lord Mikhail, and he would not hesitate in destroying her if he wished to.

Amara decided to go to the woods when there was a knock on the door. She walked over and opened it to find Iris standing there with an unrecognizable look. Amara frowned, stepping outside and shutting the door behind her. Iris was silent, biting her lip in nervousness before shutting her eyes for a while and then letting out a long sigh. Amara stared at her with her eyebrows raised in question. She couldn't understand what Iris was here for.

"I'm ready," she mumbled.

Amara was taken aback and widened her eyes. *How could she be ready so soon? Wasn't it just yesterday that she had not been sure about her being ready?* It had actually been two weeks.

"Are you sure?" She asked, confirming if this was actually the time she wanted to do this.

Iris nodded, "I'm sure. I have to do this or else my head would explode with all the visions that I've been having of your past. It is getting into my mind every now and then and I'm unable to avoid it. I want to know what happened to him and I want to reveal it to you."

"Do not get into this if you're not completely confident about yourself, Iris. This is not an easy task," said Amara.

She didn't want this to end badly. Besides Iris was still a new witch. Even though she was a fast learner, it had only been six months. However, her confidence made Amara want to beam in pride. She was beginning to admire Iris and her abilities to grasp things so easily. Iris did remind Amara of herself, in different ways of course.

"I know. I've thought about it and I don't think I can stop this any longer. I'm sure that I'll be able to do it, and you'll help me, right?" She asked, hopefully

"Of course I will." Amara nodded.

"Can we do it now?" Iris said, wanting to get this over with as soon as possible. She could not contain her mind any longer. It would go out of control and she could not let that happen. Iris had come to realize how easily her mind was used to getting distracted and she was afraid that it would get distracted again if this topic wasn't over once and for all.

"*Now?*" Amara stared at her in disbelief.

"Amara, before I let my mind wander away into the Lord's at this point – because I know it will even though he might be miles away – I want to end this. To be frank, you've had enough. You waited a hundred years. You should not have to wait any longer. You deserve the truth." Iris argued.

"I've waited a hundred years, I can wait some more but I want you to be completely confident. You know the rules, one little loss of control and everything; I mean literally everything gets destroyed. Not only will the Lord find out, you might go insane and I will never be able to forgive myself."

Amara gave a worried look as she began walking out of the castle and Iris followed. She knew where Amara was going. The woods were the only place they could peacefully do this.

"I know. I've considered everything and I am confident. I know I can do this. You made me realize what I am meant to do. I will do it," Iris said, as they entered the woods and proceeded towards the lake. But Amara took a different turn when they were nearing the lake. Iris decided to follow without question.

"If we are doing this right now, I need the safest place possible," she said and led Iris to the miniature caves that were conjured by Lord Lucifer for important and confidential meetings that only consisted of a few people. It was created for emergency purposes, and this was, as Amara thought, an emergency since there was no other place they would be able to complete this. Nobody was supposed to know about it, absolutely no one.

They walked deep into the woods, deeper than Iris had ever been to, striding on the lake-side path and reached the caves after a while. Iris observed that they were in the innermost part of the woods where it would take time for anyone to find them. She hadn't noticed when they reached the caves as she walked on observing everything around, while her heart thumped inside her chest loudly. She could hear herself getting extremely nervous inside. The task was obviously not an easy one and she was nervous, she was scared that if something went wrong she would go insane.

The only thing keeping her breathing right now was that she was assured Amara would help her and wouldn't let anything happen if it were under her control. But once she entered the time where she lost consciousness, there wasn't a chance that she would be able to help Iris, for she would be lost inside the world, forgetting that Amara was in fact conscious enough at that point of time. She only passed out hundred years ago. That didn't mean she would be unconscious at present.

But Iris metaphorically would, since she would be in another time and another place. As they stopped at the foot of the caves, Iris became more and more frightened as to what might happen even though she had enough confidence in herself. She kept repeating inside her head that she was going to be able to save herself and keep control of her mind while entering Lord Lucifer's through Amara's mind.

As impossible as the task sounded, she knew it could be done. Her powers were that strong, she was aware of that. Amara herself was nervous thinking about the fact that Iris was about to do something extremely complex. She wasn't sure if this would happen easily enough. There couldn't be a day when she was this nervous and scared for someone else. She wanted Iris to be safe. She was the closest Amara had ever gotten to anyone in the hundred years that she had been a witch.

Having Iris go insane or losing control of herself wasn't something that she wanted. The both of them stood outside the caves with nearly the same things going through their minds when Amara let out a sigh and heaved open the door of the cave. Iris stared vacantly at the space in front of her as Amara began walking inside. She stopped mid-way, turning around.

"Promise me that you are sure about this," she said to Iris who almost felt like Amara had become a part of her life, a very important part.

She felt like family and she was, in some way, deep inside aware of the fact that Amara was beginning to feel the same in spite of the lack of emotions that she showed. *She's still human*, Iris thought. How long was she going to hide her emotions? There was going to be some way for them to come out.

"I promise, Amara, I won't lose control and I am sure about this," she replied, her voice a throaty whisper which she tried so hard to hide but couldn't. It was a suicide mission she was going on and wanted to get out of it soon to tell Amara what she deserved to know. There was a little part of her that wanted to hug Iris. Amara had now a fraction of her dedicated to this childish sixteen-year-old girl whom she had begun to get mildly attached to. She stopped her emotions from coming in between and nodded, her heart going wild inside her chest. She was unsure whether or not Iris could hear it. Amara didn't want her to know how scared she was.

Amara turned around and proceeded to walk into the chamber. She lit the torches with a click of her fingers and the cave was now illuminated with a little amount of light. Iris stood at the entrance of the opening with her eyes closed as she focussed her mind to one point entirely. She then opened her eyes with a different amount of confidence that reduced all the stress that she had been experiencing until now. An unusual feeling filled her whole being and she walked over to sit on the stone chairs that were in a circle around the table in between.

Amara held her breath for a moment before turning around and settling herself opposite to Iris who showed an aura of confidence and strength around her as she sat there with a clear expression of self-assurance. She was ready. Amara regarded her with hope that it would all be okay and that she wouldn't lose control of herself. Taking a deep breath, she instructed Iris to close her eyes. Iris obeyed silently, shutting her eyes. She kept her ears alert to listen to what Amara was going to tell her.

"Take your mind back to where we stopped the last time. I am now about to open my mind to yours," she said, her voice soft and deep.

Amara closed her eyes and concentrated on the last vision that she had had. When her mind was steady on the point where they left off, she let her mind free for Iris to enter. Iris focussed her attention on the last memory she had and realized that Amara had let her mind free of the chains. Immediately, she entered through the doors and Amara, subtly enough, trapped Iris inside her mind. The doors were shut.

Amara led Iris back to the point where she lost consciousness. The part where Lord Lucifer had rescued her and now was heading to the entrance of the dungeons, ready to free the others. Iris felt as though she had entered a different realm, as though she was now in the very place that Amara was, a hundred years ago. Her mind had now travelled back in time, leaving her to the point where Lord Lucifer was lifting Amara from the floor where she had fallen, half-conscious. Iris decided that that was the point where she had to enter into Lord Lucifer's mind. Focussing her attention to the hooded figure of the Lord, she fixed her eyes metaphorically onto his being. She blocked out everything else and kept her mind solely onto Lord Lucifer. It all went in slow motion as he began lifting Amara in his arms. She was half-way into unconsciousness and a second later; Iris realized she was looking at the whole scene from another point of view entirely.

* * *

Lord Lucifer walked out of the dreaded chamber from where he had rescued Amara after slaying Zeidan. His heart was beating wildly in his chest, anticipating the fact that what his ancestors had said was about to come true. He had found the guardian of the treasures that his forefathers had given Lady Calypsa to guard. As he held her in his arms he felt a sense of pride on getting to meet the one that was going to be the greatest witch of all time. He pictured himself training her as he began proceeding to the entrance of the dungeons.

When he reached the place where the other prisoners were, he shot a glance at all the doors and they opened by themselves, setting all of the witches free. The prisoners rejoiced and rushed out of the chambers, thanking Lord Lucifer profusely and beginning to follow him. They all felt happier knowing that he had rescued Amara – the innocent girl – who had been tortured the most.

They had all seen how she had suffered every minute of everyday more than any one of them combined. The witch-hunters, as soon as they heard the commotion, left their own chambers and rushed outside to find that all the prisoners had been set free. Panicked, they pulled out their weapons and attacked everyone present. Lord Lucifer was aware that all of them would be able to save themselves and started to push through the crowd to get out of the dungeons. His priority was to save Amara and take her to a safe place. He could not afford to rescue the other prisoners. They were all capable enough and those who weren't, had a chance of losing, but on the path of saving this one important witch, he had to sacrifice the others.

There was no way he could rescue all of them. He had helped them by setting them free and that was all he could do. As he neared the entrance, the doors opened and allowed him to go out but he was stopped by a witch-hunter that began to attack him. Lord Lucifer lost grip on Amara and she fell to the floor, hitting her head on a wall and he pulled his sword out to slash the witch-hunter's neck. After doing so, he quickly picked up Amara and sprinted out of the dungeons, avoiding the cries of the war that had begun inside the chambers.

Lord Lucifer ran as fast as his feet could carry him. His powers being weak due to the long amount of strenuous travelling he had done to find Amara and rescue her, he could not teleport himself to the mountains and had to reach there by foot. When suddenly he heard hasty footsteps at his heels, Lord Lucifer turned around to find out who it was and when his eyes finally rested on the person who had captured Amara, he stopped in his tracks. He looked at the man standing behind him a few paces away, fuming.

Lord Lucifer stared at the man silently, now realizing who he was and his heart skipped a beat as he began to breathe heavily. Never in his existence had he felt this amount of helplessness as he observed the man standing before him. But he had to save Amara. He could not believe that this man would torment an innocent witch so mercilessly. With a new will to save the only hope he had, Lord Lucifer shot a disarming spell at the man and turned around to run back to the safest place he could think of. Behind him, Leo fell to the ground and groaned as pain hit his chest. Struggling, he stood up and limped behind Lord Lucifer who was now far away. He failed to notice that Lord Lucifer was a great sorcerer and could be extremely fast if he wished to.

Tightening his grip on Amara, Lord Lucifer ran along the mountain valleys struggling to reach the place faster. Once again he could hear Leo getting nearer and increased his pace, swishing past the trees and as he realized he was about to reach the mountains of Carvelli, his foot tripped and he fell heavily to the ground. The past few hours of strain had sapped his ability to teleport. Leo was getting closer and Lord Lucifer groaned, pushing his body up to standing and holding up Amara again. She had now lost complete consciousness.

He proceeded to run faster but his ankle had been twisted, which hindered his progress and his pace became slower and slower until he was gasping for air. His hold on Amara tightened, he moved towards his destination and upon reaching, dropped to the ground, exhausted. He groaned in pain, settling Amara on the grass beside a tree. They were now in the valley between the circled mountains of Carvelli.

Hearing the sound of someone groaning, Nicholas left the place where he was busy preparing a potion and rushed to where Lord Lucifer was. He sat down beside Lord Lucifer and pulled him up so he was now sitting with his back resting on the bark of a tree.

"Is she alive?" He asked, glancing at Amara once. Lord Lucifer nodded, panting. He lifted his hand to point towards something and Nicholas turned to look in that direction where Leo stood at a distance with his fingers clenched on his palm.

"Ask him to leave," Lord Lucifer whispered, shutting his eyes. Nicholas looked at him once before turning back to Leo who was now starting to walk in their direction.

"He followed you here? Why didn't you kill him?" Nicholas said, perplexed as to why Lord Lucifer hadn't gotten rid of him by now.

Of course he had that much sense as to kill a normal witch-hunter, no matter whom he had captured and how he had tortured them. Lord Lucifer simply shook his head, shutting his eyes. He was growing weaker. Frowning, Nicholas stood up and proceeded to walk towards Leo. He was about to pull out his sword and slash it across Leo's throat to kill him when Lord Lucifer screamed Nicholas's name.

He turned his face to look at Lord Lucifer, confused.

"Take him somewhere else," he said and Nicholas grew even more confused.

"Scared that I'm here, old man?" Leo snarled, taking a step forward.

He was now standing in level to Nicholas, fuming as he was well aware that someday he would have to fight this man. Lord Lucifer merely stared with bloodshot eyes at the man that stood before him.

"Scared of a petty witch-hunter?" Nicholas said, his voice as menacing as Leo's.

"Can't fight me? Too afraid that I might be more powerful than you?" said Leo, ignoring Nicholas.

Leo began to chant the hymns for the destruction of Conjurers. Nicholas shut his eyes as anger began to boil inside of him while Lord Lucifer tried not to get any weaker inside. He could not get weak, not now. Not before him.

"Silence!" bellowed Lord Lucifer, unable to hear the words that were coming out of Leo's mouth.

He knew that Leo had the power to destroy him but he was way stronger. Lord Lucifer had just lost his will to fight, seeing who it was that he was supposed to battle.

"I will destroy you. I will take my revenge, father." Leo snarled.

CHAPTER FOURTEEN

∞∞

SON OF SATAN

∞∞

*N*icholas looked back and forth between the two men. He was shocked, or maybe that was an understatement. What he felt was beyond shock. It felt like he was having a nightmare of sorts. How could Lord Lucifer be a witch-hunter's father? Of the one that had mercilessly tortured the witch he had just rescued. Lord Lucifer had not taken his eyes off his son. He looked at Leo with a varied air in his eyes. There was pain, sadness, agony, anger, shame and most of all pity for himself that he had given a man like Leo to the world; a man who had no respect for a woman, who didn't care to torture an innocent human to get what he wanted; a man whom he didn't wish to call his own.

"M'Lord?" said Nicholas, a sad but questioning expression on his face.

Lord Lucifer just blinked and hung his head before standing. He pushed himself up; taking the support of the tree he was resting on. Leo stared at him with wrathful eyes and a furious look. It was clear that there was something Nicholas didn't know. Something grave had happened between Lord Lucifer and Leo for so much of hatred to be seen on Leo's face. The son of a great sorcerer being a witch-hunter wasn't something Nicholas was expecting to see.

"*Have you not told anyone, father?*" Leo spoke, his voice dripping venom as he took a step forward.

"*What do you want me to tell them? That my son is a murderer, that he tortures innocent people for no reason?*" Lord Lucifer snarled back, his voice a dangerous whisper, as he staggered to his feet that were threatening to give away.

"*You're ashamed, aren't you?*" Leo let out a malicious laugh, throwing his head back. Nicholas dared not interrupt the intense conversation. He took a step back.

"*Yes. I am ashamed that you are a part of me.*" Lord Lucifer nodded weakly.

"*WERE YOU NOT ASHAMED WHEN YOU LEFT MY MOTHER?*" Leo howled. His voice was violent enough to shake the entire ground.

"*DID YOU NOT FEEL EVEN A BIT OF SHAME WHEN YOU ABANDONED HER AND SHE HAD NOWHERE TO GO?*" His voice was trembling with anger as he kept walking towards Lord Lucifer.

"*I REFUSE TO EXPLAIN MYSELF TO SOMEONE AS MONSTROUS AND INCONSIDERATE AS YOU!*" Lord Lucifer snarled, his eyes blazing with fear as well as anger.

"*SHE WAS SO YOUNG, FOR HEAVEN'S SAKE, YOU SCOUNDREL!*" Leo's voice dripped venom. He hated his father. He loathed Lord Lucifer.

"*How could you just leave her in the middle of nowhere and go away? How could you not think about the child that she was bearing? How could you not feel even a tiny bit of pity for that woman? She raised me all by herself, living with her mother and father who felt like she was a burden on them. She kept me away from people like you. Maybe I would never have known about what you had done if I hadn't asked her those million questions as to who my father was. . .MAYBE SHE WOULD HAVE DIED*

WITHOUT TELLING ME THE TRUTH TO SAVE YOU FROM BECOMING MY WORST ENEMY!

"But you know what, Lucifer, I found out. I searched every nook and corner but I couldn't get you. That piece of flesh lying over there," he pointed at Amara, pausing to take a breath, "I captured her so I could get to you! I knew you would come to rescue her. I knew that if I became a witch-hunter, I would be able to track you down, and kill you. I knew you were searching for her. Every single witch-hunter in the clan knew you wanted that thing. So I captured her and look where we are. You are standing in front of me and I am ready to kill you. I am ready to end you for leaving my mother just so you could practice witchcraft. You are a vile, careless, heartless imbecile. Did you know that?"

Lord Lucifer shut his eyes, stopping himself from doing something wrong. He didn't wish to kill Leo. He didn't wish to touch him. As much as he loathed him, there was some part of him that stopped him from harming his own blood. However hard he tried, he knew he had done wrong to Marzya by leaving her when she needed him the most. He hated himself for doing that to her but he was born to be a sorcerer since his forefathers were.

After they were killed in a war with witch-hunters, their lineage ceased to exist but there was a sole heir to the coven that they belonged to and that was Lord Lucifer. It was his duty to follow what his forefathers had spent their lives with. He could not keep Marzya safe with him, for his journey to power was dangerous. He had to leave her and so he did. She had let him go. He had not abandoned her but there was no way Leo would understand.

"And you feel ashamed to call me your son? Bravo, Lord Lucifer! I applaud you for your brilliance!" Leo said again, letting out a cold, humourless laugh.

"YOU ARE NO SON OF MINE!" He growled, his eyes threatening to let the tears fall. The varied emotions that he felt at the moment, he could not define them.

"Go away before I have to get your blood on my hands. I do not want to kill you," he said, taking a step back.

"Did you not hear what I said? I am your Death, Lord Lucifer and I will-"

"Nicholas! Take him away from here. Take him," Lord Lucifer cut him off, turning his back towards them.

Nicholas obeyed and shot a fainting curse at Leo before dragging him away to another valley where Lord Lucifer would be out of earshot. Lord Lucifer looked down at Amara, her innocent face covered in blood and dirt. She lay there on the ground unconscious and Lord Lucifer closed his eyes, concentrating to bring back the powers that had vanished out of him for a while. When he was sure he had enough strength, he connected his mind to the healer, Soter who had gone to fetch some herbs. After letting him know that he needed his help, Lord Lucifer looked at Amara and lifted her off the ground to place her on top of the stone table that he had conjured. He covered the table with some grass so it would not hurt her and then let her body drop gently onto the soft grass.

As soon as Soter arrived, he set himself to work. He began using healing spells and potions that he had with him inside his sack. A while later, her head was covered with a paste of herbs and she had been given the Healing Potion. Soter closed his eyes and healed the internal injuries that she had due to what Leo had done to her. All of those were difficult to cure since the duration had been very long but eventually they were all gone and she was as pure as she could ever be. She was put into a deep sleep so she would only awaken when her body felt considerably repaired of all the damage that had been done.

Lord Lucifer sat on the grass as Soter then cured his leg, which now looked as good as it was before. He left then, to prepare some other potions for Amara. Lord Lucifer stayed there on the ground, his eyes squeezed shut as a stab of pain went through his body when he realized that Leo was dead. He wanted to apologize for leaving Marzya but seeing what Leo had become, he didn't wish to make any amends. He could not believe that even after being raised by a pure soul like Marzya, his son had turned out to be so vicious and ruthless.

When Nicholas arrived, he was wiping his sword clean of the blood. He washed the sword using water from the stream that flowed in the valleys and then proceeded to sit next to Lord Lucifer after taking a look at Amara, who was peacefully asleep. Lord Lucifer looked at him silently questioning what had happened to Leo.

"Hanged," Nicholas replied. "I did have to battle him though. He wasn't as weak as we thought he was. But now he's gone."

Lord Lucifer nodded, looking down to the ground. He had failed to ask Leo how Marzya had died. Pushing her thoughts away, he concentrated on how he was going to train Amara.

"May I ask something, if the Lord permits?" Nicholas said, gently so as not to sound too curious.

Lord Lucifer gave a nod. He knew what the question would be. The only family he had left now was Nicholas, his sister's abandoned son that he took in to train. He needed Nicholas, so he was ready to answer whatever was asked.

"What he said about you leaving his mother. Was it true?" Nicholas asked, hesitating at first.

Lord Lucifer let out a sigh.

"Yes. Fifty years ago I was married when I was unaware of the legacy that my forefathers had started. My life was nothing out of the ordinary. Marzya and I shared a great life together. Then one day I met King Abraham the Third, of Acanthus. He was the successor of the great King Abraham and ruler of our land that had been hidden for centuries to protect the witches that were just beginning to establish there. He was travelling, looking for the heir of Zelos, one of the greatest sorcerers of all time. Lord Zelos was my oldest ancestor. I was fifty years old then.

"The King located me and told me everything about who I was. He asked me to join him to practice witchcraft. I did so and talked to Marzya who decided to let me go. I wanted to stay after knowing she was carrying our child. But she urged me to go on. So I did and then got trained by the King along with Lord Mikhail, who went on his own journey and has never looked back since.

"I served King Abraham till the time of his Death. King Orcus then wanted to appoint me as High Minister but I wished to create a coven of my own and began doing so, forgetting about Marzya and our child. Many years after King Abraham died; I found out that he was keeping track of Marzya and that I had a son. I wanted to have him practice witchcraft as well but was advised that it was too late. Leo began capturing witches like he said; to find me. That he had so much of hatred for me, I only realized that now. I never came in his way for the sole purpose of him being my son. But then he captured Amara and I had to save her. She has the potential of becoming the greatest witch the world has ever seen. You know the rest."

Nicholas listened silently, unable to utter a word. He wasn't expecting to hear anything of that sort and now he had nothing to say. Lord Lucifer stood up to get some peace of mind and began walking away from that area after telling Nicholas to keep an eye on Amara. He took one last glance at her and started to walk in the direction where Nicholas and Leo had been fighting, unaware of where he was going. Nicholas failed to realize where Lord Lucifer was headed and didn't think of stopping him. Lord Lucifer slowly walked ahead, his eyes wandering everywhere to get rid of the images of his beautiful wife and son whom he had left years ago. Although he was happy with the life that he had now, he did wish that he had not left her alone that way.

With the thoughts of his dead family running through his mind, he reached the clearing where Leo and Nicholas had fought. Unable to realize where he was, his eyes landed on a tree. His heart raced inside his chest, wildly thumping and he felt as though the ground beneath him had vanished. Although he was aware that his son was dead, Lord Lucifer didn't wish to see his corpse hanging on the branch of a tree with both his hands cut off.

* * *

Iris was trembling. The moment that she fell to the floor, Amara had opened her eyes and shut the doors of her mind, letting Iris out. But seeing her writhing on the floor with her eyes tightly shut, Amara began to panic. She quickly sat down beside Iris and tried to wake her but she kept trembling. Amara realized that she had not been able to get out of Lord Lucifer's mind and was still in a trance. She had lost herself in that time and was now finding it difficult to get out even though Amara had sealed her mind shut from her entering again. But Iris had mildly lost control of herself and she was beginning to lose it completely. Amara shook Iris's body. She reacted in no human way.

"Iris, wake up! WAKE UP!" Amara bellowed, shaking her body to wake her up somehow.

Her heart raced inside her chest and she was Deathly afraid of losing Iris. *What if she lost complete control and went insane?* As hard as she tried, Amara could not wake her up. When there was nothing she thought would help, she lifted her hand and slapped it across Iris's cheek so hard that her palm itself began to tremble with the force. A moment later, Iris went still and then collapsed to the floor. Amara squeezed her eyes shut in frustration before conjuring a goblet of water and splashing it on Iris's face a few times. Startled, Iris opened her eyes. She blinked to adjust her vision, almost forgetting where she was when she spotted Amara sitting next to her. It was only when Amara pulled her into a hug – clutching Iris close to her body while her eyes were squeezed shut and she almost wanted to cry – that realization dawned on Iris and she brought her mind back to the present. Amara let out a sigh of relief and relaxed, slowly letting go of Iris and resting her back on the wall behind, closing her eyes for a long while.

"Are you alright?" She asked, as Iris sat up taking support of the wall behind. She nodded. Iris was unable to put together what she had just seen.

Amara decided that it was best to let Iris get her mind back in control before asking her what she had seen. She felt as though she had just woken up after a long sleep. Iris stared at the floor with her hands slightly inducing a tremor. She was shocked. More shocked than Nicholas all that time ago. She felt as though her heart had fallen into her chest, her breath had stopped for a while. The visions kept running through her mind again and again. The voices echoed in her ears as she struggled to wrap her mind around all that she had found out. How could she tell Amara that Leo was no one else but the Lord's son? How could she even begin to explain the things that she had seen?

She felt as though a huge rock was resting on her back. Amara would be broken if she found out who Leo was. She would be angry, she would do something wrong, she would become a monster if she knew what the truth was. Iris didn't have enough strength to reveal anything to her. She knew that there was no way Amara would take this lightly. This was going to affect her badly and Iris was terrified of what might happen. The man who had rescued her was the father of the man who had tortured her. *How would I feel if this were to happen to me?* She wondered. She was afraid as to how Amara was going to react.

"Do you want anything to eat?" Amara suddenly asked, concerned.

She felt as though she had nearly lost someone important. She was afraid that Iris was going to go insane and Amara would never be able to forgive herself. Now she felt a sudden protectiveness and care for the girl sitting beside her. Iris's mind was so jumbled that she failed to notice the fact that Amara had just given her the tightest hug she had ever received. She should have been smiling in joy at that development but her mind was elsewhere. She was scared for Amara.

"No. I'm okay," said Iris, clearing her throat.

"Do you feel okay enough to tell me what you saw?"

Iris felt the colour draining from her face as the question she had been dreading, was asked. She could not even bring herself to have enough courage to tell her the truth. She was more scared than she had been before the task even began.

"Amara I. . ." she began and looked at her face.

Iris saw the desperation in her eyes, the clawing need to know the truth and the sensation of pain rushing inside of her to know what had really happened to the man who had tortured her this much. Amara deserved to know the truth. But how could Iris tell her anything? The truth was disastrous. It was harsh.

"I'm not forcing you to tell me now but. . ." Amara trailed off, biting her lip.

She was just as nervous. She could sense the fact that there was something very grave that Iris had found out. Her face said it all.

"I can't tell you what I saw," Iris finally managed to utter.

She tried to push back the heaviness inside her chest, which was rising up to her throat. She wanted to get this over with but something was stopping her entirely.

"Why?" Amara asked gently enough but it managed to send chills down Iris's spine. She wasn't looking at her.

"Be-because I just can't. It's unpleasant, Amara. It is wrong and-and I don't think if I can tell you the truth," she said, her voice cracking.

"What did you see, Iris?" Amara said impassively.

Iris felt as though she was talking to the Amara that she had met for the first time: torturous, ruthless, uncaring, vile and dangerous.

"I-" she began.

"What. Did. You. See." Amara repeated, her eyes focussed on the wall in front of her. They were darker than they had ever been.

"Please don't make me say it," Iris replied, a sob making its way up to her throat and in a moment, tears slid down her eyes. She bit her lip hard till it began to draw blood.

"What did you see?" She said once again. Suddenly it felt colder than ever and Iris was starting to shiver in fright. She was right. The old Amara was showing up. It wasn't good, not at all.

"Amara, I. . ." Iris coughed as bile rose in her throat, clogging inside.

She started to cry, her voice cracking up and the tears started to fall effortlessly. She could not bring herself to talk. She could not make herself strong enough to reveal the truth. Her whole body felt as though it was breaking apart into pieces.

"WHAT DID YOU SEE?" Amara shrieked, her voice echoing inside the small cave.

Iris sobbed harder and clutched a palm to her chest, her heart going still for a moment before it ran wild again. She opened her mouth to say the words but nothing came out. It was only when Amara turned to look at her that Iris was able to squeeze her eyes tightly shut and finally utter the words that she had choked up inside of her.

"The Lord. . ." she drew a gasp.

Amara glared at her through bloodshot eyes that sent chills right down Iris's spine. She looked murderous. Iris wanted to close her eyes and go off into a deep sleep to avoid all of this but she was well aware that she could not escape until she told Amara the truth.

"Go on," Amara ordered in a whisper. It was stern enough to make Iris afraid.

"Leo-the Lord's son-" she croaked before collapsing into the deepest cry she had ever let out.

Amara sat there with a blank, unreadable expression across her face. Her eyes were still as dark, yet not dark enough. Her hands were settled on her sides, gripping her gown with her fingers tightly. Her jaw that was clenched had now relaxed as her mind went unbelievably vacant. She dropped her stiff figure to the floor that immediately faltered. Her back was no longer resting on the wall but she sat with her shoulders slumped. There was no sound that came out of her apart from her shallow breaths.

"What did you just say?" She whispered with a little frown etching across her forehead.

"The Lord is Leo's father," Iris managed to repeat unconsciously while her tears refused to stop.

Rage boiled inside Amara and she stood up in the flash of a second. Before Iris could comprehend what was happening, she watched Amara's robes slither out of the cave.

CHAPTER FIFTEEN

∞∞∞∞∞

FIRE AND ICE

∞∞∞∞∞

Amara stood outside in the woods right next to the lake. Her mind was in shambles. She had a million thoughts running around and there seemed to be no way to control them. With every step that she had taken while coming out of the cave, her mind became more and more confused. She didn't know what to feel. She was confused, and scared, and angry, and befuddled, shell shocked and so many more things that she just could not define. Iris had not gotten a chance to tell her everything that she saw and that made her even more perplexed. She needed answers. How could the Lord be *his* father? And how could he not tell her about it? Why was she in the dark for so long? The answers to all of those questions were with the Lord and nobody else. She had never wanted to speak to him as much as she wanted to now. In all these years she had been the most loyal apprentice he could ever have, and he had been lying to her for over a hundred years.

She felt a host of emotions and they were neither showing up on her face nor were they staying inside of her. She had spent a hundred years trying to suppress her emotions and not letting them get in the way of her life, and now when she wanted them to surface, they were arduously struggling inside of her, unable to decide whether or not they were to surface. She wanted to scream, she wanted to ask questions to whoever that would come forward and she wanted to kill someone, anyone. Her jaw was clenched, eyes stinging with tears and heart hammering inside her chest with the occasional goosebumps running down her arms. She felt nauseous, she felt as though her chest was constricting her heart, and it had to go faster to circulate the blood. Her head felt heavy and she had no idea what was happening to her.

Inside the cave, Iris stood up and staggered out to the door. When she spotted Amara, she rushed in her direction and came to a standstill a few paces away from her. Amara stood with her back facing Iris, her fingers clenched around her palm. Iris took a step forward hesitantly. She didn't know what Amara was feeling at that moment. She wanted to take that pain away but she was unaware as to how she would even attempt to do that. So wiping her tears, Iris took another two steps forward and came to stand beside Amara.

"Tell me everything," said Amara, her voice cracking.

Letting out a deep breath, Iris prepared herself to reveal everything to her, deciding not to leave anything since she deserved to know it all. Clearing her throat, she began explaining every single vision that she saw from the time Amara went unconscious. She told her about how Lord Lucifer saved her, how Leo followed him and how Nicholas killed him. In the end, she proceeded to tell her about Leo being the Lord's son and while doing so, she could not stop the tears from starting to fall again. She didn't realize when that happened, and began to cry as she spoke. Amara quietly listened to everything and didn't utter a single word while Iris talked. When she was done, Iris stood there wanting to comfort Amara somehow because the rage that she was feeling had begun to show.

There was a varied amount of emotions on her face, Iris observed. A burning sensation had crept up Amara's spine and she had started to tremble with the anger that was boiling inside of her. It felt as though her bones were cracking inside and an intense pain shot up from her toes right up to her chest. She felt as though she was the victim of the pain that she inflicted on others. She felt as though her whole body was being shattered into pieces once again, just by a plain truth that had been revealed to her.

The force with which she was clenching her fingers, made blood slip out of her palm and the droplets skidded onto the ground. Iris plainly stared. She didn't have enough strength to say a word.

Without so much of a glance at Iris, Amara walked away so swiftly that Iris could not understand what had happened. Her heartbeat ran faster as she started walking in the direction Amara had gone. She heard a scream, a heart-wrenching, earth-shattering scream that sent waves of chills down her spine. Iris stood in place, closing her eyes for a moment. It felt as though the ground was shaking beneath her feet and it would only be seconds until she fell down. Holding a tree that was trembling, she stood herself in place until she was sure the ground wasn't shaking anymore. The scream continued to get louder by each second and Iris was sure everyone else was going to hear it. *The whole castle must be shaking by now,* she thought.

Moments later, the sound stopped and the wind became normal again. Iris opened her eyes and proceeded to walk further when she noticed that everyone else had rushed there from the castle. She saw Erasmus, Sienna, Fabian, Lilienne, and a few other Conjurers standing there with their eyes wide and jaws open. When she went and settled next to them, she saw Amara standing at a distance with her back towards them.

Raising her hands, she lifted her head upwards and a roar was heard, as though a lion was about to prance to attack when the familiar light started to appear. Amara stretched her hands to the sides and the light spread along. It was only a few seconds later that they all realized it.

Amara had set the woods on Fire.

The flames grew stronger as they started licking the trees and the shrubs, covering the grass that was visible and moments later, everyone had begun coughing as the Fire started to surround them. They all tried their best to use the water from the lake to stop the Fire but it was no use. The flames were too strong and violent as they engulfed Amara who was now nowhere to be seen. Iris began to panic. Her breath became shallow and she started to sprint in the direction Amara was when Erasmus grabbed her from behind by the waist, stopping her.

Everyone wondered what they could do, but nothing seemed to work at all. It was a mass panic. As they all tried to protect themselves and dodge the Fire somehow, some of them caught Fire on their clothes, and Fabian was trapped in a corner surrounded by the flames. Conjuring up some water, he diminished the Fire and rushed outside to protect himself. Lilienne tried to dodge the flames that threatened to engulf her while Marissa pushed the Fire away through wind. Erasmus tried his hardest to stop the struggling Iris, who was ready to plunge into the Fire to save Amara. There was no way they would be able to save her now.

"Don't. It's too dangerous," he said to Iris.

She only struggled harder and sobbed uncontrollably. Flinging her arms around her she screamed to set herself free and save Amara but Erasmus held her tight.

"I HAVE TO SAVE HER!" She protested against him.

"No, love, you can't go there. Breathe," he whispered softly in her ear to relax her. But she refused to listen and continued her struggle.

In a bid to save themselves, they all left the woods as soon as they could, to summon the Lord and save the whole area from being burnt down. As far as they knew, either Amara was dead or she had already saved herself and gone from there. Iris was now crying profusely and struggling harder to go to Amara. She screamed, scratching her nails into Erasmus's arms that were holding her in place and dragging her out of the woods.

"LET ME GO!" She cried and fought against him, tears sliding down her eyes.

Erasmus refused to let go of her, clutching onto her tighter than before. He knew that something grave had happened; otherwise Amara wouldn't react this way. She would not set her beloved woods on Fire. And he knew however bad it was, she would never let anything harm herself. Along with everyone else, she was aware of her importance and in absence of the Lord, she was in charge. Saving Iris and getting her back to normal was more important.

They all stood outside the woods, watching the flames dance upon the trees to burn them down. The ones that could handle the element of Water tried their hardest to reduce the Fire but to no avail. None of their efforts worked and they stood there helpless, chanting spells to stop the rage. There was nothing that worked.

"AMARA!" Iris screamed as Erasmus dragged her back in the direction of the castle. It was essential to escort her to a safe place. She was getting out of control.

As soon as he turned around to take her away, the sky went completely black. Clouds covered the whole area, engulfing it into darkness but the only light that was there was the

Fire. Erasmus turned to look up at the sky, frowning, as Iris too went silent, with her eyes focussed above. The few birds that were flying up there suddenly vanished and the sound of thunder was heard. Lightning struck and moments later, it was raining. The black droplets of water descended upon them and the Fire began to subside slowly. The rain started to pour down even faster, drenching the entire place and suddenly the Fire was gone. The woods were engulfed into darkness. The atmosphere felt like Death. Everyone went silent.

On the other side of the lake, stood a hooded figure, his face hidden with a cloak. Striding upon the water in seconds, he reached the opposite side to where the Fire was. Erasmus felt someone standing beside him and turned to find that it was Lord Lucifer.

"M'Lord," he breathed.

Iris had now rested her head on Erasmus's chest, her fingers clutched around the fabric of his cloak. She was looking at the hooded figure standing at a distance. He looked eerily familiar, as though she had seen him somewhere. The vision of someone diving into a terrible sea flashed across her eyes.

Iris blinked only to find another vision of the similar looking figure seated on the shore of a sea. The same figure that had made it rain; the black droplets of water, the gloomy atmosphere – as though someone had just died. It all felt familiar and she wanted to mull over it but her mind kept going blank every now and then. Suddenly she forgot who she was with. She didn't know what was happening and stood there, staring at nothing in particular. Erasmus wanted to let go of her but seeing her fragile and scared in his arms, he decided to keep her close. She needed someone.

"Take her inside. She looks pale," ordered Lord Lucifer, looking at Erasmus once.

Without a word, he nodded and turned around, wrapping the cloak around Iris since the air had gotten incredibly cold. Lord Lucifer looked at the destroyed woods in front of him, the burnt trees and grass that were no longer present. The owls that hooted all night were gone, the doves and crows flying around had vanished and some of them might even be in there, burnt to pieces. He walked further as everyone bowed to him and he then sauntered off, making his way to find Amara.

As soon as he had received the message from Fabian, he had teleported himself to see what had happened.

The hooded figure that was standing in the distance started to stride further as well to reach a point where Lord Lucifer met him. Amara was lying on the ground unconscious. The rain had begun to subside and everyone retreated to the castle. Lord Lucifer looked at Amara with a calmly, unable to understand what had happened, and why.

"Azrael," he whispered, looking up at the man before him.

"Yes, m'Lord?" He replied.

The sound of his voice was clear, deep and husky enough to make a person shiver in fright. The man who stood before Lord Lucifer was the one that he had trained in hiding, and who had grown up to become one of the greatest sorcerers of their time.

"Will you please escort her in the castle? I have something to take care of," Lord Lucifer said to him and Azrael nodded, turning to look at Amara.

With the swish of his fingers, he lifted her off the ground and she followed, suspended in mid-air. Proceeding in the direction of the castle, he went in through the doors as though he knew exactly where he was going, as though he had been living in the castle for years. He took Amara to the great hall where everyone was seated and conjured up a cot on which he placed her unconscious body. Everyone stared at him quietly.

Slowly, he took of his hood and Iris – who was sitting next to Erasmus holding a cup of tea shakily in her hands – looked at him. Her breath hitched at the mere sight of him.

His eyes were a dark blue, almost black but not black enough. He had hair as black as Amara's, short and cut properly. He wore a black robe, and a cloak on top of it that touched the ground effortlessly. His hands were strong, the veins clearly visible. His skin was a bit darker than white but still white enough. A slightly crooked nose that was hardly noticeable, lips that were sealed shut and he held a stoic expression. It felt as though he never smiled, as though he had never seen what happiness was like. His presence would make someone feel gloomy. It almost felt like a part of them had been ripped out of their soul.

Iris noticed that he was good looking – like the others were, but he wore no expression that a normal sorcerer would. It seemed as though there was absolutely nothing that could make him happy. His eyes were so dark that Iris felt as though they could torture by simply looking at someone. In a way he reminded her of Amara. It felt as though they were of the same species - blank, cold and emotionless.

Lord Lucifer walked into the castle and entered the great hall. Everyone stood up and waited for him to get seated. When he rested his fingers on the armrest of the throne, they all sat down in their own chairs. Amara lay on the cot in a corner, her body still drenched. Lord Lucifer looked at her just once and a gust of wind dried her completely. He then turned to look at Azrael, who was standing at a side with his arms folded across his chest.

"Have a seat," he ordered and Azrael sat himself down on a chair.

"What we have seen today was most astonishing and uncalled for. We do not know what made her set the woods on Fire but I have observed that there was some reason behind it that infuriated her.

"We all are aware that Amara would not harm anyone or anything unless given a strong cause to. Since the damage has been done, we can only find out the reason when she wakes up," he said to everyone. Ambrosius stood up from his seat to wake Amara when Lord Lucifer held up a hand to stop him.

"Not now," said he. "Let her rest."

"Meanwhile, I have to inform you that since Lord Mikhail has been gathering an army, we need one of our own. For that purpose, I have been travelling to find more Conjurers who would like to join our coven and help us. Azrael is a sorcerer whom I had been training in hiding for a long time now. He has been trained to be a very exceptional and brilliant sorcerer and I believe he will be of great use to us whenever needed. Also, I would like all of you to begin practicing your powers so they are polished when we are in need. I will be leaving again tomorrow. Erasmus, is there anything the new witch has to say?" He said, turning to look at Iris who still looked as pale as she did before.

She was no longer holding the cup of tea and sat there with her eyes fixed on the floor, unable to utter a single word. Erasmus shook his head after looking at her.

"I don't believe she is in the condition to do anything right now, m'Lord," he said. Lord Lucifer sighed, nodding and turning to look at Amara. He instructed Fabian to escort her to her chamber.

"You may all leave now," Lord Lucifer addressed them and everyone left while Fabian proceeded to take Amara back to her chamber when she stirred and opened her eyes, blinking a few times before sitting up. Fabian took a step back and glanced at Lord Lucifer once who waved a hand, gesturing him to leave.

Amara turned to look at her Lord sitting next to her and she stood up immediately, roughly forgetting what had happened. She bowed down, getting to her knees when realization struck her and she immediately lifted her head back up. Was she capable of asking questions to him? Would he answer truthfully after lying to her all this while? She struggled to get hold of her thoughts when her eyes fell on the stranger sitting in front of her. His eyes were stuck on her, as though reading her soul inside out and she suddenly felt afraid for the first time. She quickly looked back at her Lord.

"Amara?" Lord Lucifer spoke with a questioning look. She knew what he was asking, but she didn't know if she was ready to say anything at the moment.

"M'Lord, I apologize for the destruction," she said, looking down and refusing to make any sort of eye contact. She was afraid that he would see through the lie that she was about to tell him.

"The question is, what made it occur?" He replied, trying to look her in the eye so he could know what it was but she didn't look at him at all. Instead her eyes were focussed on the floor.

"I was-" she hesitated, "I thought there were witch-hunters in the area and I was meditating and I couldn't think of what to do so I set Fire to avoid them."

It was the worst lie she could ever tell. A witch as strong as her could not battle a few witch-hunters and set the woods on Fire, was anybody going to believe that? She cursed herself for saying such a silly thing but to her surprise, Lord Lucifer stared at her simply for a few seconds before he nodded. Of course, he wasn't that foolish. He knew that she was lying but this wasn't the right time to ask her the truth. He would let it go for now and ask her whenever he felt the time was right.

"Very well, but I hope this will not happen again," he said sternly.

"No, m'Lord. Of-of course not," she replied, her eyes still not meeting his.

"I have some other things I need to take care of before I leave again tomorrow. You may go now." Lord Lucifer stood up to leave when his eyes fell on Azrael and he stopped in his tracks.

Amara was now standing aside to give him way.

"Introduce yourselves. I believe the both of you will have to work together in time," he said to them before walking out of the hall. Amara turned to look at Azrael who was already looking at her.

"I didn't know the Lord's apprentices lied to him," he spoke, startling Amara. She narrowed her eyes, not liking him already.

"And who are you to tell me that?" She shot back, raising her eyebrows.

"I am one of his apprentices. He trained me in hiding. Azrael," he said, extending his arm for her in courtesy but she did nothing of that sort. She opened her mouth to say something when he spoke before her.

"Amara, I know." He nodded, pulling his hand back. She frowned, wondering as to why he was here.

"The Lord is gathering an army and I will be a part of it. Now I've heard a lot about you, Lady Amara. Your brilliance, exceptional qualities, your powers that are unmatchable but just a moment, great witch, did my powers not defeat yours, minutes ago?" He said to her, circling around.

Ridicule dripped from his tone and it clearly showed how much he was mocking her. Amara closed her eyes for a minute to contain her anger. She was right, she didn't like him a bit.

"I never said my powers are unmatchable," she replied, her voice thick with rage.

"But others have, m'lady. Like everyone says, there is no one who can defeat you. I am not close to believing that but surely I would like to tell you this, if we are going to be working together, we better accept the fact that there is going to be someone stronger than you and in this case, it would be this humble sorcerer." His hands were clasped behind his back and he bent in front of her mockingly. Amara resisted the urge to scoff at his antics.

Azrael was impressed at the strong amount of confidence that she gave off. However, he was also not in favour of her being the strongest witch there ever was. With a roll of her eyes, Amara turned her face to look at him.

"In the absence of the Lord, I am in charge of the castle, which means I have an authority over some people. In this case, you, humble sorcerer," she replied very softly, only to march past him and make her way out of the castle.

She didn't need to be answerable to someone as over-confident and vile as him. Surely he showed himself as being strong and manipulative enough but it didn't mean her powers were any weaker. She was sure about herself but not as overly as him. Being over-obsessed with one's strength wasn't something she appreciated. She wondered how she was going to work with him.

Inside the castle, Azrael stood with his hands still clasped behind his back. When Iris walked timidly out from her chamber to go to the kitchen, she looked at him from the corner of her eye and slowly enough, proceeded away so as not to get him anywhere close to her. She was as terrified of him as she had first been of Amara. Azrael stood there watching her walk past him. He looked at her quietly, his eyes focussed solely on her and as she was about to reach the door of the kitchen, she stumbled in her steps and frowned in confusion. *I haven't been physically harmed to be so weak while just walking from one chamber to another*, she wondered.

With one palm resting on a wall, she straightened herself and stepped inside the kitchen, yet her legs wobbled and they were about to fall apart. Azrael then let out a breath, taking his eyes away from her and suddenly Iris began to walk normally again, her legs feeling as usual as they did before.

∞ ∞ ∞ ∞ ∞

PART II

∞ ∞ ∞ ∞ ∞

CHAPTER SIXTEEN

∞∞∞∞∞

BATTLE OF THE WIND

∞∞∞∞∞

The water rose and fell back into the lake. It kept doing so until he rested his hands back to his sides. The wind was beginning to get colder. Winter was on its way. He stood there at the edge of the lake, his eyes scanning the surrounding when they landed on the side of the woods that had been burned down. The sound of water falling on the grass made him want to strain his ears and look closely at the foggy figure of a woman clad in a flowing grey gown, waving her hands in the air as the water fell through her fingers onto the ground. She was watering the plants so they would grow again on the barren land. Azrael began walking towards her. When he reached, Amara turned around to find him standing there with his hands clasped behind his back as he looked around quietly. Ignoring him, she continued doing her work.

Her heart broke with every place that she watered. She had set Fire to the woods that she had loved being in; the place that gave her peace and calm whenever she went there. The huge trees no longer had the lush green leaves that gave them charm. The soft grass wasn't under her feet anymore. The birds were gone. Sceiron was gone. But she wanted to take it back to the way it was before, and so kept watering the plants every day.

It had been over a week that Lord Lucifer left to travel again and she was busy with the work that he had assigned to her. Even though she was furious about the fact that he lied to her, she knew he might have had a reason for that and didn't want to find that out by risking Iris's life again. She didn't want to lose her like she nearly had last time.

She wanted to give the Lord time to finish his work and then she would ask him questions. There were plenty of them anyway. Meanwhile, she had her duty to protect the castle and the coven. A war was coming and she could not afford to get weak now. She had to keep her powers intact and in working condition to be ready to fight. Even though she still had a lot of questions to get the answers of, she was no longer getting the visions from her past again, limiting her thoughts to the present all the time. And she was glad that she had gotten rid of it all, even after a hundred years had passed with her being affected.

"How do you suppose the trees will grow back after what you did to them?" asked Azrael, running his fingers down the damaged bark of a tree.

Amara turned to look at him, a sigh coming out of her lips as she did so. The more he was around, the more she had begun to dislike him. There was no option apart from being with each other since the Lord had said they had to work together and practice for the fight. Even though he wasn't with her all day, he would suddenly show up and ask questions about the Conjurers around. He had already started to exercise his power over everyone, which wasn't going down well with Amara. As cold as she was to all the witches of the coven, she didn't act as though they were inferior to her. Azrael, on the other hand, had started to get on her nerves. He was being obnoxious every single moment of the day and she didn't like it. Also the questions that he asked were always to test her knowledge about witchcraft and so far, she had answered all of them right. But it did manage to annoy her at times.

"Nature will find its way. It does not believe in holding a grudge," she replied to him, continuing to water the plants again.

"How many elements are you capable of tackling?" He asked suddenly, after a moment of silence.

His eyes were scanning the entire area as though examining the damage that had been done. Amara tried to be as patient as she could. Not even Iris had asked so many questions as he did when she had joined.

"Every witch is expected to be able to tackle all the elements. However, we have to excel in at least two, which are the dominant ones," she said to him.

Azrael was always intrigued by the witty answers that she gave to his questions. He was prone to asking all kinds of questions that he assumed no one had the answers to, but Amara seemed to have the upper hand over all. As much as it impressed him, he also began to get a bit bothered by the knowledge that she had. At some point he would come to think as though she was really the greatest witch of their time and that everyone had not been lying when they had praised her. But he didn't want to accept that even though she gave the proof every time he spoke to her.

"What do you hold expertise in?" He asked again, curious to know if she could handle Water as good as she could handle Fire.

He had seen her ability in tackling Fire. The intensity with which the woods were being burnt, it took a lot of strength for him to subside it using the rain. It had taken him at least a few more moments than necessary to hold down the flames when he had tried to reduce the Fire. It had been too strong.

"I have been able to tackle Fire and Water better than the other elements," she told him truthfully.

He wasn't surprised. Somewhere deep inside, a feeling told him that she held the ability to tackle the same elements that he did. To an extent, he was proud about the fact that someone was capable of holding competition against him if the need arise.

"What are your thoughts on a casual battle?" He said, raising his eyebrows.

Amara stopped watering the plants and looked at him for a while, contemplating whether he meant what she had understood or not.

"Does not seem like a bad idea for practice." She shrugged, and clasped her hands together.

"Very well, then. Whenever you're ready," he said and turned to go when a wave of water crashed down on him, drenching him from head to toe.

"I'm always ready," said Amara, pulling her hands back to her sides and Azrael whipped his head around to look at her.

"I have seen you burn down the woods. Let's see how you protect it from the flames that I induce," he replied, unfazed by the water that had drenched him and raised his hands above.

He swirled them around once and a huge ball of Fire was conjured and his eyes shut. Stretching his hands behind, he threw them back ahead, letting the Fire rush hastily towards the woods. And in a moment, it was gone, for once again water had come crashing down and the smoke rose up from the Fire that had now been extinguished.

Iris sat at a distance with her legs pulled up to her chest and her chin resting on an arm. Her back was settled on the bark of a tree, her eyes stuck on the battle going on in front of her. The Fire and Water danced around together, trying to win over each other and Iris could not help but wonder how easily they depicted the personality clashes between Azrael and Amara. Both of them were equally skilled, their elements being strong enough to fight the other and the scuffle that they created around one another.

After the incident in the woods, Amara had gone back to the way she was earlier: cold. She didn't talk to Iris as much as she did before and she kept herself busy with reading, practicing her powers, watering the woods and managing the coven. She barely had any time to get Iris out of the state she was in.

Although once or twice she would ask her how she was, after a few days that had ceased as well. Iris felt more alone than ever. She had no one to talk to, not even Erasmus. He had been clawing her brain out asking what was wrong but she could not answer his questions. Amara didn't want anyone to know what had happened apart from herself and Iris. Now when she needed her the most, Amara had stopped being how she used to be. She had gone back to her cold behaviour, only speaking to Iris when necessary and she was now the same person as she was when Iris had first arrived.

At the time that she was craving for company and a friend, Amara wasn't there. But Iris didn't blame her. She hadn't gotten the answers yet. There were still so many reasons that Amara had to go back to her usual self and Iris didn't even feel an ounce of regret or anger towards her. She still respected and admired her courage. For when she put herself in Amara's place, all she could think of was deceit and betrayal from the one person that she had trusted after everything.

The Fire hurried forward and the Water began to strike back with equal force. Iris admired the amount of strength both the elements had. It only went on to explain how strong Amara and Azrael were. Their powers could easily battle one another, struggling to prove the other one weaker. It was an interesting war and Iris was too involved in watching what was going on. A while later, the Fire became so strong that the Water began to increase its force; and it created a wild chase between the two. It had started to get serious rather than casual. Both the forces had lost control and struggled to survive in front of the other.

Something made Iris concentrate hard on the battle and a gust of wind flew towards them, pushing both of them to the ground and diminishing the Fire as well as dropping the Water to the ground. It was suddenly silent. Iris had unknowingly ended the fight by her ability to tackle wind. She realized it when something made her snap back to reality. Amara was standing up and looking at Iris shockingly. She could not understand how easily Iris had managed to handle the Air and ended the battle. It had only been a while since she had started to be better in the task. With Nicholas gone, she was unsure about how much progress Iris had made by now.

Amara started to walk in her direction while Azrael stood in place observing the young witch seated there who had made absolutely no effort to end the battle, yet she succeeded. He was more impressed with Iris than he was with Amara. Then again, he had the strange grudge against her which made him want to dislike her for no apparent reason.

"D-d-did you just--?" Amara began, approaching Iris where she was seated.

"I am so sorry. I didn't mean for that to happen it just-" she stood up worriedly.

The wind had just rushed towards them without her having any control over it. She felt as though Amara and Azrael were going to torture her together and drive her insane. She began to get even more frightened when Azrael walked over to them.

"That was brilliant, Iris," said Amara, shaking her head.

She was surprised as well as impressed at the strength that Iris had when ending such a strong battle between Fire and Water. It wasn't easy to have the upper hand over two powerful elements in a battle. But then again, the advantage that Iris had was that they had been so involved in battling each other that they failed to notice the strength by which the wind was approaching. It was remarkable for a new witch like Iris.

"Indeed," Azrael interjected, standing next to Amara.

"Are you two seriously not angry with me?" Iris asked, perplexed.

"If you had not intervened, there would have been destruction," replied Amara.

"But I wonder, who taught you the skill? It's not very easy to stop a fight between two strong elements," Azrael spoke, taking a step forward.

"Nicholas taught me. But I swear, I didn't mean to interrupt the battle," Iris replied, instantly looking away from him.

She had a bad feeling about him since the beginning. She wanted to tell Amara but her distance made Iris want to be quiet all the time. Also, Azrael was quite a daunting sorcerer.

"Is that the Lord's nephew?" He looked at Amara who nodded, her eyes still on Iris.

"I have to speak to Iris for a while if you don't mind," she said to him and without waiting for an answer, grabbed Iris's arm and tugged her away where she was sure Azrael was out of earshot.

Even though she had gone back to the way that she was before, there was a tiny part of her that felt a connection to Iris. Amara wanted to make sure she was okay. And she was also aware of the fact that she had neglected Iris for a while, and she felt guilty about that. Her stopping the fight had snapped Amara's attention back to her.

Iris silently followed to where she was being led. Her eyes were wide and she glanced at Azrael, who stood there for a moment before turning around and walking away with a long look in their direction. When Amara was sure that they were somewhere safe, she let go of Iris and turned to look at her apologetically.

"I'm sorry. . ." she said to her, looking down.

Iris raised her eyebrows in question.

"Sorry?" She said, narrowing her eyes.

Why is she apologizing to me? She wondered.

". . .For avoiding you. I know it looks as though I was selfish and didn't care about what happened to you after I asked for your help. I didn't mean to do that, but-"

"It's okay, Amara," Iris said, cutting her off. "In all the time I've been here I've tried to understand you to my best. The others don't know why you are this way because they don't know what you've been through. I do. And I feel like I know you more than others, if I'm not wrong. So you don't have to apologize. I understand why you reacted the way you did and you have all the right in the world to do so. So please don't say sorry."

Amara looked at the young girl that showed such high level of maturity and understanding. She felt as though there was no one else that could understand what she had been through. But Iris did and she accepted everything that Amara gave to her. She willingly took the pain and the anguish; she gladly agreed to help her in finding out the truth about her past. She nearly went out of control only to come out stronger. After all of that when Amara ignored her, she did not seem unhappy. Not once. There was a new respect that Amara felt for Iris. She felt as though Iris was the sister that she never had. After losing her family, Iris was the closest she could ever have had. If there was anyone that could tolerate the things that

Amara did, it was Iris. She could admit that in a heartbeat. Iris had that much hope; that much strength and that much will to fight, which Amara could never build up.

For the second time after everything that happened, Amara smiled. This time, it wasn't as tiny as the last one. It looked like a real smile – a genuine one, saying she was thankful for whatever Iris had done. Iris could only grin back widely. She felt better seeing Amara smile once again, the reason being her. It was as though all her worries and all her concerns about being lonely faded away, and Iris was back to how she was before – cheerful.

Now, seeing Amara with a hint of happiness, Iris felt as though she was floating in the clouds. She felt alive again, and out of the blackness that was surrounding her for this time.

"You haven't spoken to the Lord yet, have you?" Iris asked, curious to know if there had been any confrontation.

"No. I didn't have enough time and energy to," Amara replied, looking away.

Iris nodded and they proceeded to go back to the castle when Amara started to walk in that direction. Iris thought that Amara was thinking about what she would ask when she met the Lord the next time, but Amara had something completely different in her mind. As she walked back to the castle, she could not help but be suspicious about Azrael. She had spotted someone sitting on the tree where they were talking in the woods.

Not wanting to get Iris worried, she had kept her thoughts to herself. But when they had turned to go back, she was certain that she felt a presence. It felt as though someone had just walked past them when they turned around. And she could not help but think that it was Azrael. The amount of questions that he had been asking made her suspicious every time he did so. There was something that he was hiding and she wanted to know what it was.

He seemed so different than the others that the Lord had trained, and his behaviour indicated that he was spying on them. There was something very suspicious going on and she decided to be careful around him and keep Iris away from him. She felt more protective of her and wanted to make sure nothing happened to her. Iris was someone the coven could not afford to lose. She had way too many powers – some of which she was unaware of. After seeing what she had done to stop the fight, Amara was certain that Iris would turn out to be very helpful in the war.

"May I ask you something?" Iris said, when they walked inside the castle.

Amara rolled her eyes. *Of course,* she thought. *How could Iris not ask questions?*

"Go on," she replied, proceeding towards the library.

"What powers does he have?" She asked, following her.

"Who?" Amara frowned, even though she was well aware whom Iris was talking about.

"Az-Azrael," she stuttered.

"The power of appearing out of nowhere," a voice whispered into her ear and Iris turned around in shock with one hand flying to her heart, which was beating twice as fast.

Azrael stood there contentedly and his hands behind his back as they always were whenever he was idle. Amara stopped in her tracks and looked at Azrael disinterestedly before scoffing and continuing her journey towards the library. She believed that Iris would eventually follow her and Azrael surely wasn't such a threat inside the castle. He would not do anything in presence of the entire coven if it was true what she was suspecting.

"Uh, I umm. . ." Iris stuttered, staring at him with her eyes wide.

"If you would allow me, may I ask you a few questions?" He said to her, falling into step beside her as she turned to go to her chamber instead of going to the library like she was supposed to.

"Oh I. . .okay," she replied nervously.

She felt so nervous around him and it was a surprise as to how she was normally breathing at that point.

"How long have you been here?" He said.

"Around six and a half months," she told him, avoiding his gaze.

"And what all have you learnt about witchcraft?"

"I-I have read books, lots of them. And Amara helped-helped me in some things."

She felt extremely dim-witted for stuttering like that while talking to him. *He isn't such a monster,* she thought. But that didn't mean he wasn't intimidating either. His aura itself made people feel like someone had died. All normal feelings would vanish and be replaced by fear and nervousness if he was anywhere close to five meters. But that was occasional.

"And what have you read so far? You must have good knowledge of whatever you have read."

He was now striding along with her around the passageway that led to the main door of the castle. Iris wanted him to leave her alone so she could go back to her work. It was better asking Amara questions rather than being interrogated as though she had committed a crime. She wanted to crawl back into her room and read more books to answer him confidently because even though she had the knowledge, she could not muster up the courage to give him the correct answers. Moreover, she was afraid that if she didn't answer properly, he might torture her because he seemed that threatening.

"The books about witchcraft in general, and there are a lot of things that I-I found out." She let out a breath, cursing herself for giving silly answers.

But before Azrael could ask another question, the door of the castle had been opened and there stood a beautiful witch whom Iris failed to recognize. Azrael's eyes snapped to the witch who was at the door, looking around curiously as though searching for someone when her eyes landed on him and she stared at him silently for a long moment, before her lips broke out into a grin. Iris could only stare in perplexity.

CHAPTER SEVENTEEN

∞∞∞∞∞

THE SCULPTED FAIRY

∞∞∞∞∞

A zrael stared at the witch in front of him. His eyes were stuck on her, unblinking and she was smiling at him. Iris wondered why none of them spoke a word. *Do they know each other?* She thought. *Or are they lovers?* Because the way he was looking at her, he obviously looked surprised, but his expression held so many emotions that Iris felt as though he didn't know what was happening. She looked back and forth between the two, unable to understand what was going on. The woman standing at the door was beautiful, no doubt about that. She had long red hair that reached mid-back, her eyes were a blazing blue, porcelain white skin and an average height figure, and her smile was incredible enough as well. Iris always wondered how easily these witches had beauty granted to them.

"Lea," whispered Azrael, almost to himself but Iris could hear it.

And the way the witch nodded in agreement, it seemed as she heard him as well.

"Rael," she responded and her eyes moistened a bit.

Iris took a step back as Lea rushed towards Azrael and pulled him into a hug. This was the first time Iris had seen the display of any kind of affection in the castle. There were those who had mates and were destined to be with each other but none of them even expressed an ounce of love in gatherings. This confused her, even more when Azrael actually hugged Leandra back. Iris could only stare with her eyes wide. For someone who seemed so cold and ruthless, hugging wasn't normal.

The girl dressed in a green laced gown then turned to Iris when she let go of Azrael. She smiled and said, "I'm Leandra."

Do they have the same eye colour or am I imagining it? Iris wondered.

"Iris," she replied, with a tiny smile. She stood there curiously, hoping to know who Leandra was and how she knew Azrael. Leandra looked at Iris through her shining blue eyes and pulled the strap of her sack back onto her shoulder.

"I'm his sister, if you're wondering," she cleared and Iris then gave a nod of understanding. *That is why the sudden affection,* she thought, *and they do have the same eye colour.*

"*Oh.*" Iris glanced at Azrael for a moment. He was running his slender fingers through his hair, and then rubbing the back of his neck as he looked down at the floor.

Iris felt a bit comfortable, for Leandra was extremely cheerful and it must have hurt her jaws to smile this much. After having been around all sorts of gloom, Iris felt relieved knowing she could possibly find a friend in this jovial witch.

"Lord Lucifer thinks I'd be helpful in the war," Lea said, now looking at her brother.

"Does he?" Azrael shot back, amused.

"How have you been?"

Iris decided it was best she leave the siblings in each others' company since they obviously needed some bonding time. With a faint smile, she began to walk towards her chamber.

Azrael watched Iris for a moment before turning back to his sister. "Fine, you look as tiny as you looked when you were eight," he told her with a smirk.

Lea rolled her eyes. "It's been twenty years, Rael. I'm surprised you were able to recognize me."

"Your hair is still the obvious red."

"And you still don't smile enough," she sighed.

"Why don't you go and make some friends? Get acquainted. You seem to like Iris." He pulled his cloak tighter around him and began to walk away when Lea stepped in front of him.

"Am I not allowed to talk to my brother?" She looked at him flatly.

"I have some work to do," he responded.

"Twenty years, Rael, and you still don't want to spend time with your poor little sister. What did I ever do to deserve this?" Lea faked a look of sadness, dramatically placing a hand on her heart.

"Hmm," he sighed, shaking his head in amusement. "I've missed you." He ruffled her hair and walked past her to the door of the castle.

Lea rolled her eyes and turned to look in the direction that Iris had gone, hoping to find her. She proceeded towards the passageway when the door of a chamber on her right opened, and Erasmus stepped outside.

"You must be Leandra," he said, after looking at her for a long moment.

"How do you know?" She asked, surprised.

"I just happen to know everything," he replied, smirking as he shifted to give her way.

"Then you must know where I can find Iris."

"Right beside my chamber," he said, pointing to his left. "I'm Erasmus, by the way. If you ever need anything." He smiled before leaving her next to Iris's chamber.

Lea knocked on the door of Iris's chamber. The door opened after a moment and Iris stood there holding a book close to her chest.

"May I come in?" Lea asked.

"Of course." Iris smiled, letting her in.

"I hope I'm not disturbing you," she said, walking into the chamber.

"Not at all. I rarely have company," Iris replied, putting her book away.

"Oh. Is it that lonely all the time?" Lea looked around the small chamber that had various lamps around the walls, and chimes hung near the window with a mahogany round table in between and a bed at the side, that had rumpled sheets.

"Not always," Iris said and placed her book on the intricately carved table. They proceeded to sit on the chairs and Leandra grabbed the book that Iris had kept on the table in between.

"*Ancient Witchcraft*," she said, flipping the pages of the book. "I read this when I was seventeen."

"How old are you now?" Iris asked, as Leandra put the book back on the table.

"A hundred and ten," she replied. She looked no more than twenty four in Iris's opinion. *Then again, the elixir of immortality does wonders to a witch.*

"Were you part of some other coven before you came here?"

"No. I practiced witchcraft on my own. Though I had a mentor, but she sacrificed herself fifty years ago. Since then I've been alone."

"You must be quite acquainted with this world then. I've only been here six months and I barely know anything." Iris thought about how less aware she was of her surroundings. She was inexperienced and Leandra, although young, seemed fairly smart. It seemed as though no new witches had joined after herself, and Iris always felt inferior to everyone else around.

"That's alright. It took me almost three years to get properly familiar. You'll come along," Lea gave her a smile of assurance. "So is everyone friendly here? How many Conjurers are in this coven? Do you have any good friends? Do you fancy someone?" She asked as she grinned from ear to ear.

Iris chuckled in amusement at the amount of questions she was asking. "Not everyone is friendly," she began. "I'm only friends with Erasmus and Nicholas. . ." she didn't know whether Amara could be classified as a friend. ". . .About thirty to thirty-five apprentices of the Lord are in this coven and no, I don't fancy anyone," she finished.

"You don't have any other friends?" She frowned.

Iris shook her head.

"Well then, what am I for? I'll be your friend," she grinned and clapped her hands together while Iris chuckled.

"Okay," she replied happily.

"So uh, you must know Lady Amara."

"Yes, I do."

"I've heard so much about her! Everyone talks about her brilliance and I'm so glad I could be a part of this coven to serve the Lord alongside someone as powerful as Lady Amara. She's remarkable, isn't she?" Lea let out a long sigh.

"She really is," Iris said, smiling to herself.

Iris had known Amara more than anyone else ever had, and she felt proud of herself. She felt as though she had achieved a milestone in life. Leandra began to say something when the door of Iris's chamber opened and Amara stormed in with a furious look across her face. She looked at Leandra once who was now standing up, staring wide eyed at the beautiful woman standing before her. She immediately recognized Amara at her mere presence. It wasn't difficult to recognize someone like Amara.

"I thought you were coming to the library with me," said Amara, fuming.

"I-I got caught up and forgot about it. I'm so sorry," Iris said, standing up with a look of dread.

"Don't just get out of my sight like that! Do you know how important it is to protect you?"

"I'm sorry. I-why is it important to protect me?" Iris frowned in confusion.

Amara went silent for a while, wondering whether or not she should tell Iris about her being a threat to Lord Mikhail, when her eyes fell on Leandra who was standing there looking completely star-struck. She was staring at Amara as though she were some angel. Amara frowned, not recognizing her and before she could ask Iris who she was, Leandra spoke.

"You're Lady Amara, right?" She whispered, her eyes still wide enough. Iris more or less chuckled.

"Just Amara, and you are?" Amara replied. Amara noticed that she had a similar eye colour to that of Azrael's.

"I-I'm Leandra," she said, a smile grazing her lips.

She smiles a lot, Iris thought to herself.

"She's Azrael's sister," Iris said, for Leandra was captivated under Amara's presence.

Amara nodded and looked at Leandra for a while before turning back to Iris who was trying to stifle a laugh at the way Lea was behaving at the moment. She looked like a child who had just seen her favourite toy come to life.

"I'm going to my chamber. Don't wander around anywhere without informing me," said Amara before leaving.

Iris wondered why she was being so protective over her, but then shrugged the thought, turning to Leandra who had just let out a sigh.

"Do you want a tour of the castle?" Iris said to her.

"Of course!" Lea replied and rushed out of the chamber.

Iris had never met such a cheerful witch in all the time that she had been here. She had learned to adapt to the serious environment around and didn't expect anyone even close to being as radiant as Lea was. Iris felt like she had found a good friend apart from Erasmus who seemed rather busy these days. She had been trying to talk to him but he would mostly get away saying he had some work to take care of; which again left Iris by herself. She felt at ease after having met Lea.

They passed a few chambers and met Fabian and Erasmus on the way near the meditation chamber. Iris showed the library and the ritual chambers to Leandra along with Lord Lucifer's chamber which was still sealed shut after he left to travel again. Passing the meditation and potions chamber, they went into the kitchen when Lea felt thirsty. Later, they visited the two towers at the sides of the castle, overlooking the woods and the lake. Lea looked at the surroundings gleefully since she had barely ever been in a castle. She told Iris that being alone, she had travelled a lot and never stayed in one place for long. Going to castles of covens wasn't part of her journey. She would always be in woods or mountain valleys where other witches who were not part of covens would reside.

"Do you like travelling?" Iris asked when they were sitting at the tower, looking at the lake and the burnt part of the woods that lay beneath them.

"Mm, I've seen so many beautiful lands!" She nodded. "But sometimes I just like staying at one place. It gets tiresome."

"You must have a lot of powers," Iris said after a moment of silence.

"A few, yes. I can handle the elements of Spirit and Earth. Do you want to see something?" She said, with an excited glint in her eyes.

Iris shrugged, nodding. She watched as Lea conjured up some mud and water. With her fingers waving around in circles, she mixed some water with the sludge and then lifted her hands above, which made the silt rise up and mould into the figure of a fairy, her wings spreading as though she was about to fly. Lea glided her fingers a bit more, giving proper shape to the figure and when she was sure it looked perfect, she took a step back. Iris stared in wonder at the beautiful sculpture that stood before her. Lea smiled at her reaction and clicked her fingers once, which made the leftover soil vanish from there. The sculpture looked elegant and Iris could only stare in marvel. There seemed to be no flaw in her intricate work.

Lea watched Iris in happiness. She felt as though she had found a good friend in her and it would only be hours until they started to get along even better. She let out a sigh of content, looking at the sculpture she had just created. One of the specialties of handling the element of Earth was that she could create various things out of the supplies that mother earth offered. Lea loved designing sculptures out of earth.

"This is beautiful, Leandra," Iris said, smiling.

Lea simply grinned back wider than ever as her eyes shone with excitement.

"I didn't know witches were capable of being so creative," Iris joked and Lea gave out a slight chuckle.

She glanced at the woods below, where she spotted Amara standing beside a tree. Amara lifted herself in the air and sat on one of the high branches. Lea watched as an owl flitted close to her and settled beside Amara, stroking its head on her arm.

"What else can you do?" Iris asked, snapping Lea's attention back to her.

"I can summon spirits – haven't really had the opportunity to do so for any important purposes – but it is one of my strong abilities," she replied. Iris gave a nod.

"If you don't mind me asking, why did you not get trained with your brother?"

"He left when he was eleven. I was eight years old then. Father trained me for a few years and asked me to go find a mentor on my own. Then I was trained by three other witches. Rael would send me letters at times. That continued for a few years and later it all just stopped. I was excited knowing Rael would be here when Lord Lucifer asked me to join the army. So here I am, all because of him."

They proceeded to walk towards the railing. Azrael stood beside the lake in the woods. He lifted himself in the air before diving backwards into the lake. The vision of a similar figure diving into a sea flashed in front of Iris's eyes and she blinked to focus back to reality. She silently stared at the invisible Azrael who had vanished into the water. Iris wanted to know more about him, so she turned her attention back to Lea. She was busy admiring the stretch of woods that lay before them.

"Do you mind telling me more about him?" Iris asked, and Leandra glanced at her once before looking back to the woods.

"He's one of the greatest sorcerers of our time; almost as good as Amara. He was always fascinated with witchcraft and couldn't wait until he would come of age to start practising. Father always said that he would make an incredible sorcerer. We used to be very close, but one day he suddenly left. Nobody knows why. He left to never look back. I tried to find out why, but he never gave an answer. I missed him a lot when he was gone. I got lonely. Later, I had to get used to it since my training had begun. . ." she trailed off and sadly smiled at the memory before continuing. ". . .He would steal books of witchcraft from father's library. Once I found him reading a book on black witchcraft. I didn't know what it was then. Father told me that after Rael left us, he learnt both black and white witchcraft.

"Because of that, his letters changed, the way he expressed his feelings changed. There seemed to be no happiness within him. I later realized that it was because of the knowledge of black witchcraft." She paused to take a breath and watched as Azrael's head lifted itself out of the water. "The aura that us Conjurers carry, that which we choose to show when we wish to, depends on the kind of witchcraft that we have learnt. Rael has an aura of Death, I know you might have noticed. . ." Iris was suddenly listening with rapt attention. ". . .That is because of the dark magic that he is familiar with. He chooses to keep this aura around him. In reality, he's just as normal as we are. But that's not what he wants others to think. There are so many good attributes hidden inside of him but he never reveals them. That is what makes him look so dangerous on the outside. He's strong, extremely strong and he tackles Fire and Water. He can also inflict torture. All of us can't," Lea completed, letting out a breath.

Iris could now put the pieces together. How Azrael's presence made the surroundings seem ghastly but sometimes it would feel completely normal when he was around. Her confusion about him seemed to have cleared now that Lea had explained things to her. Iris realized that most of his powers and his nature matched Amara's. They were more or less the same, yet a little different. He was someone as cold and as torturous as her, yet somehow they were two separate entities who had their own share of problems that were unknown to most. Iris was curious to know what made him leave when he was a child.

"There is one other power that I know of," said Lea, breaking Iris's train of thought.

"What is it?" Iris asked, raising her eyebrows.

"Have you ever heard of the phrase, *'If looks could kill'*?"

"Yes." Iris frowned.

"When he wants someone dead, he merely has to look at them intently enough, which either paralyzes the person, or kills them. In essence, he can manipulate you into doing what he wants you to without you realizing it. He doesn't have to invade your mind for that."

Iris looked at the figure of Azrael striding out of the lake. The image of her legs shaking when she was going to the kitchen the week before flashed across her eyes. She had noticed him looking at her, and moments later, she had staggered into the kitchen with her shaky legs. Sudden realization hit her that it wasn't her weakness acting up, but Azrael testing his powers on her.

Chapter Eighteen

∞∞∞∞∞

THE PROPHECY

∞∞∞∞∞

Iris had been spending most of her time with Leandra who was now her closest friend. Not even Erasmus could compete with that. He would try to spend with her but she was always busy with Lea. There were times when he would get upset, but then he let it go, thinking that he had no business when two women were busy with each other. He was aware of the fact that he had been avoiding her for a while since he was busy practicing his powers and keeping in contact with Nicholas to find out what exactly Lord Mikhail had been up to. But there was no such progress in the matter. That was why he had gone back to spending time with Iris but now, she was out of his grip. It had been roughly three months since Lea arrived and she had become acquainted with the castle's inhabitants nicely enough to have them all quite amused by her.

As far as Amara had observed, she had managed to make everyone happy at the time of panic since the war was coming nearer. Even Amara had to admit that Lea was very charming, and she was also relieved about the fact that because Lea was around, she didn't have to keep an eye on Iris as much. Since she was a trusted witch of the Lord, Amara had thought it was okay to leave Iris under her watch. She had even talked to

Leandra about it and she was gladly up for it. And so, Amara wasn't as worried about Iris anymore. She felt reassured as she had other things to worry about.

The apprentices of the coven had not realized the importance of the war, which meant they were not paying as much attention to strengthening their powers. Under the absence of Lord Lucifer, it was Amara's job to make sure they all understood the gravity of the situation. So she called an immediate meeting in the great hall one morning. Everyone was busy having tea outside the castle, laughing and chatting while Lea cracked jokes. Amara had sent an instant order through Fabian to summon all of them back inside. As soon as they did, Amara had wanted to whack some sense into them, but she decided to take it calmly.

"I have summoned you all here to give you a fair warning about what is going to come," she began firmly. "There isn't much time and we all need to be prepared for the war that Lord Mikhail has declared against us. I have been observant enough to notice that none of you are properly acquainted with practice for strengthening your powers. The war can strike at any point. It might even begin in a few minutes, you never know. It is mandatory for all of you to be prepared for whenever they strike. I hope you understand the danger that we are facing right now. With the Lord gone, we need to be strong enough to protect each other. We need the strength. So I would like all of you to end the chattering phase and get to work. I won't take no for an answer, and I certainly won't appreciate if you lot are busy having fun when we are facing a crisis," she concluded.

They all nodded in understanding, realizing that they had been ignorant all this while since the Lord wasn't there. If he were, the discipline would have been extensive and none of them would be sitting and laughing without a care in the world. None of them had even thought that Amara would be addressing them in place of Lord Lucifer, even though they were well aware that she was in charge. Her hold over all of them was necessary and fortunately they realized the fact. Amara watched them all, expecting some answers but they merely nodded and didn't say a word. The one that spoke, however, was Azrael who had been sitting at the far right corner of the hall, examining the walls as though he wasn't paying attention at all.

"Have *you* been practicing your powers, m'Lady?" He said, with one eyebrow raised as he looked at Amara, eyes narrowed in suspicion.

In all the time that he had been there, Amara had tried her hardest to tolerate him but to no avail. He had been as obnoxious and interfering as he had been when he first arrived. She didn't like his presence around her at all. The dislike that she felt for him was obvious and everyone around could feel the hatred burning in each of them. They clearly didn't appreciate the other. It was in the air when they were anywhere close to thirty metres around one another.

"I believe I am not answerable to you, but since you have asked. Yes, I have been practicing enough," she told him, crossing her arms across her chest.

"Why don't we see it then?" He shot back, taking a step forward.

With a curt nod in his direction, Amara proceeded to walk outside the castle and everyone else followed. Azrael sauntered forward and stood in front of her, the others circling around as though watching a duel. They were all certain that there was going to be some big argument. That, or Amara was going to end up hexing him to Death. She had raised her arms in the air to prove herself right when he stopped her, raising a hand.

"Not the elemental powers. I'm talking about your meditation powers. There are other warriors in the opposite coven who have the capability of invading minds. How good your control is over your mind, that is what we want to see," he said to her.

Amara quietly stared at him before nodding once and giving a slight shrug. She was ready for whatever he wanted to battle her with.

"Now, I will try to control your mind without entering it," he shot a glance at Iris who stood next to Lea. "And you will shield yourself, because I might end up manipulating you into damaging your soul," he completed smugly. He looked directly at Amara who let out a sigh, preparing herself for what was coming.

"Go ahead," she whispered and sat herself down, cross-legged, her eyes closed.

Azrael focussed his attention on her. There was complete silence around, apart from the rustling of the leaves on the trees. Everyone standing there held their breaths in anticipation of what was going to happen. Amara concentrated on his voice, cancelling everything else out, even the sound of her own breathing. Azrael stepped forward, right in front of her and kneeled below so he was eye-level with her. With his eyes focussed on hers, he strained his mind to keep his attention solely on her. His mind began the work, and without even blinking once, he put his powers into force.

First, he concentrated on her hand, trying to raise it in the air as the beginning step. His eyes were a blazing dark blue, as they stared right at her and Amara's hand twitched from where it was resting on her knee. The fingers moved, rising and dropping back as she resisted whatever he was trying to do. He pushed the powers stronger, and her fingers raised themselves yet again, only to drop back into position. They didn't move after. Instead in the flash of a second, he shifted his attention to her head, and in a moment, she was half-way in the air.

He had merely diverted her focus to the hand that he was concentrating on, and she hadn't realized when he managed to make her move right up from the ground. Amara now understood his strategy. Normally no one else would have, because his tactics had the ability to make one go highly baffled since he kept his attention wavering from one thing to another, rendering the victim helpless and under his control. But Amara was smart enough to get it in one go, she knew he would change his point of focus at what time, and she was prepared. She didn't try to put herself back onto the ground from where she was suspended in mid-air. Instead, she waited for his next move. She knew he would be expecting her to counter his strategy, but she did nothing of that sort.

That ended up perplexing him. But being well aware of her powers, he began to raise her body higher in the air when Amara struck back with equal force, and her legs dropped to the ground. Now she stood right up waiting for his next attack. Azrael inwardly smirked to himself, impressed. He once again focussed his attention on her in an attempt to twist her body backwards. He was sure she would resist it, and then he would snap his focus onto her hand that would grip her own neck to strangle her. With his concentration focussed on her back, he held it right there and she slowly began to bend backwards. He frowned and before he could strike another attack, Amara shot up with such a force that Azrael dropped to the ground, his head hitting the bark of a tree.

Then, she opened her eyes, the carbon black that they were. They shone so clearly that everyone around could sense the strength in her. Lea watched with admiration. She wasn't bothered about the fact that Amara had just defeated her powerful brother, who was known for his manipulative ways.

Though he gave her a tough fight, she had managed to knock him off and use his own powers against him. Iris stood there, struggling to stifle the chuckle that was about to come out. She knew there was no way he would be able to manipulate someone like Amara. It was unfeasible.

Azrael stood up, dusting his cloak off the dirt. He was more impressed than angry about the fact that she managed to defeat him using his own powers. His interpretations about her were being proven wrong. She could exceed his expectations and leave him with no answer to how she did it. There was always something unpredictable that she did, and it would have him thinking of how powerful she really was. Hard as he tried to prove them wrong – those who sung her praises – he was met with all the reasons that meant what they said was right. She was exceptional. In all his time, no one had managed to strike back so easily. There was nothing that she could not do.

Amara walked towards him with a determined expression. With her hands linked behind her back just like he did, she leaned closer and whispered, "There might be witches and great sorcerers who are capable of manipulating us, but that does not mean we are incapable of controlling ourselves."

That being said, she strolled back into the castle, leaving everyone standing there in utter shock and admiration. As galvanized as they were with Azrael's powers, they were more under the spell of the charismatic witch that managed to increase the respect that they all had for her. *Brilliant,* Iris thought and smiled to herself.

"Let's go inside," she said to Lea and turned around to leave.

"You go on. I'll be in a few," she replied and Iris shrugged before walking back into the castle.

Lea walked over to Azrael as she held a mocking grin. He responded with a scowl. She went and stood in front of him, clearing her throat in amusement when Azrael looked at her disinterestedly.

"What do you want?" He said, starting to walk into the castle.

"Why do you keep clawing her brains out every time when you know she's got the most brilliant responses?" She said to him, grinning.

"They're not *that* brilliant. I just like competing with someone who can stand before me confidently," he replied, looking down.

"Of course, wait. Does this mean you have started to fancy her?" Lea questioned with a smirk.

Azrael stopped in his tracks. She had to be cracked for saying something like that. He turned to look at her with his eyes narrowed.

"Might I ask, dear sister, what in the devil's name is wrong with your tiny brain?" He said, tapping her forehead lightly.

"Oh drop the act," she told him, in all seriousness.

"You're delusional," he responded before vanishing out of her sight.

She let out a sigh, muttering something like '*what an idiot*' and began walking back into the castle. Erasmus watched her going back inside and lingered at the window of his chamber for a while before closing it and shutting the curtains back. Closing his eyes, he connected his mind to Nicholas's and transferred a silent message to him. Nicholas, who was in the land of *Arum Commune*, busy summoning the spirit of the great witch Lilith under the orders of Lord Lucifer, got the message from Erasmus and conveyed the same to his eagle Pelagi. The eagle flew away and got to work.

* * *

Amara sat in the library reading about torturous spells, when someone slid into the seat in front of her across the table. She lifted her head to find Azrael. She shut the book and raised her eyebrows, silently questioning what he wanted. She didn't like being disturbed when she was busy reading. But Amara was well aware that nothing would stop him from intruding her personal space.

"I need to speak to you about the prophecy," he said to her in a low tone.

She was taken aback and stared at him uncertainly for a long moment. *How does he know about the prophecy?* She wondered.

"What prophecy?" She said, breaking eye-contact.

"You know what prophecy I'm talking about."

That confused Amara even more. The Lord and herself were the only ones aware about the prophecy and other than the two of them, it was only Lord Mikhail who knew that there existed some prophecy. But he didn't know what it held. Amara looked at Azrael with clear confusion.

"You're not the only one aware of what lays in the Sea of Cypress," he said.

"You know about the whole prophecy?" She looked at him dubiously.

"No, just a small part, but I reckon we need to think over it," he replied, leaning back.

How many things had the Lord lied to her about? Why did she not know that there was someone else that knew about the prophecy? The amount of things that she had been kept in the dark about, were increasing every day, and her trust began to waver. She was starting to think that the Lord had lied to her about everything, yet her loyalty and former trust stopped her from believing that. What if Azrael was lying? What if he had found out about the prophecy by manipulating the Lord?

She didn't know what to believe. Her tangled web kept getting even more complicated as she found out such things. At this rate, how was she supposed to believe anything that anyone told her?

"Tell me what you know," she said to him, not wanting to believe him just yet.

"I don't suppose this is the place to talk about that. Can we go somewhere else?" He stood up, pushing his chair back.

Amara sat there, biting her lip for a moment before standing up herself.

"The tower," she said and promptly began to tread out of the library.

Azrael followed wordlessly. When they reached the tower, Amara stood in place, watching the sculpture of a fairy standing there in a corner, the wings wrapping her body and her head bent low, as though she was mourning over something. The last time she had seen the sculpture – that Iris told her Leandra had created – it had been standing with its wings spread and ready to fly. *Am I just imagining things?* Shaking the image out of her head, she proceeded to stand next to the railing. There were more important things to discuss rather than thinking about the sculpture of a fairy.

"I know just a part of the prophecy, one which you are not aware of," said Azrael. "I don't know about the part that you do. The knowledge of the prophecy was split so as to keep it protected, since without the whole, the answer cannot be found. The Lord knows both the parts that we do. He gave us one each. Now, to decipher the complete prophecy, one needs to unite the two parts that reside with us. Only then will the seeker be capable of summoning Lady Calypsa to know the rest of the prophecy, which later will help one get closer to the treasures that are hidden in the great Sea," he concluded.

"But none of us seek the treasure. At least I don't. Then why would we want to unite the two parts?" Amara said, looking at him.

"Neither do I. The point is, Amara, that if we unite the two parts that we know of, we get closer to protecting the whole prophecy. Lady Calypsa is under threat. No doubt that she is capable of protecting the treasures, but she sometimes loses control over herself, and might get defeated, which is why we need to be strong enough to be aware of the prophecy and guard it ourselves. The Lord informed me that the Lady is in danger, and that is why he asked me to speak with you, so we can gain her trust with the two parts that we know of, which will in turn provide us with the entire prophecy so we can protect it."

"But Lady Calypsa has to be aware of who you are, and she should trust you. Otherwise even though you know both the parts, you won't get any closer if she has no faith."

"Yes. When the Lord was sure that I was trained enough and he trusted me, he made me get an audience with Lady Calypsa. I took the oath, sacrificed my blood and only then was I informed about the part of the prophecy after swearing to protect it."

Amara nodded her head in understanding. *Maybe the Lord didn't lie to me*, she thought, *but Azrael knew that I have the other part, and I was kept in the dark about him entirely.* She was unaware of who he was until he showed up three months ago. But if this meant protecting the prophecy, she would ignore the fact that her trust was starting to fade, and do her duty for which she had sworn with her blood.

"So you mean that we should divulge the parts that we know of to each other, and then go to Lady Calypsa to find out the rest?" She said to him, raising her eyebrows.

"I mean exactly that." He nodded.

"I think that transferring the message through our minds would be better rather than speaking it out loud," she told him.

"Of course," he replied.

"We'll send the message at the same time." She turned to face him completely, her attention focussed on him.

With a nod, Azrael closed his eyes and so did Amara, opening their minds to each other while shielding them from others entering. Moments later, the message settled itself into her mind and the same happened with him. Amara read the thought that had just been planted into her head.

One can die at one's own will

She held her breath, joining the two parts together. *To possess it, a loved one must be killed. One can die at one's own will.* In that context, it meant that if a loved one was killed and the seeker was in possession of the treasure, he or she will have the power of choosing when to die. But there was something missing. The part that was known to Lady Calypsa held the link to the parts that were now known to Azrael and Amara. Similar thoughts were running in his mind as soon as he received the message. There had to be a link, and the link was surely with Lady Calypsa. If they found out about it, they would be closer to knowing what the treasure really was.

Both of them opened their eyes at the same time and looked at each other.

"When do we go to the Sea of Cypress?" Amara asked, forgetting all about her dislike towards him. All she was concerned about was the prophecy and the treasure.

"Tomorrow, we'll leave early morning," he replied.

"But who will be in charge of the castle then? We don't know how long it will take."

There was a pause.

"I think it's time to ask Nicholas to return," Azrael said.

CHAPTER NINETEEN

∞∞∞∞∞

JOURNEY TO THE END

∞∞∞∞∞

T he journey was a long one. Teleporting wasn't an option since they had to save that energy for times when threats would show up. So they walked, with the wind throwing her hair into her face and his staff dropping to the ground as he lost grip over it several times. To anyone who saw them, it would look like they had been possessed by some demon. Hands hanging at their sides, shoulders slumped and hair resembling a bird's nest, along with eyes that were tired and worn out. They had not slept in three nights, and although they were used to insomnia, a long journey like this one wasn't helping their situation at all. Amara and Azrael were clearly exhausted.

It had been three days since they had left the castle to go to the Sea of Cypress. They had to travel through the huge woods and mountains to reach their destination but it wasn't easy at all. Their preparations were not that good either. They had forgotten to pack some food for the journey, which as Amara said, was the silliest thing to do for two grown adults. Even though they could create the food and use the fruits and vegetables available in the woods, it wasn't that easy to find proper things to eat when their minds were under stress. The day before they had left, Amara had talked to Erasmus about asking Nicholas to return and take care of the castle while she was gone.

Erasmus had tried his best to contact Nicholas, but his mind was involved into something very deep which rendered the connection broken. The harder he tried to connect their minds, the stronger Nicholas's mind would become, owing to the task that he was busy with. Then Erasmus had decided to tell Amara that he would be in charge until Nicholas was contacted. Hesitantly, Amara had agreed seeing the gravity of the situation. She had to go to the Sea of Cypress as soon as possible. Before the war struck, she had to make sure that the treasure that Lord Mikhail desired was thoroughly protected.

The next morning, Azrael and Amara had left without informing anyone apart from Erasmus.

"I don't want to have to answer the questions that everyone is going to ask. We don't have the time. So I'm trusting you with this and leaving you in charge. Please take care of everything until we return," she had said to him moments before they left the castle.

"I'll take care of everything. Be careful and return soon," he had replied, bidding the two of them goodbye.

After that, Azrael and Amara had begun their journey, carrying a few weapons, a map, *Healing Potion*, and the words of the prophecy neatly written on a parchment, hidden in a large book so it would be safe. They made it hard enough for anyone else to locate, if attacked by Lord Mikhail or his servants. It was kept quite safely so only the two of them knew on which page it was written. They had been walking through the woods day and night, unable to stop and get some sleep since the worry about keeping themselves and the prophecy safe rested itself as a burden on their heads. The journey – although not as long – seemed tedious enough seeing how much they had to take care of and not end up getting attacked by any chance.

"We need to stop," said Azrael, breathing heavily, three nights after they had left.

His legs were beginning to feel as though they were about to crack up and burst into pieces. Amara's situation wasn't any different. But her extreme will to keep going ahead and not resting at all – apart from a few minutes that they stopped to have some fruits on the way – made it all the more difficult for Azrael. He was starting to get annoyed.

"We don't have much time," she replied gruffly, turning to look back at him.

He was now seated on the ground with his back resting on the foot of a hill.

"If we keep walking right now, we won't have enough energy to move forward. Please, relax for a while. They won't appear suddenly and stab us," he pleaded. He was tired and sleepy after a long time.

Amara looked at him uncertainly for a while, before letting out a sigh and settling herself beside him. She had to agree that they needed to rest. It wasn't going to help if they would keep walking continuously. It would only drain out their energy and make it even harder for them to reach the Sea, which was a lot more miles to go.

"Do you need something to eat?" She asked him, resting her head on the grass and closing her eyes.

"I need water," he replied.

"I think there is a river ahead. I can hear the sound," she said, straining her ears a bit and sure enough, the sound of the waves was easily heard. The water body didn't seem far away.

"You wait here. I'll go fetch some water. Do you have a flask?" He stood up, dusting off his cloak.

Amara nodded and dug into her bag of supplies before pulling out a medium-sized flask and handing it to him. Azrael began moving ahead, following the sound of water while Amara let herself drift off into a deep sleep. The moon was beginning to get covered with grey clouds, the atmosphere becoming darker. Azrael walked faster so as to get back sooner. He was worried about Amara getting attacked while he was away. The amount of exhaustion that was plastered across her face made him think that she would not be able to handle a danger alone.

When he reached the huge river, he quickly gathered some water into the flask, filling it whole before standing up to leave again. Something made him sit back down and splash some water on his face. While he was doing that, he heard the sound of footsteps scraping across the leaves. He lifted his head up, wiping the water off of his face. He scanned the surrounding; the darkness had made it difficult for him to adjust his vision. Securing the flask around his waist using the band that was wrapped around it, he stood up and looked around once again. It was too dark. Clicking his fingers, he lighted a little flame that lingered above his palm. With a swish of his hand, he transferred the glow to a few corners. The flames stayed suspended in the air, making it easier for him to look for any intruders.

He turned around but found nothing suspicious. With another click of his fingers, the Fire extinguished, and he began walking back in the direction where Amara was. Once again, he heard the sound of footsteps approaching. Frowning, he lit the Fire again as he proceeded ahead. The light followed him where he went as he looked around for the source of the sound. Amara lay there on the ground with her eyes closed and breathing shallow. Azrael was about to reach where he had left her. As he neared the place, his eyes halted at a figure standing behind a tree. He stopped in his way.

He strained his eyes to make sure he wasn't mistaken. Before he could do anything, the figure dashed away from him and in an instant, was next to Amara. Azrael widened his eyes and proceeded forward, careful not to make a sound. He stood at a distance, watching what the person was trying to do. The cloaked figure that looked like that of a woman, bent low, close to the sleeping figure of Amara. He took a step forward to attack the woman when Amara's eyes shot open and she pushed herself away. The woman fell to the ground, her hands resting beside her. Azrael immediately rushed forward and stood next to Amara.

She opened her mouth to ask something when the woman stood up and glanced sideways for a moment. Amara and Azrael followed her gaze and a few other cloaked figures appeared with their faces covered in hoods. Soon enough they were surrounded by at least seven of them. Azrael and Amara didn't bother to ask who they were and began to defend themselves as the attacks began. The figures slashed their swords and Amara glanced at the bag of weapons resting a few feet away from her. There was no way they could grab it, they were completely surrounded.

Azrael stood there staring at two of the attackers approaching him. His gaze travelled slowly from one to the other, and the two men fell to the ground, their feet trembling as they did so. Moments later, their eyes were rolling upwards, their bodies twisting in a terrible way, hands going rigid and fingers curling up. They were paralyzed. Azrael's attention moved to another attacker who had raised his sword to attack Azrael, when Amara struck forward with equal force, an arm slamming right onto his neck. The attacker fell to the floor, petrified. Amara's arm was strong as iron as it stung across his neck, twisting it sideways, and the man went still, falling to the ground.

Azrael gave Amara a gesture to which she nodded and began to approach the woman that had first tried to attack her, while Azrael fixed his attention onto the other three attackers that were standing there, a bit terrified of what had just happened. The woman didn't notice Amara marching towards her as she dug into the bag that Amara had gotten with her. Before she could pull out anything of use, Amara had grabbed her throat in a Death grip, making it difficult for the woman to breathe. She pulled the woman up to standing, fingers clenched around her neck. Using her other hand, Amara removed the hood off of the woman's face.

She didn't recognize the woman.

"Who are you?" Amara asked, pushing the woman's body so it was pressed against the bark of a tree.

Another attacker was starting to walk towards Amara and she turned her head in his direction, lifting her leg and kicking it into his shin. The man fell down. Azrael, who was now done paralyzing the rest of the attackers, grabbed a sword from the bag and slashed it across all the attackers' necks. He stabbed his sword into the abdomen the last one that was on the ground, Amara held the woman in a tight grip, and Azrael pulled a rope out of the bag before fastening it around the woman who made no attempt or struggle to get away. Instead, she held an amused appearance, which confused the two.

"Who sent you?" He said, holding the sword in the woman's direction, its tip resting below her chin.

The woman was looking at the two of them silently, her eyes a shining green. She wore a long cloak, her hair tied up in a bun as she sat there, just looking at the two of them. Azrael stared intently at her with a piercing gaze. The woman only smirked once before transforming into smoke, setting herself free. Once out of the ropes, she took the form of a woman once again but was no longer covered in the dark cloak. Instead, she wore a long white gown, her hair a moonlit white and a smile covering her lips. The woman was beautiful and nothing like the one they had seen mere moments ago. Her emerald green eyes seemed calm now as she glanced at the dead attackers that were on the ground. They instantly vanished, leaving no trace. Azrael and Amara stared at the woman uncomprehendingly.

"Your strength surprises me, sorcerer. I am impressed," she said to Azrael.

Her voice was sultry, soft and overly calm. It could make a person content for no apparent reason. Both of them stayed quiet, unable to utter a word. The woman released a chuckle.

"I am Selene, a friend of the moon goddess Luna. I am the guardian of these woods. Do the two of you know where you are?" She said, glancing at both of them.

It seemed to her that they didn't know their location.

"We don't," Amara managed to utter.

"These woods are known as *Rosean*, surrounded by the mountains of *Romarin*. You must be wondering why you were attacked. I think you are aware of the fact that this path leads to the Sea of Cypress. Not everyone is deserving and capable enough to reach there. As one of the guardians of the Great Lady, I have the duty to test everyone who uses this path. I am aware that you are part of Lord Lucifer's coven, who is the owner of the treasures that Lady Calypsa guards, but I had to attack you out of force of habit. However, the both of you have proved your strength and I am glad to meet you two. You may proceed ahead. The Sea is not very far away," she said, a sweet smile grazing her lips.

Azrael and Amara blinked, registering whatever they had heard.

"It is an honour to have met you, Goddess Selene," said Amara. "We are thankful that you were of assistance to us. We were well aware of the route, since we do have a map of the same. Although, we did forget where we were for a while, due to the exhaustion following the journey, but we would like your permission to rest here for the night. We have been travelling for three days and haven't rested enough. We need some time to gather up the energy."

"Of course, you may rest here for as long as you like. As the guardian of this area, I will make sure you are not under any kind of threat. Do stay here for the night. It is my duty to protect travellers as well," she replied and twirled around once before vanishing off into the dark.

Azrael looked at Amara and she shrugged, gazing back at him before they sat back onto the ground.

"You did get the water," she said, breaking the deafening silence.

He glanced at the flask that was still tied around his waist and pulled it out, handing it to her.

"You're the thirsty one," she said to him and he smiled a tiny one, nearly unseen as he unscrewed the cap and drank the water.

"That doesn't mean you don't save any for me," she told him when he kept drinking.

Pulling the flask away from him, he looked at Amara silently before handing it to her. The rest of the night was spent peacefully with both of them sound asleep after the longest time. None of them had slept so calmly in the last hundred years. A subtle, yet clear realization dawned upon both of them at the same time. In all these years, the peace that they felt together was never felt before. Even though they were not on good terms with each other most of the time, somehow they felt safe when they were together. There was an invisible trust that lingered around them, with none of them realizing it.

* * *

Iris sat in the castle with Leandra, listening to the knowledge that she was providing about dark witchcraft. Iris listened to her quietly, her heart hammering inside her chest at the thought of Amara gone. She had no idea where Amara was. Erasmus had told her that she had gone somewhere with Azrael for an important task. Iris didn't trust Azrael. He seemed as dangerous as Amara yet she honestly didn't think that Amara was going to be safe with him. The man could be torturous enough, even though she was well aware of what Amara was capable of. There was no way the two could stand against each other, because none of them could defeat the other, and in the end they would end up destroying the surrounding.

She didn't want anything to happen to Amara. *If only I could see where they are and what is going on with them,* she thought. Lea blabbered on about a dark witch when she noticed Iris was paying no attention. She stopped talking and stared at Iris, who was busy looking at the foot of the rickety chair she was seated on. They were sitting in the kitchen, sipping warm lemon tea and with a few other witches bustling around. Lea cleared her throat in an attempt to grab her attention. Iris heard nothing. Lea tapped her fingers on the table between them. Again, she got no response. Iris's gaze was stuck where it was. Sighing, Lea called out her name twice before leaning across and nudging her shoulder. Iris snapped her eyes towards Lea.

"What are you thinking?" She asked.

"Nothing," Iris replied, shifting back into the chair to sit properly.

Lea didn't say anything, merely gave a flat look to her and Iris glanced away, letting out a sigh.

"I'm worried for Amara," she muttered, so softly that Leandra had to strain her ears to listen clearly.

"Why would you be worried for that lady? She's the most brilliant one I've ever seen." Lea gave a look of bewilderment, wondering why Iris would get anxious regarding someone as capable as Amara.

"I know but, she attracts trouble at times," Iris said, biting her lower lip.

"What's trouble for us is normal for her. Besides, she's with Rael and he's quite strong too. Two of them together can face a hundred other witches by themselves," she replied, shutting the book that she was holding.

"Do you...do you think Azrael would want to harm her?" It slipped out of her mouth unwillingly.

Iris didn't want to ask that question to Lea. What if she got offended? He was her brother. Of course she would not like it. Iris cursed herself for being so silly. Lea watched Iris blankly for a moment before she burst out laughing.

"Why would Rael want to harm her?" she said, stifling her laughter. "I know they don't really get along so well but that doesn't mean he would kill her. They are working together and the Lord trusts both of them with their lives. I'm sure even if they argue about something they will not kill each other."

"But-" Iris began but thought otherwise and decided to keep her mouth shut.

"Calm down, nothing is going to happen to her. She's capable of handling everything. Of all people you should know that. You are closer to her than anyone else, right?"

Iris nodded, shutting her eyes for a long moment and hoping that Amara would be safe. The vision of Amara sleeping, and someone standing beside her as though ready to attack, didn't leave her mind after the night that she had had that dream. She decided to let it go since Leandra was probably right. Amara was capable of taking care of herself. Yet, she was finding it hard to trust Azrael.

* * *

Erasmus sat inside the meditation chamber, concentrating hard on connecting his mind to Nicholas's. He was finding it harder even after three long days of trying. There was absolutely no way that he could reach Nicholas. At times, he had gotten close, almost very close that he was sure Nicholas got the connection but suddenly it would break and he would have to start right at the beginning. He was starting to get irritated and impatient. Erasmus needed him, there was no way he was capable enough of handling the castle all alone. So once again, he concentrated harder than before and his mind shot straight up to Nicholas's.

Nicholas held his breath for a moment, when his meditation was interrupted yet again. Letting out a sigh, he opened his mind to receive the message that was coming from Erasmus. As soon as the message registered itself in his brain, he stopped the meditation process and opened his eyes. He looked at the unconscious human sitting in front of him. The girl was tied to a chair, her body now numb as the spirit was just about to descend into her body. Nicholas had to stop the process. If he had been called back into the castle, he could not summon the spirit of Lilith at the moment. It was his responsibility to go back, however important the work he was doing. Without realizing the point where he had just stopped the process, he stood up and began to seal the cave, so as to keep the girl safe inside. When he was sure the place was covered in protection, he took one last look at the girl before walking out of the cave and sealing it one more time.

When the doors were shut, the lights in the cave began to dim and the wind suddenly took a halt. The earth below the girl's feet trembled and her body went rigid. Her breath stopped, her eyes sealed shut tighter than ever before, and her jaw clenched. The veins inside her throat began to appear clearer and her fingers held the arms of the chair so tight that they were close to start bleeding. A distant, bright, yet faded light shone upon her forehead, as though entering right inside her and seconds later, it vanished into her. There was a moment's pause, and the torches went out, plunging the cave into darkness. A tremor suddenly shook the girl's body, and her eyes shot open.

CHAPTER TWENTY

∞∞∞∞∞

MOMENT OF TRUTH

∞∞∞∞∞

Crimson red eyes glittered in the darkness, the only light in the otherwise blackened cave. The girl was now standing, possessed by the spirit of Lilith. She began walking towards the door of the cave. Nicholas was long gone. He had teleported and reached the castle in no time. Unaware of what the result of his mistake was, he had left without giving it a second thought. The process of summoning the spirit that he thought he left half-way had almost been completed, and Lilith's spirit was a moment away from entering the girl's body. As soon as he had left, the spirit descended, now angered by the fact that the one that had summoned her wasn't there. It was a well-known truth that an angry spirit – upon entering a body – becomes vile and malignant, even if it does not have those characteristics. The vile spirit of Lilith had now possessed the girl's body.

* * *

When Nicholas reached the castle, he was met with the news of Amara being gone along with Azrael for an important task and that he was now in charge. He had begun gathering everyone and making them practice their powers to strengthen them. Erasmus had sent a message to Amara saying that there was nothing for her to worry about since Nicholas and himself were now taking proper care of the coven. She was free to concentrate on her journey.

Azrael and Amara stood at the shore of the Sea of Cypress. Their journey was now complete; though that didn't necessarily mean that Lady Calypsa would appear.

There were chances of her not choosing to appear even though they had already had an audience with her before. The two of them had left the woods of *Rosean* the morning after they had met Goddess Selene. She had bid them goodbye with a few victuals for their journey. It took them six more hours to reach the Sea and when they did, the sun was about to set. The sun-rays shone on the darkness of the water, as the star dipped lower and lower into the horizon until it vanished out of sight. Since Lady Calypsa only appeared after midnight, they had to wait for a while before it was dark enough. Both of them were standing near the huge rocks, watching the water turn darker as the sun-rays began to disappear. For the next few hours, they sat there waiting for the night to get darker. When it was time, a gush of wind blew past them forcefully.

Amara looked at Azrael who turned to look at her as well, and they both nodded once at each other before walking further ahead so they were close to the waves. With their right legs extended, they rested their toes lightly on top of the water. It went calm instantly. It was known that whoever that had been in the presence of Lady Calypsa at least once, only had to touch their feet onto the water to tone down the waves that were ferocious most of the time. If that was successfully done, it meant that she would not take long to appear. Otherwise, they had to spend years of worshipping and magic to summon her. Due to the fact that Azrael and Amara were both trusted apprentices of Lord Lucifer, and the guardians of parts of the prophecy, there was an easier chance of them getting to see her. To some extent, Amara was certain that they would not have much trouble in getting her to meet the two of them.

She was right. As soon as they stepped on the water, smoke rose out at a distance. It whirled above, taking the shape of a hooded figure. Lady Calypsa had appeared. As she began proceeding towards her visitors, sliding across the water, her robes rippled creating mild waves in the sea. Amara and Azrael waited for her to reach them. They now retreated both their feet from the water they were touching, and took a step back. Lady Calypsa stopped a few feet away from them, examining the two. She then slid forward a little so as to be able to hear them. Amara let out a breath she was holding. Even though she had met the Great Lady once before, it made her nervous as of now thinking about what would happen next. She didn't know whether the Lady would agree to their demands, or even so listen to them. But she wanted to take her chances.

Lady Calypsa was now a few meters away from them, gliding over the water in silence. Amara and Azrael wanted to say something but they felt tongue tied. The presence of the Lady was intimidating, and they had never been so speechless before. It was always them who made others nervous. Amara now realized what the others must feel in her presence as well as Azrael's. So they stood there without saying a word. The Lady began to get impatient and quietly decided to turn around and leave, when Azrael finally uttered something.

"Great Lady, we come to seek help," he said, bowing his head.

The Lady stopped and lingered there in silence. She uttered no words, waiting for them to continue. Since everyone did come to her to seek help, it wasn't a surprise. She chose to stay quiet.

"We are the beholders of the prophecy that you guard. A part of the prophecy was given to Lord Lucifer, the message of which, divided in two other parts that were revealed to us. We come here to seek your assistance in letting us know about the rest of the prophecy that you protect," he told her, taking one step forward while Amara stood in place.

"How do you prove that you don't have the power of impersonation? How do I believe you are the true apprentices of Lord Lucifer?" Lady Calypsa replied, gliding forwards and circling around Azrael.

Her voice was deep and grave as always. She spoke ever so slowly. It was chilling.

"We would be honoured to have answered your queries about us being the true ones, Great Lady," said Amara, lifting her head.

The Lady turned to her, leaning forwards and going still for a moment before getting back to her initial position above the water. She never put a step on land.

"Reveal the parts that you know of," she said, pulling away.

"*One can die at one's own will*," Amara said, quoting the part that Azrael had been assigned with.

He glanced at her for a moment before turning back to the Lady.

"*To possess it, a loved one must be killed*," he said.

The Lady looked at them for a moment before swirling up in the air like the black smoke and coming back to their level. She moved towards Amara, beckoning her to come forward. Amara obeyed, taking a few steps ahead, her feet immersed into the water. Azrael stood there watching, hoping nothing bad would happen. Lady Calypsa was known for the changes in her behaviour.

"Do you know why a loved one must be killed?" the Lady asked, leaning close to Amara.

Amara shook her head.

"And do you, great sorcerer?" She turned to Azrael, who shook his head as well.

"To gain eternal glory, a sacrifice must be made," Lady Calypsa began. "To kill an enemy is facile, effortless. But to slay a loved one, with a love that has the power to take pain away is what takes strength. True power lies in love, it lies in Death. And Death is an unknown reality, an unheard truth, a morbid lie. If one succeeds in killing a loved soul to achieve the treasure, the love never existed at all. Love does not kill, it heals. Yet, the desire to gain a treasure that belongs not to you, to achieve it, you slay a loved one. Would you end a loved one's life?" She flew towards Amara, who stood there confused.

Amara looked at Lady Calypsa with her eyes narrowed in thought. There was something the Lady was trying to convey, something hidden underneath the words that were in the prophecy and the words that she had just said. A message was between the lines, and Amara tried to read it, straining her mind a little more than usual.

And then she spoke, "Yes, I would."

Azrael turned to look at her, frowning. *Would she?* He wondered.

"If the loved one wasn't mine, if he or she meant nothing to me. I would slay the one that is loved by someone else," she completed.

The message said that killing a loved one was necessary to gain the treasure, but it never specified that the loved one was supposed to be the seeker's own. It could be anyone. It could be a person that was truly loved by someone else and held no importance in the life of the seeker. The riddle here was to decipher the message hidden in the prophecy. If the true meaning wasn't understood, the seeker would never attain the treasure. It was highly confusing, and only someone as experienced and intelligent as Amara could have understood it. Lady Calypsa was amazed by the wit that Amara possessed. She was now assured that one part of the prophecy lay in good hands and that she was the true apprentice of Lord Lucifer.

Azrael watched the great witch that stood beside him. All his dislike towards her due to the doubts of her not being as brilliant as everyone said, were gone. Respect emerged inside of him and he now had to accept the fact that she was truly the greatest witch of their time. He could never have met a better witch in his existence, and maybe he never would. His eyes were stuck on Amara until Lady Calypsa strode in his direction and stood before him. He shifted his focus to her.

"Great sorcerer, your name makes you the Angel of Death. Do you know how the one that achieves the treasure, will have a choice in his own Death?" asked the Lady, gliding forwards and backwards once before getting back in position.

"I do not, Great Lady," he replied, looking down.

He felt ashamed of himself for not knowing the answer. *How foolish*, he thought to himself.

"But Death is the ultimate purpose of life. A mortal may gain great power, he may become the ruler of the world and he may be the one that guides the world, but what makes him the King of his own Death? What makes him seek the power to have a choice in the time of his Death? Will it give him eternal glory? Not likely, m'Lord. Will it make him the crowned head of the world? No, my dear sir, it would not. Then what would he gain? Why would he need the power to choose when the Angel takes him away?"

It was beginning to get darker. The moonlight shone upon the Sea and water glittered over the surface as darkness spread around. Azrael watched as the waves slowly moved across the otherwise silent Sea. There was no sound, not even of the wind gushing past them. It was silent, so calm yet terrifying to be in. His mind wandered around the questions that the Lady had asked. His eyes looked beneath his feet as the sand slowly but steadily began to slide down his toes and vanish into the upcoming waves.

"Power over the world does not give a man power over his life," Azrael responded with his eyes still on the sand. "The cycle of life and Death will continue and when he is aware of the fact that he will die inevitably, the power and authority will one day end, leaving him with nothing when he dies. It does not give the choice of Death to the one who gains power, but it does give eternal glory to the one who is the king of his own Death. He can live the way he wishes to. He can rule the world, he can watch generations pass as the mortals leave, and he can always be the one that holds monarchy over everything else. But if only he ends the life of a loved one, will he gain the treasure, and only when he gains the treasure, will he become the ruler of Death itself," he finished, looking up at the Lady who was listening to every word carefully.

And now, the doubts that she had about them being the true apprentices were gone. She understood how truthful and deserving they were to protect the prophecy that was given to them. There wasn't a doubt about them not being able to guard the rest of the prophecy. Being aware of the fact that she was under a threat, she had decided to reveal the complete prophecy to those who deserved to be the true guardians.

"To know what the prophecy beholds, you will have to follow me into the Sea. What you already know are interpreted parts that have been extracted from the prophecy. You will now see what the foretelling truly holds," she said, turning towards Azrael. "Lord Azrael, you are well aware of the nature of the water since you have been visiting often. You shouldn't have any trouble sailing through." She looked at Amara. "The Sea is honoured to have you here, Lady Amara. Follow me, if you will. The prophecy will be revealed along with it the secret of the treasure that I guard. But you must be prepared to keep it safe, you must sacrifice your blood once again in order to protect it," the Lady said to the both of them.

"Of course, Great Lady, we certainly will sacrifice our blood to protect the treasure and the prophecy," Amara replied, giving a nod.

Lady Calypsa said nothing and conjured a dagger out of the water. She handed it to Amara. She wasted no time in slashing it across her index finger and letting the droplets of blood descend into the water below her feet. Azrael took the dagger from her and did the same.

Then, they both spoke, "By the power vested in us by Lord Zelos and his sole heir, Lord Lucifer, we – the true apprentices of the great sorcerer – swear to protect the prophecy and the treasures for as long as we breathe this air and walk this earth, as long as we consume the water and ignite the flames. We swear to never let any dark force harm the trove. We swear to be loyal guardians."

"By the power vested in me by mother earth, lord of Air and Spirit, governor of Fire and Ale, I – the appointed guardian of the great prophecy – hereby allow the true apprentices of Lord Lucifer to enter the Sea of Cypress and I hereby pronounce them guardians alongside myself," said Lady Calypsa.

There was a wave from the sea that washed upon Amara and Azrael fiercely, as though accepting them and allowing them to achieve what they wished for. Lady Calypsa gestured for them to follow her and turned around before vanishing into the water. Azrael and Amara stole a glance at each other before proceeding behind her. Wrapping the bag of weapons and supplies tight around her waist, Amara plunged herself into the water and Azrael did the same, dropping his staff on the sand.

He knew that it would be safe until they returned. But the bag that Amara held, contained more important things which could not be left anywhere else, it had to be protected. As the water began to gush around them in wild waves, the three of them swam forward. Amara and Azrael kept trace of the Lady as they glided ahead behind her, side by side. When they started to go deeper into the waters, they noticed that the sea-bed was as dark as they had thought it would be. Although Azrael had travelled these waters before, he had never entered the deepest parts, for it was forbidden unless Lady Calypsa allowed it.

A few creatures moved past them but they carried on without losing focus on Lady Calypsa. They were now inches above the sea-bed and the plants began to tangle in their limbs as they proceeded. Amara's legs were suddenly bound by the strong leaves of a plant, and her pace stopped right there. She struggled to break free when Azrael swam backwards, keeping his eyes on the Lady as he tried to untie the tangles. Amara watched as he pulled on the plant forcefully, and a moment later her legs were free. She gave him a thankful nod and they started forward, careful not to get caught again. The Sea was just as dangerous as Lady Calypsa. One needed the approval of the Lady to let the visitors enter inside.

A while later, the Lady stopped in front of a cave. It was locked by a huge door, which had chains around the handles. Amara and Azrael looked at each other once before going ahead and waiting a few feet behind Lady Calypsa. They watched as she waved her hands in front of the door, and the chains loosened themselves, before falling onto the bed and vanishing instantly. She then proceeded to open the door, using one of her hands to do so. With a mere gesture of her hand going backwards, the door pulled open and the water around stalled. Lady Calypsa turned to glance at the two of them and gave a nod before pushing herself in through the door. The water stayed still as Amara and Azrael swam forwards. As soon as they entered, the water began to move again and the door immediately shut itself.

It was completely dry inside. They felt as though they were somewhere underground inside a castle instead of the deepest part of the sea. With a simple drying spell, Amara and Azrael stood there bone-dry. Both of them proceeded to follow the passage through which Lady Calypsa had gone. They walked ahead together. The passage was wide enough to allow two people to walk at the same time. A few minutes later, they reached an opening. They found themselves in a huge chamber at the end of the passage, where a stone table rested in the middle, with the little ball of glass resting on top of it, filled with black coloured smoke. It stood on a stand and there was nothing else but another little door in a corner which was locked, sans the chains.

Amara and Azrael stood at the entrance, with Lady Calypsa standing in the middle of the chamber next to the stone table. She waved her hands and out of thin air, appeared two throne-like chairs, which settled around the table. The Lady turned to the two visitors standing behind her. She gestured to them to get seated on the chairs. Amara and Azrael obeyed silently, walking over to the table and sitting on the chairs. Lady Calypsa stood in between them, bent low so she was level with the sphere resting on the table.

"What you see here is the prophecy record. This little globe contains the truth that you seek. It will reveal the treasure and it will answer all your questions. It will tell you why one must kill a loved one and how one will achieve the power of choosing the time of one's Death. Look into it yourselves and the answer will be revealed. Either one of you can look in, or else both of you can watch the prophecy unfold together at the same time," the Lady said, her voice even deeper than it was before.

Azrael and Amara looked at each other for a long moment, as though talking to one another through their eyes, deciding who would look. With a simple blink of both of their eyes, they shifted their gaze to the tiny sphere that held the prophecy and fixed all of their attention on what was about to be shown to them. They blocked out everything else, their focus on the black smoke moving around in front of them. Suddenly the chamber felt smaller and the globe started to become larger and larger.

Both of them watched as the colour of the smoke changed from black to green, to red and in the end it settled on white, then they heard the sound as their eyes went completely blind.

> *'Locket of the blood,*
> *Chronicle of the dead,*
> *The seeker must slay*
> *Through poison, a loved*
> *An enemy tortured, a phoenix bled*
> *All merge together*
> *To make one the slayer of Death,*
> *For you might need a Dragon,*
> *Another dead on your Manus*
> *The end of a mortal*
> *Will be the inception of your existence'*

A sudden burst of red coloured light had them thrown away from the stone table. Panting, Amara and Azrael lay on the floor, clutching the end of the chairs that they were seated on. The prophecy was a riddle that they were now trying to shape. Lady Calypsa was gone. They were surrounded by complete darkness. Amara stood up, holding the chair as she was unable to see a thing.

"Azrael?" She whispered softly.

"I'm here," he whispered back, a few feet away from her.

"There is a locket and there is a book. An *old* book," he said after a moment of silence.

Amara frowned, her mind going back to the time when she had told Iris the story of Lilith. The book of dark witchcraft was taken away by Lady Calypsa when Lilith died after taking *Phoenix Blood*. She now realized that the book was one of the treasures.

"The Chronicle, yes. The book of the darkest witchcraft there is. It belonged to the great witch Lilith. It was taken by Lady Calypsa when she died," Amara said in a low tone, wondering where the Lady had gone.

"The locket contains blood of some sort."

"*Phoenix Blood*," whispered Amara, a slight gasp escaping her lips.

"An enemy has to be tortured and a loved one has to be slain. . ." He began, getting up and walking towards Amara as she did the same.

". . .Which means that only after two mortals are killed, will the seeker be able to get closer to the locket."

She took a step forward. He took a step forward.

"*Phoenix Blood* is in the locket. But why so? *Phoenix Blood* is obtainable to almost every coven. Why would it be hidden here?" Azrael wondered.

Amara's mind went back to the part of the story that she had not revealed to Iris. The night before Lilith set herself on Fire, her blood was mixed with that of the phoenix, making her whole being pure and immortal. A little amount of her blood was taken by Lady Calypsa for it was the purest one there ever was. Nobody knew what she did with the blood.

"That is not just *Phoenix Blood*. It is mixed with the blood of Lilith," Amara answered.

She took a step forward. He took a step forward.

"And in order to kill a loved one, a dragon is needed. . ."

They now stood foot to foot.

". . .Which means that the blood from the locket must be consumed but it can only be done after taking a life through poison of the Cymmerien Dragon. And the process of torturing an enemy rests in the book of darkest witchcraft," she said.

"The three treasures: the vial of the blood of the Cymmerien dragon, *The Book of Darkest Witchcraft* and the locket of *Phoenix Blood* merged with that of Lilith's," whispered Azrael.

A moment later, the cave was lit with flames emerging from the torches around.

CHAPTER TWENTY-ONE

∞∞∞∞∞

DARK FALLS

∞∞∞∞∞

Darkness surrounded the sinister forest. Lilith's spirit was travelling through and each place she passed, the blackness increased. Wind ceased to exist; the sound of footsteps of the girl Lilith had possessed could be heard in every part. Covered by grey clouds, the moon sent no light. The girl was wearing a torn black gown, its sleeves reached up to her elbows; the skirts flowing behind her as she walked ahead. Her hair a clear brown, covered in dirt at some places and dishevelled. Her eyes were a dark red, lips dry and blood dripping from them. Her skin was pale white and wrinkled. It was a terrifying sight to behold.

The leaves below her feet made a crunching sound and nothing else was heard. An owl hooted from above a tree, somewhere in the distance, the sound echoed in the silence and then suddenly went quiet as Lilith approached. She lifted her head to find the owl resting on a high branch. It was a small one, terribly innocent looking which made Lilith smile, her teeth showing awkwardly. There was a tint of yellow in them with lines of blood in between. A moment later, the owl dropped dead beside her feet. Lifting a foot, she grazed her long toe-nails along the owl's body. She pushed the hair that was falling over her eyes back, using the wrinkled fingers that also had a hint of blood on them. Her long grey nails scratched along her cheek.

The body of a twenty-year-old mortal had been possessed by the dead spirit of Lilith, which made her look utterly different from what she used to be. Lilith continued stumbling ahead, unaware of where she was going. She was on her journey to find the one that had summoned her and left her at a time when she had almost entered the human's body. Lilith's spirit wasn't spiteful in nature. Her spirit was pure, yet the way she had died left some sort of darkness inside her that had a potential to take over. Troubled spirits had a tendency to become evil if their summoning was interrupted half-way through, or at the time when they had almost entered a body.

Unaware of the consequences, Nicholas had ended up summoning Lilith's pure spirit and stopped the process just when it was about to enter the human's body. The spirit went from its nature of benign to evil. The dark and vicious part of Lilith had taken over when the summoning was interrupted, making her spirit turn into an unpleasant and dangerous one. Instead of being of any help to Nicholas for whatever purpose he wanted to fulfil, the spirit was now out to end his life. Due to the fact that *Phoenix Blood* had rendered her mind futile, Lilith's spirit had no knowledge of the world she was in, apart from finding her conjurer and killing him.

She was passing through the mountains of Dark Falls, unmindful of her location when she spotted two blurred figures striding at a distance. Amara and Azrael were travelling slowly back to the castle, their minds flooded with various thoughts that they could not think clearly. After leaving from the Sea of Cypress, they had started to take a different route to go back. Amara had told Azrael that the course that they had used – which passed through the woods of *Rosean* – contained traces of them that could be detected by sorcerers like Lord Mikhail. In order not to take any chances of getting attacked by him or other enemies, Amara and Azrael had taken a different path.

They had left false traces in a few areas by conjuring smoke that contained imprints of their fingers to confuse any threatening beings that would want to attack them. That way, they travelled one path but had traces in others so as not to get into any kind of trouble. It was necessary for them to reach back to the castle safely. As Azrael had suggested, they had taken the route that went through the mountains of Dark Falls. The area was known for its beautiful yet terrifying waterfalls that surrounded the mountains. It was also known for being the most haunted area in Acanthus. All kinds of spirits of Conjurers resided in the caves built deep in the mountains.

Azrael and Amara heard foggy whispers of the spirits moving around them, yet not harming them in any way. They decided to take a halt and rest for a while before continuing their journey. It was three hours past midnight and eight hours after they had left the Sea of Cypress. The knowledge of the treasures that Lady Calypsa protected – and that they were to be guarded by the two of them – had left them in a trance. Both of them had similar thoughts running through their minds. Amara felt as though she was given the hardest task ever and the prophecy was to be protected at any cost. If by plain chance, any of Lord Mikhail's apprentices found out what the prophecy was; the world would be plunged into darkness.

Azrael, on the other hand, was thinking about how the two of them were going to be able to keep those treasures safe. Amara wasn't the only intelligent being that could solve the confusing riddles of the prophecy in order to reach the treasures. Lord Mikhail was under no circumstances to be underestimated. There was a lot of scope for him to find out the true meaning and gain that which was not his to own. As Azrael sat on the ground, his back resting on the bark of a huge tree, his eyes watched Amara. She settled herself opposite him at the feet of another tree. Her eyes were scanning the surrounding as she sensed a few spirits moving around her.

At a distance, she could see the figure of a woman approaching them and then suddenly taking a stop before getting out of sight. Amara frowned and looked away. It wasn't a surprise to find strange figures lurking around in the Dark Falls. She wondered whether it was safe for them to take rest in the mountains. There was a fair chance of them being attacked by evil spirits. Yet she knew that they were strong enough to battle the same. So with her eyes closed, she let her head rest on the bark of the tree while Azrael diverted his gaze. His eyes landed on the figure of a woman approaching; the same one that Amara had seen moments ago. He kept watching as the figure came closer and closer.

Without letting his eyes away from the woman, he stood up and crouched down next to the sleeping figure of Amara. He was unsure whether she really was asleep. It had only been a few moments that she had closed her eyes. The woman was now walking further in their direction. Sensing that it might be a threat, Azrael tapped on Amara's shoulder lightly. She opened her eyes to look at him.

"There's someone over there," he mouthed, gesturing in the direction of the woman who had now begun to get even closer.

They could see her gait slowly towards them. Amara stood up along with Azrael as they watched the woman approach.

"Spirits here don't take human forms," she said to him, her eyes still on the woman.

"That is what I am wondering. Do you think any witches stay here?" He asked, taking a step closer to Amara.

His sudden protective instincts in order to save her surprised him. But Amara had not noticed that. They were now standing adjacent to each other, with Azrael just one step behind her back; there was nearly no space between them.

"No. But maybe she is a traveller, like us?" She replied.

It came out more as a question. She was unsure about it herself. There were rarely any travellers that went through the Dark Falls. Everyone believed that it was a place where Conjurers were deliberately killed by evil spirits to possess their bodies. Amara and Azrael refused to have faith in the same. They were strong enough to battle spirits, if not others.

"I'm not very sure of that," he whispered back, wearing a worried look.

As they stood frozen in place, Lilith reached where they could clearly see her even in the darkness. The sound of water falling down through the mountains was heard distinctly enough in the otherwise silent area. Lilith stood there with her head tilted to the side. Her throat was dry; she felt thirsty. To quench that thirst, she needed the blood of any living thing. In front of her stood two figures that she failed to recognize; the only thing that she could think of was the smell of their blood that was surrounding her senses. Her thirst needed to be fulfilled.

Amara scrunched up her face in disgust. There was a very vile stench that had hit the air when the woman arrived. It smelt like that of a dead body decaying for years. Azrael cringed at the smell as well. His eyes were still on the woman. And then realization dawned on him as the woman took two more steps forward.

"What's that smell?" asked Amara, her voice a mere whisper.

"It's possessed. When a malign spirit enters a human, it carries around a smell that stenches like that of a dead body," he answered.

"Do we run or do we fight?"

"We can't fight a spirit that has possessed a body. It's extremely powerful, evil and incomparable. One simply can't compete," he replied.

"Then we teleport," suggested Amara.

Azrael considered it for a moment but their journey was long and they could not afford to use their strength in teleporting. If they did, they would only reach half-way to their destination. But they would also be able to get rid of the dead that was about to attack them. And if they did teleport, the false traces would be lost, making it more of a threat.

"That won't help. Wait here," he said to her and walked a little further while Amara stood there rooted in place.

The smell of fresh blood that was wafting through her senses made Lilith want to tear the two bodies apart and quench her thirst. Azrael stood a few feet away from her, his eyes focussed on the possessed body of the girl. He cleared his throat, taking a step forward, careful of not getting too close to her.

He opened his mouth to say something when Lilith proceeded ahead to silence him. She only sought blood. As her eyes turned a darker shade of red, she began walking ahead until she was standing right in front of Azrael who stood a bit taller than her. It made no difference to her. Amara watched what was happening before her as Lilith suddenly attacked Azrael, gripping his throat in her long fingers. She lifted him off the ground and held his body high up, gazing at him with a malicious grin on her lips. Amara widened her eyes before rushing in that direction to free Azrael.

The strength that Lilith had in her was tremendous. Azrael struggled to loosen the grip on his throat as he began to choke under it. Blood trickled down the back of his neck as Lilith's sharp nails pierced his skin. Before he could attempt to save himself, his eyes shut on their own as Lilith dropped him to the ground, slamming his head forcefully. It created tremors in the earth as Amara stared in complete silence. She was unaware of who the spirit was, yet she realized that it had the strength of at least four powerful witches combined. Lilith began to lean close to Azrael while raising her free hand in order to separate his head from his body, when Amara shut her eyes and grabbed his arm before using all her strength to teleport the both of them away from there.

A few moments later, they landed inside a cave. It was completely dark. Amara pushed herself up so she was now sitting, her breathing ragged as she tried to get her vision steady. She blinked a few times before looking around to find Azrael who lay unconscious at a distance from her. In an attempt to save their lives, Amara had teleported them to the mountains of Carvelli. Since it wasn't very far from the castle, it had taken all her energy to get them there and now she was completely drained out. If at all she had to conjure anything, she would need to meditate and get her powers in working condition again. Yet she began to wonder why she felt so exhausted. She had teleported the same way before and it had not drained out her powers so easily. But at that moment, she felt as though there was nothing that she could do using her powers.

It was strange. Amara thought that maybe it was because she had not been able to meditate in a while and that the visit to the Sea of Cypress was mentally as well as physically exhausting. Yet she could not help but wonder why she suddenly felt weaker than she ever had. With a shake of her head, she got up and staggered towards Azrael. There were prints of Lilith's fingers on his throat; his face looked paler than ever. Amara held his stone cold hand. She closed her eyes in order to use the remaining of her powers to heal him but nothing worked. All her strength seemed to have vanished and she didn't know what she could do.

"Wake up, Azrael," she whispered, looking at his face and holding it in her hands gently.

He was unconscious, with eyes shut and movements void. Nothing other than his chest moved up and down, nearly invisible as he breathed. Amara tried to get him back into consciousness but she could not. When there was nothing else that she thought would help, she shut her eyes for a moment and connected her mind to that of Iris's. She sent a message of help to her which travelled slowly due to the lack of her powers. Amara sat on the floor beside Azrael's unconscious body. She waited for the message to reach Iris while searching for a *Healing Potion* in her bag and pulled out the bottle. Unscrewing the cap, she began to pour some drops into his mouth when her eyes went blind and she collapsed on the floor beside him.

* * *

The castle was quiet. Everyone was either asleep or meditating inside their chambers. Leandra, Erasmus, Nicholas and Iris were seated inside Iris's chamber, discussing about Amara and Azrael's whereabouts. Iris sat there with her eyes stuck on the wall before her. She missed Amara, and hearing the news about Lord Mikhail on a hunt for something that Amara was guarding made it no better. Nicholas had gotten a message from his eagle that Lord Mikhail was trying to find out something that Amara was responsible for protecting. That made Iris more worried than ever. She didn't want anything to happen to Amara, even Azrael for that matter.

In the week that she had spent with Lea, she had come to realize that Azrael wasn't a threat to Amara and that she could trust him. Lea had told her a lot of things about him and she had begun to have faith in him. Yet her worry for Amara had not subsided. She wanted to talk to her about how Nicholas had helped her handle elements with perfection in a short time after he returned. There was so much she had to convey and it was all inside her head. She could not be open enough to anyone else apart from Amara. Even though Lea was now a good friend, she didn't feel the connection that she felt with Amara. It was like a sisterly bond, Amara was more of an elder sibling to her while Lea was the immature friend.

As they all talked about preparations for the war, Iris shuddered in her seat as something crashed into her mind. She blinked, registering the message that she had just received and stood up with a jerk, her chair toppling over. The other three observed her questioningly. Iris looked so startled that it caught all of them off guard.

"Amara needs help," she said, breaking the silence.

"You received a message?" asked Erasmus, standing up as well.

Iris nodded wordlessly.

"Where are they?" Nicholas said.

"In the mountains of Carvelli; a cave, I think," Iris replied, her eyes staring into nothingness.

"I need to go," she said before any of them could utter a word and started to walk towards the door of the chamber when Nicholas grabbed her arm and stopped her.

"You won't go alone," he said and turned to look at Erasmus and Lea who stood there in panic.

"Erasmus, stay here until we return and Lea, go to the potions chamber and get me the bag of emergency supplies," he said and walked out of the chamber along with Iris.

Lea rushed to the potions chamber and searched for the bag of potions and weapons before grabbing one and going back to where Nicholas and Iris were. She handed them the bag and Nicholas took it before looking at Erasmus.

"I will return soon," he said.

"Be careful," Erasmus replied.

A moment later, Iris and Nicholas were out of the castle, making their way to the mountains of Carvelli. Without uttering even slight a sound, Iris followed Nicholas to where he was taking her. He led her to where his horse was standing, behind the castle. Mounting himself on top of it, he handed the bag of supplies to Iris before pulling her onto the horse behind him. Soon, they were on their way to the mountains of Carvelli.

"Don't worry, Iris. Nothing is going to happen to Amara," he said; sensing the panic on Iris's face.

She nodded and let out a sigh. *Maybe I am over reacting,* she thought. Of course Amara was powerful enough to help herself but there might be some reason that she sent Iris a message. She advised herself to relax and not panic as much as she was. It was not going to help.

As they travelled ahead, Iris wondered why Azrael and Amara had not used any means of transport to get them to their destination. If Nicholas could use a horse, why did they have to travel on foot and take such a long time?

"Are you the only one who has a horse?" She asked.

"No. All of us have some means of travelling. We can conjure up carriages, use horses; dragons too at times. But they're for war purposes, or emergencies," he responded.

"Why did Amara not use anything?"

"There are some places where no wagons can be used. Going on foot is the only way to reach there. Maybe Amara and Azrael went somewhere they couldn't use a wagon." Nicholas shrugged.

The horse galloped ahead in greater speed when Nicholas silently ordered it to. The mountains of Carvelli were only a few hours journey from the castle and Nicholas had no time to waste. The wind blew past Iris as she shut her eyes and clutched Nicholas's shoulder tightly so as not to fall. The pace at which they were travelling frightened her. It got worse when rain started to drench them.

For the next few hours the rain kept falling hard and stopping in between. Nicholas halted at no place and the speed either augmented or stayed the same. Iris wondered how he was going to stop the horse that was travelling at lightning speed according to her. When they reached the mountains of Carvelli, Nicholas finally lessened the pace and they came to a halt upon entering the valleys. Iris wondered where Amara would be. There was no mention of where in the mountains the two of them were stranded.

"Where do you think they are?" Nicholas asked, looking around.

"She didn't give me the proper location," she replied, as confused as him.

"Well, connect your mind to hers. Maybe you'll find out," he told her and Iris nodded before closing her eyes and trying to reach Amara.

She had to strain her mind a lot more than necessary because she could not locate where Amara was. Iris was unable to join their minds. It seemed as though Amara was somewhere unreachable to her. After trying hard for a long time, Iris opened her eyes and let out a frustrated sigh.

"I can't. . .I can't do it." She ran a hand through her hair in frustration.

Nicholas paused for a moment before trying to connect his mind to Amara's or even to Azrael's for that matter. But nothing worked. Since Amara had lost consciousness, reaching her mind wasn't an easy task. But neither of them was aware of that.

"You said they were in a cave, right?" He asked after a while of trying and failing.

"Yes," Iris replied.

"There are five caves in these mountains. We'll have to search all of them," he said and they continued forward in search of Amara and Azrael.

* * *

There was a sound of footsteps heard inside the cave that Amara and Azrael were. The faint sound of someone walking towards them echoed in the head of the semi-conscious being of Azrael who lay there immovable. His eyes opened slightly to reveal the blurred figure of a hooded man leaning over beside his body. The man bent a little and grazed his fingers over the book that had fallen out of Amara's bag when she had looked for the *Healing Potion*. He watched with weak eyes threatening to close as the man picked up the book. A moment later, Azrael went unconscious again.

CHAPTER TWENTY-TWO

∞∞∞∞∞

FERAL MINDS

∞∞∞∞∞

It was early morning when they reached the castle. The sun was shining brightly above their heads as they entered through the doors. The morning was fresh, and it made Iris feel better after the long journey to the mountains of Carvelli. But Amara and Azrael were a different story. They seemed exhausted and had no idea why it was so. Amara had thought that maybe it was because they had passed out the night before and had to go through a long journey, but she had to admit that she had never felt this tired. It was unusual and she didn't like it.

Nicholas, on the other hand, was experiencing a strange feeling. His heart had nearly begun to constrict at times. Whenever he breathed a bit heavily or did anything exhaustive, he would feel as though there were pieces of him breaking inside of him. It was strange. Ever since he had returned from the caves after almost summoning the spirit of Lilith, he had started to have a very strange feeling that something wrong was going to happen; and how much ever hard he tried, that feeling would not go. Even though nothing had happened since, there was something that made him paranoid. And somehow it was affecting his physical being; about which he had no idea.

The night before when Nicholas had reached the cave where Amara and Azrael were lying unconscious – after having given them both a few drops of the *Fire and Ice* potion – they had woken up in a while. Iris had taken extra care to give Amara the *Healing Potion* and make her normal again. Amara had become extremely weak. Iris had never seen her that way. It saddened Iris. Azrael was experiencing something similar, his eyes felt heavy and his throat kept going dry every now and then. When they revealed the story about meeting a possessed body in the Dark Falls, Nicholas went rigid.

Something told him that he knew about the spirit, yet he could not put a finger on it. He explained the cause of Azrael's condition after. The reason that his throat kept going dry was because the grip that the spirit had was impeccable. It had sent a wave of poison inside him through the grip on his throat, which is why it kept going dry owing to the mild poison. Although harmless, the poison had a potential to make him weak. The remedy for that was to have the *Fire and Ice* potion once a day. They had then left the caves after Amara had thoroughly checked her bag of supplies to see if everything was in place. Azrael had given her a warning that he had seen someone when he was half-conscious. Whether it was a dream or reality, he was unsure. Yet for safety purposes, Amara had ensured everything. There was no damage and nothing seemed to be out of place.

Azrael reflected that maybe it was a dream after all. Yet, he could not get the image of the hooded figure that sat next to him, out of his mind. It felt real, but blurred enough to be a dream. After a while he had let go. All four of them had then left to return to the castle on foot. Nicholas tagged his horse along as they strode in the direction of the castle. Amara and Azrael were strangely quiet which worried Iris immensely. Although they were usually not the ones to talk, the atmosphere seemed to have altered with them around.

She hadn't known Azrael as much, but she knew that there was something wrong that kept Amara at bay. There was a missing link that could not be connected how much ever hard she tried. For a fact, she could figure out that something had happened where had been to; something that had made her aloof from not just Iris, but everything else. It was not normal and Iris wanted to know what it was that changed things all of a sudden. No one uttered a word except for when necessary until they reached the castle. Amara had retreated to go to her chamber and Azrael had done the same, leaving Iris and Nicholas at the door, wondering what was wrong. Nicholas was busy speculating what it was that was bothering him so, but Iris had only one thing in mind.

Iris couldn't understand what had happened to Amara. Letting out a sigh, she started walking to her chamber to get some rest.

Nicholas left through the castle doors and went up to the tower. He stood there with his hands resting on the railing when his eyes fell on the fairy carved out of soil. Lea's creation stood in the tower even after a few months had passed. Strangely enough, it kept changing its position. Each time Nicholas or Amara saw it, the fairy had either taken a flying stance, or that of hiding herself. He had made it a point to ask Lea the reason for the movements. He always seemed to forget about it.

* * *

In the castle, Amara sat inside her chamber after taking a cold shower to calm her nerves. She still felt weak. She had never been *this* weak. When it became unbearable, she rushed to the kitchen to energize herself with something to eat. Impatiently she grabbed all that she thought would get her back to normal and began feeding herself. She sat inside the kitchen on a chair, all the food placed before her on the table. Her eyes seemed to start watering all the sudden. She could not understand what was happening. It had never happened to her before. How much ever she ate, she just did not feel active enough. It was the same, a little better but all the same and Amara didn't like it at all.

Frustrated, she threw the plate on the floor and held her head in her hands. Whatever was happening to her, it wasn't good. Amara stood up to go out of the kitchen when she turned around and blindly hit her head on someone's chest. Azrael stood there with his eyebrows raised, clearing his throat since it felt dry. He grabbed a glass of water and gulped it down while Amara took a step back. He then looked at her. The frustrated expression that she held didn't go unnoticed. He frowned.

"What's wrong with you?" He said, grabbing an apple from the table beside him.

"Nothing! I have to go," she replied, unable to meet his piercing gaze and walked across from him to go out of the kitchen.

"You should get some sleep," he said softly to her, following closely behind. He didn't know why he was going behind her but something made him want to. Amara was wondering the same and yet she wanted him to accompany to her. Being alone was exasperating when she was on the verge of setting something on Fire.

"I don't feel like sleeping," she said, swiftly treading ahead. She had unknowingly taken the back door that led to the woods behind the castle. Her feet had led her there all by themselves and she didn't know what she was going to do next.

Azrael was still following her, unaware of the reason. He didn't feel as weak as Amara did. Maybe it was because of the *Fire and Ice* potion that he was taking, and he felt as though his brain was functioning better than ever. It felt as though he had a strange but good feeling inside him that didn't make him as serious and grave as he was before. In a way, he felt sort of alive; something that he hadn't felt in a long, long time.

Amara stood in the woods outside the lake, her head flooded with a million questions as to why she was feeling that way. Her whole body seemed to be on a sabbatical. It felt as though none of her organs were in working condition, more so her mind. It seemed to be playing tricks on her which she didn't appreciate. She wanted to kill someone. She wanted to get rid of that feeling.

"Amara!" said Azrael for the third time when she hadn't paid attention even once. He was standing in front of her, clearly annoyed. He didn't seem to like the fact that she was frustrated. He wanted her to be okay, the reason to which he could not figure out. It was strange but that didn't stop him. Amara looked at him quietly with her eyebrows raised. She hadn't heard him until now.

"You need to calm down," he said.

Amara stared at him silently for a moment, her breathing becoming a bit normal again. She closed her eyes for a long while before looking at him again.

"I do." She breathed, letting out a sigh.

Azrael gave her a slight smile and a nod before taking her hand and leading her to a deeper part of the woods. Amara blindly followed without questioning him once. When he was sure about where he was, Azrael let go of her hand and asked her to take a seat on the grass below. It was a bit moist and cool, which made Amara's nerves a little calmer than they were before. She did not feel like slamming her head on a wall. Azrael then sat in front of her.

"Now tell me what's wrong," he said to her softly.

Amara was puzzled whether or not she should tell him. After contemplating her choices for a while she gave in. *There isn't much I can do now,* she thought before letting out a breath. "It's strange. My head feels like it's about to explode and I'm capable of doing absolutely nothing. I feel like a mortal with no powers," she revealed.

Azrael internally chuckled at the word '*mortal*'. Amara was far from mortal. She was the perfect witch. There was nothing even remotely mortal about her. She had the distinct ability to stand out in a crowd of great Conjurers.

"You're not even close to being mortal. You know that. Also, the capability that you have is a gazillion times more than that of a mortal. Why don't you try out something? Use your powers. Try conjuring some water," he told her.

"I don't think I can," she replied pathetically. She felt worthless.

"One day of unconsciousness and you feel as though you can't do anything. Have you really forgotten who you are, Amara?" He raised an eyebrow disbelievingly.

Amara looked at him for a moment before glancing away, only to stare at the lake. With her eyes focussed on the water, she concentrated her mind and a wave started to rise up. A smile threatened to hit Amara's lips when suddenly the water fell back in. A disappointed look etched upon her face. That had never happened to her. Her powers seemed to be dying; which was not good.

"Don't lose hope. Try again," said Azrael, giving her an encouraging nod. But Amara felt that there was something really wrong. Why did her powers seem to have faded away like that? That was something out of the usual.

"This doesn't happen," she said to herself but he heard her.

"There's a first time for everything. You can't give up so easily, oh great witch. They know you for your brilliance. You can't protect the prophecy and the treasures if you sit here doing nothing. This is only because of the long journey we had. It was exhausting, mentally as well. So you just have to try a little harder."

Amara regarded him silently. She didn't know what she was supposed to do or say. It was different being in the woods with Azrael. But in a way that felt natural to her. All she was worried about was her powers that seemed to have gone somewhere.

Azrael hoped that his words had made some kind of difference to her. He watched as she looked away from him and towards the water again. She let out a sigh, closing her eyes for a moment before turning back to him. "Do you think meditation would help? I haven't gotten a chance to meditate in a while," she told him hopefully.

"Of course it will," Azrael replied, with an encouraging nod in her direction. Amara bit her lip, she knew that she wanted to meditate. She needed rest. For her, rest had always been meditation. Sleep could not give her the peace that she needed; but meditation could.

"I'll leave you alone then," said Azrael, getting up.

Amara looked up at him thankfully and smiled for his help. Maybe if he had not calmed her down, she would have set the woods on Fire again. Her frustration was at its peak when she had left the castle. But after Azrael helped her get her mind alert, she felt lighter. Her head didn't seem as heavy as it did before and she could peacefully meditate. She didn't say anything to him, just smiled; and Azrael smiled back, taking steps backwards and then turning around. Moments later, he vanished out of sight. Amara was still staring where his footsteps had been. Something she had failed to notice was that the one person that she had disliked the most had suddenly changed and was helping her. In her frustration, she had let that go unnoticed. Her attention was elsewhere.

She then stood up, making her way closer to the lake. Letting her feet drop into the cool water, she placed both her hands on her knees. Her eyes closed again, the sun shone above her face as she let her mind drift into a meditative state.

* * *

Iris stood in the potions chamber with Leandra as the latter practiced her skills of creating different kinds of potions. As Lea chatted away about what ingredients she was adding into the potions, Iris barely listened. Her mind was crammed with thoughts of why Amara was behaving oddly. It had been only a few hours that they had returned from the mountains of Carvelli; yet her worry had not faded even after Erasmus had assured her that it was just exhaustion that was holding Amara back. He had told her that she would get back to normal soon. But Iris wasn't listening. Her intuitions said to her that something was wrong. It wasn't just because Amara was acting strange, the reason she thought that way was because the moment they had returned, Azrael had become something she had never thought he would be. His presence was cheerful; which Iris noticed wasn't the case before.

He had a similar kind of behaviour as Amara, yet a bit different. The aura that he gave off was of Death. Why had suddenly all the darkness inside him vanished? When she talked to Erasmus about it the hour before, he had told her that those were the side-effects of the *Fire and Ice* potion. It had the ability to jumble up one's thoughts. If the brain was stalled or a person was under shock, the potion would restore the workings back to how they were. But if consumed in excess amount for some reasons, it behaved like alcohol did for humans. Although the *Fire and Ice* potion was far from alcoholic effects, it gave an exhilarating sensation. It made changes in one's behaviour.

But Iris refused to accept that it was because of the potion he was consuming, owing to the effects of the evil spirit that had nearly killed him. There was something she wasn't ready to accept. Suddenly all the trust that had developed for him was starting to go away. She had no explanation as to why that was happening. She did not have a reason to do so, but it still worried her. She was holding Azrael responsible for the changes in Amara's behaviour. The changes that were only going to stay for a while, yet she refused to accept the fact that it was just because of the exhaustive journey that the two of them had been through.

"Hello, dear sister of mine."

Iris snapped her attention to Azrael's deep and husky voice as he entered the potions chamber and stood next to a babbling Lea who had not quieted down for the last half hour. She turned to look at him, grinning as she did so.

"Look what I made; its *Filoris* potion," she told him, holding up a vial of the potion.

"And what is it used for?" He asked.

"I was just telling Iris about it. She'll explain it to you while I look for that pesky book of *Unusual Potions* that I haven't found in ages. I'm going to the library," she said before dashing out of the potions chamber.

Iris was amused at the amount of energy that girl had. She was always this fast and impatient.

Azrael looked at Iris, waiting for her to explain what the potion was about. She turned to him after Lea had gone. "Well?" He probed, raising his eyebrows. He had never really spoken to Iris properly. Whenever he tried, something came in between. Iris didn't exactly like his presence, now more than ever. His behaviour lately was very confusing for her. It seemed to her that suddenly the air around the castle had changed. Even Nicholas was acting aloof all the sudden which was frustrating Iris.

"Are you going to tell me or should I just make you do it?" He said when she didn't reply. Iris blinked. *What was his question again?*

"I'm sorry. I uh. . .I don't really know what Lea was talking about. I wasn't listening. She talks a lot," she told him. A nervous chuckle escaped her lips as she said the last bit, in the end biting her lip. She was half-expecting him to get angry.

"As a matter of fact, she does. Half the time I don't listen to her at all," he replied, chuckling along with her. And all the sudden Iris felt comfortable, something which she had never felt around him before. But that didn't change the fact that she suspected him of having done some sorcery over Amara's mind to make her act strange.

"Besides, I know what this potion is used for," he said lifting the vial of the *Filoris* potion.

He looked at its contents – a subtle yellow with a hint of smoke swirling in its neck – intently for a long moment before placing it back on the table. Iris's eyes were stuck on the vial as well. It seemed rather common yet unusual. The transparent yellow liquid stood out of all the potions. There were various other yellow coloured potions but *Filoris* seemed an entirely different one from those.

"It helps in reducing the fear of something. When a terrifying incident happens; for instance, you experience a nightmare that doesn't leave your mind for days on end, this potion helps in recovery. It restores the adrenaline to a normal level. Quite useless if you ask me. I don't think reducing fear requires a potion," he told her, shrugging in the end.

But Iris felt intrigued by that tiny vial. It seemed interesting even though its usage wasn't that great. Although, she did agree with Azrael on some points; she did not think the rate of fear would be so high that it would need a potion to get rid of.

They began walking out of the potions chamber when they were both done discussing about the potion. As Iris and Azrael walked ahead after closing the door of the chamber, Iris's mind went numb for a long moment. She stopped walking. Her feet stumbled and she involuntarily rested her hand on the wall for support. It didn't help. She fell to the floor as her insides went completely numb. She could not move. And then suddenly her senses went back to normal. Azrael was crouched down before her with his hand on her shoulder.

"Are you alright?" He asked, with a look of concern. Iris nodded silently. She pushed herself up to standing, unable to understand what had happened. For a moment, she looked at Azrael suspiciously. He had done that before. He had paralyzed her. But what she had felt then was different. It hadn't made her *mind* numb as such. Azrael was just manipulative, but could he have done this? She wondered and started walking further, leaving Azrael behind. He shrugged to himself and walked in the opposite direction.

Iris reached the entrance of the great hall where Nicholas was sitting with Erasmus and someone else beside him. She frowned. The man in front of Nicholas was someone she failed to recognize. *Is he a new addition to the army?* She wondered. Taking a step forward, she tried to look at his face closely, but could barely see it. Erasmus then looked up to find Iris standing there with her eyes stuck on their visitor.

"Iris, come in," he told her. Iris snapped her head towards him and without a thought, headed in further to where they were sitting. The visitor was now looking at her when his conversation with Nicholas was interrupted. His eyebrows were raised as he watched Iris settle herself on the chair in front of him.

"Iris, I would like you to meet someone," said Nicholas. "This is Eridanus. He is joining the coven," he told her. "Eridanus, this is Iris. She is brilliant at reading minds," he said to the visitor, smiling. Iris looked at Eridanus and he grinned, which she returned.

"You were the one that paralyzed me just now," she said to him. Her eyes were solely focussed on him and she suddenly had a vision of him connecting his mind to hers without her knowledge. Eridanus looked at her, amused as well as impressed. Iris observed that he was rather similar to Nicholas in behaviour. Although she had known him for less than a minute, she could make out how he supposedly was.

Eridanus had hazel eyes, dull yet magnificent. They were his most attractive feature. His hair was brown, with a hint of blonde in them. He had a square jaw, a tiny nose, broad shoulders and a tall frame as far as Iris could judge since he was sitting. A smirk was covering his features as he observed Iris and she noticed that he had a manly build, with a boyish charm. It was a strange blend, but not unpleasant to look at.

"He *paralyzed* you?" asked Nicholas, frowning as he looked back and forth between the two. Iris nodded, without taking her eyes off of Eridanus. They held a piercing gaze.

"He has similar powers like me. He created a connection between our minds. I think it's probably because there was no other mind that he thought was weak enough to invade, since all of you here are quite experienced in blocking your minds and protecting them, unlike me. I'm still the mastering the art," she said. Her gaze was still focussed on him.

"Brightest witch indeed," said Eridanus, smiling.

CHAPTER TWENTY-THREE

∞∞∞∞∞

MONSTROSITY

∞∞∞∞∞

I t had been three days after the night that Lord Mikhail had accidentally found Amara and Azrael in the mountains of Carvelli. He had been resting in a cave when he had heard the sound of someone landing into another. Since he was tired after the journey that he had to take to meet the one that would help him with the prophecy and Lady Calypsa, he had decided to ignore the notice and carry on resting. But his mind told him to find out who it was. So he followed the sound and reached the cave where Amara and Azrael were.

Suddenly, all his restlessness seemed to vanish at the sight of them. Azrael had fainted and Amara was trying to wake him up by using a *Healing Potion* when Lord Mikhail used a weakening spell that made her pass out instantly. He then approached the pair and crouched before them to find an open bag that had some of the supplies fallen out. He looked through the two weapons and a bottle of potions in the darkness when his hands landed on a book. Since he was unable to read it in the dark, he closed his eyes and tried to decipher what was written inside it when his mind caught on to the fact that there was a protection around the book. Sensing that it was something important that Amara would want to hide, he had started to pick up the book and leave when he heard footsteps approaching the cave.

In an instant, he vanished from there and landed back into the cave that he was in before. He sent a subtle message to his messenger that informed the same about something important being in the book; and that it needed to be found out. His messenger, after receiving it had set to work immediately. And then Lord Mikhail had decided to continue his journey; he was aware of the fact that his work would be done and that he would receive a message soon enough. On his journey, he reached the Dark Falls, wandering around to find a place of meditation when he spotted the figure of a woman lurking around the waterfalls. To get a closer look, he walked further only to find that the woman was no one else but a hungry spirit that had possessed a human body. He wondered who it could be.

Muttering a spell, he put on a shield of protection around himself so as to guard him if the spirit attacked. Then he proceeded in her direction. Sensing the smell of blood, the spirit turned around to find Lord Mikhail standing at a distance. Lilith stared at the ready bait with her eyes wide and head tilted to the side as she smirked menacingly at her prey. She was getting her fill that night. Taking a few steps forward she stood in front of Lord Mikhail, who was trying hard to understand who it was that had possessed the body of the human girl that stood before him. The horrible stench made him want to vomit but he controlled it. Lilith raised her hand, her wrinkled fingers with long nails touched Lord Mikhail's face. In his years of experience he had learned that when a spirit like hers was about to attack, making any kind of sound or movement could get the victim into trouble.

So he stayed still, even though Lilith's fingers were cold and piercing and even though he felt like burning himself alive. He kept his position intact as Lilith was getting ready to attack. At that instant, Lord Mikhail shot a spell that stilled the spirit in place. Lilith stood there with her teeth showing, her hand raised and her head tilted to the side. Stepping away from the spirit, Lord Mikhail closed his eyes and connected his mind to hers. In moments, he realized that the spirit had turned malignant instead of keeping its usual nature of being pure. He understood that it was old; one that had started to exist over a few hundred years ago and had been summoned only recently.

Yet he could not figure out whose spirit it was. Since the spirit itself had forgotten its own identity after it turned evil, it was difficult to find out the same. Lord Mikhail knew that his spell would only last for a few moments before she would attack even harder. So with the information that he had in hand, Lord Mikhail teleported himself out of the Dark Falls, leaving the hungry spirit of Lilith more aggravated than it was before. When Lilith regained her position, her eyes turned redder and darker. The thirst for blood had increased, and due to the fact that she could not get her hands on any of the prey that she had found, it made her stronger and more prone to attack.

Now the only blood that she sought was of the one that had summoned her. Had she not been summoned, she would not have been left this thirsty. That was the only thought that crossed her mind and Lilith then ascended to find the one that had summoned her. The senses began to work better and her mind became alert. Unaware of where she was, and unknown to the identity of her caller, she followed the trail of her thirst, which led her ahead. There was only blood and murder that she sought, and it became her path to Nicholas.

* * *

Nicholas was busy talking to the new sorcerer that had joined the coven. Eridanus listened to Nicholas with his gaze stuck on Iris, who stood at a distance with another witch, that he had been told was called Leandra. They were conversing. He noticed that only Leandra was chatting away while Iris stood there staring at nothing in particular. Nicholas and Eridanus stood at the gate of the graveyard outside the castle as the former explained about the shields that Amara had put up to protect them from threats. She wanted to ensure proper protection if any of Lord Mikhail's servants decided to attack or send another threat to them. The shields were invisible, yet their presence was felt easily.

Iris stood listening to Lea explaining about how spirits were summoned. Her right side rested on the bark of a huge tree while Lea sat on the ground. Iris listened to her attentively, nodding every now and then but her eyes were travelling from one place to another before they landed on Eridanus. He was already looking at her. Noticing her gaze on him, he winked. Iris rolled her eyes and looked away. He was charming, that was for sure. But he also made Iris want to slam his head on a tree for being able to paralyze her without her noticing it. She did not like competition. His abilities were similar to hers and he had the experience of ninety years which gave him an advantage over her.

That fact hurt her ego badly. In the three days that he had been there, Iris had come to understand that he was around ninety-five-years old and had the ability to manipulate minds to an extent that could procure serious harm to the victim. Iris, on the other hand, had only just learnt how to invade a mind without the knowledge of the victim. Eridanus had so much experience in that field that it made Iris want to scream in frustration whenever he showed off his skills. All she could do was roll her eyes and walk away from him.

The most annoying part of it all was that he refused to leave her alone. He was everywhere, and it didn't help that Nicholas had given her the task of helping him around since he was new. However, Eridanus seemed to have no interest in the castle and its workings. He would only talk endlessly about how he had practiced manipulation when he was a wanderer getting trained by all kinds of Conjurers.

He had highly extensive knowledge about the world of Conjurers and Iris again felt extremely jealous of him. Needless to say, she was not fond of him. She certainly did not appreciate the fact that he had stopped talking to Nicholas and was now approaching to where she was stood. When he reached her, he gave a brilliant smile. Iris returned it with a cynical one of her own. Lea suddenly stopped talking and watched the two of them looking at each other with completely different expressions. Iris had the feeling of kicking him in the gut while Eridanus watched her as calmly as he could. Lea inwardly chuckled and decided to leave them alone. She stood up and walked away noticing that none of them were paying attention to her.

"Nice evening, ain't it?" said Eridanus.

The smile was still plastered across his face and it didn't make Iris happy at all.

"It was until you showed up," she muttered thinking that he had not heard her.

He chuckled in response, proving her wrong.

"Anyway, I was hoping you would show me the potions chamber," he told her.

Iris frowned. *Do I have to?* Letting out a sigh, she thought that she might as well get it done and over with. Maybe then he would leave her alone.

"Sure. Follow me," she replied and turned around to walk back into the castle.

Glancing at Nicholas who was standing next to a grave looking up at the sky, Iris proceeded and entered the castle followed by Eridanus. They walked in the direction of the potions chamber and Iris opened the door to let them in.

Outside in the graveyard, Nicholas stood with his eyes focussed on the sky that had started to turn darker. It looked as though some unknown being was close. The protective shields had the tendency to turn dark in colour whenever a threat was noticed. Frowning, Nicholas walked into the castle and made his way to the library where he knew Amara was present. After she had returned from the journey with Azrael, Amara had kept herself busy in reading books from the library and meditating most of the time. She would rarely speak to anyone and kept to herself. She had also not spoken to Iris properly after returning, which had been bothering the latter yet Iris chose to ignore it thinking it was Amara's choice.

Amara, on the other hand, had all her concentration on coming up with a reason for her weakness. The long hours that she spent on meditation to gain back her strength seemed to work fine; but there was some kind of invisible glitch that kept her from gaining back her usual self. In a bid to understand the reason behind this, she had started reading books. There was no progress in the matter though. She had not been able to find out what it was that kept making her feel like she was growing weaker by every passing day. She didn't lose hope. She knew that there was some way to find out the reason behind it all and she was not going to stop searching for the same.

When Nicholas stood in front of her across from the table that she was reading the book on, she looked at him with her eyebrows raised in question. She didn't want to be disturbed, and she had made that quite clear by staying away from everyone including Azrael. Although he had offered to help, she had declined saying, *"I want to battle this on my own. We will talk about this when I have an answer."*

To which Azrael had shrugged and decided to concentrate on his own work of making plans to guard the prophecy and its treasures. That kept him busy.

"You need to come outside," said Nicholas. He held a look of panic and his instincts told him that there was a dangerous threat that was trying to enter.

Amara immediately stood up at the look on his face. She realized that it was something grave and the two of them rushed out to the graveyard where the sky had now turned completely black. Frowning, Amara turned to Nicholas.

"Get Azrael, now," she said in urgency.

Nicholas instantly retreated into the castle and found Azrael sitting in the great hall, practicing a few spells. He looked at Nicholas, who gestured to him to go outside with him and Azrael left what he was doing and they reached to where Amara stood in the graveyard. She was staring at the sky, muttering a spell to strengthen the protection because whoever it was, the threat seemed to be a very powerful and dangerous one.

"Can you tell me what this threat could be?" She asked Azrael.

He was staring up at the sky as the shields started to spread around evenly to ensure added protection when a cracking sound was heard; as though the foot of a table had bent or been broken. The sound meant that the threat was trying to break the shield.

"So much strength can mean two things," Azrael replied, realizing what it was.

"What?" Amara said, frowning.

"It's either an extremely strong sorcerer like the Lord and Lord Mikhail. Or it is an evil spirit. Either of the two have enough power to create a crack in the shields so strong," he said.

Chills ran down Nicholas's spine at Azrael's words and he stumbled at his feet. His throat suddenly went dry, eyes still, and hands numb. There was a stinging pain that went through his body and his mind felt as though it had stopped. The possibilities of it being the Lord were slim to none, because the shields allowed him to enter the castle whenever he wished to. They would only get in motion if a threat was detected; and Lord Lucifer wasn't a threat.

"Lord Mikhail is a threat of course, but not so malign that the shields turn completely black. I think it is a spirit," Azrael said after looking at the sky with increased concentration.

Another crack was heard and a sudden gush of air struck the three of them, making them fall to the ground. Nicholas lay there without moving an inch as realization sank into him. His mind dragged itself to the memory of him summoning the spirit of Lilith and leaving it at a point where the spirit was about to enter. He snapped his head to look at Azrael, who was on the ground beside him.

"What are the results of summoning a spirit and stopping the ritual in process?" He asked.

Frowning, Azrael looked back at Nicholas.

"The spirit turns malignant and enters the body it was to be summoned in," he replied.

Amara looked at the two of them in perplexity. She wondered why Nicholas was asking such a question.

"It's the spirit of Lilith," whispered Nicholas, all to himself as he realized what he had done.

"What?" Amara stood up with her eyes wide in shock.

But Nicholas did not reply. The repercussions of what he had unknowingly done were clear before him. He had left the summoning at the time when he was not sure whether or not the spirit was entering the body. His duty to the castle was more important to him than his task of summoning Lilith's spirit on Lord Lucifer's orders. He had failed to realize what it would cost.

Before Azrael or Amara could enquire about what Nicholas meant, the doors of the graveyard creaked open to reveal the dark figure of a woman entering inside. Lilith took slow steps towards the blood that invited her. She understood that it was the blood of her caller that had led her to him. Her strength had been tested due to the shields around the castle but that didn't stop her from entering. The quest of blood had the power to break any shield, however strong it may be. Nicholas went rigid at the sight of Lilith. She was getting closer, thereby increasing Nicholas's uneasiness.

"It's the spirit that attacked us in the Dark Falls," Amara whispered to Azrael.

He nodded in agreement.

"We have to do something," he told her and began to walk towards Lilith when Amara grabbed his arm and forcefully tugged him back to where she was standing.

Startled, Azrael stumbled on his feet and frowned at her.

"No. Not you. I'll do something," she said to him.

"Don't be silly." Azrael scoffed. "You can't battle an evil spirit as strong as this one. Didn't you hear what he said? It's the spirit of Lilith. We all know how strong a witch she was. It's natural that her spirit would be stronger." He shook his head.

"I'm capable enough of battling an evil spirit. You were the one that got caught in her grasp and fainted," she replied, offended.

In their argument, they failed to notice that Lilith had now come to stand right at Nicholas's feet from where he was awkwardly lying on the ground. It was only when the stench struck their senses that they snapped their heads to look at the scene.

"Oh dear," muttered Amara and pushed Azrael aside to save Nicholas, who was completely numb by that point.

"Holy goddess of the Earth, I pray to thee. Weaken the evil and triumph the good. Birth of the dead and doom of the soul. I pray to thee, guard the weak and destroy the evil. Holy goddess, I pray to thee. Weaken the evil and triumph the good. Save the soul and end the spirit. I pray to thee. . ." Amara chanted.

It was loud enough for the spirit of Lilith to hear. Lilith craned her neck to the side. Her appearance was more terrifying now that she had heard the spell of weakening her. She widened her eyes that were the darkest shade of red. They pierced into Amara's soul as she continued to chant the spell. Azrael stood behind her chanting the same spell to increase the effect. Lilith's insides began to stir as she let out a deafening scream that shook the walls of the entire castle. The scream was violent enough to have Amara and Azrael thrown far away from where Lilith and Nicholas were.

They were slammed onto a grave, their heads hitting the stone hard enough to make them faint but they regained their consciousness in a moment's time due to the strength of the spell that had been uttered. All of those who were in the castle had either stumbled or fallen to the ground and most of the books in the library had dropped from the highest shelves. The kitchen where a few witches were seated had been shook so badly that the vessels had all clanked and dropped to the floor. The meditation chamber was disturbed. In the chambers of the witches all tables and chairs and fallen. In the potions chamber, where Iris and Eridanus were, a few bottles of potions had cracked and Iris had also stumbled and descended to the floor.

Lilith's scream continued to vibrate the walls as the spell started to burn her inside. Everyone in the castle shut their ears and cringed at the horrible and frightening sound. Eridanus grabbed Iris by the arm and pulled her up to standing. She struggled to stand straight and held his shoulder to gain her composure. Her eyes were squeezed shut at the sound of the scream that ran shrill into her ears. Eridanus held Iris and the pair walked out of the potions chamber to find out what it was that had such an effect. Along with the two of them, all others including Erasmus and Lea followed outside at the source of the sound.

Lilith was now holding Nicholas by his neck, high in the air just the way she had done with Azrael in the Dark Falls. Her nails pierced his throat and his eyes rolled upwards as pain shot up through his spine. His powers were gone. They had vanished entirely and there was no way he could gain them back since his mind had gone numb. His body was paralyzed as Lilith slammed his back to the bark of a tree forcefully. She then dragged his body down to the ground. The bark scraped Nicholas's skin and he cringed in pain, ready to scream for help but no sound came out of his mouth. He struggled to breathe but his lungs had constricted.

Lilith grinned maliciously at the one that had called her from her peaceful afterlife, which seemed to have been lost from her mind. Yet she was aware that she did not belong in this world. Her life on earth was over and the *Goddess of Earth* would never let her stay there for long if the spells were chanted again. She had to finish her task as soon as she could. Once she had the blood of her caller, she would descend back to where she had come from. But if there was no one who could send her spirit back, she would forever wander around in search of blood of all those who were related to the one that summoned her. So Lilith raised her other arm to bury her nails into his flesh when all the members of coven reached the graveyard. Amara and Azrael had joined as well.

"Repeat what I'm saying," ordered Amara and all of them began to recite the chant that she had uttered before.

The strength of the spell was now high since everyone had gathered for the same. It sent Lilith into frenzy. She now sought blood as well as revenge from all of them. The spell was burning her on the inside as the coven surrounded her and Nicholas. Lilith wanted to scream again but her strength began to subside slowly. She lowered her hand to plunge her sharp nails into Nicholas's flesh when someone caught her wrist in a tight grip. Azrael stood behind her, chanting the spell while pushing her hand away from Nicholas and Amara tried her best to release Nicholas's neck from Lilith's grasp.

By some means, Lilith gathered her strength to scream out loud once again. It shook the ground and everyone dropped down. Even though it was not as powerful, the scream was strong enough to paralyze a few of them. Amara had been pushed away from Nicholas, and Azrael lost his grip on Lilith's wrist. Immediately she plunged her fingers into Nicholas's chest. His eyes went still and his breath caught as her nails descended down to his abdomen, tearing into his flesh. Before the others could begin to chant the spell again or save Nicholas, she let go of his neck and tore his body into two parts using all her strength.

There was complete silence. Everyone watched the scene unfold before them without moving an inch. Iris was blank. Amara let out a tired sigh and her shoulders drooped as she witnessed the sight. Azrael squeezed his eyes shut, cringing and Erasmus stared at his best friend's body with eyes wide, unblinking and void of all senses as realization struck him like a bolt of lightning.

Nicholas was dead.

CHAPTER TWENTY-FOUR

∞∞∞∞∞

LIBERATION OF SOULS

∞∞∞∞∞

T he sound of flute playing softly echoed in everyone's ears. As Lilith quenched her thirst through Nicholas's blood, there was absolute silence around apart from the sound of the flute that Sienna was playing. The music seemed to have a slow yet harsh effect on the spirit of Lilith. She began to tremble. Sienna stood at the far corner next to the castle gates, away from the rest of them. The sound that was soothing to everyone else's ears was poison to Lilith's. The flute had been enchanted with spells had the power to drive away all kinds of evil spirits. There was a distinct way of playing the instrument as it was used for many other purposes. To drive away evil spirits, a melodious but intimidating tune was used, which could infuriate the spirit and push it far away from vicinity.

Sienna was skilled in the same. She had the ability to play the flute in such a manner that it could instantly get rid of every evil thing around her. All bad vibrations, even the air would become pure creating a stilling and unadulterated aura everywhere. Lilith's spirit was starting to burn on the inside. She stood up, forced to leave the graveyard and go somewhere far away to a place she knew not. Sienna played the flute effortlessly and Lilith began to tremble even more.

The others were still in their positions. The aftershock of what had happened in front of them had not left their minds and the sound of the flute made their thoughts stall in one place rendering them unable to travel anywhere else.

As the music began to increase its swiftness, Lilith's feet started moving backwards. On one hand she had her desire unfulfilled, her thirst unquenched, and on the other there was a burning sensation that was torturing her spirit more than it had when Amara was chanting the spell. Sienna began to move forward and the sound, greater than before, was beginning to torture Lilith. Her head tilted upwards as she resisted the urge to run away from there and quench her thirst. Her trembling body moved backwards on its own accord. Sienna took another step forward. Then Lilith began to sprint away. Her feet carried her to the gate of the graveyard so as to set herself free from the agony. Her weakness made it difficult for her to even scream.

Lilith stumbled and fell as the sound of the flute refused to leave her ears. Struggling on her feet, she stood up and then ran out of the graveyard, dragging her feet as fast as she could, and leaving the area of the castle to go somewhere far where she could not hear the sound. When she was away from the terrifying music, her mind began to process what had happened and she fell to the ground in the woods. After that, the only thing that occupied her mind was revenge. Now she did not seek the blood of the one that had summoned her; she sought the blood of the coven of Conjurers who had driven her out of there. She sought murder.

The moment that Sienna's flute stopped playing, the long silence was broken by an ear splitting shriek. Iris was on the ground, tears running furiously down her eyes as she screamed in sorrow. Reality hit her straight in the chest and it felt as though her lungs had constricted rendering her breathless. She opened her mouth to say something, call out Nicholas's name but nothing other than her cries was heard. The moment that they had witnessed the killing of their Lord's nephew, a few witches had fainted at the sight. Others were struggling not to express their sorrow. Their minds were numb after watching everything. Sienna stood behind the crowd unable to see Nicholas's body. Nobody knew her sorrow apart from Erasmus, who was mind numbingly cold at that point of time. His best friend's body was right in front of him, ripped apart.

Every memory that he had ever shared with Nicholas, every day that they had spent in learning witchcraft, the hundred years that they had been friends; it all flashed before his eyes at once. But he made no sound, he made no movement. The silence was long gone as the others began to sob along with the terrible screams that Iris produced. She had seen Death but not of someone close. Never in her wildest dreams had she thought that she would witness the horrific Death of her mentor and friend. Nicholas had been her guide in the world of Conjurers. He had taught her so many things. He had been her trainer, her mentor, someone she could rely on apart from Erasmus. He had helped her in getting rid of the thoughts of her human life. He had made her a better person, a better witch.

If he had not been there when she had to get trained for Amara's task, she would never have been able to do it. She owed him her life. He gave her strength and he gave her hope. To watch his body get torn into two pieces right in front of her eyes was traumatic. She failed to realize how she fell to the ground, when Leandra ran towards her and pulled her into a hug, and she failed to realize when Eridanus took her back into the castle after he had seen and heard enough of her cries.

Amara watched as Eridanus pulled Iris away from the view. Had she not felt a ticklish sensation on her cheek, she would not have realized that a tear had stealthily slipped out of her eye. She looked at Nicholas's body, his eyes that lay open, rolled upwards; his hands that were limp on his sides up to his shredded waist. The other part of his body that contained just his legs lay at a distance. Amara looked at it and another tear escaped until she was biting her lip to stop them. *How many years have passed since I've cried?* There was such pain inside of her and yet she had managed to control her emotions. But now as she sat there with her shoulders drooped, eyes moist and stuck on the body of the man who had helped her get trained along with the Lord, all the pain that she had hidden inside of her in the hundred years came crashing down.

She could no longer contain them. It felt as though her heart was about to burst of all the pain that she had forced inside of her. Her chest felt heavy, throat tightened and she struggled not to let out a scream similar to that of Iris's. Although she was now in the castle, Iris's cries echoed inside Amara's ears clearly enough to break her soul inside. She then glanced at Azrael who sat opposite to her with his right arm leaning on a grave. His head hung low and eyes stared unblinkingly down at the ground. Amara blinked and looked away. Ambrosius stepped forward, clearing his throat and proceeded towards Nicholas's body. He glanced at Fabian who stood at a side. He immediately followed Ambrosius and they picked up both parts of Nicholas's body.

Fabian cringed at the sight, composing himself back to normal as he carried the body towards Ambrosius.

"We have to go to the sacrificial chamber," he said to Fabian, who nodded in agreement.

They then carried both parts of his body back into the castle and in the sacrificial chamber. The others followed suit. When a witch or sorcerer was murdered in such a brutal way, it was a custom for everyone in the coven to be present in the sacrificial chamber where they would sacrifice the body of the victim to Isiah: the God of salvation. Only then would the soul be set free. For someone who had been murdered so mercilessly, the soul would reside on earth for years, passing through four stages of afterlife before it was free to travel to the portal of independence from the world.

The first stage was of the *wanderer*: one where the soul would search for another wandering soul that had been killed similarly. The second was of *emulation:* one where after finding the other wanderer, the two souls would together proceed to the third stage of *helper:* one where the souls would provide help to a seeker (a stranded, helpless witch or sorcerer in dire need of direction). When that stage was covered by both the souls, they would then reach the fourth and last stage of *salvation:* one where the souls would go on separate ways to find their own doors of the portal that would free their souls for eternity.

It took years to complete the first stage of afterlife. The journey was never an easy one. That was one of the reasons there were so many lost souls in the woods behind the castle. They were all looking for their pair of wanderer that would lead them to the second stage. Only some of them would find the other wanderer, others would remain lost in the world. For Nicholas, it would be a hard task. A Death like that of Nicholas's made it harder for his soul to achieve salvation. As all of them approached the sacrificial chamber inside the castle, silence followed suit. Their heads hung low, void of any sound apart from their feet on the concrete floor.

Amara and Azrael walked together behind everyone else. No one uttered a word. Amara felt as though she had failed. She had failed in saving the one that had helped her become what she was. She had failed in saving his life after he had helped her achieve one for herself. The pain that she felt in her chest was that of her disdain upon not being able to fight back. She no longer considered herself to be as powerful as everyone thought she was. She no longer thought that she was strong enough to do anything else, if she was unable to battle one evil spirit to save her mentor. Instead, she was now walking to the chamber where his soul was to be set free of his body.

Although Azrael had not been acquainted with Nicholas as much, there had been times when he had helped him during his time of training. Whenever Lord Lucifer had other important tasks to take care of, Nicholas would substitute. He was the one that had taught Azrael the art of creating an aura around him. Azrael had then learnt to create one of Death. Every witch and sorcerer had an aura that travelled with them everywhere they went; that aura was a guarding shield. It portrayed their true nature. Azrael's was that of Death, since he had almost been greeted by the same when he was a child. And now, seeing the Death of someone who had been there at times for him, he felt lost.

Iris and Eridanus were in the latter's chamber. He handed Iris a cup of the *Fire and Ice* potion to bring her back from her semi-conscious state. Iris had now stopped crying, there were dried tears that stuck to her skin. Her eyes were bloodshot, throat was dry and as she drank the potion, her senses began to return slowly. Eridanus stood near the window, looking out at the woods behind that had turned darker than they had ever been. It seemed as though the trees and shrubs were grieving for the Death of Nicholas, as though they felt what the others were feeling. Eridanus blinked and turned to look at Iris, who was seated on a chair, her knees drawn up to her chest. She was staring at the foot of the chair without blinking. Eridanus received a message from Fabian to summon at the sacrificial chamber.

"Iris?" He whispered, crouching below in front of her on the floor and tilting his head to look at her.

Iris glanced up at him, her vacant face sent waves of pain into his eyes. The sorrow that she felt was evident even though she was not showing it anymore.

"We've been called to the sacrificial chamber. Will you be able to come?" He said to her, raising his eyebrows in concern.

Iris stayed silent, watching him for a while and then nodded. He took the cup from her hands and placed it on a table nearby before they proceeded to go to the said chamber. Upon reaching, they heard the chants coming from Ambrosius who was sat on the floor. Iris had been to the sacrificial chamber for the first time. The chamber was a round one, similar to the great hall. It was dark apart from the few torches of fire that rested on the walls. In the middle, there was a huge circle that surrounded a star. Candles rested on each point of intersection, and one right in the middle of the star. Nicholas's body lay there before Ambrosius, who was chanting the sacrificial hymns to call for the god Isiah.

"Behold the power, the valour, the strength, the calmness. Descend the Lord of salvation, of doom, of light of that of the moon. We bow down to thee, great Lord, to set the soul free. We pray for salvation, we pray for redemption. Descend the Lord of deliverance, of liberation. Behold the power. Behold the valour. Behold the spirit. . ."

Ambrosius continued to chant the hymns until the light from the torches went out, plunging the chamber into complete darkness. Moments later, a silver gleam appeared right behind the star. It illuminated the chamber and blinded each and everyone there. The light then turned into the shape of a sword that descended right into Nicholas's body. A second later, it vanished and the chamber went completely black once again. Then the torches lit up by themselves. Nicholas's body that had been split into two was now there on the floor, clean of all the wounds and blood with the two parts joined. His face looked serene and pale white. There was a sudden chill inside the chamber that created a cold atmosphere.

Not a single drop of blood rested on Nicholas's body. That was when they all realized that his soul had left his body. What remained was just flesh and bones that had no spirit inside. Ambrosius stood up and conjured a coffin. With the help of Fabian, he lifted Nicholas's body that seemed extremely heavy. They did not wish to levitate his body. He deserved a proper burying. When the body was placed in the coffin, Ambrosius and Fabian carried it outside along with Erasmus and other sorcerers that helped. When they reached the graveyard, Azrael dug into the soil and in moments, created a space for the coffin to fit. Ambrosius and Fabian placed the coffin into the pit before covering it with the mud again.

They all muttered their respective words in his memory to themselves before retreating into the castle. Eridanus was at Iris's side the whole time to make sure nothing happened to her. Erasmus stood with his eyes staring at the grave that had consumed his best friend's body so effortlessly. Sienna was right beside him, tears dropping down her eyes fluently as she made no movement. When everyone else was gone, Erasmus and Sienna sat on the ground beside the grave. She placed her forehead on the stone, now shaking with her sobs echoing around.

Erasmus struggled not to let his tears fall, but as he began to inhale the air that no longer had Nicholas in it, his cries joined that of Sienna's.

"He never belonged to me, did he?" asked Sienna hoarsely, raising her head from the stone to look at Erasmus. He turned his head towards her.

"As merry and happy he was with his life, he never had a place for love," he replied.

"I wish he had loved me the way I loved him," she said, biting her lip.

"He never had faith in love. His mother left to go with the murderer of his father. That day on, he refused to believe in love. He always told me, that if something as pure as a mother's love is foul enough to make her abandon her own child, then there is no such thing as true love. He masked his pain with the cheerfulness. But I know how much he suffered. I saw him suffer through my own eyes."

The memories of a fifteen-year-old Nicholas wailing for his mother to return to him haunted Erasmus a lot of times. Nicholas's father was killed by a witch-hunter whom his mother had been in love with. After his father's Death, Nicholas's mother left with the witch-hunter and handed over Nicholas's responsibility to Lord Lucifer. He taught Nicholas to mask emotions. Then he became the happiest sorcerer the coven had ever come across. Nicholas learned to cover his emotions with his never ending smile. That way, no one apart from Erasmus could ever know how broken he really was inside. When he met Sienna, he was no more than ninety-years-old. She was a new witch that had joined the coven. He was a charmer, but he never so much as even touched a witch. Yet most of them tended to fall for him. The one that got caught in his charm even after resisting a lot was Sienna.

She wished to be with him but each time she tried, he refused. To get some help, she would ask Erasmus as to why Nicholas avoided being someone's mate. The only answer she ever got was '*It's the way he chooses to be*'. Even after Sienna and Nicholas became good friends, she could never even get close to why he avoided love despite of being so gleeful and charming. For someone who had witches falling at his feet, *he* never fell for one.

"He did love you. He just wasn't ready to accept it," said Erasmus, after a while of silence.

Sienna said nothing. Her mind was busy thinking of all the time that she had spent with Nicholas. Each and every memory of his was stuck inside her head. The way he teased her for being so naïve, how he listened to her cribbing about the other witches that were so much better than her, the way he politely told her to keep away from him, for he could never love her back; everything stabbed Sienna inside. She felt lonely without him. She felt weak. His memories were all she now had to survive with; and the one memory that would never leave her was of him teaching her the art of playing the flute.

CHAPTER TWENTY-FIVE

∞∞∞∞

MOMENTS OF REMORSE

∞∞∞∞

*I*t was midnight when she woke up. There was a beautiful
stream beside her; its waves glistened in the moonlight. Her
eyes opened to find the night sky shining above her and a distant
sense of peace filled her inside. She pushed her body up so she was
sitting. There was a damp paste across her forehead and the wound
stung as she sat up. She blinked a few times to get rid of her blurry
surroundings. When she was sure that she could see properly, she
started to stand up.

"Need any help?" a voice called and Amara turned her head
in the direction softly so as not to hurt her head again. It stung
as it is.

A man stood before her; someone that she failed to recognize.
He had striking blue eyes and a handsome face. He stood tall and
his face held a sort of calmness that Amara found to be safe. She
cleared her throat to find her voice and began to stand up again
when the man took a few steps towards her and gave her a hand
to help her up. She flinched upon touching his hand, her mind
going back to the tormenting touch of Leo and she took a hasty,
stumbling step behind, only to fall back on the stone table. The
man blinked once and gave her a warm smile, as a silent assurance

that it was safe. He extended his arm again and this time she grabbed it to pull herself up to standing, still a bit weak.

"I'm Nicholas," *he said to her as she struggled to stand properly. It seemed as though years had passed that she had stood on her feet. Amara felt tired even after having been asleep for possibly a long time.*

"I-" *she started to ask him something when her mind was hit with the memory of Leo and what he had done to her.*

She stumbled at her feet and then another vision flashed across her eyes, one that had her being rescued by someone. After that, she remembered nothing. How long it had been, what had happened to Leo, she knew not. Nicholas steadied an arm around her waist to keep her in place.

"Do you want to sit down?" *He asked and Amara shook her head timidly, but sat down anyway because Nicholas pushed her onto the stone table again. Amara could not understand where she was.*

"What has happened? Where am I?" *she asked in a haze.*

"Are you aware that you are a witch?" *Nicholas questioned and Amara nodded her head in response.*

He was now standing before her as she sat on the stone table with her hands clutching the edges.

"My uncle, Lord Lucifer, rescued you. He is a well-known and powerful sorcerer. We're in the mountains of Carvelli. We'll be going to Acanthus someday. That is where we reside," *he told her.*

"I... what happened to him?" *she asked, hoping he would understand that she was talking about Leo.*

She did not wish to speak his name.

"The one that captured you?" *He replied with his eyebrows raised. Amara nodded.*

"He's not any of our concern now, Amara. You're safe with us. Nothing can harm you," *he said to her and she opened her mouth to ask him more about Leo when he shook his head and* she understood that it was best that she not speak anything more about him.

"What am I supposed to do now?" She managed to ask.

"You will be trained in witchcraft. We will enhance all the skills that you were born with. Your mind will be more powerful than that of humans, much more powerful. You will be extremely strong than what you are now. You will learn to handle elements, battle witch-hunters and a lot of other powers that you wouldn't have imagined as a mortal," he answered, sitting beside her on the mossy grass atop the stone table.

"Am I capable of doing all of that?" she asked, unsure of herself.

"More than capable. You don't know your strengths yet," he told her with a reassuring smile.

"Will I ever know what happened to-"

Nicholas shook his head.

"No, Amara. That is past now. You won't think about it anymore. You're reborn as a witch. You've left the mortal world. No memory of that world should stay with you," he said to her and she blinked, looking down.

There were so many questions that she wanted to ask but she knew that there would be no answer.

"Lord Lucifer will be here soon and your training will begin. You may get some sleep until tomorrow morning," Nicholas said and stood up from beside her.

"I don't want to sleep anymore," she replied.

"Then you're free to take a walk around, if you wish. It's safe here and we won't let any harm come to you," he said and took a few steps back before disappearing.

Despite the surroundings that were dark and dead calm, Amara did not feel even a fraction of scare. She felt peaceful. This was a well-deserved peace after all the torture that she had gone through when in the dungeons with Leo. She shut her eyes for a *long moment and let out a deep breath before standing up. With her legs now supporting her fragile frame, Amara began to take a few steps forward and towards the stream. She stood on the wet marsh, the coldness seeping in through her toes and slowly touching every part of her body. Placing her right arm on her left shoulder, she pulled off the torn gown that she was wearing, one that Leo had so mercilessly ripped off her body like a beast.*

Amara pealed the clothes from her body in a hurry, not wanting to be in them anymore. If she were to leave everything behind, it had to begin with each and every speck of those memories. She then lifted a foot and immersed it into the cool water before her. She took slow steps inside, engulfing the waves into her skin as the water entered the very brink of her soul and she dipped her head inside, reaching the deeper parts. With her eyes closed, she washed off every touch, every feel of Leo's skin on her body; her face, her hair, her limbs. He had only touched her body, not her soul. Her soul was pure, it was clean, serene.

She felt the old memories leaving her physical being. Everything began to vanish out of her. Her eyes opened and she felt a sense of relief and peace as she absorbed her purified self. When she was sure about leaving the water, Amara turned around and walked out onto the wet grass, only to find a new set of fabrics set on the side atop the dry area. Amara held the long black gown in her hands, the colour was entirely different from what she usually wore. Her mother always asked her to wear those creamy white gowns that enhanced her features. She never wore black. Lifting the fabric in her hands, she slid it over her body.

It fit her properly, covering her arms in the long sleeves and cascaded down through her feet behind her in soft waves. Amara grazed her clean fingers through her wet hair and shook the tangles. She then left her tresses hanging down her back instead of braiding them as she always did. Her mother never liked her hair let down. Amara then pushed her feet into the boots that lay before her on the grass. She had never worn boots. Her mother always told her that they were for men. They hugged her legs up to her knees and she began to walk ahead with a sense of pride as she left every memory behind and started to walk around the valleys of the mountains of Carvelli.

The wind gushed around her, making the atmosphere colder and colder. But Amara did not feel the chilly sensation that she would have otherwise felt. Instead, it felt as though she was finally home. She was where she was supposed to be. A familiar sense of acceptance entered inside her, as though this new world was taking her in the way she was, as though it was going to make her strong to face every other battle, as though she was going to become new.

Amara then realized that this was where she truly belonged.

* * *

Iris stared at the rippling water in front of her. The chilly air made her embrace herself as she stood in the forest, watching the lake before her. The sunlight shone upon the water, the early morning hue surrounding her as the sun started to rise above the horizon. December had arrived and she had barely noticed it. The witch calendar certainly did not give exact dates and months of the normal human calendar. It worked according to the movements of the sun and the moon. It was quite medieval in Iris's opinion. She wondered how the Conjurers judged their birthdays. Nicholas had once told her that Conjurers aged one year where humans aged a hundred. The *Elixir of Immortality* played a part in that. The human calendar was an entirely different story. However, it didn't really matter to her. What mattered was that it had been about a month after Nicholas's Death and nothing had changed.

Upon hearing of his nephew's murder, Lord Lucifer had returned immediately. He had spent three nights locked inside his chamber, not meeting anyone and not speaking a single word. The castle was destroyed; mentally and emotionally. Iris could see the walls losing their colour, the air going slow and the trees in the forest muttering silent cries as if mourning for the Death of a very beloved companion. The one that was struck the most was Lord Lucifer and after him, Amara. The former had returned after Nicholas had been buried. He had then sat next to Nicholas's grave and expressed his silent sorrow by hanging his head low.

Lord Lucifer blamed himself. It was on his orders that Nicholas had summoned the spirit of Lilith so that she – being the one whose blood rested in the locket – could help Amara and Azrael in suggesting ways of protection; but since the process had gone wrong, it had ended in his nephew's Death. Lord Lucifer could not stop blaming himself. If not for him, Nicholas would have been alive, hale and hearty, making the castle lively again. He had lost his only family. Nicholas was gone, and it was as though he took away all the limited happiness and the joy that was around because of him. It was all gone.

For three nights, Lord Lucifer had not left his chamber. He spent hours in conjuring up blazing Fire to punish himself for killing his nephew, but to his utter sorrow, nothing worked. His body was immune to all kinds of flames due to the countless number of times that he had practiced shielding his being. That shield now had the power to work all by itself and Lord Lucifer had no control over it. Later when he thought that the castle needed to be protected and taken care of due to the fact that Lord Mikhail could strike any second, Lord Lucifer had left his chamber to resume his journey of including more Conjurers in his coven. He had decided that they had no time to waste and he could not afford to lose any more people after having lost Nicholas.

After instructing Amara about it, Lord Lucifer had left. Even a month later, Amara had kept herself aloof. Iris had recovered with help of Eridanus but Amara had failed to. Eridanus had proved to be a good friend to Iris even though he was still as annoying as he could be. But his will to try his best to make Iris laugh or even smile a little made her build a sort of friendship with him. Erasmus was always away. He had started to travel and complete the quests that Nicholas had taken in hand and left incomplete. Sienna spent her time playing the flute and trying to distract herself. But each time she looked around, she would spot a figure at a distance, as though watching her and then disappearing whenever she took a single step forward.

The rest of the coven had learnt to adapt to the now dull environment, and had become a bit normal, yet a sense of loss lingered inside of them. No one had realized what Nicholas actually meant to all of them without being personally related to any. He had taken away something close to their hearts: happiness, which was in the castle because of him and no one seemed to notice it before. Azrael had made himself busy in spending all his time reading books in the library and mulling over ways to protect the prophecy. Amara was helping him do the same but most of her time was spent in her own chamber. Leandra helped Eridanus in bringing Iris back to normal and the two of them together kept her company nearly all the time. She was rarely left alone.

Whenever she was alone, Iris would try her best to talk to Amara. Even though she was always around, Iris missed her. It had been a long time that she had properly talked to Amara and that made her feel gloomier than having lost Nicholas. She did not want to lose Amara as well even though that would be in a different way. Once, after two weeks of Nicholas being gone, Iris had ventured around the castle aimlessly when

Eridanus was in the mediation chamber and Lea was asleep. She had found herself on Amara's doorstep. When she raised her hand to knock, she heard the faint sound of a cry.

To Iris's utter shock, Amara was inside her chamber, crying. Nobody knew about it, because whenever Amara was locked inside her chamber, no one dared to approach her; that was apart from Iris. She had immediately wanted to go inside but Iris stopped herself and retraced her steps. In the one year that she had been there, she had seen Amara scream in agony and smile in content; but never had she witnessed her sobs. And it stabbed her in the heart, knowing that the Death of someone who wasn't close to her, had made her break down so easily.

That moment on, Iris had understood that all the pain that Amara had pushed inside her in the hundred years had suddenly started to pour out uncontrollably after she had witnessed Nicholas's Death. It did not matter that he wasn't close to her. Just the fact that his Death made all her emotions rush out of her furiously was what worried Iris. Amara had started to lose control over herself. The control that she had mastered by a lot of hard work, she was starting to lose it. And Iris wasn't the only one who felt that.

Amara was internally destroyed by Nicholas's Death. For weeks she had been unable to control her tears that fell unconsciously down her eyes. Whenever she tried to help Azrael in thinking of ways to protect Lady Calypsa and the prophecy, she would end up breaking down and running back to her chamber. It was like a plague had struck her and was now refusing to go away. She felt every bit of pain that she had felt when she was in the dungeons getting tortured by Leo. She felt the loss of her soul, she felt the pain constrict her chest, she felt her head break into tiny pieces, she felt the agony that had struck her when her spiritual training had begun almost a century ago, and she felt all the feelings, all the emotions and all the pain that she had stored inside her for ages.

It all came back like rocks falling on top of her. And it hurt a lot. There was nothing that she thought would take the pain away. She was confused as to why she had become this vulnerable and weak upon Nicholas's Death. She knew that she wasn't as weak, yet it made her feel so small that she could not decipher it. Her powers that had started to weaken when she had returned from the trip to the Sea of Cypress had still not come back to her. She tried to meditate, but it did no good. She was always interrupted by the sudden pain that went through her each time she tried to distract herself.

She felt tired all the time. She felt exhausted and lost. Maybe it was because she felt inferior upon being unable to save a fellow apprentice from an evil spirit. What was the use of so many struggles to gain power? What was the result of the praises that they sung of her bravery and strength? Was it all a lie? Was it all worthless? The questions that ran through her mind refused to leave and she thought that maybe that was why she had lost the will to get up and fight again. On Lord Lucifer's orders she had begun to manage the castle again, but Azrael helped her in the same and she barely had any work to do. He had taken everything in his hands.

He would make all Conjurers practice their powers and he would give them proper nourishment so they were strong and he would also spend time in thinking of the prophecy and the treasures. Amara, yet again felt worthless, for she was unable to do a single thing. Azrael offered to help her, but she declined every time. Known for being such a strong witch, her powers were so far gone that she had absolutely no recollection of what had happened to her. She began to hate herself and she began to loathe herself. A month had passed after Nicholas's Death, and Amara was in her chamber, wiping the remnants of tears from her cheeks. Shutting her eyes in frustration, she stood up barged out of the chamber to go to the forest. She had had enough.

She could not handle the pain anymore. It felt as though she was back to the human that she had been when the Lord had rescued her, as though her training was starting yet again. As she proceeded to the forest, she spotted Iris standing there with her left side leaning onto the bark of a tree, the side of her head resting on the same. Amara took a few hasty steps ahead. How long had it been since she had spoken to Iris? After having made her gone through so much by letting her invade minds and find out things of her past, Amara felt as though she had been a horrible person by abandoning her. *Why? How?*

"Iris?" she called out upon reaching a few feet away from her.

Iris turned around. Amara observed how grown the sixteen-year-old looked. Maybe she was now seventeen; a year had passed and Amara had failed to notice. Wearing a red coloured long sleeved gown, Iris had no hint of childishness on her face anymore. She looked mature, brave and someone identical to what Amara had been when she had learnt witchcraft. Her blonde hair was longer now, reaching up to her waist in soft curls. Her eyes were paler than they had been before and her face was dull yet beautiful. Amara noticed how she resembled the old her. And suddenly all the memories of how she had been trained and how she turned into what she was came flooding back to her.

* * *

Training was difficult. Lord Lucifer wasn't one to take no for an answer and Amara was the perfect student. She always seemed eager to work. Whether it was rigorous rounds of physical training or the time inducing meditations, she took it all willingly. Lord Lucifer was impressed, and he knew that she was strong enough to deal with all. It did not come as a surprise to him when she wholeheartedly accepted all the tasks that she was given. Nicholas, however, was a bit surprised. He had never seen a witch this eager to learn every difficult skill put forth. It was a challenge and Amara seemed to love those.

After everything that she had been through, her zeal to act upon all the tasks willingly was something he had never seen in a witch. However, he had not come across a witch who had been through something so tormenting. Amara was different, given the circumstances she had emerged from. She was determined to achieve something; something that would lead her to greater heights. She would never look back. Nicholas could see it in her eyes. Amara was going to be stronger than many, better than every other witch of their age, and she was going to surpass all expectations. She was exactly what Lord Lucifer needed.

It began with physical training. The night after she had let go of her past and decided to adapt this new life, Amara had surfaced stronger than ever. Lord Lucifer had made sure that she wasn't weak before they began training, but he needed no confirmation. Amara had asked him to start right away. She did not believe in wasting time. Lord Lucifer wanted her to learn meditation skills before anything else but Amara was adamant. She wanted the physical training prior to others. She insisted that it would only make her concentrate on meditation better.

Lord Lucifer did not mind. He began with teaching her the art of fighting without weapons. He taught her to dodge her enemies, disappear into thin air, strike a blow out of nowhere and be merciless while killing. She was unsure of how she would be able to kill mercilessly. It reminded her of how she was shown no mercy.

"If they don't value the virtue of mercy, you don't either. Be ruthless, be vile, be inconsiderate when facing enemies.

They are a threat to your existence, and nothing is more important than yours and your coven's existence," *Lord Lucifer had told her.*

It took time for her to get that fact into her mind entirely. At times it was hard. Sometimes she would have nightmares that reminded her of her past. She was scared of falling asleep. But sleep was necessary. It only gave her enough strength to wake up the next morning and fight braver. Lord Lucifer's words would help her a lot. He pushed her to the point that she would be exhausted. Amara did not like being exhausted.

"Don't let your memories be your weakness. Make them your strength; make them the force that motivates you. They're your enemy, disable them, disarm them; kill them. But never be scared of them. For if you are ever scared of your enemies, you will fail," *he would say.*

"But never underestimate your enemy. If you are strong, they are struggling to get stronger. Don't let them achieve that," *he said to her one day when she had woken up at sunrise with a scream.*

She had had a nightmare. Amara would spend nights crying at times when she remembered how Leo had tormented her. How he had killed her mother and father, how he had killed Arion. Oh how she missed her little brother. She missed the way he would create nuisance, the way he would spoil all her knitting work and the way mother scolded her, how she would get angry with him for being such a spoilt brat and how then she would end up kissing his cheeks. Her little brother was gone. Leo had ended her all in moments.

She never let her Lord find out that she would sometimes become weak and succumb to those memories, that she would let her guard down at times when she was unable to control it. Unknown to her, Lord Lucifer would watch her from a distance and a stab of guilt would run through him knowing that it had been his own son that had given his apprentice such pain. He could see that Amara would put up a mask the next morning when the training commenced.

Sometimes she wished she would never sleep and train all night as well. She did not care about getting rest. She wanted to get rid of those nightmares. But Lord Lucifer had taught her to be brave. He had taught her to face her fears.

"Fear is a door that shuts all your passages to victory. Be mindful of your enemies' strength, but never be fearful of them. Dread makes you weak. You can never be weak," *he said to her once when she was unsuccessful at disappearing from her opponent's sight.*

Nicholas would act as an enemy most of the time. There were safe ways to fight that ensured no major harm occurred. Amara wasn't trained enough to fight enemies firsthand. She still had a lot to learn. Lord Lucifer had to give Amara motivating words, he had to push her forward at times when she felt her strength drain and her mind giving way. She feared that she would not be able to fulfill her Lord's expectations. He was kind yet stubborn, and a strong force that helped her survive and Amara felt indebted to him. She saw Azar in him sometimes. When he would effortlessly handle elements, when he would show her how easy it was to achieve elemental powers once trained. She felt closer to her father.

Lord Lucifer managed to fill the void in Amara's life. But a nagging sensation of not knowing how Leo died, whether he really died or was still out there somewhere, torturing another innocent, never left Amara's mind. She wanted so many times to ask Lord Lucifer about it but she knew that topic was not to be discussed. She had to leave everything behind but how much ever hard she tried, Amara could not get those horrific nightmares out of her mind. She spent sleepless nights wandering around the valleys of the mountains that they would train in. They travelled at times, to far off places and rivers and seas. They would train her in different locations with the different weather conditions. Amara enjoyed the thrill of teleporting with her Lord. He had taught her a few beginning ways of teleportation.

It was quite interesting. At times she would feel like laughing, but nothing seemed to surface. She wanted to smile, she wanted to be happy but something always held her back. Whenever she thought about happy memories, she thought of Leo. He was the happy memory of her life since the time she was old enough to understand what happiness truly meant. Her memories involved Leo all the time. He was in her good ones, he was in her bad ones and he was the worst one. Hard as she tried to forget him, she could not. She failed every time.

And it had only been a year.

They were yet to go to Acanthus. Amara was told that Lord Lucifer had a coven there. There were many lands of Conjurers, but Acanthus was the one that held the most skilled and brilliant ones. Lord Lucifer would often go to visit for a few days and until then Nicholas would train her. Nicholas was a friendly sorcerer and Amara felt herself warming up towards him. But she could never pluck up the courage to get closer to any male henceforth. She was frightened of them. Her Lord had told her to lose fears. There was no place for fears within the world of witchcraft.

But this fear did not seem to leave her. She could get rid of every other frightening memory, but not one that involved her being close to a promising male. There was no part of her that needed that kind of a bond again. She would consider being friends, but even that much of closeness scared her.

Amara was only capable of being as close as she was to her Lord, because he reminded her of her father. She preferred staying away from the others. Being close to sorcerers was not her concern. Her concern was her existence as a witch. She wanted to become what her Lord expected her to. He wished for her to reach heights that no other witch ever had. He wished for the people to sing praises of her. He wished for her to be brilliant, fearless and gallant. He wished for her to be a warrior.

And Amara was going to be that. For her, Lord Lucifer's wishes were her father's wishes. They were a constant reminder of Azar. He was a constant reminder of her father. That was the only memory that she wanted to keep with her. All others were painful and brought her sorrow. But all others did not leave her either. They had a grip on her that she tried to loosen every time she was hit with them, but all was in vain.

She would still try, however hard it was, she had pledged to try her best.

~ ~ ~

"Elements are a witch's greatest power," *Nicholas was saying to her.* "They are what make our being. Earth is the base of all life inside of us. Fire is the unseen force that drives us forward. Air is what we survive on. Water is the force that helps create balance with the Fire, and Spirit is what you are. It is your identity. A witch that can handle all elements is a conqueror. There has never been a witch who has been able to tackle each and every element; nor has there been any sorcerer capable enough. The most we can handle is three. Managing at least two elements is the most important skill of a witch. Once you master the art, you are capable of anything and everything; good or bad. It is up to you to choose the right one." *It had been ten years after her physical training.*

It had finally come to an end and she was given the Elixir of Immortality *before her spiritual training as a witch began. She was given books to read while her physical training was going on. She had read so many things about witchcraft and witches in general, that Amara now had a proper idea of how this world worked. She was strong; stronger than she had ever been.*

Her physical training had morphed her into something entirely different from what she was, ten years ago in the mortal world.

Her arms were stronger, legs were slender, eyes sharper and mind on high alert. She could run faster than a horse, dodge dangers within the blink of an eye, appear out of nowhere to strike her enemy, and she could kill effortlessly. She was yet to master the art of being merciless. But she was quite sure that she would be able to do it once her elemental powers were in practice and she had learned to control her mind. It was going to be difficult, of course, but along with her physical training, Lord Lucifer had begun to teach her the meditation skills simultaneously. It was helpful in concentration during combat.

She had learned archery, sword-fighting, poisoning, and killing with a single touch on a nerve. It wasn't as difficult as she had imagined it would be. She had only read about it and heard about it from her Lord. But she was yet to do it in reality. Amara's first kill was a vile witch-hunter who had come to attack Nicholas. Purposefully, the sorcerer had handed the responsibility of fighting the hunter to Amara. She had wasted no time in battling him and then ending his life by twisting his neck. The end result was a flawless kill. Lord Lucifer and Nicholas were impressed. No witch had been able to do that in the first attempt.

Amara was already on her way to greatness.

Now that she was learning the elemental powers and Lord Lucifer had gone to train another one of his apprentices, Amara was being trained by Nicholas. He had given the book of elements to Amara so she could read it a few months prior to the actual training. She had read on it extensively and could not wait to learn the art of handling elements.

"I will teach you to handle all the elements. In the end you have to choose two of them that you wish to master. They will depict who you are," he said to her and Amara nodded. "What is the first element that you wish to tackle?"

"Air," she responded. One would think that since she was so drawn to the element of Fire, she would want to learn to tackle it before the others, but Amara wanted to save Fire as the last. That was what she wanted to master the art of, but she knew that only if she were able to tackle other elements, would she be able to touch Fire. Because as mentioned in the Book of Elements, Fire was the trickiest one of all; and she loved that challenge.

Nicholas began telling her the oldest tricks in the book for handling Air and Amara learned it all quickly. Soon enough, she was able to handle Air and then proceeded to go towards Spirit. The element of Spirit was the most sensitive one and Amara found it difficult to deal with. But she tried her best and as Nicholas concluded that she was better at handling Spirit than she was at Air. It surprised her since she hoped that she would have been better at Air.

It was the same with Earth. Amara was as efficient in handling the Earth as she was in Air. Though Spirit continued to remain her forte. When the time came for Water, Amara's strength seemed to be tenfold. Her concentration was the highest and her mind unmoving. She realized that she was much better at managing Water than she was at Spirit. Water held a higher rank than Spirit at this point.

The last one was Fire, as she had wanted it to be. The trickiest, the hardest and the most notorious element of all; Amara loved the thrill of dodging flames and conjuring them out of nowhere. Every time she produced Fire, her mind went back to how Azar had shown her glorious visions of those flames. There was a glint in her eyes when she played with Fire. Lord Lucifer trained her in handling Water and Fire, since those were not Nicholas's strong suit. He could only observe her in admiration as to how quickly she was learning.

No witch had been able to learn the art of tackling elements in two years. Amara was brilliant. When asked what elements *she would like to excel in, to no one's surprise, she chose Fire and Water.*

Nicholas and Lord Lucifer knew how strong she was in handling those. It was time for them to return to Acanthus and introduce Amara as a new coven member.

The coven saw her strength when she battled ten witch-hunters at a time without any help. It was marvellous to watch Amara flawlessly kill them all. The entire coven became instant admirers of her skills. And nobody failed to notice the coldness that surrounded them whenever she was around. Her limited, almost non-existent interaction with the coven members was apparent to everyone around. They all understood soon enough that she was not one to mingle with the lot. She liked being unaided; she enjoyed isolation.

Not long after, the coven members began to distance themselves from her, realizing that nothing was going to change her behaviour towards them. But not a single witch and sorcerer failed to see the evident strength that had increased because of her. The coven was stronger and it was indomitable in her presence. Acanthus knew that.

* * *

"Amara?" Iris held her shoulder and Amara snapped back into reality, blinking a few times and running a hand through her tousled hair.

"I'm sorry," muttered Amara, looking down and biting her lower lip.

"*What?*" Iris retorted with an evident frown.

"For the second time, I abandoned you when you needed me and I- I'm sorry, Iris. It was wrong of me. I'm a heartless person. You did such a big favour to me and I repaid you by leaving you in the middle of nowhere. I'm selfish. I'm sorry,

Iris, I really am. I promise I won't do that again. I found a friend in you for the first time in a hundred years and I. . .you don't deserve this. You're so young, so innocent and you were thrown into this dark world where you had no one and I left you. It's as if I used you for my own good and then-"

"Amara!" Iris bellowed.

Iris held Amara by the shoulders to steady her. Amara was unable to stop her tears. She fell to the floor and Iris immediately pulled her into a hug. *She isn't selfish,* Iris thought to herself. *She's broken and that detached her from everything else.* It was terrifying, to say the least, and Iris understood that as she had her arms wrapped around Amara's shoulders with one of her hands resting on her head trying to calm her down. Iris did not understand how *she* was managing to control her tears at such a point. Maybe she had become emotionless herself, and maybe the tables had turned. Maybe Amara was now at the breaking point that Iris had been when she had arrived.

The vulnerability that Iris had had a year ago was now transferred to Amara. Iris stroked her head softly while she cried. Amara rested her head on Iris's shoulder and let the tears fall profusely, not trying to control them anymore. In a way, she was sure that she was going to feel better after talking to Iris. There was an invisible connection that the two of them shared and no matter how far apart they would be; the connection would never leave them, for it was of the mind. Iris had seen what Amara had been through and she had felt her pain through invading Amara's mind, which made her closer to Amara than anyone had ever been. She felt every emotion that Amara felt and understood everything without Amara uttering a single word. And that was what made their connection strong and unbreakable.

Amara pulled away from Iris while wiping her tears. Iris rubbed Amara's arm in a soothing manner and told herself that her only purpose in life was to bring any sort of happy emotion inside of Amara that would carry her out of the darkness that she had fallen into. Iris took it upon her that she would do anything to get Amara back to normal, and a better normal at that. She smiled at Amara as she let out a deep breath.

"You're not selfish. But I will make sure I enter your mind and manipulate it next time you stop talking to me," said Iris with a smile.

Amara stared at her with a confused frown. *Did she say manipulate?*

As though reading her mind, Iris said, "Eridanus taught me the art of manipulation while you were away. I'm on the beginners' stage but I can deal with it."

"You can manipulate minds and I don't know about it?" Amara replied, half-shocked, half-impressed, her eyebrows raised, and saddened about the fact that she was unaware of the same.

Iris just shrugged.

"Wait. Who is Eridanus?" Amara suddenly asked.

Iris looked at her for a long moment before letting out an amused laugh. Amara had been so tangled up in her own world that she was unaware of the new addition to the coven and the army.

"He joined the army about a month ago. His powers are mostly similar to mine with some extra ones. He can read minds, manipulate them and he also has the power of premonition. He did have a feeling that something bad was going to happen, hours before Nicholas's Death but before he could get the whole plot, Nicholas was already gone," she said, looking down as she said the last words about Nicholas.

"Oh. I haven't really met him," Amara replied, frowning to herself.

She did not know how she had missed that. Something told her she had seen him or talked to him, but then her mind was so boggled the last month that she remembered only faded parts of it.

"I think I should go to the meditation chamber. My powers seem to have died," saying, Amara stood up and dusted the back of her grey gown.

Iris followed suit.

"Wait. I have a question," Iris said when Amara was about to leave.

A moment later, Amara smiled, nodding once in Iris's direction to which she frowned.

"Why are you smiling?" She asked.

"You haven't asked me questions in a while, which you usually do whenever I'm around," Amara replied and Iris rolled her eyes, smiling back.

"Never-mind, I wanted to ask you why there is an eagle hovering about your window every day and why it always sits next to Nicholas's grave before flying to your chamber," said Iris.

For a month, she had seen the same eagle fluttering about Nicholas's grave, also shedding a tear or two at times before it flew towards Amara's chamber and hovered around the window as though it wanted to get noticed. She had wanted to ask Erasmus about it but he was travelling. Other than him, nobody knew why the eagle behaved so.

"Pelagi," muttered Amara, distractedly.

She shut her eyes for a moment. Nicholas's pet eagle, his messenger had lost his master and she was one of the few people that knew how close the two were. She felt terrible for not having paid attention to the sound of knocking on her window-glass every day. Pelagi was obviously devastated. How could she have forgotten about that? Who else was it supposed to deliver messages to if not Amara after its master had gone?

"Pelagi?" Iris repeated, snapping Amara out of her thoughts.

"Nicholas's pet eagle; Iris, do me a favour, find him. He must be somewhere in the forest or around the castle. I need to go and meditate. I really do. Just find him and try to get him to me somehow. It's important," she told Iris before rushing back into the castle and barging into the meditation chamber.

Pelagi had something important to say; Amara was sure of that. But without meditating and getting her powers back in working condition, she would not be able to understand what it was that he wanted to reveal.

After Amara had vanished, Iris shrugged and began walking around to find the eagle called Pelagi that was apparently Nicholas's pet. Thinking that since Amara had been so panicked about it, there might have been something important, Iris lifted her head to look about and find the magnificent eagle that had not failed to go unnoticed by her, every time it appeared. There was a discrete charm to him that was attractive. He more or less resembled Nicholas in a way: charming and majestic.

As Iris sauntered to find the eagle, Eridanus appeared out of nowhere and stood beside her while giving her a smile. She raised an eyebrow. Even though he was helping her learn the art of manipulation and being friendly, he was still a bit annoying. Besides, he would not stop telling her that she was beautiful and possessed a remarkable physique, which made her want to slam his head on a wall at times; although contradictory to her annoyance, she enjoyed the same and didn't complain most of the time. It helped in distracting her from Nicholas.

"Were you looking for me?" he asked her, smirking as she strode ahead, ignoring him and continuing to look for the eagle. At his words, she stopped and looked at him.

"If you are a flying eagle, then yes I *was* particularly looking for you," she replied, rolling her eyes in the end.

"I would gladly become an eagle for you," he said, winking.

Very annoying. She stopped herself from hitting him across the face and did not let her attention waver from the task that she was doing.

"Can you stop being a waste of time for once and help me look for a beautiful eagle?" She told him before he could utter another line.

"I will ignore the objectionable comment for now and ask you why you're looking for an eagle." He slapped a hand on his chest mockingly and gave her a disheartened look.

"I'll tell you when we find him. For now, make yourself useful," she said to him before moving ahead and Eridanus chuckled to himself, following her behind.

* * *

Azrael was rushing around looking for Amara and asking everyone whether they had seen her. He had checked her chamber, the two towers, the library, the potions chamber, the kitchen, and everywhere else apart from the meditation chamber. He was about to go in the direction of the same when he bumped into Leandra who was carrying a pile of books back to the library. She fell to the floor and as did all her books. Azrael looked at the numerous books of potions and spells and who knows what, which were scattered around him. Lea looked up at him lividly.

"Are you going to help me?" she asked him when he stood there still, while she picked up all the books again.

"Sorry. I was in a hurry. Have you seen Amara?" he said, bending down and grabbing the books off the floor.

"I saw her run into the meditation chamber," she replied as he helped her carry all the books to the library hastily.

He was about to trip and fall due to walking too fast when Lea grabbed his arm and steadied him.

"Why are you in such a hurry? Is everything okay?" She asked him, placing the books on a table as they reached the library.

"I just need to find Amara. I'll talk to you later," he replied before storming out of the library and to the meditation chamber.

Lea stared after him in confusion before she shifted back to doing her work. She had a lot of research to do about unusual potions. There were books to read and she had taken up on herself to get knowledge about all the most unusual things in witchcraft. So ignoring her strange brother, Lea got herself busy.

Azrael now rushed to the meditation chamber and looked in all the doors to find Amara seated inside the last one with her eyes tightly shut. Surrounding her was an aura of positive energy that could be felt by Azrael as soon as he opened the door. His interruption had no effect on her though; she continued her meditation. Not willing to disturb her, Azrael decided to leave the chamber when he thought of the important thing that he had to talk to her about. It could not wait. Her meditation had to be interrupted no matter how deep her mind was into it.

Hesitantly, the sorcerer took a step ahead and tapped on Amara's shoulder. She did not react. Impatient, he called out her name along with tapping on her shoulder again. She gave no desired response. Amara was engrossed. Frustrated, he shut his eyes before gathering all his strength to shake her shoulder, and yelled out, "Amara!"

Her eyes shot open. Azrael was thankful that there was no one else meditating around or he would have had to face the wrath of disturbed witches. Amara was already staring at him viciously.

"What the devil do you want, sorcerer?" she said to him, venom dripping out of her tone.

Azrael cleared his throat, ignoring the fact that she was obviously angry, and concentrated on the important message that he had to give to her. He paused for the fraction of a second.

"The eagle. Nicholas's eagle. He gave me a message," he finally revealed and in an instant, Amara realized that it was something extremely grave. Colour drained out of her face as she stood up and the both of them left the meditation chamber.

CHAPTER TWENTY-SIX

∞∞∞∞∞

SPIRITS

∞∞∞∞∞

The eagle stood before them on the railing of the tower, turning his head all around as though looking for something. When Azrael and Amara reached the top of the tower, Pelagi fixed his eyes onto them. He looked at Amara, who was following Azrael as he approached the eagle. There was an incomprehensible expression that she held. She was unable to build up how she would react upon hearing the message that the eagle was about to give to her. Azrael, already aware of the same did not wish to reveal it, but preferred getting it delivered from the source itself.

Amara now stood right in front of Pelagi, who fluttered his wings and raised himself so he rested on her extended arm. For the eagle, Amara was his next owner and he would now answer to her and only her. She looked at him as he raised his head and then in hushed whispers – an unrecognizable language that no human would understand – delivered the message that he had to give, and then bowed down in grace. Amara blinked, registering the message and then looked back at Azrael. He stood there patiently.

"M-Lord Mikhail-Lord Mikhail has taken Lilith's spirit under control?" She uttered in a whisper.

Azrael looked at her for a long moment before nodding in agreement.

"I don't know how, but he has the spirit under his influence after she killed Nicholas. Now he's stronger. Also Lilith was supposed to help us with the prophecy as the Lord had said but now she might end up helping Lord Mikhail if he uses his powers to get her mind under his control. This is dangerous."

"We need to do something about this. If at all Lilith reveals the prophecy to him it could end everything."

Amara was panicking. She knew what the repercussions of Lord Mikhail getting Lilith under control would be. The coven would be doomed, the treasures would be in peril and Acanthus would be destroyed. Everything would then be under Lord Mikhail's control if he figured out the riddles that were hidden in the prophecy. If at all Lord Mikhail got the treasures, he would spread darkness all over the world. Not a human would be spared and white witchcraft would cease to exist. His power would make him vile, more than he already was and it would make him a threat to all things living. The strength of the three treasures was such that they could change the entire personality of the possessor. Even if the one that achieved them was an innocent by heart, they could make one evil and insatiable.

The treasures had a power to create two different individuals in one. For a while, the possessor would be calm like silent water, and then he/she would morph into something entirely different and dangerous. If the treasures granted immense power and authority to one, they were also capable of manipulating one's mind to an extent that one would never return from that state. And that could lead to extreme destruction, which worried Amara more than ever. She was afraid, Deathly afraid of what would happen if Lord Mikhail succeeded.

* * *

He was in the deep waters of Carinelle, seated on the bed of the river as black coloured fumes shot up from his fingers. The water was cold, chilling, frightening and it ironically burned one on the inside. Located far away from Acanthus, the river Carinelle was under the scrutiny of a beautiful land called Heletes. It was a tiny village where the oldest Conjurers resided, who spent their time in meditation, who had abandoned the world entirely and only concentrated on meditation and achieving salvation without Death. The Conjurers there would have such power and energy while meditating that they could somehow liberate their souls without damaging the body in any way. Those who succeeded were known as the *Mortuis*. It took a lot of years of meditation and unbreakable concentration. Only a few most powerful ones were capable of performing the same.

Lord Mikhail decided that the place would be safe to summon the spirit of the one that had slain Nicholas. The moment that Nicholas had been killed, Lord Mikhail had received the message from his messenger when he was in the mountains of Carvelli, still trying to understand what it was that Amara was hiding in the book that he had almost gotten his hands on. The moment that he received the message, Lord Mikhail had left to go to Heletes. Diving deep into the river of Carinelle, he had rested on the bed and begun his call for the spirit – unknown of its identity.

Lord Mikhail realized whose spirit it really was when it arrived. The reason he had summoned Lilith under the water was that it was the safest possible place and he knew nobody could interrupt him in the silent land of Heletes where no witch or sorcerer was allowed unless it was for meditation. The silence there was precise, and it never broke because of the calmness that it set forth. It was only a place for meditation. Not a single soul talked. And that was what Lord Mikhail needed when he would try to find out the reason for which Nicholas had summoned the spirit of Lilith, and how she had ended up murdering him.

As soon as Lilith stood in the water before him, Lord Mikhail had sealed her mind. He then began to manipulate it into finding out who she really was and what task she was supposed to perform upon reaching back to earth, where she did not belong. Due to the malign nature of Lilith and her forgetting her own identity, it was difficult to get her mind under his control. Lord Mikhail needed patience, a lot of patience. However, he did not have much time. He was assured that there was something extremely useful in the spirit of Lilith, which he intended to find out as soon as he could.

* * *

Amara knew that Lord Mikhail was intelligent enough to find out why Lilith's spirit had been summoned. She was well aware of his capabilities. The only thing that she did not know was his whereabouts. She thought of asking the same to Pelagi, but a bird could only be of so much assistance. He was asked to give the information of what Lord Mikhail was up to, but the eagle could not explain the exact location, neither could it lead them there. The task ahead was difficult, and Amara had no idea how she was going to solve the puzzle.

"What are we going to do?" She turned to Azrael who looked equally confused as they sat opposite to each other in the library after Pelagi had left to quench his hunger.

Amara and Azrael retreated to the library to try to come to a solution. They were lost. Amara had informed Iris that she had already found Pelagi so Iris wasn't looking for the bird anymore. Rather, she was busy in the meditation chamber with Eridanus where he was helping her master the technique of manipulation.

Eridanus stood there watching her as she shut her eyes and concentrated on invading his mind. He rested his back on the wall behind and let out a sigh. His thoughts were interrupted by a wave of visions flashing across his eyes and he suddenly collapsed on the ground. He blinked. Once, twice, thrice and the visions appeared yet again, blinding him. He saw fumes of black smoke rising from inside a river and then he saw the figure of a woman lifting herself from the water, as though being pulled by a rope and then falling back inside. The cycle continued for a while and then his mind was snapped into another vision where he saw the figure of a man descending into a huge sea and emerging amidst a Fire that surrounded him.

A moment later, the visions were gone. Eridanus blinked again, now adjusting his eyes. Standing up, he glanced at a meditating Iris once before dashing out of the chamber and making his way to the library where Amara and Azrael were. Their eyes shot up to him when he settled himself on a chair beside Azrael and opposite to Amara who looked at him quizzically.

"I need to know what message the eagle gave to you," he told them with a panic-stricken expression as he looked back and forth between the two.

"Why?" asked Azrael, frowning.

"I saw a vision. . .I-there is some danger out there and I know you two are in trouble. Just tell me what the eagle told you. I saw him meeting the two of you and delivering an important message, I just don't know what it was."

"Would you mind telling me who you are?" said Amara, raising her eyebrows.

"I'm Eridanus. I have the power of premonition and I just had a vision of Lord Mikhail entering a huge sea and then being surrounded by flames inside a cave. I know this is something important and you two need to know about it. What did the eagle say?"

He held a worried look while Amara stared at him wide eyed. *Did he say cave? And why does he look so familiar?* She pushed those stray thoughts aside since there were more important things to take care of.

"Is this about to happen or has Lord Mikhail already done what you saw?" Azrael said as Amara was too lost to even utter a word.

"No. Usually I get a vision long before it happens. I'm sure there is time but it is going to happen. Did the eagle mention any of this?" Eridanus replied, looking at Azrael.

"It just said that Lord Mikhail had the spirit of Lilith under control," he said and Eridanus let out a sigh, biting his lower lip in thought.

"Something needs to be done about this as soon as possible. I sense a danger."

"I realize that, and we are trying to find a solution for this but it's not that easy," Amara uttered, as she gazed at the books before her, lost.

Eridanus looked at her for a long moment before blinking and then nodding once.

"Okay. There is one thing that can be done," he replied after thinking for a while.

"What?" Amara asked eagerly.

"We could try to get Lilith's spirit under control, if anyone is well aware of summoning spirits. I could help you find out when and at what point Lord Mikhail is not paying much attention to the spirit because I'm sure that would happen. Getting a spirit completely under control is a very complicated and strenuous task. Only highly powerful sorcerers or ancient witches are capable of doing the same. Lilith has already taken the vow of destroying our coven because we didn't let her finish her meal of Nicholas so she'll come back for revenge and Lord Mikhail could use that to his advantage.

"Though it'll take time for him to actually find out the cause of her being here, we need to do something immediately." He paused to take a breath. "Since Lilith isn't actually very fond of our coven, we would have to manipulate her mind so she doesn't know who is calling her. If that can happen, then someone who is capable of summoning spirits can get her under our power."

Amara stared at him, contemplating what he had said. She could think of some way to bring the spirit under control. There were two people sitting right in front of her, who were capable of manipulation and Iris too, was well aware of a few ways of manipulation. Whereas summoning a spirit was concerned, she was trained in the task but wasn't strong enough and would surely need assistance. She did not know who would be of help.

"I believe Azrael is skilled enough in manipulation. Of the physical being, I mean." Amara looked at Eridanus. "You and Iris could help him in controlling Lilith's mind. But I'm not sure how the spirit could be summoned here. I can do the task to some extent but I'm not as strong. I would need someone," she finished.

Azrael narrowed his eyes for a moment as though in thought, before he turned his head around, and caught sight of someone he was hoping to find in the library.

"Lea," he called out softly so as not to disturb the other witches that were busy reading.

Leandra turned her head to look at her brother. She raised her eyebrows, questioning what he wanted. Azrael beckoned her towards him. Snapping the book shut, she placed it back on the table before getting up and proceeding to walk towards her sibling.

"Sit," he said to her and Lea took a seat.

"She can summon spirits. It's one of her dominant skills," Azrael revealed to the others.

Amara looked at Lea, who sat there clueless. She had never really spoken to Lea. Mostly it would only be to ask about Iris, but nothing serious as such. Amara was unaware of what powers Lea possessed and what elements she was capable of handling. She did not even know how experienced Lea was.

"What am I being talked about for?" asked Lea, piping in out of curiosity.

"How skilled are you in summoning spirits?" Amara said before any of them could reply.

Although a bit nervous around Amara, Lea had now mastered the art of keeping her nervousness hidden under her ever present smile. Amara was intimidating, which rather scared Lea a bit around her, even though there was nothing remotely dangerous that Amara could do to her. Yet the mere presence of the powerful witch made her nervous. She kept it hidden skillfully enough and was relieved about the fact that she was barely ever addressed to apart from a few times that she was asked about Iris. Although, this time, it seemed as though there was something important since Amara was directly addressing her.

"I've been practicing for around ninety years now. I believe I am good enough," she replied, shrugging.

"If I were to say that we need to summon the spirit of Lilith, would you be able to?" Amara retorted and Lea stared at her in utter shock.

Summon the spirit of the one that killed Nicholas?

"You're joking, right?" She let out a nervous chuckle and looked at the three of them. They had entirely serious expressions across their faces. None of them replied.

"You're telling me that we have to summon the spirit of the evil witch who murdered Nicholas?" She glanced at the three of them again to make sure they were not making some joke. "She's the most powerful spirit I've ever seen! I don't think anyone would be capable of summoning a hungry spirit like hers."

"That's exactly why we can't do it alone," Azrael said. "We need a team. A strong, capable group of us who can successfully summon her spirit so as to stop her from going to the wrong people. Lord Mikhail already has summoned her and we need to stop him somehow."

"How is that possible?" Lea asked.

"Well, Eridanus, Iris and I will try manipulating the spirit," Azrael said. "Iris and Eridanus will do it through the mind, while I will help you in summoning her here physically. Eridanus can cease her mind so she wouldn't realize where she's being summoned. You and Amara together can perform the rituals needed to summon the spirit. That way we can get her under our control."

Lea listened to him silently, contemplating everything that he had just said to her and then blinked, glancing at Amara once.

"Easier said than done," she said, and then turned to look at Amara. "The two of us can't possibly summon such a strong spirit after it has already been manipulated twice. We are going to need more assistance and strength."

"ERIDANUS, YOU SCOUNDREL! I've been looking all over for you! I was supposed to invade a certain mind but you vanished out of sight. I was left wondering where in the devil's name, my mind was supposed to go!"

Everyone snapped their heads towards Iris, who stood there, fuming. Her eyes were focussed on Eridanus as she glared at him. He cleared his throat and looked at her sheepishly.

"I'm sorry I had to leave like that. There was something important that-wait, sit down. We need to talk to you," he replied.

Frowning, Iris opened her mouth to say something when she noticed the serious looks that the lot held and quietly sat down. She waited for them to tell her something and Amara decided to explain everything to her. Iris listened silently, understanding whatever was being said to her. When Amara was done, she let out a sigh and Iris kept her gaze locked onto her.

"You want me to manipulate the mind of *Lilith*?" She replied, astonished.

"Yes. You won't be alone," replied Azrael.

"What about the assistance that we might need in summoning the spirit?" Lea asked when Iris was about to say something.

"Right. Who else is skilled in summoning spirits?" Eridanus said, scratching his chin.

"Fabian?" Offered Lea, for she had heard that he was trained in the same.

"No, he's not strong enough. We need someone experienced," Azrael said.

"What about Ambrosius? He sacrifices souls, correct?" Eridanus spoke.

"No, he isn't as useful." Amara denied.

Iris sat there pondering over what was going on as the others thought of those who could help.

"Sienna!" Iris exclaimed suddenly, and all of them turned to look at her.

"Why her?" Lea questioned.

"She drove Lilith's spirit away. The flute is skilled in summoning spirits as well. I'm sure she can help," Iris replied.

"That could work," Amara agreed, nodding.

"Let's talk to her then." Eridanus stood up and the others followed.

After searching the entire castle for Sienna, all of them split up to look for her. Amara found herself on the tower where Lea's sculpted fairy stood, now with her wings in a flying stance. She watched the fairy for a moment before her eyes flitted to Sienna who sat there with her eyes staring off into space.

Amara approached Sienna and cleared her throat, but the latter did not react.

"Sienna?" Amara called out.

CHAPTER TWENTY-SEVEN

∞∞∞∞∞

THE FALLEN WARRIOR

∞∞∞∞∞

A mara watched as Sienna stood up and dusted off the back of her gown, sniffling while wiping her cheeks. She then turned to look at Amara who stood there silently.

"Yes?" said Sienna, startling Amara.

She cleared her throat and asked, "Are you okay?" Amara hesitated.

Never before had she interacted with Sienna apart from times when it was necessary. There were no friendly relations between the two that would give Amara a reason to ask if she was okay. And that took Sienna aback. She felt that it was awkward and strange for Amara to ask her something like that out of the blue.

"I'm fine. Is there something you need?" Sienna replied, pushing a strand of hair behind her ear.

"Yes. It's quite important so. . .I just don't want to disturb you if you're not ready for this." Amara hesitantly looked at her.

"I'm alright, Amara. You can tell me whatever it is." Sienna let out a humourless laugh as she spoke.

Amara hoped it wasn't spiteful on her part and then asked Sienna to follow her back to the library while sending messages to the others that she had found Sienna. When the two of them reached the library, they found that the others were already present. Apart from the five of them, the library was empty as Azrael had asked everyone else to leave. Sienna looked at them curiously as she sat down on a chair beside Iris. As soon as she had settled, Azrael spoke, "I hope we didn't disturb you if you were busy."

"I don't think crying about the fact that the man I love is dead, particularly counts as being busy," replied Sienna, chuckling in the end.

The others did not react. They were unsure whether or not it was a laughing matter. It felt extremely strange for Sienna to have spoken like that. *Maybe she's in trauma,* Iris thought sadly.

Eridanus cleared his throat to break the silence and then began explaining to Sienna what their plan was. She listened to him silently and when Eridanus was done talking, she let out a sigh, furrowing her forehead as though thinking of something. She did not know what good would come out of getting Lilith's spirit under control – it did not mean that Nicholas would come back – but she knew that if the spirit was under Lord Mikhail's control, it would result in serious damage.

"Alright, I'll help you summon the spirit. When and where are we going to do this?" She said.

"We haven't decided that yet," Amara replied, in deep thought.

"For now, I suggest we go and give our minds some rest through meditation. We have to prepare for what we are going to do. It isn't a simple task and we need to be focussed," Azrael said, and stood up.

"He's right. We should go and meditate for a while. We'll assemble again to prepare the day and time of our task," said Lea and they all stood up to leave.

Sienna was the first to get out of the library followed by Iris and Leandra. When Eridanus left as well, Azrael stood back as Amara began to make her way out. He grabbed her arm and gestured to her to follow him outside into the woods. Amara did not question as the look on his face meant that it was something important. So she walked in the direction that was leading her. When they reached the woods, Azrael turned to face her and Amara waited for him to talk.

"Since the others are not aware of what actual purpose we have of summoning the spirit of Lilith, I needed to speak with you alone. In the days after we returned from the Sea of Cypress, I have been doing my research about constituting a way to protect the prophecy. After a lot of thinking I have reached a conclusion and I want to know if you approve of it," he told her, resting his back on the bark of a tree.

"Go on," she urged, giving him a nod.

Azrael let out a sigh and began explaining what he had thought of.

"Lady Calypsa isn't strong enough as the both of us are aware of it. In order to protect her, we need a team of spirits of old witches who have been the strongest of their time. They can create a protective shield around the Sea of Cypress, which would put restrictions on the wrong seekers entering the sea and attacking the lady; but sorcerers as strong as Lord Mikhail can easily enter after battling those spirits, especially if he has Lilith's spirit on his side. In any way, we need Lilith's spirit with us. Besides that, we will require more spirits that are not malign and safe enough to cater to our demands. If there is a strong team of spirits protecting Lady Calypsa, it will be difficult for Lord Mikhail to break the wall. For this purpose, we cannot use help of the others because all of this is not supposed to be revealed to them. But I think we could use Sienna's help. What is your opinion on that?"

Amara registered his words and pondered over them for a long moment. She bit her lower lip, blinking as she understood his point. It was quite useful, to say the least. Creating a barrier of spirits around the Sea of Cypress meant that Lady Calypsa did not have to divide her time of protecting the treasures as well as the sea. If the spirits guarded the sea, the Lady could devote all her time in guarding the treasures, which she was fairly capable of, and would not need extra help with. But involving another witch meant revealing everything; because without that no sane person would agree for summoning a whole team of spirits. It wasn't a simple task.

Though, if asking Sienna to help them meant ensuring complete protection of the treasures, then Amara was ready to do the same. Revealing the prophecy to Sienna was far better than letting it be known to Lord Mikhail.

"I suppose that could help. But we will have to be careful about this. If she has to help us, she will have to sacrifice her blood and we'll have to speak with the Lord and Lady Calypsa as well. Without their consent we cannot reveal the prophecy to Sienna. It is not our right to decide that," Amara said after a while of thinking.

"That is correct. I have sent a message to the Lord about instructing us about this. If it is possible, we will go to see Lady Calypsa again. Otherwise she would not be able to believe us even though she has enough trust," he replied, agreeing with a nod.

"When do we inform the Lord then? And how do we know Sienna will agree to help?" Amara asked.

She did not know whether or not she would be able to convince Sienna into this task. Her reaction was something unknown to Amara since she had not known her so closely. A task like this meant having enough trust on Sienna and Sienna having enough trust on Amara and Azrael. Because none of them anywhere close to knowing her, Amara could not tell whether or not she would be of help. The task of being revealed the prophecy to was an extremely complicated and confidential one. If at all there was even a tiny glitch, everything would fall apart. Amara did not want that.

"That is another question. I have a theory that if Iris gets to know Sienna, our task would be easy." Azrael offered, raising his eyebrows.

Amara regarded him impassively for a moment.

"But that means involving another person," she said.

"Iris wouldn't question you if her life depended on it. That much I have understood in the time I've been here," he told her, assured of the fact that there was no way Iris would ever want to get into details if she was advised not to. Besides, she trusted Amara with every nerve of her body.

"That seems about right. I'll talk to her," she said to him with a nod of assurance.

She did have enough confidence in Iris being a perfect person to do this job. Amara trusted her as much as Iris did Amara. So they left to go back into the castle, and Azrael retreated to his chamber while Amara walked to Iris's. She knocked on the door to find Lea opening it.

"Is Iris here?" She asked, standing at the door.

Lea nodded with a tiny smile and stepped aside to let Amara enter.

"Iris, can I speak with you for a moment?" said Amara, entering inside.

Iris was standing next to a table, going through a book of spells when Amara addressed her. She immediately turned around and nodded before following her outside.

"I'll be right back," she told Leandra and then walked outside to where Amara was leading her.

Lea shut the door of Iris's chamber and strode back to where she was seated, picking up the book that Iris was reading. Outside, Iris and Amara walked to the potions chamber where the latter was sure there was no one at the given moment to interrupt them.

"There is something important I want to talk to you about, and I want you not to reveal it to anyone. What I'm about to tell you is something that will stay between the two of us and Azrael. Alright?" She said to Iris when they were in the potions chamber, all alone.

"I promise not to reveal it to anyone," replied Iris with a nod.

"I want you to get to know Sienna. Find out how strong her relations were with Nicholas. Also try to know for how long she has been a witch, what powers she has, where her expertise lies and what all major tasks she has performed under the orders of the Lord. Tell me if she can be trusted with any kind of grave matter. I want to know everything."

"Okay, may I ask why?" Iris frowned curiously.

"I can't tell you that. But it is extremely important that I need you to do this. Can you help me?" Amara asked, raising her eyebrows hopefully.

She was sure Iris would agree, but a part of her said that being the inquisitive person that Iris was, she would ask more questions. Yet Amara knew Iris was quite obedient when it came to important tasks.

"Of course I can. I would even manipulate her into telling me everything, if you want me to," Iris said, jokingly as she added a slight chuckle in the end.

Amara watched her for a moment in all seriousness, which made Iris shut her mouth and her grin vanished. Then Amara flashed the ghost of a smile before rolling her eyes and walking past Iris who bit back a laugh.

"I'll let you know if manipulation is required." Amara turned to look at Iris from the door. "For now, bring me the desired information; and don't get too curious."

"Yes, m'Lady," Iris replied and the two of them left the potions chamber.

Outside the window of the chamber, the silhouette of a figure shifted away from vicinity as soon as the pair left.

Amara proceeded to go to her chamber while Iris went to her own, humming a soft tune to herself and thinking of how she would get to know Sienna. She had absolutely no idea how Sienna would react. What if she would get angry and not talk to her at all? What if she wasn't friendly enough? What if she got to know more than she was supposed to?

"Good evening, m'Lady," a voice whispered into Iris's ear and she whipped her head around so fast that she lost her balance, and fell to the floor.

With a scowl, Iris lifted her head to find Eridanus standing there as he struggled to bite back a laugh but could not control it for long. Instead of helping her up like he should have, Eridanus burst out laughing while holding his stomach. Iris sat on the ground rolling her eyes in frustration and rubbing her backside, for it hurt badly. She placed her hand on the wall beside her and stood up, dusting off her robes since Eridanus didn't seem like he was going to help her anyway. *Why did I even think that he was going to be a gentleman?*

Iris waited for a moment to see if he would apologize, but since he was busy laughing she turned around and stalked off, letting out a sigh of disappointment. However, before she could reach her chamber, Eridanus placed a hand on her shoulder and turned her around to face him. He was no longer laughing, but that did not make Iris any less annoyed.

"What is it that you want?" She asked him, irately. Eridanus was sure that he was going to get beaten up if he did not apologize as soon as possible.

"I'm sorry. I shouldn't have laughed like that, but you looked so funny on the floor, I just. . ."

He trailed off looking at the obviously irritated expression on Iris's face that told him his apology had gone unnoticed due to the sentence that had followed after. Clearing his throat, Eridanus scratched the back of his neck and Iris rolled her eyes before turning to leave again.

"I'm extremely sorry, Iris. It was wrong of me to laugh like that. Forgive me?" He told her, stopping her by grabbing her arm. Iris pulled her hand away from him and stepped farther from where he was stood right in front of her.

"I have things to do, if you'll just excuse me." She turned and left.

Eridanus did not stop her this time and let out an exasperated sigh as Iris walked off. In another passageway right opposite to where Eridanus and Iris were, Amara had watched the whole scene and could not help but shake her head in disapproval when Eridanus spotted her there. He gave her a sheepish grin to which she shrugged and turned to go to her chamber when she was stopped by her name being called. When she looked in the direction of the sound, she saw Eridanus jogging towards her.

As she looked at his face a little closely and clearly for the first time, without any other thing interrupting her, she realized he seemed vaguely familiar. Whether she had seen him in the castle when Nicholas died, or before that, she did not know. But in a way he seemed familiar. It was as though she had met him before and talked to him yet she was unsure of the same. She thought that she might have spoken to him some time and did not remember about it, but it felt like a foggy memory to her.

"I'm not sure if I should address you as Amara or Lady Amara. You are a very experienced and a better witch than many of course. So I'm not sure how I should be addressing you," he told her when he reached to where she was stood.

"You can call me Amara. I don't desire any title to my name. Is there anything else you need?" She asked, raising her eyebrows.

"Yes-I mean no-actually I-" he stammered.

"Talk to me when you're not speech impaired," she said, rolling her eyes at his nervousness.

She began to walk away. At times, it infuriated her when others acted this terrified of her for no apparent reason. She had done nothing to harm them nor had she ever been so threatening for everyone to be intimidated by her. She did not know how she could change that.

"I was thinking that maybe you would want to talk to me," he called out. Amara stopped at a distance and turned to look at him. He was fidgeting with his fingers, staring at them distractedly.

"I've been a here for a month and you haven't made any effort to speak with me, which I find really strange. I mean it is *me*, you would know me," he said to her.

"And what exactly is that supposed to mean?" She asked him, perplexed.

"I. . .never mind. I'll let you be on your own," he told her with a stoic expression before taking a few steps back and turning around to leave.

Amara watched his retreating figure, puzzled. She didn't quite understand what he meant by that, yet her mind told her that she knew what he was talking about. There was a missing piece that she could not put her finger on. She wanted to talk to him again but something stopped her. She took a step forward to follow him and ask him what he meant by whatever he said, but then she thought better of it and walked back to where she was going after leaving a lingering look where Eridanus had just been. Not only did she find it strange, she found his argument fairly genuine as well, but what it meant, she could not understand. That frustrated her. Thinking that it was not as important, Amara entered her chamber and let go of the thoughts. She picked up her sword that was kept safely inside the trunk in a corner of the chamber, and left to go to the woods.

She spotted the foggy figure of Azrael creating flames into the water of the lake when she reached outside. Amara glanced around at the woods, which had begun to grow back a few of the shrubs and plants that had been burnt by her. That day on, she had watered the woods every day, hoping they would be as they were before, and some of her hopes were being fulfilled. She silently thanked the *Goddess of the Earth* for being of help to her and then proceeded to walk towards the lake: on the banks of which she would practice her sword-fighting skills.

Azrael turned his head to look at Amara, who stood there watching the flames that he had created. As soon as he spotted the sword in her hands, his concentration wavered and the flames dashed down into the water, letting out smoke. Amara coughed and gave him a look of disapproval to which he grunted in frustration, for his concentration had faded.

"It's your fault. Had I not seen the sword in your hands. . ." he trailed off, gawking at the weapon.

"Blaming others for the fault in your focus is the most unimpressive thing coming from someone like you, great sorcerer," Amara retorted bemusedly.

Azrael scowled at her and looked away.

"Let me challenge you for a duel then," he told her as Amara pulled the sword out of its case.

She raised an eyebrow and then shrugged.

"I don't mind that."

Azrael raised his hands in front of him, palms facing upwards and closed his eyes, muttering something softly. In a moment, a sword appeared on his extended hands and he opened his eyes. He then turned to look at Amara, who was standing there ready to battle him.

The duel began. Both of them swung their swords forward and the metal clashed together creating an array of sounds. Amara raised herself and whooshed above Azrael and landed back on the ground right behind him. Swinging his sword backwards he turned around and slammed it into Amara's. She pushed his sword downwards using all her force and Azrael resisted with all his might. For the fraction of a moment, he let her push his sword to the ground and then threw it in direction of her legs. Amara lifted herself to avoid the blow and Azrael immediately grabbed her free arm, turning her around cogently and her back was now against his chest; his sword on hers as both the weapons rested right next to her neck. Her arm was twisted backwards as both of them stood there trying to catch their breaths.

"You're not the strongest, great witch. You can lose focus too," he whispered, smirking.

Amara scoffed and pushed his sword away using hers as she kicked his leg from behind, making him drop to the ground.

"Impressive," he told her and she let out a breath, holding out an arm for him. Azrael ignored the offer and pushed himself up to standing.

Once again, the swords clashed together and they battled for a while before Azrael extended his leg, pushing it into Amara's, and she fell onto the ground; her grip lost itself on her sword and she dropped it along with her, losing the battle. Immediately, Azrael placed his sword onto her neck and held it there with an arrogant smirk. But Amara's eyes were elsewhere. When Azrael followed her vision upwards to the sky, he spotted the largest bird that he had ever seen. It flew above them, the wings flapping and creating a sound of a terrorizing wind. Azrael frowned and pulled his sword away from Amara.

She sat up, a look of horror etching across her face as she watched the creature circling above her.

"What is it?" Azrael asked as he noticed the look on Amara's face. She gulped in fear.

"The Lord; he's in danger," whispered Amara.

CHAPTER TWENTY-EIGHT

∞∞∞∞∞

THE GRIM

∞∞∞∞∞

There were black and white stripes on its wings, which were only visible when it flew. Its face and body was that of a magnificent and fierce horse. The overall black coloured creature had a red eye that shone brightly in darkness. It had various symbols on its body that remained covered when it wasn't flapping its wings. It had a long tail and giant wings. The creature that now stood before Amara and Azrael was the largest one Azrael had ever seen. He had read about them but never sighted one.

Amara watched the giant bird worriedly.

For she knew that it was the Lord's pet, who was only sent without the Lord if he were in danger. She could understand that something was wrong and that the Lord was in need of help. So she took a few steps forward when the bird landed before her, and she stroked its head when it bowed to her. She then took a step back.

"Is the Lord in danger? Is there something wrong?" She asked him softly.

The bird nodded once, looking down. Azrael stepped ahead adjacent to Amara.

"Is there any message from him?" She asked again.

It then flipped open its wings and produced a roll of parchment that fell to the ground. Amara picked it up and opened it. On the parchment were two words that she read out loud.

"*Noctia Stella*," it read in a loopy, yet clumsy manner, making Amara frown.

Sudden realization hit her. She dropped the parchment on the ground and induced a flame that burnt it to ashes. Then she turned to Azrael.

"We have to go," she told him.

"What is going on?" He asked.

"The Lord needs us. I'll tell you all about it on the journey. Right now, we need to leave. I'll go get my bag of supplies and inform the others. I think we're going to need Iris as well."

With that, Amara stalked back into the castle while Azrael stood there, confused out of his mind. He could not even pick up the parchment and read what was written on it, for it was already destroyed for safety purposes. So he stood there waiting for Amara to return as he watched the giant creature before him. It turned around and walked towards the lake to drink some water out of it until Amara was back. Inside the castle, Amara had grabbed her bag of supplies and rushed to Iris's chamber where the latter was busy talking to Leandra about how idiotic Eridanus was. As soon as she saw Amara barging into the chamber, she knew something was up.

Iris was immediately on her feet.

"You need to come with me. We're travelling," said Amara.

"Travelling where?" Iris questioned.

"Just be quiet and follow me. There's no time for queries," she said and pulled Iris outside by her arm. Then she stopped mid-way and turned to Leandra.

"Please inform Sienna and Eridanus that we are leaving and will be back soon. Meanwhile, the three of you can prepare everything that is needed for summoning Lilith's spirit," she said.

"Of course, I'll be on it right away," Lea replied with an obedient nod and Amara rushed out of the chamber, dragging Iris along with her.

Iris followed Amara confusedly and had a million questions to ask but she saved them for later. It wasn't the right time to ask anything to Amara since she was in panic mode. When they had reached back to the woods, Amara let go of Iris's hand.

"Wh-what is *that?*" gasped Iris as she spotted the huge creature that stood at a distance from her.

Amara ignored Iris's reaction and kept walking. Iris's eyes were wide as she had not seen anything so huge in her entire existence. It was terrifying, to say the least. She held dazed look as she blindly walked ahead with Amara. Her eyes were stuck on the bird before her. Azrael turned to find Amara walking forward followed by Iris and he took a few steps ahead.

"Do you mind explaining to me what exactly that is?" Iris asked with her eyes wide.

"No time for questions, Iris," Amara replied while securing the bag of supplies around her waist.

"Okay. Mount on top of it," she instructed to Iris who snapped her head in Amara's direction and gave her a bewildered look.

"Most certainly NOT!" replied Iris, horrified.

"Iris, we have no time!" Amara told her, irritated.

"You're asking me to sit on that thing and-wait, is it going to fly?" She shot back, taking a few steps backwards.

Amara was far more than angry now. She was infuriated.

"At the speed of lightning; now get on it or I'll have you unconscious right this minute!" warned Amara, sternly.

Impatient with all the commotion, Azrael rolled his eyes as Iris began to take a few more steps back in terror. He stalked up to her, grabbed her by the waist, and effortlessly tossed her on top of the creature that was waiting for them to climb on. Iris squealed in horror as she saw herself settled on the soft yet firm body of the creature. She still held a terrified look on her face as she realized that they were going to fly. Iris had always been afraid of heights. It scared her to no limit. And having to fly on a giant horse-like bird that apparently ran at lightning speed wasn't making her feel any better.

As soon as Amara mounted on the bird followed by Azrael who settled behind with Iris between the both of them, the wings were extended and the horse began to run. Iris shut her eyes tightly as they rushed ahead with what seemed like immeasurable speed to her, and then without her noticing, they were in the air. The giant wings flapped on the creature's sides as they began to go higher and higher until the ground beneath them disappeared. Iris clutched onto Amara's shoulders with her eyes still tightly shut.

"Now do you mind telling me what this huge thing is and why we are flying to a place I have no idea about?" She asked, gathering all her strength.

Fortunately for her, the bird had lowered its speed when they were high enough and Iris no longer had to scream due to the wind. Amara let out a sigh. Iris never gave up on her questions. She was the most curious being Amara had ever come across. Thinking that the girl was never going to let her live in peace if she did not answer her queries, Amara started explaining to Iris about what the creature actually was. Azrael sat behind them stretching his arms to his sides and yawning.

"This creature is known as Equus. It is the Lord's pet and these kinds of creatures are only found in the world of Conjurers. No human is aware of them. Equus are very rare birds. The first one was created by a powerful sorcerer called Philinarmus Estrado, thousands of years ago. Since then these creatures have naturally bred. Though a few of them were destroyed by dark witchcraft due to their great powers, there are some left that produce themselves from time to time. Equus are born out of the earth. They can only be destroyed through dark witchcraft, otherwise they are immortal. But if and when their Lord dies or they are abandoned, the creatures crash into the earth and break into shards.

"And when they desire a new Lord, the shards buried into the earth assemble again to form another giant bird. They don't grow physically; they create themselves back to the giant forms. It is a very fascinating process to watch them grow back. It is nearly the same as a phoenix but rather different. Equus have powers that are unbeatable. They emit a sound so horrible that it can paralyze the victim for twenty-four hours. Also they let out smoke that can blind the victim as well. They have highly poisonous nails that are brought out only upon their Lord's orders. The nails are capable of killing the enemy with a single scratch on their body. Fighting an Equus is very difficult. Only powerful sorcerers or witches are capable of the same; and besides them, the ones who are skilled in dark witchcraft."

Azrael had read about Equus when he was sixteen and was learning about witchcraft. But since he had not witnessed them in reality, he was surprised to be in the presence of one. Iris's eyes were wide in amazement as she heard what Amara was describing. But she wasn't satisfied. She had more questions to ask.

"And what does the Lord call his pet?" She asked, raising her eyebrows.

Amara let out a sigh, shaking her head. It was no use getting annoyed; she should have become rather used to Iris's questions since they never seemed to end.

"Sparnai," replied Amara.

"What is it supposed to mean?" Iris frowned.

"Why don't you ask that to the Lord? It's his pet after all."
Amara shrugged in response. Iris shut the question away. *Ask
the Lord?* That itself terrified her. She did not have enough
strength to speak to someone as powerful and intimidating as
Lord Lucifer. It was not her cup of tea.

"Okay. Now, can you please tell me where we're going?"
Iris questioned.

"The Lord only sends his pet alone when he is in danger.
So we're going to help him wherever Sparnai takes us," Amara
replied.

"Why do you need me for that?"

"I don't know. I just felt like I needed you."

"Ladies, if you two are finished with your interesting
conversation, I have something to ask Amara,"

Azrael interrupted before Iris could open her mouth to say
something else. She quieted down when he leaned forward so
his words could reach Amara.

"Now what do *you* want?" said Amara, letting out a
frustrated sigh. She was tired of answering questions. Although
she knew that being irritated was not going to stop Azrael from
saying what he wanted to.

"Apologies for being an annoyance, but I would like to
know what was written on the parchment that you destroyed,"
he told her.

They were now travelling a bit faster. The sky around
them was dark and Iris wondered how the Equus was able to
look without any source of light. Then again she thought that
it might be one of the creature's powers. As Sparnai flew faster,
Amara noticed that they were about to reach their destination.
She figured she might as well have answered the question
before they reach.

"Noctia Stella."

"Huh?" Azrael gasped as he heard that name.

"Excuse-me, but could someone please enlighten me further!" Iris exclaimed, thoroughly annoyed at their mutual level of understanding.

"Noctia Stella is a *Mortuis*. She is more than a thousand years old and has been practicing dark witchcraft for ages now. Through the message that the Lord sent, I assume it has something to do with her since she is an extremely powerful witch. She can't move a single finger due to old age but her strength lies in her eyes. She can do terrible things: things that can damage our world to no extent. But she had been caged by King Abraham the First using a shield of spells that are invincible.

"No amount of dark witchcraft can damage that shield. So she cannot destroy anything major on her own; but she has power enough to give her teachings to others enabling them to do her work. The glitch in that is it would take centuries until Conjurers become as strong as her and finish what she wants to do. But the problem is, nobody knows whom she has trained," Amara revealed.

They were starting to descend back to the ground. Iris clutched Amara's shoulders again when the speed increased. Moments later, they were on the land, softly paddling onto the grass. Iris observed her surroundings. There was absolutely no sound that she heard. Not even the wind flowing through the leaves of trees made any sort of noise. It was a deadly calm. They had entered a clearing where there were tiny huts of various kinds settled at a few paces ahead of them. There was a considerable distance between all the huts that were covered with stacks of hay. It seemed like a quaint village, but there not being a single sound was frightening in a way.

As the Equus came to a halt, Amara was the first to get down. Then Azrael followed suit. Iris was still atop Sparnai, gulping as she could not bring herself to descend. Azrael had to grab her by the arm and pull her down in one go, holding her waist to steady her so as not to let her fall. Iris dared not make a sound. She thought that she would be tortured if she uttered a single syllable. When Azrael was sure she was conscious enough to stand on her own, he let her feet touch the ground and released his hold on her waist. Iris pushed the hair falling over her face back, and started to follow Amara as she walked ahead. The Equus retreated and left to go to a river that was at a distance behind them.

"Where are we?" Iris whispered, leaning close to Amara's ear.

"The village of Heletes," replied Amara just as softly.

Iris did not ask anything else. She decided that she would save the rest of her questions for when they returned. At that moment, the more important task was to rescue the Lord. Amara walked ahead looking around to find any hint of Lord Lucifer but he was nowhere in sight. The path was lit with a few torches of fire that rested on trees. Azrael searched for Lord Lucifer as well, but to no avail. Then suddenly Amara stopped and turned to Iris.

"Can you find out where the Lord is?" She whispered.

Iris looked at her for a moment and then nodded. She shut her eyes in an attempt to connect her mind to Lord Lucifer's. She had never done that before. There were other minds that she had invaded and connected to, but not Lord Lucifer's. Neither did she ever dare to, nor had a chance like that occurred.

The air around them was cold. But Iris did not feel a thing, for her mind was focussed on something else. When she was sure her mind could locate Lord Lucifer's, she strained it so as to find out where he was. Iris realized that Lord Lucifer was not in his proper senses. She saw a vision of him inside one of those huts, but far away from where most were present. That hut was the gloomiest one out of all. It was bigger and the walls were a clear black with the strangest symbols around them. They gave off a dreadful vibe. Iris saw Lord Lucifer bound in chains on top of a chair, trembling. She immediately opened her eyes.

Without a word, she began walking in direction of the hut. Amara and Azrael glanced at each other before following her. They walked farther away from the shacks that were closely there and were now in an isolated area. Huge trees were in their surroundings, but there wasn't a single leaf on them. The air was disturbing. It gave off an extremely grim vibe. Iris blindly walked towards the shack and stood in front of it. The wind came to a standstill. The atmosphere was gloomy, creepy and frightening. It made Amara shudder in dread. Azrael scrunched his face up in disgust at the stench that had begun to waft through the air.

It was similar to the one that Lilith carried; only this time it was worse. Iris snapped back into her conscious state of mind at the horrible smell. The area around the hut was deserted and petrifying, to say the least. It scared Iris a lot more than necessary. She had never been to a place as gloomy as that one. It was worse than any place possible. She glanced at Azrael who was standing beside her, and then at Amara who was staring at the symbols on the hut. As they began to enter, the smell augmented and the atmosphere became darker and darker. A single candle was lit inside, illuminating the rest of the place in a soft glow.

Iris inadvertently grabbed Azrael's arm as they ventured further in. Soft chants of spells were heard that made Iris cringe. Azrael glanced at Iris once and placed a hand on hers to assure that he was there. She failed to notice and clutched his arm tighter, her nails digging into his flesh. Amara walked ahead to find Lord Lucifer tied to a chair. He was shuddering uncontrollably and right opposite to him was a woman. The appearance of her was hideous, sickening. Iris wanted to scream at the sight, it made her shut her eyes to never open them again. It was far worse than Lilith's.

The *Mortuis*, Noctia Stella, was nightmarish. Her hair was dishevelled, sticking up in every corner, gray and black; the bushy mane pushed back so it did not fall on her wrinkled forehead. Her skin was white underneath specks of black. Eyes a shade of dark red: cold and monstrous. Her nose was a crooked one, again wrinkled. Cheeks were covered in spots of blood and hanging loosely in crumpled lines. Lips were a dark purple; almost black and exceptionally dry. Her hands were crinkled and they trembled on her knees as she chanted spells. Nails were crooked, asymmetric and longer than usual. With lines of blood on them, her nails were settled on the robe that she wore: torn and old. It was tainted and worn, a black coloured robe that had holes in the sleeves that stretched to her elbows. Ripped from the waist a bit, crumpled as she sat still with her eyes boring into Lord Lucifer's trembling being.

Amara's gaze snapped towards Lord Lucifer and she immediately began muttering the purest spells to free him. Azrael proceeded ahead and joined in along with her while Iris stood there shivering beside him. She hid her face into his shoulder with her eyes tightly shut. Amara and Azrael chanted the spells but even though Noctia Stella had noticed them, she did not take her eyes off of Lord Lucifer, for she was quick enough to know that her concentration loss would render the process useless. So instead of disabling her opponents, she continued the attack on her victim.

"Gods of power of the wind and earth, the trembling flames and salient waters, spirits of the pure and the great ones, give us

the power to defeat the evil. End the sinful and slay the iniquitous. Give us a soul purer than virtuous, a tranquil strength to vanquish the impure and to trounce over the absolute. . ." Amara thus continued chanting along with Azrael.

Amara shut her eyes and chanted the spells louder. She then grabbed Iris's arm, and through her mind, sent a silent message of manipulating Noctia Stella's mind. Iris looked horrified. How could she handle the brain of more than a thousand year old witch who was skilled in dark witchcraft? That seemed like the silliest idea to her. But seeing the impatience on Amara's face, Iris shut her eyes and began to apply all the teachings that Eridanus had taught her. She was a fast learner, no doubt, but she had never manipulated any complicated mind of a normal witch, to have been skilled in doing the same for a *Mortuis* like Noctia Stella.

Amara sent Iris another message saying that since the witch's concentration was solely on Lord Lucifer and in trying to beat her opponents, it would not be as difficult to invade her mind. Iris took that as a confidence boost and let out a sigh before shooting a straight arrow through her mind into that of Noctia Stella's. Iris realized that due to the amount of years that the witch had existed, her mind was a weak one. She could only perform dark witchcraft, but was incapable of having enough control over her mind. That made Iris's task easier.

Noctia Stella failed to realize when her mind had been invaded. She only understood what had happened when Lord Lucifer suddenly stopped trembling in his seat. His eyes that had rolled upwards had gotten back to normal, and shut by themselves. Iris had shot her best manipulation skill into shutting Noctia Stella's mind to an extent that ceased her process of torturing Lord Lucifer. Amara immediately set Lord Lucifer free while Azrael pulled out the *Healing Potion* from Amara's bag and poured a few drops down Lord Lucifer's tongue.

However, Iris was still stuck. Her eyes were closed, mind blocked and it tackled that of the *Mortuis* and she stood stone still. When Amara looked at her, she immediately rushed towards Iris only to find Noctia Stella's eyes now focussed on her. The witch was staring right into Iris as though trying to paralyze her while Amara tried her best to counter the process. Azrael had noticed what was happening and since Lord Lucifer had now woken up, although weak, he glanced for a moment at Noctia Stella and then rushed towards Iris and Amara along with Azrael by his side. He grabbed Iris's arm and Azrael did the same with Amara. Lord Lucifer gave a nod in Azrael's direction and a moment later, the four of them vanished from the cottage. They landed forcefully on the ground beside the river Carinelle that was outside the village of Heletes.

The Equus was immediately by their side and Lord Lucifer instructed Azrael to help Amara who was struggling to stand up, for her head had been hit while he looked at Iris and was about to help her up. But she had fainted.

CHAPTER TWENTY-NINE

∞∞

FLAMES OF DESTRUCTION

∞∞

Her head was throbbing. Lights blinded her eyes that were half closed. Someone was shaking her shoulder as though trying to wake her up. But she did not want to wake up. She wanted to sleep a little more. The pounding in her head refused to go away and she was certain that all she needed was a tiny bit of sleep and it would all be okay. Nothing seemed to work and she started to wake up as much as she did not wish to. Her eyes opened slightly more and she heard a faint voice calling her name followed by a foggy sentence that echoed in her ears.

It sounded something like *"Why is she not waking up?"*

And slowly her eyes began to flutter. Her mind came back into its senses and she seemed to hear the voices clearly.

"If you use the word 'dead' right now I'm going to destroy everything!" the voice exclaimed.

It only increased the pain in her head, as though someone was hitting a huge rock on the inside.

"Will you calm down? She isn't dead! She's going to wake up!" said another voice.

She understood that it was a male voice from the sound. Then there was a female voice but she failed to recognize it.

"Both of you, shut up! She's fine! Look."

She squeezed her eyes shut as the pain increased. Just as she was about to open her eyes, she saw something. It was a woman, a nightmare-inducing woman that made a chilling sensation crawl up inch by inch into her body as though consuming her. The woman was walking towards her. Her eyes red, hair dishevelled, lips worn, voice hoarse, deep and frightening. The woman had wrinkled arms, forehead and a slightly crooked nose. The appearance was ghastly and it scared her to no limit.

She wanted to run somewhere, anywhere but there was no way out. She was locked inside a circled room that had no door. It was pitch black yet she could see the woman clearly. She tried to take a step back but was met with a wall. Her face turned in every possible way to find some door or window or anything that could get her out. The woman started to mutter something as she neared her.

"You will see Deaths of loved ones, of great ones and of brave ones. You will see them get tortured and destroyed until you are the only one alive!"

She was shaking in fear. Her breath caught, heartbeat hastening as she tried to find a way out but there was nothing she could do. As the woman came closer, raising her hand to grab her throat, she screamed as loud as she could, now sitting bolt upright with her eyes wide open. She breathed heavily. Drops of sweat trickled down her forehead and she let out gasps of breath. Everything was foggy around her as her eyes began to water. She felt an arm circle across her shoulder and her forehead crashed into a chest as she let the tears fall.

"It's okay, Iris, you're okay. You're alright," Eridanus whispered into her ear softly.

He smoothed his fingers down her hair, his other hand holding her close to him as she clutched the fabric of his cloak and sobbed. She held on tightly to him, the image of the woman still in her mind.

Amara let out a sigh, letting her back rest on the wall behind as she pressed a palm onto her forehead, squeezing her eyes shut for a moment. She was in Iris's chamber along with Leandra, Azrael, Eridanus and Soter. The moment that they had returned from the village of Heletes with an unconscious Iris, Amara had rushed to find the healer because Iris refused to wake up at any cost. They had tried water, *Healing Potion*, and a whole lot of things that were in the bag of supplies that Amara had taken. Nothing seemed to work. Iris had lain still between Azrael and Amara as they travelled back to the castle with Lord Lucifer.

They had no time to ask him what had happened and how he had ended up trapped on a chair in the shack of a devilish dark witch. Iris was more important at that point. Amara was surprised as to why the *Healing Potion* wasn't working. As soon as they had reached the castle, the first one to rush towards them was Eridanus who had already begun to take Iris in his arms and run inside. Prior to them returning, he had gotten a vision of Iris fainting. It worried him to no extent. Then the moment that they were back, he had wanted to wake her up in any possible way. He had absolutely no patience as the hours ticked by and Soter worked his way into healing Iris.

Soter had told them that she was going to be alright, but a mind and body that had been meddled with by a *Mortuis*, was hard to recover from. It was difficult, but Soter was assured that he would be able to do it if Eridanus would leave him alone for even a second. However, Eridanus refused to leave Iris's side. He sat there not moving an inch and watching everyone coming and going out the chamber while Soter did everything he could. Eridanus waited for hours, days and then a week until there was some progress. He did not leave the chamber till the time Iris started responding after a long week. In the meantime, Leandra and Sienna had begun to plan the summoning of Lilith's spirit along with help from Lord Lucifer who was also getting healed after getting attacked by the *Mortuis*. The story behind it, however, was a mystery.

Amara had been trying to meditate to be strong enough when they summoned those spirits but her mind always kept going back to Iris and whether or not she was going to recover. She was aware of the fact that Soter was entirely capable of healing her but the nagging sensation of having to lose Iris would not leave her mind. Though, Azrael was always by her side whenever Iris's condition worsened and Amara felt like breaking down. He was there to help her concentrate on meditation and he was there to talk to her about things that bothered her. He was there when she felt exhausted of all the stress and needed a good night's rest. Azrael had unknowingly helped her recover from the traumas in so many ways that Amara failed to comprehend it all. He had been the one she had gotten closest to after Iris.

Azrael gave her peace, he gave her assurance and slowly and steadily Amara began to develop a thin layer of trust on him. Because he was there when she accidentally went back to having visions of her past while resting on the branch of a tree; he was there to hold her hand when she was about to fall off the branch. He was there when she let a single tear fall, the time Iris was on the verge of dying, on the third night after they had returned. And he was there, the moment Iris woke up and Amara was on the verge of collapsing out of exhaustion.

He held her hand when she rested her back on the wall behind, pressing a palm to her forehead. He was beside her in a moment, gently gripping her hand and giving her the silent assurance that it was okay. Surprisingly, it calmed her immediately and she returned the ghost of a smile that he had given to her.

Eridanus had now relaxed; his eyes were skimming with tears, imagining what would have happened if he had lost Iris but having her in his arms was enough of an assurance. As he hugged her close to him and she cried, he smiled in content. She was still there. The week had been agonizing for him.

Watching Soter run around trying to find ways of healing her and attempting all sorts of things to make her alright was frustrating for him. In the times that Iris showed no progress, Eridanus felt like hexing himself to Death. What was the use of him being in the castle if he could not help her learn the power of manipulation? What was the use of him mastering the art himself if he could not tell her the limits to which minds could be meddled with? What was the use of him being there for nearly four months if he could not be of help to the girl that he had become so attached to; if he could not tell her that he was hopelessly in love for the very first time in his life?

It was only when Iris's tears stopped falling that she was able to let go of Eridanus, who held her in a tight grip close to him. She coughed, wiping her tears and pushing back the strands of hair stuck to her face. Soter sat beside her on a chair, holding a palm on her forehead that no longer seemed to be heating up with fever. It was normal. He gave her a smile.

"How do you feel?" He asked.

"Horrible. My head is aching and I need it to go away," she replied in a hoarse voice that sounded irritable to her own ears.

She could only imagine how it sounded to the others. Eridanus stood there grinning wide as though he had just won a war and was about to dance in celebration. Iris frowned at his expression but her eyes darted towards Amara, who stood opposite to her with her back resting on a wall, her eyes looking back at Iris. She held a relieved expression. Iris gave a light smile and Amara smiled back, closing her eyes for a moment. Iris then was about to look back at Soter who was filling up a glass full of some liquid when her gaze caught onto something that she found extremely strange yet wonderful. Azrael and Amara were holding hands.

Her smile widened as she looked at Azrael whose eyes were stuck on Amara. There was a look of adoration on his face as he gazed at her. Iris then glanced at Lea, who stood at the foot of the bed, grinning at her. She looked happy to see Iris awake. Iris snapped her eyes in direction of Amara and Azrael, and Lea frowned, turning around and fixing her gaze onto the two hands that were clasped together. Then she smirked, looking back at Iris with a mischievous glint in her eyes. They silently agreed upon discussing about it later. Soter had now shoved the glass full of green coloured liquid in Iris's direction.

"What is that?" She asked, scrunching up her face in disgust.

From the looks of it, she knew it would taste very bad.

"For your headache," replied Soter.

"I am not drinking that. It looks like poison." She shook her head with pleading eyes.

Soter responded with a flat look and extended the glass in her direction. Her head pounded yet again and she reluctantly took the glass from his hands and brought it to her lips. She shut her eyes and took a sip before spluttering it out.

"Are you trying to kill me?" She gasped, coughing.

"Iris, don't be a child," said Soter. "It's a higher dose of the *Healing Potion*. You need to drink it before the headache gets worse. It could be serious." He was looking at her sternly and Iris could do nothing but obey.

"*Higher* dose? I've been out for no more than a day!" she replied, bewildered.

Then she glanced at everyone hopefully. They said nothing but Lea and Eridanus's grin vanished, Amara and Azrael were no longer holding hands; the latter wasn't in the chamber and Amara was walking towards her bed to stand next to Lea.

"How long have I been sleeping? What happened to me?" She asked in a whisper.

Eridanus let out a sigh, slumping back onto his chair beside her bed. Amara scratched her forehead and Lea looked away.

"Drink that first. You'll have your answers then," said Lea.

Iris sighed and shut her eyes before gulping down the disgusting potion in one go. She then coughed while Soter took the glass back and placed it on the table beside her bed.

"Remind me to never drink that again," she said, shaking her head to get rid of the taste.

Her head began to feel lighter and she was relieved of the weight that she had been holding as the potion made its way into her system.

"*Now* can I get my answers?" She asked, looking at everyone.

"You were unconscious for a week and three days," Soter began. "We've been trying to get you to wake up since the night you returned from wherever you had gone with Amara and the others. Obviously you don't remember anything since your mind has been meddled with. It's going to take time till you fully recover." Perplexed, Iris stared at him.

"Unconscious? For a week? Where had I gone and with whom? What is going on?" She panicked, now sitting up straight as her head felt better.

"Wait, wait, just wait a minute," said Eridanus, holding up a hand. "Why did you wake up screaming?" He asked her.

She snapped her head towards him and blinked. She had forgotten. She did not remember what she had seen to have her wake up screaming. *Was it a nightmare? Did I see someone die? Was it a vision from past or future?* She struggled to find out why she had woken up like that, but there was no trail of it.

"I-I don't remember," she stuttered.

"Do *you* know why she woke up screaming?" Eridanus turned to Soter.

He nodded, letting out a sigh.

"She must have had the nightmare," he said. "But I don't know the details. Someone needs to tell her what happened from the beginning. She won't remember otherwise."

Amara looked at Eridanus and then at Lea. She gestured Lea to follow her outside. Realizing what they were doing, Soter stood up as well, to leave the chamber. He turned to Eridanus.

"Tell her," he said.

Eridanus nodded and then looked at an impatient Iris. She looked scared. Eridanus got up from the chair he was sitting on and settled himself beside her on the bed. She was sitting with her legs sprawled before her on the bed with the sheet covering up to her waist.

"Relax," he whispered, placing a hand on hers.

Iris let out a breath she was holding. Something in his voice calmed her.

"Just calm down and listen to me without interrupting. Okay?" He told her with a reassuring smile. Iris nodded in response.

Eridanus began telling her everything that had happened from the moment that she had left with Amara. He had been told all the details by Azrael when they had returned. Iris silently listened to him, opening her mouth to say something whenever she thought she heard something familiar. Her mind struggled to find a trace of what had happened in that one night. She only remembered a few parts of it. When he described to her that they were in the hut of a *Mortuis*, her ears had perked up. Her eyes glistened with the visions of a dreadful woman, and suddenly the nightmare that had occurred to her came flashing before her eyes.

She panicked. Her hands began to tremble in fear and paranoia. As soon as Eridanus noticed that, he held both her hands and shushed her.

"It's okay now. Don't be scared. I'm here and you're safe. Nothing is going to harm you," he told her in hushed whispers, reassuringly.

Iris was still trembling on the inside. She swallowed the lump in her throat and shut her eyes, taking a deep breath. Eridanus held her hands tightly, repeating that she was going to be alright. Iris calmed down. She did not remember everything that had happened that night apart from the terrifying woman that she kept seeing.

She felt as though she had seen the *Mortuis* lot of times but Eridanus told her that it was only a nightmare. The fact that she could not recall anything else bothered her. It frustrated her and she wanted to know what exactly had happened, instead of hearing it from someone else.

"Give that tiny brain of yours a bit of rest. It'll come back to you. Just don't think about all that now. We have other things to take care of," he said to her.

Iris nodded in understanding. She realized that they had the task of summoning Lilith's spirit.

"But I've been out for more than a week. What if Lord Mikhail already has Lilith's spirit under control?" She asked, raising her eyebrows.

"Lea has been keeping an eye on Lilith. She tells us the spirit is not responding particularly the way Lord Mikhail wants it to. There has been some progress but we'll be able to redeem it. The plan is already prepared. We just have to wait until you have recovered completely and then we can start the process. The Lord has also agreed to help so we're stronger now," said Eridanus, smiling.

Iris finally calmed down. She sighed in relief and then looked back at Eridanus. Leaning forward she threw her arms around his neck in a hug. He responded with a shock at first and then returned the affection.

"Thank you," she told him, pulling away.

"For what?" He frowned. "For being so devilishly charming and handsome?" He said before she could reply.

Iris narrowed her eyes and gave him a flat look before slapping his arm.

"You're such a pain," she said, shaking her head. He winked in response.

"Now go get a bath," he told her, standing up from the bed. "You smell of muck."

Iris threw a pillow at him as he bolted out of the door with a smirk. She pushed the covers off of her and stood up, stumbling at her feet. Keeping a hand on the wall next to her she steadied herself and blinked to adjust her vision. When she was sure she was able to walk, Iris proceeded towards the bathroom in her chamber.

She left to go to the kitchen when she was done cleaning herself and dressed into a light-blue gown. Her hair was down her shoulders in damp tangles when she muttered a drying spell and shook her now dry hair before entering the kitchen.

"Tea, my lady?" said Eridanus, appearing out of nowhere when she entered through the door.

He was holding a cup of steaming hot tea in his hands, extending it towards her.

"Who knows, you might have poisoned it," she replied and walked past him.

"I wouldn't dare," he told her, placing a hand on his heart, feigning horror. He followed her as she looked for something to eat. Iris rolled her eyes at him.

Grabbing an apple, she began munching on it while Eridanus started to tell her something. The door of the kitchen opened and in walked Amara, Lea, and Azrael.

"How are you feeling now?" asked Amara.

"Hungry," she replied and Lea rushed in her direction, pulling her into a tight hug.

"You'll break my bones, Lea," said Iris with a chuckle.

"Sorry," Lea replied, letting go of her.

"Feel okay, little one?" Azrael spoke as he held a smile.

Iris had a foggy vision of her clutching his hand while in the chamber of the *Mortuis*. She nodded in reply. Without wasting another moment, Amara began talking to Iris about the important task that they were supposed to perform.

"Alright then, Iris, we don't have much time for the process of summoning Lilith's spirit now. And we are thinking of starting it tonight; but we have created a plan in a way that if you don't feel up to it, we try to make our forces stronger with the Lord's help. You shall only be involved if your health is suitable and if Soter gives us the assurance that you will be okay. Of course we will be helping you in every possible way but you have to be completely in your senses for this. Are you going to be able to do this?" She said.

"I don't know but I'll try. I do want to help with this, Amara. I can't let you lot do this alone. By tonight, I promise I'll recover. I will have to," she replied.

"No, Iris. This is not a compulsion. With your help we'll obviously be stronger and it becomes easier but you won't force yourself into this. It's not easy," Eridanus said with a serious look.

"I appreciate your concern but I-I want to do this. I've prepared myself for it even though I've been asleep for more than a week. I know that since you all are with me there is no way I will be harmed. This is as important to me as it is to every one of you." Iris protested.

"Are you perfectly sure?" asked Azrael, raising his eyebrows in concern.

"Yes," Iris said.

There was a confident look that she held even though she wasn't much assured inside. She had wanted this task done the moment that she had been told about it. She had no other option. It was necessary that she be of any help to Amara. It was a vow that she had taken for the rest of her existence. And it was not to be let down.

"Okay then. Eridanus, help her get prepared for this," Amara said, sighing. "Meanwhile, Sienna and I will set up the sacrificial chamber. Azrael, please inform the Lord that we begin at three a.m. sharp. Also tell the others not to be anywhere around the sacrificial chamber tonight. The library will be closed and the whole passage downstairs needs to be shut down. Leandra, you get the required books for the spells that we need."

With that, the four of them vanished out of sight, leaving Eridanus and Iris standing in the kitchen while Iris finished the apple that she was eating. After she was done filling her stomach and was sure that she had enough energy to begin, Iris and Eridanus left for the meditation chamber to prepare her for the task that night.

* * *

Amara and Sienna got themselves busy in planning the whole process once again while setting up the sacrificial chamber. By nightfall, the chamber was plunged into darkness. Then the candles were lit, surrounding the points inside the huge circle with a star. Enchantments were spread on the walls as the atmosphere went to a still-calm. The single window in the chamber was shut, leaving just enough space for air to sweep in; curtains were drawn, books kept outside the circle of light as Leandra, Sienna and Amara stood there at midnight. When they were sure all preparations were done, three of them left the chamber and then spread enchantments around the whole area covering Lord Lucifer's chamber and the library.

Then they went to the meditation chamber and prepared themselves for the next three hours. At exactly three in the morning when the clock struck, the lot descended down to the sacrificial chamber along with Lord Lucifer. The passage had been sealed and the ritual began.

CHAPTER THIRTY

∞∞∞∞∞∞

THE DANCE OF THE SOUL

∞∞∞∞∞∞

L it by a single torch of fire, the sacrificial chamber was amiss a darkness that surrounded it for nearly two hours. The door had been enchanted in protection so as to keep the sounds coming from the chamber unheard. For the sounds were a music that no one was able to contain. They were horrific and chilling. It was not a normal night. Inside the chamber, sat three witches surrounding the circle of Fire between them. The candles that rested on the points of the star within were now blazing with flames as the wax melted furiously. Yet they did not diminish. All the candles remained the usual size.

Amara, Leandra and Sienna were chanting innumerable spells so as to summon the Lord of souls, Isiah. Azrael and Eridanus were busy trying to connect their minds to that of Lilith's so as to manipulate her, while Iris and Lord Lucifer sat in one side of the chamber, watching everything in silence. At times when sounds of the chants grew louder and clearer, they scared Iris. She would flinch every now and then but after a while she began to adapt to them. Lord Lucifer was unaffected.

He sat there transferring some of his energy to the three witches whenever it felt like they were losing strength.

Summoning an evil spirit from the clutches of a Lord like Lord Mikhail wasn't easy. It was tiring and they had been at it for almost two hours. Various lights flew around as the chants grew louder. Sometimes blue indicating progress, sometimes red: that showed a barrier that the witches had to fight in order to go ahead; and sometimes it went completely black, saying that the spirit was starting to respond.

"Give us your power, holy Lord of Death, of salvation, of doom. Send us the soul that is evil and impure. We pray to thee, Lord of greatness, of spirits. Help us to the evil and to the Deathly. Give us your power to summon the grave soul. Holy Lord of salvation, of doom, give us your strength to take the vile in our grasp. We pray to thee. . ."

On went the hymns, echoing around the chamber, the sounds inducing slight tremors in the walls. Iris watched as the chants continued and Azrael and Eridanus concentrated their best in manipulating the spirit.

* * *

Far away in a small cave of the Dark Falls, the body that Lilith's spirit had possessed was shivering. She lay on the stone floor where Lord Mikhail had left her a night ago. After ensuring protection around the cave, he had left to go and meet with Lord Zachariah to let him know the progress that had been made. Lord Mikhail had not received any message from his source in the castle of Lord Lucifer and it confused him in some ways. He was aware that something big was about to happen, yet he had not been informed about it.

Although, letting Lord Zachariah and his apprentices know what task they were to do was more important than not receiving information from his source. He was now in the court of King Orcus after a long and tiring journey from the village of Heletes, to the caves of Dark Falls and then back to Acanthus, at five in the morning. The court of King Orcus was eerily quiet. When Lord Mikhail approached the King, he was seated on the throne wearily.

"Your highness?" He expressed with concern.

He wasn't expecting the court to be summoned so early in the morning. The usual time was always after seven. Seeing the looks that everyone held, it seemed to Lord Mikhail that something grave had happened. When King Orcus raised his head, it was comprehensible that there was a grave matter that needed to be discussed. The court would not be summoned otherwise.

"Lord Mikhail," said the King, relieved that the Minister was back.

He hoped there would be some help from him.

"What is the matter, your highness?" Lord Mikhail asked, frowning.

"We have lost Lord Zachariah," replied the King.

Lord Mikhail stared. He merely stared at the King vacantly. Lord Zachariah was the eldest sorcerer in Acanthus, and Lord Mikhail's mentor. He had been the source of information and help that Lord Mikhail needed. *Lost?* He wondered. How was that possible?

"What do you mean lost?" He whispered.

Lord Zachariah was the most learned sorcerer of their time. He was old but powerful. He had enough strength to paralyze someone at once. Defeating him was a difficult task, and only extremely strong sorcerers or witches were capable of doing that.

"We buried him a few hours ago."

Upon hearing that, Lord Mikhail's heart dropped in his chest. Lord Zachariah was dead? He asked himself a million questions as to how that was possible but he could never get the answers. He knew nothing of what had happened in the court after he left to look for the one who would help him gain the prophecy by summoning Lady Calypsa. He had enough information about everything that went on in the castle of Lord Lucifer but he was unaware of what occurred in his own.

"How did this happen?" He asked.

"There is no clue of how he died," the King began. "We found his body in the mountains of *Rosean*. Two nights ago, he told us that he would be travelling for some important message that he had to give to you, said he would only do that in person. He refused to have any guards or our apprentices sent with him and insisted on going alone. We tried to stop him but he would hear nothing. Then hours later, I received a distorted message from him saying that he needed help. By the time we located him and found him in *Rosean*, he was gone. We suspect that he was attacked but there was no trace of any hex or injury. He was clean. It seems to be that he lost strength or-"

"Lord Zachariah is not weak enough to lose strength while travelling," Lord Mikhail cut him off, snapping.

He could not believe what he was hearing. It was strange and most mysterious to have Lord Zachariah dead all the sudden. What was the message that he wanted to give to Lord Mikhail? Lord Mikhail gave a lot of thought to it. Lord Zachariah would not have left the court to meet him in person if it were not extremely important. Now there was no way that Lord Mikhail could find out what the message was. Summoning the spirit of Lord Zachariah was also not a choice since his soul would still be in the process of the after-life and during that, it would be of no use. It could be years until he would find out what the message was.

"That is what we believe as well, Lord Mikhail. But his Death is most confusing. We have been trying to think of the cause but there is no answer. If you could tell us any possibility," King Orcus trailed off.

There was a pregnant pause. Lord Mikhail sat down as he gazed at the floor in confusion. He gave it deep thought. As grieved as he was at the Death of his only mentor, it confused him to no limit for not knowing the cause of his Death. An extremely powerful and learned sorcerer like Lord Zachariah could not die so easily. There had to be someone as strong in competition to defeat him. Who was it that had enough power to defeat Lord Zachariah? Who could have that much influence?

"Lord Lucifer," he suddenly breathed.

"I beg your pardon?" said the King.

His eyebrows were raised in astonishment. Had he heard what he thought he had?

"It could only be him. You said there were no injuries of hex evidences, correct?" asked Lord Mikhail, looking up at the confused King. The rest of the court, although silent, held similar expressions as that of their King.

"He was clean. It seemed like an unharmed Death," replied the King.

"Lord Lord Lucifer is the only one that can kill someone without a single harm to the victim. Although, Lord Zachariah is not so weak to have been under influence of Lord Lucifer; what confuses me is how he let Lord Lucifer attack. He could be the only one," Lord Mikhail muttered in deep thought.

"But why would Lord Lucifer do something like that?" asked Lord Gabriel.

"That is another question." Lord Mikhail sighed. "We need to find that out somehow."

"Are you sure that it was Lord Lucifer?" the King said.

"Not completely, but the evidences point that way. I'm going to have to meet him."

With that, Lord Mikhail stood up to go to the castle of Lord Lucifer when the King stopped him.

"Lord Mikhail, this does not seem like a bright plan. We have not any proof of whether Lord Lucifer has committed this. If he has, it is punishable of course, for Lord Zachariah was one of the greatest sorcerers we have had. For him to be killed it is most astounding, but we cannot blame Lord Lucifer for it without a single proof. There is no existent evidence of this. You have just arrived. Do rest for a while. We know your journey was tiring. I suggest you take some rest and then we shall discuss on this matter thoroughly. It is my request, Lord Mikhail, please return to your chamber. I shall send assistance to you right away for refreshments."

"We do not have time for *refreshments* and *rest*, your highness!" Lord Mikhail snapped with annoyance. "There is a war that I have declared; I have to gather an army. I have an important task to take care of. I cannot sit in my chamber and rest at this moment. Lord Zachariah is dead and you expect me to take rest?"

"Lord Mikhail, you are under a lot of stress. Nothing can function this way. We need you to be stable right now. For that you need to rest. I give you a direct order as your King. You have to obey me and go rest right this moment."

There was a stern look that King Orcus held, one that Lord Mikhail had seen for the first time in many years. King Orcus was known for being weak and irresponsible. He had never used his authority of being King over anybody. He always took advice of his Ministers before taking a single decision, even though it might be of less importance. Whether it was his kindness or weakness, nobody knew. Yet the Ministers respected him enough since he was the descendant of King Abraham. Lord Mikhail stared blankly at King Orcus, unable to utter a word.

"To your chamber, Lord Mikhail, now." He repeated.

A moment later, Lord Mikhail was out of the court and back into his chamber. It seemed as though he had not been there for ages. Only months had passed since he had visited his chamber, after he left to travel. It was comforting to him in a few ways, yet he was so disturbed at the Death of Lord Zachariah, that he did not know what exactly he felt. He was perplexed as well. He did not know whether Lord Lucifer had really been the one that killed Lord Zachariah, or if it was someone else. And if it was Lord Lucifer, what was the reason behind it? What was the message that Lord Zachariah wanted to give to him?

As he rested himself on the bed, he stared above at the ceiling with various thoughts running across his mind. Questions that he could not find out the answers to were lurking in his brain as his eyes shut themselves and he descended into a deep sleep after weeks; nearly forgetting about the spirit of Lilith that was being summoned from the Dark Falls, right to the castle that wasn't very far from where he was.

* * *

Lilith's body was now being tossed around in the cave, hitting the walls and the floor tremendously as it tried to dodge the protection that had been created around the cave. It was being called somewhere, and the call was powerful enough to have rendered her helpless and out of its own control. Lilith was partly influenced by Lord Mikhail after he had tried to release her mind with all the vile thoughts, replacing them with the prior thoughts of what she really was; and she was partly influenced by the chants that were echoing into her ears, pulling her towards the source. The control of Lord Mikhail was stronger, and it stopped her from breaking the protections and travelling to where she was being called.

As her limp body smashed across walls, her red eyes rolled upwards, mouth open and a horrific sound erupting from her throat, Lilith heard another sound that began to break the protection slowly and steadily. She fought it; Lord Mikhail's control over her tried to fight harder but the sound that she was hearing started to become clearer. The melody of a flute ·pierced her ears and mind, rendering all her control useless as she struggled to keep still inside the cave.

All the sudden, Lord Mikhail's protective shields cracked and Lilith's eyes burned furiously. She stood still for a moment, eyes wide and hands stuck to her sides. Something made her rush towards the entrance of the cave that had been sealed shut with a huge rock. Lilith began to push the rock using all her strength; unaware of how much her body was being injured. Her fragile fingers applied all their strength onto the rock that refused to budge, for it was too heavy.

Miles away in the castle, Azrael and Eridanus were trying their best to manipulate Lilith into leaving the cave that she was trapped in and reaching the castle but so far, they had only managed to move her body from wall to wall and then back to the floor, injuring her profusely. But as soon as Sienna had picked up the flute and started to send out various melodies from it, the protective shields that were around Lilith broke and Eridanus immediately entered Lilith's mind, then manipulating her into trying to get rid of the rock that was covering the entrance. When they were sure that it would injure her more and make it difficult for them to make her travel all the way to Acanthus from the Dark Falls, Azrael raised one of his hands, keeping his concentration on Lilith.

The gesture of his hand being raised meant that Iris had to intervene at that point. Since she was weak after having fainted from the journey to the village of Heletes, they had not let her join them until it was extremely necessary and had no option. As soon as Iris saw Azrael's hand up, she rushed to sit beside him and shut her eyes immediately. Meanwhile, Lea and Amara were in a trance. Their chants were no longer heard, but they were silently praying to the God Isiah so as to keep the sacrificial chamber ready for when the spirit arrived.

Azrael created a link between his mind and that of Iris's to help her form a clear connection to Lilith. Iris used all of her strength to do the same. She let her mind get focussed on the spirit that was to be summoned and concentrated hard as she could. Lilith went awfully silent. No sound came out of her, no movement occurred. The cave was quiet, eerily quiet apart from the sound of the flute that echoed around. Lilith's eyes scanned the cave. It was sealed shut. There was no escape. Moments later, she closed her eyes. Her hands raised themselves on their own accord. Her feet moved backwards a few paces.

With slow movements, Lilith's lips moved and a spell came out of her mouth that shattered the rock on the entrance of the cave, a blinding red light glittering from the stretch of her fingers. Wind rushed inside the cave as soon as the barrier was gone and Lilith then proceeded to walk out of the chamber. Iris let out a breath that she was holding. She had entered Lilith's mind, keeping a firm hold to the link with Azrael's so as not to lose herself in the spirit that she was handling. With that, she had made Lilith break the rock down into pieces instead of using physical strength. Meanwhile Eridanus had helped her cease Lilith's mind to not let any other force enter.

What Iris had done was remarkable, in Azrael's opinion. He made a mental note to applaud her for that. He then started to make Lilith's body move in direction of the castle while Eridanus made sure that she was going on the right path, and Iris kept a hold over the spirit's mind so as not to let it wander around anywhere that was unnecessary. And Lilith walked as she was being made to. The sound of the flute led her into an ecstasy that nobody was able to understand. It mesmerized her and made her lose herself in the sound. The melody that Sienna was producing had immense power to bring Lilith to the castle.

Lord Lucifer watched the whole process with relief. He could see the strength that was his coven. In those six Conjurers, he saw a power that assured him that his coven was going to be one of the greatest of their time. Five elements described the power of his apprentices in the chamber with him. Iris was the Fire that had strength to destroy as well as illuminate. Azrael was the Water that ensured peace and could wipe out dangers of all kinds. Eridanus was the Earth that gave a base to their strength and held them on ground. Sienna and Leandra were Wind, both strong and made their presence felt, although invisible; and Amara was the Spirit that held the rest of them together and ruled over all.

It was astonishing as to how none of them needed his help in summoning a spirit as strong and vile as that of Lilith's. As he sat there watching the whole process unfold before him, the window of the chamber flung open, shattering the glass everywhere and indicating an arrival. Amara, Leandra, Azrael and Iris's eyes shot open to find the spirit of Lilith enclosed in the body of a human staggering towards them slowly. Iris looked at the one that had killed Nicholas. She did not know how she felt. Sienna still had her eyes closed with the flute playing and Eridanus was exhausted as he slumped on the wall beside him, his eyes slightly open.

Amara watched as the spirit of Lilith crashed before her between the circle of light. Then there was a deafening silence.

∞ ∞ ∞ ∞ ∞ ∞

PART III

∞ ∞ ∞ ∞ ∞ ∞

CHAPTER THIRTY-ONE

∞∞∞∞∞∞

THE LOST APPRENTICE

∞∞∞∞∞∞∞

The spirit of Lilith was trapped inside the sacrificial chamber. Lord Lucifer had paralyzed the body of the possessed and sealed her in the chamber with immense protection around her to protect her from being summoned by Lord Mikhail again. The shields were stronger and better than what Lord Mikhail had done. Ambrosius was asked to patrol around the chamber to make sure no harm occurred. The castle was then calmer and more peaceful than ever before. It was four days later that the doors of the castle were flung open and in walked the King's men along with an injured prisoner.

Lord Lucifer stood up from his throne. The others were seated around him in a meeting for the preparation of the war. As everyone turned to look at the intruders, a groaning sound was heard while the guards dragged him in and threw him on the floor between the circled residents of the castle. Everyone frowned in confusion.

"Lord Lucifer, is this your apprentice?" asked one of the three King's guards, lifting the prisoner's face through his cloak's collar.

He groaned in pain once again and Iris winced at the familiar sound. Her eyes were wider than ever when she saw who it was.

There lay Erasmus, with his face covered in blood, a cut on the side of his lip, an injured eye, hair dishevelled and one hand twisted in a very painful way that made it obvious it was broken. His cloak was torn, blood dripping from a wound in his leg. The sight was unbelievable. He wasn't the Erasmus that Iris had been with before. He was someone completely different and Iris was astounded.

"Erasmus?" uttered Lord Lucifer, a look of disbelief etched upon his features.

"Well since that has been established. The King has asked for an audience with you this evening, Lord Lucifer. And your apprentice here has been arrested," another guard spoke.

"What is. . .may I ask as to why he is being imprisoned?" Lord Lucifer asked.

"We are unaware of the same. The King has summoned you and his highness will let you know the reason," replied the guard.

"But-" Lord Lucifer started to protest.

"Get him off of the floor," the guard cut him off.

Then before anyone could say anything, Erasmus was lifted up and dragged out once again, to everyone's shock. Iris stared at the whole scene in front of her wordlessly, trying to contain the sudden shock that she was experiencing. She wanted to say something and stop those guards from dragging Erasmus out of the castle but no sound came. They were all silent. None of them had been able to contemplate what had just happened. It all had gotten over so fast that it was impossible to put the entire process together.

"Take your seats," said Lord Lucifer, breaking the silence and then settling himself on his throne.

"My Lord?" asked Azrael, perplexed.

"We aren't aware of what has happened so I can't say anything at the moment. It will only be understood when I meet the King in about two hours," he replied.

Every one of them had worried expressions mixed with those of confusion. Nobody knew what was going to happen at the King's palace. Moreover, why Erasmus had been arrested was a mystery.

"M'Lord, I would suggest you to take someone with you. We cannot risk your safety at this sensitive hour," said Amara from where she was seated beside Eridanus.

Iris sat on the opposite side with Leandra and Azrael, her eyes fixed at the marble floor, as though in deep thought.

"There is no need for that, Amara. I don't think going to the King's palace will be dangerous." Lord Lucifer shook his head in denial.

"I volunteer to go with you, m'Lord. We insist that you have at least one of us to accompany you," Azrael offered.

Lord Lucifer let out a sigh and then nodded in agreement. It seemed like a logical and sensible thing to do at a point where one of his apprentices was being imprisoned by the King, for a reason that nobody was yet aware of. The meeting was then dismissed after Lord Lucifer left the main hall and retreated to his chamber, leaving Iris, Azrael, Amara and Eridanus there. Iris was silent, her eyes still on the floor. Her eyes were a bit moist and there was a strange expression that she held, something that the others failed to comprehend.

"Why is Erasmus being imprisoned?" She suddenly asked, breaking the silence.

The rest of them turned to look at her.

"We don't know yet, Iris. We will only know when the Lord returns from the King's court," said Eridanus calmly, from where he was standing next to a window.

As he looked at Iris, he realized that he had failed to confess his feelings for her yet. What stopped him was something he could not put a finger on. Maybe it was a fear of not being reciprocated with, for Iris showed no signs of similar feelings towards him. And he did not wish to impose himself on her if she did not feel the same. But that would not stop him from wishing of being seated beside her right now, giving her an assurance that the first friend she had after entering the castle was going to be okay. He knew that although Erasmus had not been in the castle for a while and that he and Iris had not exactly communicated in the last two months, Erasmus was an important person in Iris's life, no matter the consequences.

"Why is Erasmus being imprisoned?" Iris uttered again, lost in thought.

Amara and Azrael looked at her in perplexity. They glanced at one another worriedly. Why was Iris repeating the question when she had already been answered? Amara opened her mouth to say something when Iris spoke again.

"Why is he being imprisoned if he was only trying to defend himself?"

Amara realized that Iris had been having visions of what might have happened with Erasmus.

"Iris, what have you seen?" She asked, getting up and heading in her direction.

Iris still kept her gaze locked onto the floor, as though in a trance.

"He was only trying to save himself. Is that a crime?" She said, not realizing that Amara was sitting right in front of her on the floor with her hands on Iris's knees.

"Iris!" Amara bellowed.

Iris snapped her eyes in her direction. Amara watched Iris's face with concern.

"What?" She said, as though pulling herself out of a daze; she blinked thrice while looking at everyone.

Eridanus stood where he was, wondering what Iris had seen as he tried to push his way into her mind but she shot a warning glare in his direction and blocked his path. He looked away. Azrael glanced between the two of them and despite the sensitive situation at hand; he smiled slightly to himself at the exchange that had happened. He found Iris and Eridanus to be an interesting pair. But that wasn't his concern at the moment. He was baffled about the fact that one of Lord Lucifer's most trusted apprentices was being imprisoned.

"What have you seen that concerns Erasmus?" asked Amara, snapping Azrael out of his thoughts.

"I'm not sure. All I saw was him trying to defend himself. I don't exactly know what it was. But there was another man, I don't recognize the face but it was someone old. Erasmus was being attacked and- I don't know," replied Iris, dazedly.

She ran a hand through her hair, tucking a strand behind her ear in the process.

"Alright. If you see any more visions just let me know, okay?" Amara gave a determined look and Iris nodded in response.

Amara then stood up and took a few steps back before walking out of the hall and to her own chamber. Azrael let out a sigh and strode over to Eridanus who stood there with his eyes focussed on Iris. She was now getting up to go to her chamber as well. There were a few books that she had to read along with Leandra. She was waiting for Iris. Without glancing at Eridanus as he was expecting her to, she walked past him and disappeared. He let out an audible sigh, which Azrael noticed and raised his eyebrows at.

"Have you ever loved someone?" He said to Azrael.

"Describe love," replied Azrael, leaning on the wall and crossing his arms on his chest.

"I don't know. But if you haven't, then I suggest you don't, because it is very exhaustive when you aren't sure whether she is going to throw a curse at you or accept you wholeheartedly."

With that, Eridanus gave Azrael a fleeting look of despair before wandering off outside the castle. Azrael blinked, staring at the floor beneath his feet. *Could it be?* He wondered and then shook his head as he rolled his eyes in denial. *No it cannot be.* Then he proceeded to walk to his own chamber and wait until it was time to join the Lord to the King's court.

* * *

Two hours later, Lord Lucifer found himself standing before King Orcus in the court, surrounded by various other Ministers including Lord Mikhail. He was staring at Lord Lucifer with a piercing gaze that said he had just one thing on his mind: murder. Lord Lucifer bowed in respect to King Orcus along with Azrael who stood behind him amidst the crowd of enemies that they were going to have war with. It seemed nearly surreal to him as he watched the faces of those that he would have to battle in a matter of time. And seeing the looks on their faces, the war did not seem very far away. It was close, and he knew that the protection of Lady Calypsa was now their utmost priority after they left the King's court, whether with or without Erasmus.

The King gave a nod in Lord Lucifer's direction.

"Have a seat, Lord Lucifer," he said.

Shaking his head in disagreement, Lord Lucifer stood there with his staff held in his right hand, his robe sprawling behind him.

"What is it that has happened, your highness?" He asked, eager to know the cause of his apprentice being arrested.

"It is with utmost sadness that I inform you about the demise of our great Lord Zachariah. We have lost a very vital part of our Ministry," said the King.

Lord Lucifer's eyes widened in shock before he lowered his head in remorse, wondering how that had anything to do with Erasmus being imprisoned. He was aware of how powerful Lord Zachariah was. He had played a role in Lord Lucifer's training along with King Abraham. The loss was surely saddening, but having Erasmus arrested was something he still could not understand.

"Lord Lucifer, your coven has been a very important part of Acanthus," the King continued. "We have worked together in protecting the Kingdom from attacks of witch-hunters and other creatures that would be of harm. We have existed in harmony since the days of my forefathers. However, taking into account recent events, war is imminent, which is of course of great concern to the Kingdom as well as the Ministry. But of course, the privilege of depending on the Ministry's help resides with my great Ministers solely.

"The Death of Lord Zachariah is most sorrowful, since he had nothing to do with the war. For him to have been harmed is unacceptable and the killer will be sentenced. Lord Zachariah was one of the greatest sorcerers from the time of King Abraham the Second. His killing through the hands of one of your apprentices is alarming; given the respect that Lord Zachariah has received in all these years.

"Today we have arrested your apprentice by the name of Erasmus Carcius Lehfe'r under the accusation of him being the one that has slain our respected Lord. Four nights ago we discovered the body of Lord Zachariah in the mountains of *Rosean* and since then Lord Mikhail has left no stone unturned in finding out who it was that killed the Lord. After two days of searching the vast areas of *Rosean*, he has come to the conclusion that your apprentice had been meditating in the mountains when Lord Zachariah met him. The accused has left a trail of him since he resided there for a week which is why we could understand that it was him that was present at the time Lord Zachariah died. We found him in the mountains after Lord Mikhail sent us the message regarding the same.

"The accused has agreed to his crime but refuses to divulge the information as to how he managed to slay someone as great as Lord Zachariah. We all are aware of his power although he was of old age. Killing a powerful sorcerer like him is not a facile task. He is to be sentenced for life imprisonment in the dungeons for committing a crime of such intensity. Tonight, I summon you here to help us in deciphering as to why the accused has slain Lord Zachariah. If you will kindly cooperate, Lord Lucifer."

For the three minutes that the King spoke, Lord Lucifer listened to him with rapt attention and so did Azrael. Their shock upon knowing that Erasmus was the one to kill Lord Zachariah was obvious enough to everyone else around. Lord Mikhail was still shooting daggers in their direction and Azrael decided to ignore it even though he had noticed, unlike Lord Lucifer who wasn't as much under shock as Azrael was. Lord Lucifer was well aware of how strong Erasmus was, although his power was not exactly focussed on and shown to others.

He believed in keeping his powers hidden and only revealing them when extremely necessary. Killing Lord Zachariah might have had a reason behind it, since Erasmus was not one to kill a well-known and powerful sorcerer. What appalled Lord Lucifer was the cause of it. He wanted to know why Erasmus had taken such a drastic step. The injuries that he had were obvious enough to tell Lord Lucifer that he had been tortured into revealing the reason he killed Lord Zachariah and how he managed to do so. Yet Erasmus had not uttered a word about it.

"Your highness, it is with great remorse that I express my sorrow for the Death of a great sorcerer of the likes of Lord Zachariah. May his soul find salvation soon in the after-life. I do not know why my apprentice has killed the Lord. I assure you it wasn't under my orders or anyone else's from my coven. Erasmus has been away for about a month after the tragic Death of my nephew and part of the coven, Nicholas. Erasmus's whereabouts were unknown to us. I would be honoured to be of any help to the Ministry. But your highness, we cannot ignore the possibility of a conflict that might have happened between the two. I do not see any evidence that would state that Erasmus was the only one at fault. I am not accusing the great Lord of being wrong, but Erasmus is a trusted apprentice and I have to question this. I believe he had a concrete reason to do what he did," said Lord Lucifer calmly.

"You are correct, Lord Lucifer. If he were not at fault, the accused would have divulged the cause, free of fear. But since he hasn't, doubts are bound to arise," the King replied just as softly.

"I understand that my apprentice will have to be questioned in the court," Lord Lucifer said.

"It is as custom goes, Lord Lucifer. We shall summon the accused." The King nodded and started to order a guard to bring Erasmus into the court when Azrael stepped forward.

"If I may interrupt, your highness," said Azrael, glancing at Lord Mikhail for a moment. "I am Azrael, another apprentice of Lord Lucifer. Forgive me for the intrusion, but will your majesty permit us to speak to Erasmus in private?"

Lord Lucifer snapped his head in Azrael's direction with a warning look. What he had proposed was most unacceptable and there were chances that Lord Mikhail would be enraged and get Azrael imprisoned as well for going against the rules of the law; given Lord Mikhail's influence over the King. Lord Lucifer did not wish to lose any more of his apprentices from the coven. The war was coming sooner.

He was not surprised when all the Ministers rose from their seats and began to talk loudly, grumbling and protesting against what Azrael had just said. Lord Mikhail stood there, fuming as he tried to stop himself from not hexing Azrael and Lord Lucifer right then and there. The King silenced the court as he raised his palm.

"Please, great Lords. Take your seats," he said.

Everyone quieted down; although they did not stop staring at Azrael who had stayed perfectly calm during the whole chaos.

"You do realize that you are speaking against the law?" said the King, looking at Azrael.

"I do, your highness. But the reason I suggest this is that for days the accused has faced persecution in front of the King and the Ministry without revealing what has been asked of him. Speaking to him in isolation would perhaps prove favourable. I can only offer such proposals your highness, the rest is always your decision," explained Azrael.

The King listened to him silently and then nodded his head in understanding.

"It does not sound any worse than what we have tried already. Very well, we shall go to the dungeons and meet with the accused right away. Lord Lucifer, I will accompany you and your apprentice along with one guard as the custom goes."

"Your highness, this is against the law!" Protested Minister Gabriel. "His Grace cannot possibly agree to such a request from a mere sorcerer that is part of Lord Lucifer's coven. The Ministry is responsible for making crucial decisions and not some stray resident of the Kingdom!" He stood up and the other Ministers agreed.

"Lord Gabriel," the King drawled, "The decision has been made by the King and not a stray resident of the Kingdom. We have not broken any law. '*The Binding of Sorcerer's land*' states clearly that changes may be made in the law as long as it is of no harm to the Kingdom. This is not a very crucial matter per se. It is only to meet the accused and I do not see any harm in the same. I would suggest you not to speak against the King in such manner. You may have the power to make decisions for the Kingdom but the power of disbanding you resides with the King."

With that, the King left the court followed by Lord Lucifer and Azrael, while the rest of the Ministers watched their disappearing figures. Lord Mikhail sat on his throne controlling his anger. It was unacceptable and suddenly the King had become independent and wasn't taking any orders from Lord Mikhail or other Minister like he used to before. It struck Lord Mikhail that the King might be taking the staunch meditation training from Lord Zachariah to have found such confidence. It was not a bad thing but it bothered Lord Mikhail nonetheless, for he had started to lose power over the King at a time when he was starting to lose a lot of other things including Lord Zachariah.

The King's guard led the way down as they progressed towards the cell that Erasmus was kept in. The dungeons were located four floors below the courtroom. They walked through a series of corridors and long winding passageways as they made their descent. As they neared the dungeons, groans of pain were heard from a distance. There was a vile stench looming in the air. As they neared Erasmus's cell, one of the guards shoved the door open and Lord Lucifer spotted his apprentice lying on the cold floor of the dark cell with his eyes shut as tears rolled down slowly and steadily through them. His hands and legs were bound in chains as he wept and cried as pain ensued right from his toes up to his head. The pain that he had been going through for two days was something only he would understand. No other soul would know the torture that was being inflicted upon him for long hours. He could not sleep, or eat, or even crawl away from where he was trapped. Neither could he breathe normally. His chest heaved up and down as he struggled to breathe in the cell that had no sufficient amount of air inside.

It was not like the usual jail. There were no bars. A huge circled wall along with a single window with iron bars on top of the wall right below the ceiling allowed just a bit of air to get in. A metal door was shut using protective shields to prevent prisoners from escaping. They were bewitched to stop the prisoners from using spells to break out. Inside, Erasmus's head pounded in pain. His eyes were tightly shut as he tried to get rid of the nightmare that flashed before his eyes every time he attempted to sleep. It was a haunting sight that reminded him of what he had done every minute as it passed.

* * *

The wind echoed around his ears as he breathed deeply with his eyes closed and back straight, resting on the bark of a tree behind. After the Death of his best friend, Erasmus had left the castle to finish the tasks that Nicholas had started. There were witches that he was training in hiding, books that Lord Lucifer had asked him to hide and endangered creatures that he was protecting. All those incomplete tasks that Lord Lucifer had assigned to Nicholas were to be taken care of and Erasmus was going to do the same. As he trudged along the path in the mountains of Rosean, the grass beneath his feet felt soft and inviting. *Erasmus settled himself there after a month long travel where he had resumed most of the tasks that Nicholas had left. In* Rosean, *he was supposed to train a new witch that Nicholas had begun the training of, and now was undergoing a serious meditation process.*

Erasmus decided to look for the witch after a while. He needed to rest a bit. As he sat beneath the tree he was resting on, he heard the sound of footsteps approaching. Opening his eyes, Erasmus turned around to look for the source. Moments later, there stood in front of him one of the Ministers of the King's court that he had seen once. He recognized the Minister as being a very old and powerful sorcerer.

"Lord Zachariah, is it?" He questioned, bowing in respect.

Lord Zachariah walked ahead carrying his staff with him, taking slow steps as he was unable to walk like he did when he was younger.

"You!" he roared, pointing a finger in Erasmus's direction furiously.

Erasmus frowned and began to say something when Lord Zachariah walked a bit faster towards him and stood right in front of him.

"Are you not Lord Lucifer's apprentice?" He asked, still as furious.

"Yes, great Lord, I am," replied Erasmus, perplexed.

"The foul, loathsome of a Lord, Lucifer. He has raised a coven of weaklings! And he expects to protect not only Acanthus but also the prophecy that Lady Calypsa guards. Tell your foolish Lord that Mikhail will take everything from him! The witch that you call brilliant shall never be able to guard the prophecy!" he bellowed.

There was a stutter in his voice and his body shivered as he spoke. Maybe it is due to old age, or maybe the air is just too chilly, *Erasmus thought to himself.*

He stared at Lord Zachariah in confusion. What was he talking about? A prophecy? And why would he call Lord Lucifer names?

"Great Lord, I am unaware of what prophecy you speak of. But I assure you, our coven does not consist of weak Conjurers. Whatever it is that Lord Lucifer is protecting, it will be guarded with utmost care if it is of such importance," he said to the Lord, calmly as he could.

"Mikhail will be informed of the treachery that the spirit has committed. The spirit is gone! The weaklings have taken it under control – it is gone! The spirit will assist. But Lucifer will never see the light of the day when I inform Mikhail of the happening! The war will end the reign and Acanthus will be destroyed! Mikhail shall sail through the sea and gain the secret prophecy that the weak witch is guarding. And I shall help him do so. You, apprentice of the fool that is Lucifer, you must leave those feeble ones and join Mikhail in the quest of eternal glory! You shall be rewarded, young one. Join the coven of Mikhail and let go of the frail!"

Erasmus watched the sorcerer speak in undertone and then shook his head in denial, a silent chuckle escaping his lips.

"Leave the coven of the great Lord Lucifer? Sir, for being one of the greatest sorcerers you speak such malarkey. I have sworn my life to the coven of Lord Lucifer and will never betray the Lord."

A moment later, he was thrown to the ground as Lord Zachariah shot a curse at Erasmus. He pushed himself up to standing. There was a wrathful look on the Lord's face as he continued to attack. Erasmus then stepped away and hid behind a tree.

"I do not wish to fight you, great Lord. Do not compel me to do so."

But his plea was unheard. Lord Zachariah struck a blow once again and Erasmus was tossed away. In an attempt to save himself,

Erasmus stood up and decided to teleport from the location but another blow caught him and as he fought to defend himself, he unknowingly shot the silent and strongest curse of paralysis towards the Lord. Soon he was on the ground, his eyes rolled upwards and hands stiff on his sides. Erasmus rushed towards Lord Zachariah to revive him from the curse but due to the evident strong force that he had sent the curse with, the paralysis had taken a worse turn. He had paralyzed Lord Zachariah into killing his own self. It was known that if a paralyzing curse went wrong by an inch, it would mentally affect the victim into ceasing his/her own bodily functions leading to Death. It did not create any injuries or harm to the body, but the victim would be mentally distraught and unable to bring himself back to the normal state.

Due to his old age and weakness after shooting various spells at Erasmus, Lord Zachariah could not counter the curse that Erasmus had shot him with. It was a strong curse and a very covert one that frightened Erasmus to no limit. However strong or capable a Conjurer might be, the paralyzing curse – if gone wrong – had the power to kill in no time. It not only affected the victim, but the killer as well. As Erasmus watched the dead body that lay before him and realization struck him that he had unknowingly killed one of the greatest sorcerers of all time, his eyes were filled with various illusions that blinded him. But he ran. He began to run to wherever his feet dragged him. Visions of Lord Zachariah silently suffering in pain flashed across his eyes as he tried to run faster and faster out of fright. But moments later, his foot tripped over a rock and he fell to the ground into unconsciousness.

* * *

CHAPTER THIRTY-TWO

∞∞∞∞∞

HIDDEN VIRTUES

∞∞∞∞∞

The King, true to his word left Lord Lucifer and Azrael alone in the cell where Erasmus lay searing in pain, and swiftly walked back to await their return in the shadows of the gaol.

Erasmus lay on the floor, writhing in what seemed like unbearable throbbing while Lord Lucifer and Azrael merely stood there with their minds vacant. The door of the cell was closed to give the three of them enough privacy, hoping that Erasmus would divulge everything. The King stood outside with his guard waiting for the session to get over. Inside, Lord Lucifer struggled to get hold of Erasmus to make him steady but nothing worked. He was shivering in pain and his eyes were tightly shut, drawing tears from them. His groans made Lord Lucifer wince. Nothing had affected him so, he wondered why Erasmus's pain seemed so infiltrating to him. Maybe it was because he was reminded of Nicholas when he looked at Erasmus. Or maybe the pain that his apprentice felt was far too agonizing to him and he could not take it.

"M'Lord, allow me to wake him up. He's probably experiencing a nightmare," said Azrael, kneeling down beside Lord Lucifer who was still busy trying to get Erasmus to open his eyes.

He pushed himself away and rested his back on the wall behind, his eyes stuck on Erasmus. Azrael settled himself beside Erasmus and closed his eyes. Connecting both their minds, he pulled Erasmus out of the nightmare that he was having, using his manipulation skills. Erasmus suddenly stopped shivering. His groans turned into shallow breathing, and slowly his eyes opened. Azrael stepped away and Lord Lucifer leaned forward.

"Erasmus?" said Lord Lucifer as he held a concerned look.

None of the injuries had been cured and Erasmus still looked the way he had when he was dragged into the castle, if not worse. Erasmus blinked, his eyes switching from Azrael to Lord Lucifer.

"M'Lord-" he croaked, trying to push himself up so he could sit. Lord Lucifer placed a hand on his shoulder and shook his head.

"How are you, Erasmus?" asked Lord Lucifer, although he knew it was a silly question and the answer to that was quite obvious before him.

"Not good, I assume," he answered, chuckling slightly.

It amazed Lord Lucifer as to how Erasmus could joke even when he was in so much pain.

"Why have you not informed the King of why you killed Lord Zachariah?" Lord Lucifer said, coming straight to the point.

There was no time to talk about anything else other than the required information.

"I didn't think it was safe to divulge it in presence of Lord Mikhail," replied Erasmus, his voice hoarse and crooked.

"You could have told the King in private then."

Erasmus shook his head.

"The King would have informed Lord Mikhail. But I understand that it is pointless anyway, since Lord Mikhail will find out sooner or later by his own means."

"Tell us, then?" Lord Lucifer raised his eyebrows.

"The King will ask you what I said. It's not safe to speak." Erasmus shook his head again. "Do you have a quill and a piece of parchment?" He looked at Azrael hopefully.

Azrael nodded and pulled out a quill from inside his cloak along with a tiny parchment that he carried everywhere with him, should need arise. He handed the equipment to Erasmus. With trembling hands, Erasmus pushed himself to a half-sitting position so he could write and began scribbling something on the parchment.

"Tell the King that I said nothing and keep this parchment with you until you reach the castle. Read it and then destroy it. We can't risk anything," he said while writing slowly on the parchment with his trembling fingers.

Lord Lucifer nodded and then took the written parchment from Erasmus before handing it to Azrael who safely hid it under his cloak.

"Is there any way that we can set you free from here?" asked Lord Lucifer.

"Lord Mikhail would never let me go if I'm not being killed for what has happened. I'm going to be tortured for eternity. Hopefully that helps killing me." He let out a humourless chuckle. "But m'Lord, I want to stay alive until after the war gets over. I won't be able to fight, which I apologize for, but if I can get messages through owls – I would want to keep up with whatever is going on, if it's alright," he replied.

"Of course, we'll make sure the owls reach you without being detected by guards. Meanwhile I shall try my best to set you free," Lord Lucifer said, with a slight reassuring grin before getting up.

"Be careful," Erasmus said to Azrael and he nodded in agreement.

Moments later, they walked out of the cell and back into the dungeons. The King was seated at a distance outside an empty cell with his guards standing on either side of him. He looked up spotting the two of them coming out of Erasmus's cell.

"Any progress?" He asked, eyebrows raised, standing up.

"No, your highness; he refuses to even open his eyes. We tried everything we could," Lord Lucifer replied, shaking his head.

"We've been facing the same." The King sighed in defeat.

"I'm sorry, your highness." Lord Lucifer hung his head.

"We should return," the King said.

The rest of them followed him back up to the courtroom silently. They were met with a quiet atmosphere in the court as well. Everyone stood up when the King entered. He proceeded to his throne. As soon as he was seated, Lord Mikhail stepped forward.

"I assume that there was nothing Lord Lucifer could find," he said, his back towards Lord Lucifer and Azrael.

"I'm afraid not. But we will keep trying until he reveals everything. I presume that the war is coming soon?" the King said, raising his eyebrows and glancing back and forth between Lord Mikhail and Lord Lucifer.

"I give Lord Lucifer a fortnight to prepare. The attack will strike any time after that," Lord Mikhail answered.

"Lord High Minister," said the King. "Before you attack, as custom goes, should you not offer a white flag?"

"Your highness, I do not have any such arrangement in mind but since a custom has to be followed. . ." Lord Mikhail trailed off.

"A private meeting between the two of you has to take place before the battle strikes," the King said and glanced at a silent Lord Lucifer.

"Of course, your highness," said Lord Lucifer. "Whenever it is suitable."

"Then I suggest that Lord Lucifer meet us in His Grace's private courtroom tomorrow at dusk," Lord Mikhail suggested and the King nodded in response.

"As the King commands," Lord Lucifer bent his head in respect.

"Very well, the court is dismissed." With that, the King stood up and left the courtroom.

Lord Lucifer retraced his steps towards the door. Azrael followed suit and the two of them left the King's court, making their way back to the castle. Azrael left a fleeting look in Lord Mikhail's direction before stalking out of the court.

* * *

Amara sat in the library with Iris. She was asking her about Sienna and Iris was giving her the desired answers. After being asked to befriend Sienna and get all information that Amara desired, Iris had gotten busy with other things that restricted her from talking to Sienna directly and slowly extracting all necessary information from her, which led to Iris invading Sienna's mind. But there was no expected result out of that.

"I invaded Erasmus's mind," said Iris, scratching her forehead with a sheepish look.

"Why would you invade *his* mind?" Amara frowned.

"Because he knows everything about everyone, and if I invaded his mind I could find out whatever you needed to know about Sienna," Iris replied.

"He's under imprisonment right now!" Amara protested disbelievingly.

"When I got the information, I didn't know that he was being arrested. I just invaded his mind restricting myself from straying anywhere else and just stuck to Sienna," she said, hoping Amara would not get angry with her for what she had done.

Of course she loathed herself for invading Erasmus's mind when he was being arrested. Now that she knew Lord Lucifer and Azrael were back with the truth that Erasmus had given to them, she felt even worse. But it did not stop her from resuming the work, for the war was approaching and there was no time to sit and cry about things. It was time to start working.

"Alright," Amara sighed. "What have you got?" She placed both her hands on the table in front of her and leaned forward to listen.

"She was trained by the Lord starting from the age of ten along with Erasmus and Nicholas. She started fancying Nicholas when she turned eighteen and he was about twenty then. Nicholas and Erasmus were inseparable and wouldn't pay much attention to her. She was mostly on her own and made friends with this other witch that died for some reason that I am not aware of. Nicholas never reciprocated her feelings. Somehow they got together but then Nicholas left to travel for all tasks that he had to do and left her alone. Erasmus has tried to be there for her as a friend since. She can handle the elements of Spirit and Fire. She speaks to spirits at times; benign ones. Not being skilled in anything else as such, she has this brilliant power of handling Spirits which I think you are aware of.

"And of course, the flute. Doesn't have anything against you but isn't exactly fond of you. She thinks you are too cruel. But she has a lot of faith in the Lord and what he stands for, so I think she would prove useful for whatever it is that you want her to help with. And she dislikes Leandra. I don't know why though. I didn't think it was necessary to find out why."

Amara nodded in understanding after Iris finished talking.

"Do you think I can trust her with something confidential?" She asked, raising her eyebrows hopefully.

"I don't think it would be a problem. No harm." Iris shook her head in the end.

"And will *she* trust me with this?"

"If you communicate through the Lord then it would prove fruitful, I think. That would give you more strength," Iris said.

"Alright. I'll do that." Amara nodded and then pushed her chair back to stand up.

"You should go and get some rest. Your tiny brain is too pressured these days," Amara said, ruffling Iris's hair lightly before heading out of the library.

Iris sighed and then proceeded to go to her chamber while smiling slightly to herself despite the gruesome events that had been happening. Amara walked out to the woods to see Sceiron. She had not met him for a long while. As she walked further in, she heard footsteps approaching. Frowning, she walked ahead and looked around only to have her head bump into a wall. She glanced up to find Azrael standing before her. He glanced down at her bemusedly as she took a step back and away from him.

"What are you doing here?" She asked him.

"I was looking for you," he replied, falling into step beside her as she ventured into the woods to find Sceiron.

"Why?" She asked, tilting her head to spot Sceiron somewhere.

"Any progress on Sienna?" He enquired.

"Iris tells me that if we talk to her through the Lord, maybe she would agree to the task that we want her to help us with."

"I was thinking along the similar lines," said Azrael.

"How is Erasmus?" She asked.

"I've sent some *Healing Potion* to him through an owl. He will be alright in a matter of time. The Lord says he'll be our spy in the castle. It's better to have one, and he can act as though he's in pain. So it's not as much of a trouble now that we know what happened between him and the sorcerer," he told her and suddenly Amara shot up to a high branch of a tree in the matter of a single moment.

He blinked and looked at her. She was seated on the branch with a little owl settled on her arm as she stroked its head softly. Azrael smiled and then followed her up, sitting beside her carefully, for they were on quite a height. Amara turned to look at him.

"Sorry. I just hadn't seen him in a while. I didn't mean to ignore you," she told him.

"He's quite magnificent, your owl," he replied, looking at Sceiron with adoration.

"Sceiron, oh, yes, I found him in the woods a few years ago. He had an injured wing. I mended it and since then he has been with me," Amara said, smiling at Sceiron.

"How old is he?"

"Three years."

She kissed Sceiron's head softly before Sceiron settled itself on her knee.

"How old are *you*?" Azrael then asked with a smirk.

Amara glanced at him once before turning back to look at the vast stretched lake before them.

"What do you think?" She replied, not looking back at him.

"I would guess over two hundred?" He offered and Amara gave him a flat look.

"Do I really look that old?" She shot back.

"A bit," he whispered.

"I'm only a hundred-and-nineteen, great sorcerer."

"That's it?" He said, chuckling.

And before she knew it, Amara was chuckling along with him. How long had it been since she had had a good laugh? There was no reason for her to be laughing at the moment. Just a silly joke about her age and she was laughing as though it was the last thing she would do. Why was it so easy with him? That without a single effort from his side she was ready to give in? She had smiled before because of Iris. But apart from her there was no one who could induce a single grin from Amara. Then what was it that made her laugh with Azrael?

"You should laugh more. It makes you look less intimidating," said Azrael, when they were done cackling.

For him, it wasn't as surprising. He knew it was always this simple with Amara. Though they had never had such a pointless conversation which induced a laugh for no apparent reason, he knew he was more comfortable with Amara than he was with anyone else. He had never had friends, he was just like her. He was intimidating and dangerous and frightening and powerful and always so grave but never had he ever felt so much at ease with anyone else. Amara was an exception. Even the silence was comforting to him. There was nothing that he would want more than to spend time with her. Whether it was for summoning spirits or talking about protecting the prophecy or just nothing in particular, he felt at ease. He had the sudden urge to smile with her, talk about pleasant things that he had not done with others before, not even with Lea for a long time.

It gave him this strange but fuzzy feeling inside whenever he was with Amara. Spending time with her made him lighter in the head. There was no stress. He did not mind silence either. There was this invisible contact established between the two of them which created a strange aura around them that neither recognized. But Azrael knew that Amara felt it as well; for he could see the clear difference between when she was with others and when she was alone with him. They had two different personalities when within the eyes of others and when they were together. Somehow he felt safe with her and so did Amara. She felt safer than she had ever felt before. It was surprisingly strange but she did not seem to mind it.

That unknown trust lingering around them gave the both of them some sort of an assurance; assurance of trusting each other with their lives. None of them were aware of it, but it was there, hidden somewhere in the back of their minds and they refused to accept it. The presence of it was felt every time they were together.

"You're more intimidating than I am," said Amara, breaking Azrael's chain of thought.

He blinked and then looked at her.

"Am I? You set Fire to the woods when I arrived here. I had to get it all under control. You're too dangerous for your own good," he told her, rolling his eyes.

Amara grimaced at the memory of the time that she had set her woods on Fire. The shrubs and trees had started to grow back once again, but it was a slow progress. At the moment, she sat on the opposite side of the burnt part where there were enough trees and shrubs to make her feel like she did before. The wandering spirits still made their presence felt around her, and Scerion was with her which made her feel much better about herself.

"As far as I remember, you thought that I wasn't as good of a witch as others claimed," she said to him, raising a brow.

"That was just to test you. I found out that you were quite similar to me. Besides we've had mind duels as well as sword duels, so I know how strong you are. Not to mention the way you deciphered the riddles that Lady Calypsa offered when we went to see her. I have to admit, that was impressive," he told her, amazed as he recalled the memory.

"Why thank you, sir. But that doesn't change the fact that you're not as dangerous as I am." She smiled.

The snowy-white owl trotted upon Amara's knee slowly as his eyes switched between the two of them. It seemed as though he was enjoying the conversation that was happening. Then again, so were Amara and Azrael.

"I'm not. You're the most brilliant witch of our age. People sing your praises," he told her.

"Who exactly has sung my praises? I've always wondered. Everyone tells me that they think I'm this extremely accomplished witch, but what have I even done to achieve that?" She frowned.

She was genuinely confused about why there was so much praise for her. It had always been a mystery to her since she had never made the effort to find out why. It wasn't a matter of high concern but she was curious to know.

"Young Conjurers. They hear about you from their parents and mentors. I was in the village of Jarram a few years ago. There was a family of a sorcerer that gave me shelter for a night. I was travelling. A little witch of ten told me that her mother had sung praises of this brilliant witch called Amara from the coven of Lord Lucifer. Her mother says that you saved a group of young witches that were being attacked by a few lions in the mountains of Carvelli. You destroyed many witch-hunters all by yourself when they were in force years ago. You ended the realm of dangerous warlocks that were terrorizing Acanthus. You saved Lord Mikhail when he was being attacked by ten witch-hunters at the same time – yet he still wants you dead – you-"

"Alright, I think that is enough for now. I didn't do all of that alone. I had help. The Lord was mostly there with me and there were others from our coven too," Amara cut him off when it went beyond her expectations.

She did not wish to hear all of those things. To her, none of those deeds sounded great enough to be sung praises of.

"Yes, but you were the one that did most of the work. If you want to be so modest then I have something that would make you feel quite better. I've also heard that you are far too cold while killing. And you don't like being around people much. Once when a young sorcerer tried to make fun of this other witch, you gave him such an intimidating look that it frightened him to no limit and he never spoke to that female again; nor did he ever face you, for that matter," he chuckled as he said that. "They have seen you slay doves, which stabbed their hearts into pieces but you had not a single ounce of pain on your face as you did that. You also-"

"Azrael?" She said softly, cutting him off.

"Yes?" He whispered back with his eyebrows raised.

"You may stop talking about me now," she told him and Azrael laughed lightly, shaking his head.

"My point is, Amara, you don't know how brilliant yet dangerous you are," he told her in all seriousness.

His eyes were now fixed on Amara as she stared back at him with equal intensity. "And you're far too beautiful, of which you aren't aware either," he then whispered so softly that it was unheard.

But Amara could hear every word, every syllable that he had said to her. And it gave her these extremely strange and never experienced chills through her spine as she listened to him. That feeling was something she had not known before, and it made her feel alive inside every part of her. Sceiron hooted from where he was seated on Amara's knee and both of their eyes snapped away from one another. Amara blinked once. . .twice. . .thrice to register what had just happened and she could not believe it. How long had it been since someone had so genuinely talked about her right in front of her, without a single worry about how she would react? Not only had Azrael talked highly of her, he had not hesitated in telling her how cold and ruthless she behaved at times. And it did not bother her for a single moment.

She turned to look at him after a long while of silence and smiled. Azrael returned the smile with one of his own and then the two of them retreated to the ground, leaving Sceiron on the branch; for the wind was too chilly up there. They decided to sit under the tree for a while before going back to the castle. But as the night became darker and the moon shone above them in all its grace, Amara and Azrael continued to talk about all kinds of pointless things that made them feel so much better given everything that was going on lately.

"Why did you have to save Lord Mikhail from a few witch-hunters and why does he dislike you this much to have declared war?" Azrael asked as Amara twiddled with the grass beside her bare feet.

"It happened in the mountains of *Lunaire*," Amara said. "I was assisting Soter and Lilienne in collecting some herbs for a few potions when we realized that there were witch-hunters in the vicinity. I left the work and found Lord Mikhail and a few other Ministers there battling about twenty witch-hunters. Lord Mikhail was trapped between ten of them and the rest of the Ministers were busy trying to save themselves. I helped him and killed most of the hunters, which for some reason infuriated Lord Mikhail and the Ministers. The Lord later told me that it was because they were ashamed of themselves since they couldn't help their High Minister and had to take help of a young witch to save them. So apparently, he isn't fond of me." She shrugged in the end.

"He dislikes you because you're more powerful than him and the other Ministers combined, which is why he declared war," Azrael concluded. "See, this is why people sing praises." He smirked.

"Our *coven* is more powerful than his. That is why he wants to destroy us," Amara said truthfully. "That and he also has an ulterior motive of gaining the prophecy..."

"People sing *your* praises, not the coven's."

"There is nothing to be sung praises of!" Amara sighed in exasperation.

"Let me elaborate..."

And so, the pressure of the war and the protection of the prophecy escaped their minds for those few hours as they sat under the tree, both of their backs resting on the huge bark of the Giant Sequoia. None of them realized when their eyes shut themselves on their own accord, and Amara's head fell onto Azrael's shoulder as they drifted off into the most peaceful sleep that they had had in a long while.

CHAPTER THIRTY-THREE

∞∞∞∞∞

FROM DAWN TO DUSK

∞∞∞∞∞∞

The King's private courtroom wasn't as huge as the general one. It was the size of the great hall of Lord Lucifer's castle. The walls were adorned with various symbols representing the culture and glory of Acanthus. It was a custom to have ancient symbols in the palace of the King. It depicted several stories of witchcraft: the downfall and the revival, when it was at its peak, when wars were fought, everything was comprised into those symbols and designs all across the walls. Lord Lucifer sat in the courtroom with Lord Mikhail sitting opposite to him. Both of them were silent. They knew why they were there, they knew what was supposed to be said to the King, and they knew why they were on this dreadful war.

The first battle was yet to strike. None of them thought that the other was prepared enough for the war. For it was a mystery to the both of them as to who all were in their respective armies. Although Lord Mikhail was aware of a few secretive things from the castle with the help of his messenger, he was not as sure of it since he had not gotten any recent messages. Or maybe he had not bothered to contact the messenger in the first place.

As they sat there waiting for the King – unable to look each other in the eye for they feared that they would end up in a duel – they wondered how the war was going to end up. Would Lord Lucifer and Amara succeed in protecting the prophecy? Would Lord Mikhail be able to find out what the prophecy held? Would Lord Lucifer's coven be destroyed? Or would Lord Mikhail end up dead? Similar questions ran through both their minds. Lord Lucifer had received a message from Erasmus on the previous day saying Lord Mikhail had realized that Lilith's spirit was no longer where he had hidden it; which had infuriated Lord Mikhail to no limit and he had ended up punishing a few of his coven members in frustration.

Whether he was frustrated with himself or his army, Erasmus did not know. But so far, Lord Mikhail had not tried to get Lilith's spirit back for he knew it was under extra protection than it was when he had it under control. Besides, the war was about to start, and if Lord Mikhail won, he would surely get Lilith back under control to help him with the prophecy.

When King Orcus walked in along with Minister Leontues, and the guards closed the doors, Lord Lucifer and Lord Mikhail stood up.

"Your highness," said Lord Lucifer, bowing his head in respect.

The King offered a smile and settled himself on his throne. Lord Lucifer and Lord Mikhail sat back down on their respective ones followed by Minister Leontues.

"Good evening, Lord Mikhail, Lord Lucifer," the King said, giving a nod of acknowledgement to the both of them.

"Your highness, let us not waste time and proceed with the meeting," said Lord Mikhail, stoically.

"Certainly. Lord Mikhail, please tell us what the war is about," the King said and Minister Leontues flipped the parchments on his table, holding the quill in place to begin writing.

"The Ministry believes that Lord Lucifer is trying to win the throne by creating a strong coven under the alleged reason of guarding Acanthus," said Lord Mikhail and Minister Leontues scribbled on the parchment.

"What does Lord Lucifer have to say to that?" The King turned to Lord Lucifer.

"I only wish to protect our land and if that means starting a monarchy of my own, I would not hesitate in agreeing to what our High Minister has said," Lord Lucifer responded.

"Describe the strength of the respective armies," the King said.

"Three covens assist our army, your highness, Lord Alistair and Lord Riordan from the land of Silene Noeturna and Lord Vane from Adiantum."

"And you, Lord Lucifer?"

"From Murier Albys, the covens of Lord Theodore, Lady Nysa and Lord Vincent, your highness" answered Lord Lucifer.

"Where will the battles take place?"

"The battlefield of Artemisia is at the borders of Acanthus, your highness," said Lord Mikhail. "The Ministry believes it would be suitable."

"Very well." The King nodded as Minister Leontues scribbled away on his parchment.

"Do you, Lord Lucifer, wish to extend a white flag of peace to solve this dispute, avoiding destruction?" The King turned to Lord Lucifer.

"I do, your highness," replied Lord Lucifer. "If Lord Mikhail and the Ministry agree to it, I am ready to extend a hand of peace where my coven peacefully guards Acanthus and the Kingdom can function just as normally as it does as of now."

"Do you, Lord Mikhail, wish to accept this flag of peace?" King Orcus hoped that Lord Mikhail would agree to this and settle the dispute mutually instead of raising a cry of war. It was better that way, nobody needed destruction. But his prayers went unanswered.

"I do not, your highness," said Lord Mikhail. "The Ministry believes that Lord Lucifer's coven is too intrusive regarding the protection of the land and a war is essential to end this once and for all."

The King sighed in defeat. Lord Mikhail could not be stopped and he knew it.

"The battle strikes anytime after the fortnight, correct?" King Orcus questioned.

"Yes, your highness," said Lord Mikhail.

"Well then, if there is nothing else left to say, the court is dismissed."

The King left the courtroom, and Minister Leontues pressed the hot seal onto the parchment that he had sealed in an envelope, before following the King.

Lord Lucifer left to go back to his castle, pulling the hood of his cloak onto his head. Lord Mikhail stared at the fading figure of Lord Lucifer and vowed to end his existence when the war began. For it was due to him, that Lord Mikhail had lost all the glory that he could have gotten.

* * *

"What are you talking about?" said Amara, pushing past Iris and walking out of the kitchen chamber where she was busy having tea.

Chuckling, Iris followed her out and fell into step beside her.

"Amara, I was the one that woke you up from your beautiful dreamland with Azrael. I saw the way you two were asleep all night," she said to Amara who suddenly turned red in the face as she attempted to hide it by looking away.

When have I ever blushed in a hundred years? She wondered.

"We were talking about some important things and must have fallen asleep due to exhaustion. You know a lot has been going on these days," she answered, stuttering as she searched for words in her mind.

What was she going to tell Iris? That she had talked about the silliest things with Azrael and they had fallen asleep with her head resting on his shoulder? How could she possibly tell Iris that she had done something inane the night before? It was something that she had never done in her entire existence as a witch.

"Of course I do. But that does not change the fact that you were sitting in such close proximity with a male. In my time here I haven't seen you do that with anyone," Iris said slyly.

"Iris, nothing happened. I might have lost track of where I was and my silly head must have fallen on his silly shoulder sometime during the night. Why is it such a huge matter?" said Amara as she stopped walking and let out a frustrated sigh.

Iris was being a pain at the moment and Amara had a lot of important things to do. *What happened to those important things while talking complete nonsense with Azrael,* she thought and mentally hit herself.

"I never said something happened, Amara," Iris replied, smirking.

Amara stared at Iris for a long moment with disbelief before rolling her eyes and turning around to leave. Iris was purely delighted when she had found Amara and Azrael peacefully asleep in the woods, the time that she had gone to look for Amara at dawn. Iris wanted to talk to her about

Erasmus, but upon encountering the couple in the woods, she had forgotten all her worries and a beautiful smile had graced her lips. For years-she knew Amara had never developed so much of a simple conversation with a male, let alone fallen asleep so carelessly. Iris knew Amara had never been able to sleep so easily. Seeing her sound asleep with such content was a priceless moment, and Iris would cherish it for her entire existence. She was happy to see Amara with Azrael and she could sense that unbreakable bond developing between the two even though it wasn't the slightest bit of obvious.

And if Amara was happy with Azrael, Iris would be all for it. After having faced worse things in her life, Amara deserved all the happiness that she could get. If it was Azrael who would give that lost smile back to Amara, then Iris would worship him for eternity and beyond. As she watched Amara walk away, a tear full of glee slipped out of her eye and she smiled in content. Sighing, Iris returned to her chamber where Leandra had promised they would meet after she had grilled Azrael. Of course she had told Lea about what she had seen. It was only fair that she knew what her brother had been up to.

There was no doubt about how happy Lea was. As soon as Iris had given the news, she had rushed to find Azrael. He was heading out of his chamber, drying his hair after a bath. When his eyes fell on Lea skipping towards him like a little girl, he frowned in confusion and dreaded that Iris had informed his sister of what she had seen in the morning. He waited for her to reach him and when she did, he was pulled into a tight hug.

"Do you plan on crushing my bones, Lea?" He asked.

Lea chuckled and let go of him. She dragged him back into his chamber and they sat on two chairs opposite to each other.

"I will crush your bones if you don't tell me how you ended up in the woods with Amara all night," she said to him as she smirked.

"We have a war to fight and you are asking me about something so silly and unimportant?" He raised his eyebrows in disbelief.

But of course it wasn't a surprise. He did not know how he had ended up resting his head on Amara's all night. It was strange, but it was the best feeling he had ever experienced in a long while. Never had a woman done something close to touching him apart from Lea. Never had he felt what he had felt with Amara. He wanted to feel that again and again, because it was the most beautiful thing he had ever experienced. But he had to push all of those thoughts away, for there was a battle to fight and a prophecy to protect.

"The war is a fortnight away, Rael. But I won't ask you anything more and waste your time. Just tell me one thing. Do you or do you not fancy Amara? Because I know you, even though it has been twenty years since we met. You are my brother so I am well aware about the amount of time you spend with a witch. Falling asleep with one is just unbelievable, so you *do* fancy her, don't you?" She said with a glint of mischief in her eyes.

"I am not going to tell you anything of that sort. We were talking about something important and fell asleep because we were tired. It is only natural. I would have slept so peacefully if I were in my chamber. So it isn't anything new," he told her.

But he knew how much of a lie that was. It was nothing important that they were talking about, neither was it because they were tired that they fell asleep. Azrael was well aware of the fact that none of them would have had such a peaceful sleep if they had been in their own chambers that night. For it was that invisible lingering trust that made them feel so safe with one another, and nothing else.

"*Oh* come now, Rael. You've fancied her for a while now. You're just not ready to accept it." Lea threw her arms in the air in frustration. Her brother was an idiot.

Azrael rolled his eyes.

"Am I allowed to go now? I have to meet Amara and discuss something important," he told her.

"Of course you do. By all means, dear brother, go on." Lea smirked deviously.

Azrael just shook his head and left the chamber with a grinning Lea. Smiling softly to himself he made his way towards the library where he knew Amara was.

There she was, seated on a chair behind a table in the farthermost corner of the library. She held a huge book in her hands, but both of them knew that she wasn't reading it. Her mind was obviously elsewhere. They had not exchanged a single word after the morning when they had woken up, startled to find themselves sitting that close to one another. Amara had avoided his eye and so had Azrael, for it was extremely strange for the both of them and they did not know what they would say to each other. But now there were essentially some vital things to be talked of. As he made his way towards Amara, Azrael could not help but wonder how effortlessly beautiful the witch was. Shaking all of those stray thoughts out of his mind and telling himself to concentrate on what he was there to do, Azrael proceeded towards her. Amara looked up at him when he settled himself beside her on a chair.

"What are you reading?" He asked.

"Nothing," she replied and shut the book of Spirits of the Doomed.

"Anyway, I wanted to talk to you about the summoning of spirits for guarding Lady Calypsa," he told her.

"The Lord is going to talk to Sienna tonight. I think he already is, since he's returned from the King's palace. He will let us know," she said, looking away.

She did not know how to look at him without getting her face to flame. It was awkward for her. She knew it was the same for him. But it was not important right now. They had a war to fight, which was soon to come.

"Alright. Is there any-anything else that you want to talk about? About the protection I mean," he said, scratching the back of his head.

"No," she replied, shifting in her seat.

Why was it making her so uncomfortable? Why was talking to him so complicated suddenly even though she felt better than she did with anyone? She wanted to get rid of those thoughts but they would just not leave her.

"Amara, I don't want things to be uncomfortable between us. We-" he began.

But before he could continue, Sienna walked into the library and proceeded towards the two of them. Azrael and Amara looked up at her. She settled herself on the chair opposite to them across the table and let out a sigh. Amara and Azrael raised their eyebrows in question.

"The Lord spoke to me," she said, clearing their doubt.

"About the. . ." Amara trailed off.

". . . Spirits for guarding the Sea of Cypress," Sienna completed, nodding. "I have a suggestion though."

"What?" Amara and Azrael asked at the same time.

They glanced at each other for a second before turning back to Sienna.

"We won't need to summon those spirits. Back in the woods there are a lot of wanderers. I have been acquainted with them a long time. If I request them, maybe they would help us. Besides, Amara also is quite friendly with a few of those spirits, aren't you?" She said.

"To some extent," replied Amara.

"We need a team. I reckon at least ten spirits will be necessary," Azrael suggested, glancing at the two witches.

"No matter, I think I can convince them with the help of Amara," Sienna said.

"Well alright then. When do we do this?" Amara asked.

"I think we can start right now, if you don't mind," said Sienna.

With a nod of agreement, Amara stood up and so did Sienna. Azrael bade them goodbye and the two of them left the library while he sat there wondering why he felt so empty after Amara left. Shaking his head, he blinked and then sighed before grabbing a book and starting to read. He had to spend some time until Amara returned and they proceeded to the Sea of Cypress together. He was hoping they would go together. Why, he had no idea.

Out in the woods, Amara and Sienna stood in the deeper parts, looking around and wondering as to how many wandering spirits were lingering there. Their eyes were closed as they took in the surroundings. Sienna opened her eyes first and turned to Amara.

"There's plenty. Do you want me to communicate or do you want to help?" She asked.

"You do it," Amara replied, beckoning Sienna to go ahead with the process.

Nodding, Sienna closed her eyes and took in a deep breath, exhaling it out slowly. With her mind focused on the spirits that she had befriended, she pulled out her flute from inside her cloak and began to play the soft melody that echoed around them in the woods. The sound of the gentle winds mingled with the music and created a beautiful symphony that calmed Amara's ears. It was a different melody than the one that Sienna had played when summoning Lilith's spirit, and while driving it away after Nicholas's Death. Yet it was just as soothing as it had been before. Amara leaned on the tree beside her, listening to the sound silently.

The air around her suddenly seemed to change. Amara felt the souls whirl with the wind as though rushing towards something. Then a few silhouettes appeared. They were suspended in mid-air, right in front of Sienna in a semi-circle. It felt as though they were communicating to Sienna in soft whispers when she stopped playing the flute. The spirits stood there hovering above them in the air as they communicated with Sienna. Amara could not hear a thing. Whether it was the normal language they were conversing in, or it was some secret one, she did not know. Sienna then turned to look at Amara, gesturing her to go forward.

"They ask why Lady Calypsa needs to be guarded by them," she whispered closely to Amara.

"It is for protection since the war is about to start. The Lord and I won't be able to guard Lady Calypsa so efficiently with the battles going on. The Lady requires added protection in times like these," Amara whispered back.

Sienna gave a nod and then whispered something to the spirits; something that Amara neither understood nor heard properly.

"They agree. They would like an audience with the Lady," Sienna said.

"That is perfectly alright. We shall leave whenever we can," replied Amara.

Moments later, the two witches were back into the castle after having talked to the spirits. They parted ways and Amara left to go to her chamber when she bumped into Azrael who was walking along the passageway with Eridanus.

"What happened in the woods?" He asked, stopping Amara.

"They agreed. We'll leave when the Lord says so," she replied.

"Okay. And I had to tell you something. We have a new addition to the coven," he told her.

CHAPTER THIRTY-FOUR

∞∞∞∞∞

ILLUSIONS OF THE PSYCHE

∞∞∞∞∞

T he man who stood at the door of the castle had a sinister appearance, Iris observed. Starting from his hair that was a dirty shade of brown, his forehead was wrinkled and his eyes a sapphire blue. It was a strange combination and his eyes stood out the most, making him look even ominous than he actually seemed to be. He had a dark complexion, his beard stretched down to his chest along with his hair that was tied behind his head in sort of a bun. He wore long grey coloured robes and no footwear. He was evidently plump. Iris would call him something on the uglier side but other than that, he seemed quite different from the rest that she had seen in Acanthus. She wondered who he was, for most of the recruits in the coven were young. Younger than what he seemed to be.

She had not met anyone like him. It gave off a strange vibe as he walked past her carrying his staff that he softly stomped on the floor as he stepped ahead. Iris watched him walk by as did everyone else. When he went and stood in front of Lord Lucifer in the hall, the silence followed. Everyone turned their heads towards the centre of the hall, waiting to know what was about to happen. Amara and Azrael stood beside Iris. Eridanus stood opposite to them along with the other members of the coven.

"Welcome, m'Lord," said Lord Lucifer, standing up and bowing his head in respect.

"I would like you to be introduced to my coven. We have the army of thirty-five Conjurers who will fight for us in this war," Lord Lucifer said and gestured the man to turn around and look at everyone.

He then extended his arm to his right, indicating Ambrosius. "This is Ambrosius, my closest servant and the only one who is allowed to enter my chambers. He is very skilled at sacrificial rituals. Then we have Lilienne, the potion maker. She has been making potions since a hundred and ten years. Firdos here belongs to the nomadic sorcerers who have been practicing the element of Air for about two hundred and fifty years. Then there is Eridanus, our manipulation warrior who has nearly similar powers to that of our other young recruit, Iris." Lord Lucifer looked towards her and so did the man.

She awkwardly blinked and gave a small smile in his direction. But the man's expression was impassive. He did not react. His eyes merely flickered from one end to another as Lord Lucifer introduced all the other members of the coven. In the end he stopped at Amara.

"Amara happens to be our most skilled and powerful warrior. Water and Fire are her best elements. Sword-fighting is another one of her powers."

Lord Lucifer's voice trailed off in Amara's mind as Azrael immediately shifted his head to look at her and slightly smirked. She glanced at him through the corner of her eye and struggled not to roll her eyes. He was thinking of the duel that they had had before they left to rescue Lord Lucifer from the clutches of the *Mortuis* Noctia Stella. How completely interesting that duel had been was something fresh in both of their minds. Every strange uncomfortable feeling that they were having since the past two days was now gone. The moment that Azrael had informed Amara about a new addition to the coven, the two of them had gotten busy in finding out who it was and later talking to Sienna about how they were going to help the spirits travel to the Sea of Cypress to protect Lady Calypsa, without being detected by Lord Mikhail.

Since then, they had shared a few moments like the ones during the night they spent in the woods, and had been comfortable around each other after that. Now there seemed to be no discomfort between them. Mostly because there was a war coming and they had to protect Lady Calypsa. Other than that, maybe it was because it did not matter anymore, the two of them had vaguely enough accepted the fact that there was some invisible string between them that held them together, however loose it may be; it was there. And both of them were sure of it.

"I would like to get all of you acquainted with our most elderly and learned member of the coven, Lord Khshathra Vairya. He won't be fighting in the war, for he is a priest; and one of the most knowledgeable. He is here to ensure protection of the castle while we fight," said Lord Lucifer, after he was done introducing Amara to Lord Vairya.

"He does not speak. Lord Vairya took the vow fifty years ago," Lord Lucifer informed them.

"Ambrosius, escort the Lord to his chambers."

When Ambrosius left with Lord Vairya, Lord Lucifer turned to the rest and instructed them to leave, only apart from Sienna, Azrael and Amara. As they were leaving, Eridanus grabbed Iris's arm and pulled her in the direction of his own chambers. Amara watched the two leave and frowned in confusion before turning back to look at Lord Lucifer who stood there patiently waiting for the others to leave. When everyone else was gone, he switched his attention to the three apprentices that stood before him.

"When do you three plan on leaving for the Sea of Cypress?" He asked, sitting on his throne his fingertips joined together as he tried to collect his thoughts.

"We were thinking tonight, m'Lord," said Azrael, glancing at the two women once. "Would you accompany us?" He raised his eyebrows.

"Is it required? I have been travelling a lot for the past month. It is exhausting and a war is coming. I cannot lose any strength at this moment. If it is really necessary. . ." he trailed off.

"No it is not," said Amara. "It's not so necessary, m'Lord. I think we can handle ourselves."

She nervously looked at the other two. They looked at her disbelievingly. Of course it was required that the Lord accompanied them. They were not sure enough that they would be able to carry about ten spirits to the Sea of Cypress without being detected. It was a long journey and they needed a higher force. It would take all three of them to guard the spirits. To lead the way and fight off threats wasn't something they would be capable of while handling ten souls. They had to protect each other as well.

"Are you sure?" Lord Lucifer asked, raising his eyebrows in suspicion.

He looked at all three of them pointedly.

"Yes, my Lord. You don't have to worry. We shall leave tonight and return as soon as we can," replied Amara, nodding in assurance.

"Alright then," Lord Lucifer sighed. "I need to start preparing for the war now. Discuss strategies with the coven. Since the three of you may not return until the next few days, I will hold meetings again for you. But for now we need the preparations to begin. Try to return as soon as you can. And if you need anyone else to go with you then by all means do so. Keep the details to a minimum but other than that you can escort whomever you need. Do inform me of the same. Sienna, you may leave now. I have to speak to the two of them privately."

Nodding her head, Sienna turned around and left with a lingering look in Amara's direction, for everyone knew that she had made a foolish decision of not including Lord Lucifer with them. He was needed. It was unsafe without him.

"Lord Vairya is here to protect the spirit of Lilith; to keep an eye on any intrusions from Lord Mikhail and helping in guarding it. Being a very experienced priest, he has informed me about a trouble that we might be facing here. There is a spy that we have in the castle. Someone who is part of the coven; he couldn't tell me the identity of the person, but he is assured that there is someone who has been sending messages to Lord Mikhail about confidential things. Things that only the two of you are aware of; I need the both of you to keep an eye on each and every member from now on, and find out whoever it is that is betraying us. Make sure you find the traitor."

He stood up with a menacing look as he took a few steps forward and stared right at the two of them.

"I do not trust anybody at the moment and I want you to do the same. Trust no one, for it is crucial information that has been revealed to Lord Mikhail. I could sense it in the King's court. And when I say anybody, I mean that if it turns out to be the ones I trust the most, the consequences of the same will be destructive. Be careful," he whispered before vanishing out of sight.

Amara and Azrael stood there with chills running down their spines as the air suddenly turned cold. For a few long moments none of them spoke a single word. Then Azrael turned to her and offered a sad smile before walking off slowly. *Trust no one*, the Lord had said. Could she trust Azrael?

Sighing, Amara turned around and walked back to her chamber for gathering the required things for the trip to the Sea of Cypress. She took an enchanted bag, threw in her sword, a dagger and a box of the smallest needle like poisonous weapons that could be inserted into skin and end a life instantly. They were to be used only for extremely important and dangerous attackers. Amara concluded that they might face some problems on the way, so she sealed the box properly and carefully placed it in her bag. Moments later, she was out of her chamber, locking it securely before she rushed to the potions chamber. Sienna was already there, gathering the required potions for the journey into another small bag. When she spotted Amara walking in, she stopped doing her work and turned to face Amara.

"What is wrong with you? You are supposed to be one intelligent and brilliant witch. How could you say that we don't need the Lord with us? Of course we need him! It could be dangerous! We need a powerful force with us if any attack occurs. Do you even realize the intensity of the situation? There are ten spirits that we are going to be carrying with us on a long journey where anything could happen. Those spirits could turn malignant if not given proper care to. The three of us alone cannot just-"

"Enough," said Amara, raising her hand and cutting her off. "Do I come off as a fool to you? When I denied the Lord I had thought about what I was saying. He needs to be here. We have an elderly priest who is going to protect the spirit of Lilith. If he is protecting that dangerous spirit, we need to guard the protector as well. And only the Lord can do that. Nobody else in this coven is capable enough of handling spirits as much as you are. With you gone, no one else will be able to contain this. The castle needs the Lord more than we do. He told us that we can take others for our protection. I am sure we can. Leandra is also good at handling spirits. We can take her with us. She is young and she is strong. We can ask Iris as well, or even Eridanus. All three of them are strong enough to help us. This is not the time to argue amongst us. We have a war to fight."

Sienna stared at Amara silently. *She has a point,* she thought.

"Women having arguments is always so fascinating. Did I miss something?" Azrael waltzed into the chamber carrying a bag of his own slung around his shoulder.

He stood beside Amara who sighed.

"Do you have everything we need?" He asked Sienna.

"Almost, I'll meet you both at the horse-barn at midnight," she replied.

"Why there?" He frowned.

"Aren't we travelling on horses?" She asked, turning to them.

"No. We can't. We'll have to walk. The route to the Sea of Cypress is not something horses can handle. Or any wagon for that matter; it is required that the travellers walk if they have to reach Lady Calypsa," answered Amara.

"Great," Sienna rolled her eyes.

"Well someone could always carry you if needed." Azrael shrugged nonchalantly in response.

"Yes. Get a dragon for me," replied Sienna, smiling slyly as she walked past him swiftly.

Amara stared at Azrael. It was as though she was going to stab a dagger through his ribs. He raised his eyebrows in question. She just shook her head and ventured out of the chamber so fast, he had only just blinked. Azrael followed her outside and stopped her in the passageway.

"Is everything okay?" He asked, concerned.

Humans or sorcerers, males are always dim-witted, she thought to herself.

"Spectacular," she replied, sarcasm dripping out of her tone.

She did not know what made her do that. She did not know why she had spoken that way and why she suddenly felt so angry. All she knew was that she did not like Sienna anymore, or maybe it was Azrael whom she wanted to kill repeatedly, for heaven knew what reason.

"You appear anything but spectacular," he told her.

"Why do you care?" She snapped, walking away and he followed trying to keep up.

"I'm not entirely sure if I understand that question," he said.

"Wouldn't you rather get a dragon for Sienna instead of talking about silly things to me?" She stopped and turned to him with a feral expression that nearly scared Azrael for a moment.

And then suddenly a smirk hit his face as he realized what Amara was feeling at that point of time. *How could I be so shallow?* He thought. It wasn't even his *idea* to make her jealous in the first place. What seemed like him being over-friendly to Sienna was actually him just offering a silly suggestion as a joke, which ended up in Amara feeling jealous.

"Get that smile away or I will hex you." Amara pointed an index finger in his face before storming off, leaving Azrael standing there as he laughed his heart out at how interesting Amara was. Despite of putting up the tough and intimidating personality in front of everyone, there was still an ounce of a vulnerable girl inside that was ready to pounce whenever he was around her.

Shaking his head, Azrael walked back to his chamber and Amara cursed herself for feeling what she felt. Was it even sane? Was it necessary for him to affect her so much? He was just a coven member, someone that she was working with, and he should not matter to her at all. But was he just all of that? Or had things miraculously changed? She failed to understand a single thing. Deliberately, she pushed those thoughts away from her mind and began to approach Iris's chamber. She knocked on the door once before entering. Leandra and Iris sat inside, talking in hushed whispers about something and giggling as they did so. Amara cleared her throat to get their attention.

"Amara," Iris said, standing up.

There was a silly grin that she held, and it refused to go away. It rather annoyed Amara, for she had an idea as to what they had been talking about, and why she was smiling in that manner. Choosing to ignore it, Amara informed Iris about the journey and that it would be helpful if she accompanied her along.

"Leandra can join us if she wishes to," she said, looking at Leandra who seemed eager enough to go with them.

"Well, okay. I don't think we have anything else to do," said Iris, nodding in agreement.

"Of course! We will join you," Leandra said, smiling.

"Alright then, meet me at the gate in an hour. Gather whatever supplies you think will be necessary for the journey."

With that, Amara turned around and left the chamber while Lea and Iris got themselves busy in preparing for the journey. An hour later, the five of them were assembled outside the castle gate, carrying one bag each.

"Everyone ready?" asked Azrael, looking at all of them.

They nodded and began to walk in the desired direction. Unknown to Lea and Iris, the ten spirits that Sienna had gathered invisibly followed them, settled all around them in a circle as though in guard. As they all strode ahead, Iris's curiosity sprung up.

"Why are we going there?" She asked.

"Not to be disclosed, Iris. Your questions cannot be answered at this moment," said Azrael, offering her a smile.

Iris sheepishly looked away, disappointed.

"Hopefully they will confess their feelings to each other," Lea whispered to Iris who chuckled and nodded in response.

"Speaking of confessions. . ." Iris trailed off and Lea widened her eyes, turning to look at her curiously.

"What?" She said, excitedly.

"I was talking to Eridanus after the meeting in the great hall," Iris began.

"Shush," Amara hissed at the two of them before turning away.

The both of them then kept quiet and followed the other three in silence.

They had been travelling for the past four hours and when it seemed like they needed to rest, Azrael stopped in the valleys of some mountain. Throwing his bag down to the ground, he turned around to face the others.

"We'll rest here for an hour. You two can get some sleep while we keep watch on any dangers," he said to Iris and Lea who seemed eager enough to sleep since they felt quite tired after having walked for so long.

Soon they were sound asleep under a tree. Azrael then turned to Sienna, grabbed her arm and led her away from Iris and Lea so they would not overhear.

"There is a cave here. You could go and give the spirits some rest," he told her quietly and she nodded in response.

Amara pushed herself to the ground, resting her back on the foot of a hill. She glanced at Azrael and Sienna. A pinching feeling struck her on the inside watching his hand on her arm. She turned away, ignoring the two along with the unknown feeling that was creeping inside of her. Letting out a sigh, she dug into her bag and pulled out a flask of water before gulping down some.

"May I have that?" said Azrael, extending his arm and pointing to the flask.

He sat before her, crouched down to his knees as he spoke. Without a word, Amara handed him the flask and looked away. Once again – unaware of what had made her so ignorant towards him – Azrael frowned in confusion as he gave the flask back to her and she refused to look in his direction, uninterestedly taking the flask and shoving it into her bag.

"You seem quite restless," he said to her, settling right beside her at the foot of the hill.

His arm brushed the side of hers and she shifted away realizing that a certain chill ran down her skin at his touch. Amara mentally cursed herself for feeling things that she should not be feeling. It was silly. She decided not to look at him suspecting that her flaming cheeks would be obvious even in the darkness.

"Do I?" She replied, impassively.

"Are you really bothered about the fact that I talked to Sienna?" He asked, almost cursing himself for directly asking such a silly question to her when he knew what the answer was and how she was going to react.

"Why would I be bothered about something like that? Do I look like a twelve-year old?" She snapped, a bit annoyed.

Azrael struggled to bite back a chuckle.

"I'm sorry. I shouldn't have said that," he told her, looking down.

"Just be quiet and get some rest," she whispered back calmly before resting her head behind and closing her eyes.

Azrael looked at her for a long moment, smiled, and then sat up properly so he could keep watch while the others rested.

* * *

They had not faced any dangers so far and were now stood at the Sea of Cypress, one day later. The spirits were all safe and everyone was quite tired yet content to arrive at their destination without having to face any qualms. The sun rose up from the east as they set foot in front of the huge sea where Lady Calypsa resided. There was a beautiful light that surrounded the Sea. Since it was early morning and Lady Calypsa would not see them before midnight, the lot decided to get some food and rest until the day ended. Sienna left to find a cave along with Lea who had been helping all this while, although unaware of the spirits. It was quite evident that there were some other companions with them - since Leandra herself dealt with spirits, she could sense the same but did not say so.

With her help, Sienna had been able to keep the spirits in control while the others enhanced the protection. Iris and Amara now sat on top of a huge rock, pulling out a few food items from the bag that Lea had prepared in the kitchen before they had left. There were a few fruits which Amara handed to Azrael and Iris before taking some for herself. Azrael sat on another rock with his legs extended in front of him.

"Iris," he called out when she was busy talking to Amara about white witchcraft.

"Yes?" She turned to him, raising her eyebrows.

"Do you think you will be okay here alone?" He asked, stepping down from the rock that he was seated on.

She frowned.

"I think so. . ." she hesitated, glancing at a confused Amara.

"It's safe, don't worry. Besides, Lea is here, see," he told her, in the end pointing at Leandra who was heading in their direction.

Iris shrugged in response.

"Lea, take care of her and don't go wandering," he said to her.

"Are you going somewhere?" She asked.

"Yes. Just be careful," he replied before looking at Amara.

"Amara," he spoke. She looked at him.

"Walk with me," he said.

"Why?"

She narrowed her eyes in suspicion. She did not know what sort of suspicion it was, but nonetheless.

"Just walk with me," he said again while Lea and Iris exchanged knowing looks, trying to hide their smirks. Sighing, Amara stepped down from the rock and began walking to where Azrael led her. Iris chuckled and looked at Lea as she sat next to Iris bemusedly. At a distance, Azrael led her away from there and silently they proceeded along the shore of the Sea.

"Do you have any doubts about who it could be?" He suddenly asked.

"Lord Mikhail's messenger, you mean?" She replied, admiring the light of the sun that shone upon the Sea. He nodded in response.

"I'm not sure. It could be anyone." She shrugged.

"Before we begin looking for the traitor, I need one thing cleared between us, since we have the task of revealing the same. I don't how much you trust me. We don't exactly know each other that well."

He stopped walking and turned to her. "I don't doubt you on that, nobody would doubt upon the fact that you could be the messenger, it's just not possible. I, on the other hand, have joined the coven only recently. So if you want to know whether I am the traitor, I offer myself for any test that is needed. And when I pass that test, I want you to trust me completely so together we can find out who it is."

He stepped forward and intently looked straight into her eyes. She stared back. Something inside her told her that it could not be him. At any cost, it wasn't Azrael. She knew it. It was unclear to her how much she trusted him, but she knew for a fact that he wasn't the traitor they were looking for. Yet the confirmation was required.

"I'm letting you into my mind. You can see whatever you need to," he whispered.

With that, he opened the doors and Amara unintentionally entered his mind.

CHAPTER THIRTY-FIVE

∞∞∞∞∞

POSSESSED

∞∞∞∞∞

There was an ocean of visions that Amara saw when she entered Azrael's mind. She saw a million things all at once. There was a jumbled version of his childhood but she was unable to understand a single thing, for it came and went too fast. Then she saw a flicker of his training by Lord Lucifer, a glimpse of Nicholas, and then suddenly he was in the castle with her. Amara could not contemplate a single thing. She was then rushed into another vision where Azrael was with Lord Lucifer, getting trained. This time it was clear and slow. She could see the devotion in his eyes. She could see his powers coming into force, how he easily acquired the strength of handling the same elements as she did. It was incredible. But she did not see a single vision where he was in any way associated with Lord Mikhail. And it all but confirmed her trust on him. She knew it wasn't him. It could never be him.

A moment later, as she tried to pull herself out of his mind, she involuntarily stopped at his conscious and subconscious thoughts. The majority of his thoughts were clouded by just one person: Amara. And it filled her with this strange but wonderful feeling. It made her smile. Unwilling to look any further, she closed the doors of her own mind to conceal her approach ahead. Then Azrael's mind shut itself for her. Both of their eyes opened. They were standing at the shore, away from the rest of the group, staring at each other as though there was nothing else they could do. Amara watched Azrael in awe. She wasn't expecting herself to be in his thoughts. And to contain most of them, it was something overwhelming for her.

When a wave crashed upon their feet, they blinked and looked away. Amara tucked a strand of hair behind her ear and suddenly noticed that her heart was racing. A smile found its way on her face and she glanced at Azrael once. He was looking at the Sea.

"I haven't trusted anyone apart from the Lord, and now Iris," she said quietly. "It has always been difficult for me to develop any sort of trust on someone. I don't know you. I don't know you at all."

She kept her eyes on her feet as she said that. The water cascaded down from under her toes slowly.

"I gathered that. But I don't need you to know me. I want you to trust me by knowing what I am now, not by knowing what I was in the past; because revealing the past is a choice, not a rule. I want to be a part of your future. I want your trust to be there with me until the day I die," he said to her, now gazing at her with what seemed like utmost content and adoration.

Amara looked at him. His words had reached the deepest parts of her soul and she smiled back at him.

"I don't know if I trust you with everything in me. Maybe that will take time. But I trust you enough to know that you are not a traitor. And this trust may develop into something bigger and more beautiful further in our future," she told him truthfully.

For a moment, there was silence, and then Azrael turned to look at her again.

"Are you suggesting that something is going to happen between us in future?" He asked with a mischievous glint in his eyes.

Amara was taken aback. Her embarrassment was about to show up when she looked at his face and realized that he wasn't being serious. But despite of the joke he intended it as; she knew there was a seriousness hidden in those words. They just did not want to accept it at the moment, suspecting that it would all shatter.

"Maybe that is just something in your head, sorcerer," she told him before turning around to walk in the opposite direction.

"I never said the walk was over," he called out and she looked at him again.

"Don't we have more important things to do?" She raised her eyebrows.

"Not until midnight."

And with that they were walking together again. As they treaded, a silence followed. It wasn't an uncomfortable one. They listened to the sound of birds chirping, the view of the sun shining upon the water, and the wind rushing around them in circles. They walked further and further along the shore of the Sea and they failed to notice the wall that was in between – stopping them from accepting what they felt for each other – was now gone. It had ceased to exist and both of them knew what they actually meant to each other. The only difference was that none of them were ready to reveal the same.

For a long time, they walked along the shore and then returned to where the others were. Sienna was still in an isolated area giving the spirits some rest, while Lea and Iris were fast asleep on the rock that they had been seated on. It was nearing noon when Amara and Azrael settled themselves back to where they were before. They spent the rest of the day in a bit of meditation among other things. Lea and Iris got busy chatting about one thing or another and exploring the shore while Amara and Azrael discussed war strategies and how much practice was needed.

When midnight came, Lea and Iris were sent away since an audience with Lady Calypsa was only meant for Amara and Azrael. Sienna was asked to be there, for the spirits were to be taken care of while they spoke. They stood there with the sound of the waves crashing into their ears. The sky was darker than before, the moon invisible amidst the grey clouds that had surrounded. Amara and Azrael raised their right legs before resting their toes on the water. It suddenly went calm. The waves diminished and the wind seemed to slow down. Sienna watched as black coloured smoke rose at a distance from the middle of the sea. It reached high above before contorting into the figure of a woman. As she approached further, Sienna observed that there was no face to be seen. It became an even foggy and a smoky appearance instead of being clearer.

Lady Calypsa now stood in front of Amara and Azrael who bent in respect and Sienna followed suit. She stood adjacent to Amara while Azrael stood on the other side of the latter.

"Great Lady, we come to offer you guardians," said Amara.

"Guardians?" asked the lady with a hint of curiosity in her tone mixed with annoyance.

Why would someone as powerful as Lady Calypsa need guardians?

"Yes, Great Lady. Since the war is about to begin, we need to ensure proper protection for you. The prophecy is under your watch but we bring guardians to offer you protection so your attention remains solely on the prophecy. Lord Lucifer has sent orders for your guard," Azrael spoke.

Lady Calypsa seemed to think for a while before she circled Amara and Azrael, stopping at Sienna in the end.

"And who would you be?" She hissed in Sienna's ear.

Sienna shut her eyes at the sound echoing in her ears. Lady Calypsa was intimidating enough to her since it was the first time that she had been in her acquaintance.

"She is the carrier of your guardians," answered Amara.

"Where are the guardians?" asked the Lady.

"These are invisible spirits, Great Lady. Ten spirits will be your guardians and protect the sea from any harm," Amara said.

"Lord Lucifer trusts these spirits?"

"Essentially so," said Azrael, nodding.

"It is Lord Lucifer because of whom I choose to believe you. I did receive a message from him saying that his apprentices would be visiting. The assurance was needed to be careful of imposters," replied Lady Calypsa, now going back in position on top of the water as her robes slithered into the water behind her.

"Of course, Great Lady. It is most necessary," Amara said.

"Leave the guardians here. I shall not require your assistance further than this. The spirits and I need to communicate in privacy to ensure that every sort of protection is covered. You are free to leave."

With that, the Lady vanished. From around Sienna, the spirits rushed away and in the direction of the Sea like a wild gush of wind. She realized that they retreated into the sea along with Lady Calypsa.

The waves began to crash upon the shore again and the wind started to rush around them.

"We can leave now," Amara said and turned to Azrael and Sienna who nodded in response.

The three of them then left to find Iris and Leandra before leaving the Sea of Cypress. As instructed, the two witches were supposed to be in the woods adjoining the sea, from where they were to leave to go back to the castle. Amara had strictly asked the two to be seated under the giant oak tree, which was easy to spot. But the spot under the oak tree was empty. Neither were there any trails of footsteps for them to be there. Amara and Azrael cast a glance in each other's direction while Sienna followed behind them.

"Are they here?" Sienna asked.

Amara turned to look at her worriedly.

"No. They're not," she replied.

Sienna hurried to where Amara and Azrael were.

"They might be somewhere around here. Let's look for them," he said, giving Amara a reassuring smile.

She nodded in reply silently. They headed in different directions calling out Iris and Lea's names in a bid to locate them but nothing worked. Azrael stopped at a point, returning to where they were when he found no source of his sister and Iris. Amara stood under the oak, looking around to find where Iris was. The feeling of sheer panic refused to go away. Iris was way too important to her and if a single harm occurred, Amara did not know what she would do.

"Amara," Azrael said quietly when he reached her.

She turned to him hopefully but upon finding that there was nobody accompanying him, she looked away.

"Amara," he said again, holding her shoulders and turning her to his side. "We'll find them. Don't worry."

He tried his best to give her enough assurance but nothing worked.

"Listen to me," he told her when she looked away again.

"Connect your mind to Iris's. Maybe then you can find her location," he said.

"Right! We could do that," she replied and shut her eyes immediately.

With her concentration focussed on Iris completely, Amara established a link between both of their minds. It took a few long moments to locate Iris's mind, but when she did, Amara found that Iris was alone. Leandra was nowhere around her. Blindly, she followed where Iris's mind led her to. Amara could not understand as to where Iris exactly was and what condition she was in or what she was doing. All she could sense was fear that came through Iris's mind into hers. So she followed the vision silently. As he saw her walk away from him, Azrael began to follow her in a bid to ask where she was going. But one look at her vacant and uncomprehending eyes, and he decided to walk with her without a question.

They reached a clearing. He sent a message to Sienna telling her where they were. Sienna appeared soon enough. Amara stopped at a distance. Below her was a pit. There were iron bars covering the pit. It was dark, nothing could be seen. But Amara heard a sound; a wailing sound – someone asking for help, someone crying. Amara suddenly snapped out of her connection to Iris's mind. She looked down. Another wailing sound was heard, this one louder than before. Letting out a breath Amara bent to her knees and gazed into the pit. Azrael and Sienna imitated her, looking down in the pit through the iron bars.

"Iris," Amara whispered, recognizing the sound.

The pit was deep. Iris would have been somewhere below out of eyesight.

"She's in there," she said again, when Azrael merely stared down into the pit.

"How did-"

"Get her out of there!" Amara cut him off with a screech.

There was a pounding in her head. She knew, she just knew that Iris was being tortured. Who it was; how it happened and why it was being done, she was unaware. She cared not. All she cared about was Iris. Iris in pain. . .Iris being trapped under the pit . . .Iris in danger. There was nothing else on her mind.

"Amara," Azrael began.

He wanted to calm her down but Amara refused to listen. She shook her head.

"Rescue her! Do something!" she told him, panicked.

Her eyes were moist, a pained look she held as she looked back and forth between Azrael and the pit from where Iris's wails were still echoing. But before Azrael could do a single thing, Sienna had already weakened the iron bars by conjuring a sharp metal blade. She started to scrape the blade over the bars using all her strength and soon enough, they began to crack. Immediately Azrael conjured another one before starting to cut through the bars himself. But Amara was blank. She could not think of a single thing to do. Sitting there she stared at the pit. She tried to locate Iris to get her out somehow, in any possible way. The worry of losing Iris was seeping inside of her slowly and steadily burning all her insides. If anything were to happen to Iris, Amara did not know what she would do.

Her attention wavered when she heard a thud. Blinking, she lifted her head to find Eridanus on the ground at a distance. She stood up, frowning. Azrael and Sienna looked up in confusion while cutting through the bars.

"What are you doing here?" Amara asked Eridanus who pushed himself off of the ground and sprinted to where they were.

"Iris," he panted. "She sent me a message," he said between breaths.

"She sent a message to *you*?" Amara questioned.

It surprised her as to why Iris would send Eridanus a message. He was far away in the castle. Instead of doing the same to Amara, Azrael or Sienna who were close enough to her, she sent a message to him. Amara found it strange.

"Where is she? What is happening?" He asked worriedly.

He looked at Azrael, then at Amara, at the pit and then at Sienna in panic.

"Amara, conjure a rope. I'm going into the pit," Azrael said.

Instantly there was a long rope right before them. Azrael grabbed it, pulled off his hooded cloak, tied the rope around his waist and jumped into the pit while Sienna held the rope in her hands. Azrael descended down the mud walls around him and they began to get wider as he approached the bottom. Iris's voice became clearer, louder as he descended below. He wondered where Leandra was. Maybe she was with Iris, or maybe she was somewhere else in trouble. Who did whatever they did and why, Azrael didn't know. He had no time to think over it. He had to save Iris.

There was a foul smell that surrounded him when he reached the bottom. It was a passage ahead of him. Letting go of the rope, he conjured up a torch of fire before following Iris's cries. The passage opened to reveal a larger clearing where he spotted two figures. One was Iris, on the floor, wailing in pain. Her eyes were rolled upwards, her limbs twisted in a very strange way. Her body was shivering.

Opposite to her sat a horrific sight. Noctia Stella. Azrael recognized the *Mortuis* upon looking at the hideous appearance. He cursed under his breath before rushing towards Iris. Noctia Stella's eyes did not waver from her victim. Her blazing red gaze was on Iris, yet she knew that there was someone else in the pit trying to rescue the prey. Azrael wondered how Noctia had left the village of Heletes and come far to the path leading to the Sea of Cypress. It was impossible for a *Mortuis* to leave their residence and go somewhere else, unless they had help from an immortal. He wondered who it was that had helped Noctia Stella.

With his mind focussed on Noctia Stella, he used all his powers and created an invisible shield around Iris to keep her safe. Since most of his strength had been used due to the amount of powers Noctia possessed, he could not carry an unconscious Iris out of the pit all by himself. A faded message then rushed out of his mind and reached Amara. Due to the force by which the message hit her, she stumbled on her feet and took a step back. In moments, she started to rush down the pit. Without a question, Sienna immediately bound the rope around a tree behind them and gave the other half to Amara. She tied it around her waist and descended down the pit.

Breathing heavily she reached the passage where Azrael, Iris and Noctia Stella were. A rage boiled inside of her when she spotted the *Mortuis* seated there trying to break the shield that Azrael had created. Sprinting to where the two were, she grabbed Iris by the waist, held Azrael's arm and led them back to where the ropes were. She pushed Azrael and Iris together, tied the rope around both of them and tugged on it to send a signal to Sienna, who started pulling on the rope along with the help of Eridanus.

Amara watched as Azrael and Iris ascended back up the pit. But along with Azrael, the shield that he created was gone. Noctia Stella's attention was now focussed on Amara. It would take some amount of time until Azrael and Iris reached the top and she would be able to go. Until then, Amara was in the pit alone with Noctia who was now starting to create barriers that would weaken Amara so she would not be able to leave. There was a fury that built up inside her and she could destroy anything and everything that came in way, but not someone as strong as Noctia Stella. Amara could not do that alone.

She fought the unseen barriers with any strength that she could. But she had to save some power to go back to the top. It was difficult fighting the *Mortuis* all by herself. She needed help; any powerful Conjurer would need help since it was not easy to battle *Mortuis*. And witches that practiced dark witchcraft were always more powerful than others. Something started to blind Amara's vision. She stumbled, ready to fall but she resisted it. Her hands were plastered on the walls around her, trying to keep her feet steady but Stella was stronger. Amara's eyes began to view black and grey patches and she blinked to adjust her vision but nothing worked.

She felt the rope touch her shoulder as it fell down to let her up. But she could not bring herself to let go of the wall and grab the rope – or even so, tie it around herself to go back. She panted, her breath seemed to give way and it felt like there was no air in the pit. Suffocation began to enter her senses and she gasped for air while struggling to keep her eyes steady with vision. Just as she was about to give up and descend to the floor, an arm was wrapped around her waist and she felt herself being pulled towards someone. And then her feet left the ground. She was being lifted upwards and in moments, there was enough air to let her breathe. Her head fell backwards and she was laid to the ground when Azrael released his hold on her.

Sienna pulled out a bottle of *Healing Potion* before letting some drop into Amara's mouth as she had done with Azrael and Iris. Eridanus was now embracing Iris with her head resting on his chest as they sat under a tree. He stroked her head softly and held her close to him as she breathed shallow breaths. She was weak, her eyes shut and her fingers clasped around his cloak in a tight grip.

"It's alright. You're alright," he whispered softly into her ear.

Ever since he had confessed his feelings to her in the castle before she left for the Sea of Cypress, he felt even more protective of her than he had ever felt. She had not replied to him at that time, Lea had interrupted and she didn't get a chance to tell him what he wanted to hear. Now with her resting in his arms, he felt content. There was absolutely nothing else that he seemed to care about at that point of time.

When Amara's eyes fluttered open, she coughed and pushed herself up so she was sitting. Azrael sat in front of her apprehensively.

"Are you alright?" He asked her, raising his hand and pushing a stray strand of hair behind her ear.

Even in her weakness, Amara felt his touch send a strange sensation down her spine. And it rather disappointed her when he pulled his hand away suddenly, clearing his throat.

"I'm okay," she croaked. "Where is Iris?" She asked, her eyes landing on Iris who was covered with Eridanus's cloak that he had wrapped around her.

Despite herself, a smile etched across her face as she looked at the caring expression that Eridanus had when he held Iris. And then suddenly a thought struck her.

"Leandra," she breathed, turning to look at Azrael.

Sienna's head snapped towards her as realization struck her that Lea was nowhere to be seen.

CHAPTER THIRTY-SIX

∞∞

REVELATIONS

∞∞

There was little time to dwell over how Leandra had ended up where she was. Under the Sea of Cypress, she lay on the bed with blood flowing around her mixed with the water. There was a gash on her abdomen, blood dripped out of it furiously. When Azrael had received a message from Lady Calypsa saying a witch had been found in the sea bloodied, they had all rushed back to the Sea and he had jumped inside immediately. Eridanus left Iris with Amara and followed after Azrael. Amara and Sienna waited at the shore with a sleepy Iris resting on Amara's shoulder. Eridanus's cloak was still wrapped around Iris, who mumbled incoherent words softly. Eridanus and Azrael searched for Lea and spotted her far in the sea at the bed. Azrael picked her up and started to ascend above with her, holding her close to his chest. They swam towards the shore and upon reaching, Azrael let Lea drop on top of the sand.

Sienna rushed towards them and pulled the *Healing Potion* out of her bag. It had started to finish since it had been used for Amara, Azrael as well as Iris. To heal the wound on Lea's abdomen would be difficult. Nevertheless, Sienna let the remaining potion drop into her mouth. Unconscious, Leandra coughed out water and drew a gasp. Her eyes opened for a few moments before they rolled upwards and shut again. Azrael sat there watching his sister breathe heavily as the *Healing Potion* began to work its way into her system. Eridanus muttered a drying spell and all of them were no longer dripping with water. Amara had skidded to a halt before them with Iris still resting on her body. Eridanus looked up at her and gestured to hand Iris to him. Amara pushed the half-asleep Iris towards him and he immediately wrapped his arms around her in an embrace.

Amara sat beside Azrael and watched his face contort into a saddened one as Lea refused to open her eyes.

"We need to go back to the castle, now," said Sienna. "Soter will have a solution. We can't do anything without the resources."

"We can't teleport. Not all of us. But it's necessary to get Leandra back to the castle immediately. I can create a false trail for a few of us so she can be escorted back by teleporting," Amara replied.

"Eridanus, you can teleport out of here with Iris. She needs to return too. I need someone with me here. Either Azrael takes Leandra and Sienna stays with me, or otherwise."

She looked back and forth between Azrael and Sienna. Sienna was busy trying to wake up Lea while Azrael held a vacant look, something which Amara could not decipher. Eridanus looked at her and nodded to beckon Amara towards him. She swiftly walked in his direction and stood before him.

"He needs you. Sienna will come with us. You take care of him," he said to her quietly while Iris mumbled something that Amara stressed her ears to catch.

"Are you sure the two of you will be able to manage them alone?" She asked.

"We'll be fine. But if Azrael comes with us it'll be difficult to handle his emotions as well as these two," he told her truthfully.

Amara nodded in understanding. As much as she wanted Azrael to be with his sister while she was in that condition, she also wanted him to be okay. And looking at the way he was behaving at the moment, she did not think it would be wise to send him off with two injured to take care of, one of which included his sister. He needed to calm himself before reaching the castle.

"Alright then. I'll create the false trails. Also, Azrael is the only person who can help me do that since his false trails are quite powerful so I'm going to need him. You be careful and take care of Iris and Leandra. We'll be there soon," she said and Eridanus nodded in reply.

She then turned to look at Sienna.

"Sienna," she called out and Sienna looked at Amara with her eyebrows raised.

"Will it be okay for you to go with Leandra?" She asked.

"Of course, I'll go," Sienna replied and packed everything back into her bag of supplies before she stood up.

She then hoisted Lea and held her in place with arms around her. Sienna had managed to stop the blood from flowing too fast but Lea was still unconscious. As soon as the four of them were about to leave, Leandra let out a gasp and her eyes opened. They were bloodshot, her head was titled backwards and she breathed heavily. Azrael's head shot up towards her and he stood to go near his sister.

"Lea?" He whispered.

He placed his hands on her cheeks and brought her head back to level. She stared at him transfixed, but spoke nothing. Just as Sienna opened her mouth to tell them that they had to leave, Leandra muttered something under her breath. Frowning, Azrael leaned forward to listen.

"S-s-spirits. . ." she gasped.

"Lea-what? Spirits?" Azrael asked, confused.

"T-the s-spirits. . ." she mumbled again and then her eyes shut once again.

Azrael let his hands drop from her face and sighed.

"We'll get to know what she said later. Right now she needs to be saved. It could get really worse," Sienna said impatiently as she pressed on Lea's abdomen to stop the blood.

"But she-" Azrael began to protest when Amara placed a hand on his shoulder to pull him back.

"They need to leave," she told him and he reluctantly stepped away to let them leave.

"Rael. . ." whispered Leandra, her eyes fluttering open and close.

Azrael snapped his head back to his sister and extended his arm to grab hold of her when Sienna vanished along with Eridanus and Iris. Azrael watched the empty space, unblinking. His eyes started to get moist. What had Lea meant when she spoke of spirits? She needed him. She had called out his name. His little sister needed him. He started to shut his eyes to teleport when Amara grabbed his arm and pulled him back towards her forcefully. He crashed into her and they were about to fall but Amara steadied him in place with both her arms on his shoulders. It was a bit difficult since he was quite taller than her, but she managed.

"You need to breathe. Leandra is going to be okay. Right now we have to create the false trails before Lady Calypsa finds out that someone teleported out of here. It is forbidden. She might react wrongly. It won't be long until she realizes what has happened. And you have to calm down. We will be at the castle soon enough and everything will be fine. Soter might already be working on making Leandra and Iris okay. Your little sister is safe in the castle," she said to him softly.

He looked at her with uncertainty before letting out a sigh and nodding in understanding. They needed to save themselves and create false trails. Only then would it be okay to leave for the castle.

"Breathe," whispered Amara when he held one.

He blinked and failed to understand when and how his arms lifted themselves from his side, extended towards Amara and were wrapped around her waist. She was swiftly pulled in his direction and before she realized what had happened, he was embracing her. It was only when his arms tightened around her and he buried his face in her neck that she felt how fast her heart was beating. There was a strange chilly sensation that crawled up her spine as she processed what was happening. Without her knowledge, her arms were now around his neck, her feet lifted a little above the ground because of his height, and then she shut her eyes.

She rested her head on his shoulder hesitantly. He breathed into her neck in contentment. Azrael realized then what he had done. But he did not wish to let go. He wanted to stay that way. All his worries seemed to vanish when he held her. He was at ease, he felt safe. It was as though she had a shield that was around him. He knew that if ever he was in pain, she would be there. She would protect him. He was the most vulnerable with Amara. He was under her safety. He did not need to worry about anything harming him. She was like his guardian, his protector, and the one he had inevitably and unknowingly fallen in love with. When he would accept that, he knew not.

"Rael," she whispered when they stayed that way for none knew how long.

Azrael opened his eyes at the tone she had used. It sounded beautiful to his ears. It made him smile. Never had his name sounded so dear to him. Lea called him that too, but it did not feel the way it did when Amara spoke. It was different, very different from what Lea used to say. And it was different from how his mother used to call him. For a moment, he went back to those thoughts about his childhood when Amara slowly pulled away and he was brought back to the present as he looked at her face. His arms then reluctantly dropped from her waist. There was a crimson hue on Amara's cheeks as she looked back at him.

It made him feel as though he had accomplished something. Who had ever succeeded in making Amara blush apart from him, as far as he knew?

"We have to go," she told him and then he rushed into reality.

They had to leave. They had to set the false trails for the rest of the lot so nothing would happen. It would become difficult to go back to the castle otherwise. He could wonder all about Amara on the way back. But at the moment, there were other important things to do.

"Yes, I'm sorry. Let's go," he replied and the both of them left the shore immediately.

A few moments later when they were at a distance, they created the false trails for Eridanus, Sienna, Iris and Leandra to make it look like they had used the route that was required to go back to the castle, instead of teleporting or using a wagon which wasn't allowed. The route to the Sea of Cypress did not allow any other means of transport apart from walking. It did not matter from how afar one was travelling. And if false trails were not created at times of emergency when teleporting was necessary, it could anger Lady Calypsa leading to torturous results.

When the trails had been successfully created, Amara and Azrael left to go back to the castle. On the way, Azrael strained his mind to figure out why Lea had spoken about the spirits. Were they in danger? How had she ended up in the Sea of Cypress? Why was Iris under Noctia Stella's control? There were various questions that ran through his mind as the two of them walked ahead. Dawn had now approached. The sun was rising above the horizon and then the forest was drenched in sunlight. Amara walked behind Azrael with her eyes wedged on his back. The cloak that he wore was flowing behind him as he took steps ahead. She watched him with mixed feelings.

For a moment, she felt like smiling at what had happened back at the shore of the Sea; at the same time she felt worried for Leandra and Iris. Suddenly her thoughts were clouded with delight as she remembered the way he had opened up to her and she had started to trust him more than she had trusted anyone. But could she do that? Could she trust a man after what Leo had done to her? Could she trust Azrael after her own Lord had not told her about him being Leo's father? Was it possible for her to fall for someone when she had been betrayed so brutally before? It didn't matter that a hundred years had passed. The most she had come to trusting someone was Iris and Lord Lucifer. Trusting Azrael did seem like a viable thing to do, but something always seemed to pull her back. She could not do it, much as she wanted to.

With a shake of her head, she pushed those thoughts away from her mind. Now was not the time to think about Azrael. It was important to understand what Leandra had meant when she had spoken of the spirits. They had to find out how and why Iris had ended up with Noctia Stella and how Leandra had been left injured in the Sea of Cypress. They had a battle to fight and there was no time to dwell on futile things that held no importance before what was coming.

"What do you think?"

She was snapped out of her thoughts when Azrael turned around and spoke to her. She frowned in confusion. *What do I think about what?*

"You didn't hear me, did you?" He asked, chuckling slightly.

Amara sheepishly shook her head in response.

"I was asking what your thoughts are on Noctia Stella being in this region all the way from Heletes," he told her as she fell into step beside him.

They walked adjacent to one another now and Amara decided to give it a thought. What could it be that brought that *Mortuis* near the Sea of Cypress?

"She couldn't have arrived all by herself. That is not possible," she told him.

"Yes. She would have needed a powerful Conjurer for this purpose. She would have needed a wagon. And getting a wagon here without being detected is quite difficult. Who could have done it?" Azrael wondered.

It was like a riddle that they could not decipher easily. There was something missing that they were unable to put a finger on. It was nagging their brains but they found no definite answer.

"It could be Lord Mikhail," Amara suggested.

"Witches like Noctia Stella do not mingle with those who are not her servants. This has to be someone who has been trained in all sorts of dark witchcraft by her. And Lord Mikhail is not very skilled at dark witchcraft," said Azrael.

"How do you know that?" Amara looked at him in confusion.

"If he was trained by Noctia Stella he would have achieved the prophecy already. Our coven would have been destroyed. But he doesn't know anything about the prophecy. He *wants* to know. His belief that he can easily defeat the Lord and get what he needs is quite obvious. He wouldn't resort to such dark witchcraft without even knowing what the prophecy holds. Also, getting help from a *Mortuis* has its repercussions. He already declared war against us. Now if he used Noctia Stella as bait, it would hurt his reputation. He's one of the King's Ministers after all," he replied in all honesty.

Amara nodded in understanding. He did have a point. If Lord Mikhail was acquainted with Noctia Stella, everyone would have known about it. His strength would be tenfold. And he would not send her to harm Iris or Leandra. As far as Amara could understand, Noctia had her own intentions in hurting Iris. After having rescued Lord Lucifer from her with the help of Iris since she had succeeded in blocking Noctia's mind, it was obvious enough that the evil witch would want some sort of vengeance. But the question still remained. Who had helped her in leaving Heletes?

"Well then, who else is that powerful?" She asked Azrael.

"That is what bothers me. I can't figure out who it could be. Moreover, why would she want to harm Lea?"

"What if it was someone else that harmed Leandra? Noctia Stella doesn't have anything personal against *her*, but she does in case of Iris."

"True. But whoever harmed Lea had something to do with Noctia. Her talking about spirits is very curious though. I don't understand what she meant by that." Azrael scratched his forehead, perplexed.

"Maybe all of this is interconnected. We should join the dots. The moment we left the spirits with Lady Calypsa, Iris and Leandra disappeared. Iris was found with Noctia Stella while Leandra lands in the Sea of Cypress and we are informed about it through Lady Calypsa. As far as we know, she was supposed to be busy having a meeting with the spirits. We then find Leandra who talks about the spirits. There has got to be some sort of link between all of this," she told him thoughtfully.

"But it still doesn't make sense as to how Noctia Stella ended up here and took Iris." He shook his head in reply.

"This is too complicated. I think we should wait till we get back to the castle and we'll hear what Leandra and Iris have to say." Amara sighed.

It was complicated indeed. Their minds were occupied by a lot of things and there was nothing that they could get a conclusion out of. They had a journey to finish whilst creating false trails every now and then so they would be safe. And they had to reach the castle as soon as they could. There wasn't enough time left. In a week or two, Lord Mikhail would attack with his army. They all needed practice. Their powers had to be exercised.

"I hope Lea is okay," muttered Azrael, looking down as he walked.

"She's probably already awake and talking incessantly with Iris," Amara said to him with a reassuring smile in his direction. "Don't worry. She'll be okay. Your sister is safe."

Azrael looked back at her and returned her smile with one of his own. One thing he had realized in the time he spent with Amara was that he smiled more than he had ever done before. Lea used to complain about the fact that he never smiled as much; not after he left home. But with Amara, his smile never seemed to go. It was always that easy with her, he didn't know how.

"Thank you," he told her truthfully.

His eyes scanned hers. He wanted to know whether she had the same feelings when she was with him or it was just his imagination. But there were so many things that were trapped in those eyes of hers that he could not keep his concentration on one thing. All he noticed was that they were expressive, there were a million things that they wanted to say but she had everything chained inside. And he wanted to free those chains. She said nothing in reply but just smiled and then looked away.

* * *

A day later, they were stood before the gates of the castle, tired and exhausted mentally as well as physically. Amara let out a sigh when they stopped at the gates of the graveyard. But Azrael didn't wait. He was worried for his sister. So before the gates even opened completely, he rushed inside and into the castle doors. Amara followed him in slowly walking ahead since there was no energy left in her. She needed to sleep. They had not stopped to rest at all on the way. One whole day and night they had spent in walking and had only stopped for a few moments to find something to eat so they could venture ahead. Amara did not know how Azrael had enough strength to run into the castle.

She knew Iris and Leandra were safe there. She did not want to worry about them because they had a lot of people around. Soter was fully capable of taking care of the both of them. But the thought of Azrael worrying about losing his sister made her want to rush towards him, for he needed someone beside him. If anything were to happen to Leandra, she could only wonder how he would cope. So Amara increased her pace a bit and reached the castle after passing the graveyard. Once inside, she went in the direction of Iris's chamber hoping both Leandra and Iris would be there.

When she entered inside, she found Eridanus sitting beside Iris on the floor and Leandra lying on the bed with Soter beside her. Azrael stood at the foot of the bed, staring at his sister as she breathed shallow breaths. Iris looked up at Amara and she walked ahead.

"Are you okay?" Iris asked, pushing herself up from the floor and standing in front of Amara.

"Am *I* okay? You were caught by a dead witch. I should ask *you* if you're okay," she replied.

"I'm fine. But Lea isn't," Iris said.

She looked at Leandra's comatose body while Soter mixed up some ingredients into a paste. Amara took a few steps ahead and looked at Leandra. Her face was pale, the gash on her abdomen was covered in a bandage with a brown coloured paste and her breathing was shallow. Amara went and stood beside Azrael. Eridanus stood up from where he was sitting on the floor and came next to Iris.

"Soter, how long has she been unconscious?" Amara asked.

Soter looked up at her from his work.

"She hasn't woken up since they got here. I've been trying but her response seems to come and go in flashes. Her wound isn't that deep but some mental impact has rendered her still," he replied.

"Iris, what happened there?" Amara turned to Iris.

"I don't exactly remember, but Lea and I were standing below the oak tree that you had asked us to. Suddenly she sensed some dark force around her and told me about it. But we decided to stay there until you people returned. Then something happened and I passed out. I don't know what happened after that but when I woke up I was in this dark pit with the dead witch. She stared at me with those terrible red eyes of hers and I was really frightened. I was terrified." She winced at the memory. "And then I started to go blind. I couldn't see a thing. My eyes were open but I saw nothing. Then there was this unbearable pain. It was. . ." she trailed off, blinking and clearing her throat that had gone dry. The memory still scared her.

Eridanus slipped his fingers into hers, holding her hand tightly in reassurance. She glanced at him once and then turned back to Amara.

"Then before I realized, I was out of the pit." She finished.

But there was one lingering question in Amara's mind that she needed an answer to.

"Why did you send a message to Eridanus instead of me or Azrael?" She asked.

Iris frowned.

"I didn't send a message to anyone," she replied.

Amara was about to question her back for what she had meant when they heard a gasp and Leandra's eyes flew open.

∞∞∞∞∞

CHAPTER THIRTY-SEVEN

BETRAYAL

∞∞∞∞∞

Lea coughed as Soter helped her sit up. He pushed a pillow behind her and she rested her back on it, leaning her head on the wall. Azrael immediately rushed to her side and sat beside her on the bed. Lea shut her eyes for a long moment before turning to Azrael and giving him a tired smile. He held her hand.

"How are you feeling?" He asked in a whisper.

"I'm fine," she replied, her voice raspy.

"I'll get you something to eat," Soter said and stood up to go to the kitchen.

Amara and Iris headed towards the bed and Iris offered a reassuring grin to Leandra who returned it with one of her own exhausted smile. Her face looked paler than ever, Iris observed. Her eyes had dark patches under them; overall she seemed weak since she had not eaten in three days.

"Do you remember what happened?" Azrael asked cautiously, not wanting to make her feel like he was burdening her right when she woke up.

"Let her eat first, Rael. She'll answer your questions later," said Amara, taking a step forward.

Leandra snapped her head towards Amara. *Since when did she start calling him Rael?* She wondered but decided that now wasn't the time to bring up that issue. There were other things to be taken care of.

"No, I'm alright," Leandra croaked.

"Are you sure?" Amara asked with concern and she nodded in response.

Iris picked up a glass of water and extended it in Lea's direction before she began talking. At least that was due until Soter got the food. Lea gulped down the water in urgency. Her throat that had been feeling dry and parched now seemed soothed. She let out a sigh, putting the glass away. Azrael continued to hold one of her hands in his own, not wanting to let go. He did not intend to lose his sister again.

"While we were waiting at the place you had asked us to," she began. "We were busy chatting and then I felt this strange presence around me. I couldn't understand what it was. It seemed weird but there was something; something bad. I tried to sense what it was but nothing helped. That presence lingered around us for a while before Iris passed out. I tried to wake her up but the invisible force was concealing me from doing so. I tried a lot. That force began to push me away from her. But as I struggled to get closer to Iris, I was thrown afar. By the time I recovered and reached back, she was already gone. I panicked and started looking for her.

"I looked in every possible place I could but it felt like something was stopping me from going much further. Then I waited. I stopped at a place and waited to try to understand what the force was. It was so strong that it had ceased my voice. I couldn't speak. Then I was being lifted above. It was as though there were chains around my body. That force took me higher into the air, it all happened so fast I couldn't even send any messages. I struggled then something crashed into my abdomen and before I knew it, I was on the ground. By this time I think you all had realized that Iris and I had disappeared. But I was far from the tree we were supposed to be waiting under.

"After that I was dragged to the Sea of Cypress. I struggled a lot but the strength the force had was impossible to battle all by myself. So I concentrated on identifying what it was. Right before I was thrown into the sea, I sensed that it was a spirit. Whether it was the spirit that we were carrying or some other one, I'm not sure. But I know that it was an extremely powerful one. And that's it. You know the rest."

When she finished, Soter walked in with a tray of fruits and a vegetable salad. Everyone made way for him to go in and he placed the food in Leandra's lap. A moment later, she was busy savouring the food kept before her. Amara decided to leave the chamber to ponder upon why a spirit would so attack Leandra. Was it sent by Noctia Stella to make Leandra leave Iris? Had it been sent by Lord Mikhail to distract Leandra so Iris could be harmed? He had wanted to harm Iris and Erasmus anyway. Now that Erasmus was already trapped, it was easier for him to hurt Iris to accomplish his task since she could turn out to be the brightest witch there ever was. What could it have been?

It was quite disturbing to have such an attack happening when a battle was about to strike. It only made sense that the spirit and Noctia Stella were sent by Lord Mikhail so he could weaken the army. As she walked out of the chamber, Eridanus followed after her leaving Iris and Azrael with Leandra to take care of. He knew there was no point in staying with Iris when she was busy with her injured best friend. It only made sense to leave them alone along with Leandra's brother who needed to be with his sister at that moment. Eridanus walked out of the chamber and shut the door behind him, looking for Amara in the process. She was going towards the great hall and he began to proceed after her.

"Amara," he called out.

But she didn't respond. She kept walking. Eridanus sprinted in her direction and stood before her in the hall.

"Amara," he said again and she looked up from where she was staring at the floor wondering about the questions that were bothering her.

"Yes?" She asked, raising her eyebrows.

"The Lord asked me to tell you that he wants to see you as soon as you return," he told her.

"Why did you not tell me before?" She said and started to turn for going towards Lord Lucifer's chamber when Eridanus grabbed her arm to stop her.

"Wait," he told her, going in front of her again.

When he did not let go of her arm involuntarily, Amara shot him an intimidating glare that made him step away instantly. Just because she was being normal towards him did not mean that he could make any sort of close contact with her. She knew he didn't mean any harm nor did he have any wrong intentions. But there was a stature that Amara had to maintain and no one but Azrael and Iris were allowed to crash it down. She had not expected that to happen with Azrael either, but things seemed to have suddenly changed.

"I'm sorry," Eridanus said sheepishly.

"What do you need?" She asked impatiently.

If the Lord had asked to see her immediately then she had no time to spare. It had to be important.

"Do you think those spirits were sent by Lady Calypsa?" He asked, perplexed.

Amara was taken aback. She had not thought of something like that. Why would Lady Calypsa send spirits to harm Iris and Leandra? There was nothing remotely close to what they had done that would be of any issue to her. But could it be that Iris and Leandra were not welcome at the Sea of Cypress and that angered Lady Calypsa? Although, Amara knew that there was enough trust, so the Lady would talk to Amara or Azrael directly if it were a problem.

"Why do you say that?" She asked with a frown.

"I'm not sure. I mean, Iris and Leandra got attacked near the Sea of Cypress and Leandra was found in the Sea itself. It's sort of curious. Also if Lea says it was a sprit that harmed them, it's only natural to wonder that the spirits could have been the ones that we carried and that Lady Calypsa asked one to attack," he replied.

"Okay, look, I have to meet the Lord at the moment. We'll think about this when I return. Until then you try come up with some conclusion for this, okay?" She told him.

Eridanus nodded in response and Amara pushed past him to rush towards Lord Lucifer's chamber. She knocked on the door thrice upon reaching. It was opened by Ambrosius who asked her what she needed.

"The Lord asked me to meet him after I returned," she told him.

Ambrosius disappeared for a moment and then Lord Lucifer walked outside the chamber, shutting the door behind him.

"Follow me," he said to her and she silently obeyed, walking after him to where he led her.

They were going towards the sacrificial chamber and Lord Lucifer stopped at the closed door.

"Lilith's spirit is in there, Amara," he said. "Lord Vairya tells me that the spirit is very uncertain. It has started to descend to the afterlife and a part of her keeps pulling her back to the world. It is most dangerous for she is malign as well as safe at the same time. We need to be more careful. The battle will start in the next two weeks. The two covens that are going to be our allies will be here by tomorrow night.

We discuss strategies thereafter. But if Lilith's spirit is not controlled properly, it will destroy everything.

"The three treasures will be threatened once again, for they will be out in the open. It won't take time for Lord Mikhail to resurrect himself and achieve what he wants to. I need you to put your protective shields around this chamber for protection. Lord Vairya will be inside at all times. To safeguard him and to make sure that nobody from the enemies finds out he is here, we need to guard this area thoroughly. Will you perform the required spells?" He completed and Amara immediately nodded in response.

"Of course, m'Lord. I will begin right away," she replied.

"What of the two young witches? Are they alright?" He then asked.

"At the moment, yes. But m'Lord, may I discuss something with you?" She said.

"Go on," he told her and they began to walk away from the chamber to get seated somewhere.

Amara led him to the library where they sat opposite to one another.

"Leandra says that there was a spirit that attacked Iris and herself. We are quite confused about where the spirit might have come from. Also, Iris was captured by Noctia Stella, who was supposed to be in Heletes but somehow she reached the Sea of Cypress, which is most curious. I am not sure if I can come up with an answer. What are your thoughts on this, m'Lord?" She asked.

"Well, it is perplexing, to say the least. As far as the spirit attacking Leandra is concerned, I have my doubts on Lord Mikhail. Maybe he wanted to harm her so he sent some unidentifiable spirit. Leandra is strong enough to battle a Conjurer as far as I have seen her strength. But fighting a spirit all alone is very difficult even for someone stronger. I do keep my doubts on Lord Mikhail. Since we cannot prove anything at the moment, I think this should be left to ponder upon until after the battle. Maybe we get some clues that tell us it was him.

"Then there is Noctia Stella. She would have needed a very powerful someone to help her reach the Sea of Cypress. I don't think that had anything to do with Lord Mikhail but we cannot underestimate him at that. Noctia Stella, however, had her own motives in wanting to harm Iris. Who brought her there is the question. I have my doubts on the traitor. Have you been able to find out who it is?"

"No, my Lord. There hasn't been much time for that but we are trying," she told him with remorse.

"M'Lord, may I ask you something else?" Amara said before he could say anything else. Lord Lucifer nodded in response.

"Why did Noctia Stella capture you?" she said, hesitantly, not wanting to seem too interfering.

Lord Lucifer sighed. "Noctia Stella is one that created the *book of Darkest Witchcraft* and she found out about it being one of the treasures that Lady Calypsa guards. She has trained someone in dark witchcraft and I assume that it could be our traitor since that is the only person who has any idea about what the prophecy holds apart from you and Azrael. There is a connection between these two, and I happened to be in the land of Heletes for some rest during my travel. That is when she must have realized that I was there and captured me to extract information."

"The traitor must be found. . . ." Amara breathed, realizing the intensity of the situation.

The battle would prove futile if they failed to find the traitor. Whoever it was would know the battle strategies and it would then be sent to Lord Mikhail so he could break everything easily. It was important to find out who it was immediately for the other covens would arrive the next night.

"Yes, we don't have much time. Erasmus sent a message saying that the war strategies are being planned out discreetly in Lord Mikhail's chambers. The traitor is probably the one that helped Noctia Stella and is the only connection between Lord Mikhail and the *Mortuis*. Everything will then fall into place."

That being said, Lord Lucifer got up and left the library leaving Amara in utter worry about how she was going to find out who the traitor was. Sighing, she stood up and started walking back to the great hall where she was going to meet Eridanus. When she spotted him sitting on a chair in the hall, she walked over to him and settled beside him.

"Any results?" She asked.

He was sitting with his head resting on his fists, elbows on his knees. When Amara spoke, he looked up at her distractedly.

"Nothing," he told her.

Amara sighed in response, looking away.

"I have to talk to Azrael. Keep thinking," she told him and left to go back to Leandra's chamber.

She could not tell him about the traitor that Lord Lucifer had talked about. Who knew if Eridanus was the one anyway? She headed forwards, about to bump into Iris who was busy staring at the floor as she walked.

"Iris," Amara said and she snapped her head upwards, coming to a halt.

"Amara," Iris breathed.

"Are you alright?" She asked looking at the uncertain expression Iris bore.

"I'm fine. I'm okay. I just-I need some water," she said and placed her hand on her throat.

"Okay," Amara replied blankly, nodding.

When she started to walk past Iris, Amara was pulled back to where she was before. She frowned, looking down at Iris, who let out a breath.

"Lea and Azrael are having an argument. I don't exactly know what it is about because I was busy talking to Soter. He just left to get some herbs for Lea. And I had to leave because I felt thirsty and didn't want to disrupt their conversation," she said with uncertainty.

"An *argument*? Between Azrael and Leandra?" Amara shot back with equal confusion and worry.

It was hard to believe. Those two had such adoration and love for each other that thinking of them fighting or arguing over something seemed completely absurd and strange. Just a day ago, Leandra had spoken Azrael's name in her unconscious state and Azrael had been so scared for her that it took a hug to calm him down along with a few more reassuring words. Now that she was awake and alright, they were arguing?

Maybe it is just a normal sibling dispute, Amara wondered. But it was still hard to believe. So she decided to go and see what was happening. An injured Leandra arguing with her brother did not seem like a very safe thing to do given their state of mind.

"You go get your water. I'll see what's going on," she said to Iris who nodded in reply and then Amara proceeded towards Leandra's chamber. She stopped at the door, hesitating whether or not to open it and go inside. She did not want to interrupt their discussion, it was personal. But the sounds coming from inside were not being of any help to her. So letting out a sigh, Amara slowly opened the door. She did not wish to eavesdrop, but hearing what the argument was about before she barged in to stop it seemed like a sensible thing to do. So with her head leaning on the slightly ajar door, she paid attention to what was being said. She heard Leandra's voice first, filled with angst.

". . .Accept it. Accept that it was you who tried to get Erasmus into trouble. Be brave, Rael, tell them that it was you who sent a message to the King's Minister so they could find Lord Zachariah," she was saying.

Amara's breath stopped. Her eyes were wide and panic covered her face as she tried to understand what was going on.

"You don't mean that, Lea," said Azrael.

Amara sensed a sorrowful tone in his voice.

"I do, I do mean it. It's only fair to accept that it was you who helped Noctia Stella reach the Sea of Cypress so she could harm Iris. It was you!" Bellowed Leandra, and at that moment Amara's head began to spin. She clutched the handle of the door for support trying to digest what she was hearing.

"It was you who let the Lord get into the clutches of Noctia Stella and you tried to deceive them by going with Amara to rescue him! How long will you lie? How long will you act like you are not the messenger of Lord Mikhail? For how long will this betrayal go on?"

"Lea, you need to shut up right now!" Azrael threatened.

His voice was now frightening, and it made Amara want to go in and save Leandra if at all he were to do something silly. But she did not know what she was supposed to do. Was Leandra telling the truth? Was Azrael the traitor that they were looking for?

"No, I won't! What is your beloved Amara going to say to this? Do you think she'll be happy upon knowing that you're the one threat who is living in the same castle with her and luring her into falling for you? Don't think I don't see the way you're meddling with her feelings. I see it, and I see that she has started to fall for you. You're that brilliant, aren't you? You acted like the one person that she could trust and when she finds out who you really are, what is going to happen?"

That was when Amara began to hyperventilate; that was when Iris reached to where she was and looking at Amara's expressions, she started to go inside the chamber when Amara held her hand in place to stop her. Her grip was so tight that it began to hurt Iris but she dared not make a single sound.

"Lea, enough! I won't hear another word-"

"No! I'm going to tell the truth to the Lord. I cannot believe you would do this. I didn't know my brother was a traitor," Leandra hissed and Amara sensed footsteps ascending towards the door, and before she could step away and leave or go inside herself, the door was slammed open to reveal a limping Leandra holding the door and Azrael standing at a distance with his head hanging.

Amara's eyes were stuck on him. Was everything that she just heard true? Had Azrael broken her trust? Had she made the same mistake again? Was he really the traitor? Should she believe what Leandra had said? Her head was spinning out of control as she stared at Azrael who now looked up. His eyes were bloodshot, he held a murderous look and before she knew it, he had lunged towards Leandra in an attacking stance when Iris pulled her away only to fall to the floor along with Azrael. His eyes then lifted themselves to find Amara standing before him.

He seemed to have regained control then as he stood up. He opened his mouth to speak something when Amara cut him off.

"Is this true?" She whispered, staring at him blankly while Iris lifted Leandra off the floor.

"Amara I-"

"Is everything that Leandra just said, true?" She spoke again, her voice a bit louder.

"There is nothing that I would-"

"Are you the traitor?" She asked, still as cold and blank.

"I-"

"ARE YOU THE TRAITOR?" She now screamed.

The walls shook by the force of her tone of voice. It rang in Azrael's ears and he flinched, taking a step back. Never had he seen Amara that angry. And now he knew that if he did not answer her questions, there would be destruction. He glanced at Leandra once before turning back to Amara.

Letting out a breath, he mumbled, "Yes."

That was all it took for Amara to grab his throat and push him backwards to a wall. He did not struggle against it. By now, Eridanus, Sienna, Fabian and Ambrosius had arrived, for Amara's voice had given the message to everyone that there was something grave that had happened.

"WHY? THE LORD TRUSTED YOU! *I* TRUSTED YOU!" she said, an agonizing tone in her speech.

There was a strange pain that was crawling up inside of her and she could not shake it away hard as she tried.

"I'm sorry," was all Azrael said and Amara slammed his head on the wall behind.

It did not hurt him as much as the fact that what he was saying did Amara. He shut his eyes at the pain only to open them back in moments.

"Why?" She whispered with her eyes moist.

She could not believe it. It was painful; extremely painful. Hearing Leandra say the words and hearing Azrael do the same had a lot of difference. He admitted it, he agreed to it. And that was what killed her inside, knowing that he was the traitor they had been looking for. How could it be?

"I'm sorry," he said again, looking down.

Amara stared at him long and hard before she let go of him and he was thrown to the floor. Those questions were to be asked by the Lord, she concluded.

"Inform the Lord that the traitor has been found," she announced.

Ambrosius frowned. *What traitor?* He wondered. Nobody knew that there was a traitor apart from Amara, Azrael and Lord Lucifer. So it was quite obvious that Ambrosius would be clueless.

"GO!" she ordered and Ambrosius left immediately, not wanting to anger her anymore.

Azrael lay on the floor, staring at nothing in particular. Everyone had questions but no one dared to say a word. No one wanted to face Amara's wrath. When Lord Lucifer entered the chamber, he glanced around everywhere from Eridanus to Iris to Leandra to Azrael and then his eyes stopped at Amara.

"The traitor has been found, m'Lord," she whispered, gesturing towards Azrael.

Lord Lucifer turned his head towards his apprentice that lay on the floor, blank. He then turned to Amara but she was already gone. He did not want to question her. He was well aware of the fact that it would not be without cause that Amara had pointed out Azrael as the traitor. He trusted Amara far more than he did Azrael.

"Get the guards. Open the cellar, and take him," he ordered coldly while staring at Azrael.

Moments later, three guards were in the chamber, pulling Azrael to his feet and dragging him outside. There was no movement that he made by himself. But as he was being dragged out of the chamber, his eyes flickered over to the side to find someone offering him a triumphant grin.

It was Leandra.

CHAPTER THIRTY-EIGHT

∞∞∞∞∞

TRUE LIES

∞∞∞∞∞

It was cold where he was. The icy air nipped at the very brink of his soul as he dropped his constant struggle to set himself free. He wanted to tell her the truth. He wanted to let everything out so badly that he just could not seem to control it. But there was nothing that he could do. Along with the chains that bound his hands and legs, his mind was trapped as well. It had been nothing short of painful when the guards had mercilessly dragged him down to the lowest floor of the castle a night ago, before opening the door of a chamber that remained shut all along – and pushing him inside, only to open another lid on the floor that stretched into what looked like a never-ending pit. The steps led him down deeper inside and then they reached an opening where there were a few cells located in a semi-circle. It was a small enclosed space where no other prisoners remained.

The cellar was the coldest, most haunting and dreadful part of Lord Lucifer's castle. Hardly any prisoner was known to have survived. What rode them to a torturous Death was unknown to everyone. But Azrael was about to find out. When the guards opened the bars of a cell and threw him inside, he crashed onto the floor with a groan; it his head on the side.

He was then pulled up to sitting, his hands fastened together with shackles covering his wrists and then they bound the same around his legs. The worst part was when Lord Lucifer had come to see him. He had stood outside the cell callously, something that was reserved only for those he felt immense hatred and loathing for. Azrael did not like it being directed towards him.

"I will not ask how and why Amara came to this conclusion," Lord Lucifer had said. "But since you were the one person that I had trusted the most after her, I will let you know this, I did not, for the slightest bit of me, fathom that it would be *you* of all people. I treated you like my own son. But I had always wondered whether or not you would trace your father's footsteps. And you did. Until the war gets over, you will remain in this cellar and then we will decide what has to be done. All your powers are hereby sealed. They will no longer work. The cellar does not allow that. And no sort of dark magic can defeat it. You cannot send messages to anyone. You are, from this moment on, as worthless as a mortal to us."

With that, he had vanished. Azrael had listened quietly, not uttering a single sound. His face was unresponsive, his eyes cold and blank. He felt not a single thing apart from wanting to be with the one person he thought he was safe with: Amara. Azrael needed her. Now as he sat with his head leaning onto the chilly wall on his side, his eyes focussed on the bars of the cell, all he could think of was how Amara would never trust a single soul after what had happened. She had barely begun to trust him, and now that it was revealed that he was the traitor, he was well aware that there was no way that she would ever be the same. Not only had he lost the chance to spend time with someone whom he had started to care for, he had also lost the Amara that he had pulled out of the fake mask that she wore.

He had lost her, and she wasn't going to come back. That much he was quite sure of. No amount of explanation would bring her back. Neither would *he* go back to the way he was with Amara. He had lost himself too. Till eternity, if that was for how long he existed. Or maybe he would slowly fade into an agonizing Death in the cellar, like the others did.

The smell of Death was lingering around him, entering his senses and blinding him of all light. It made him weak, it made him cough and splutter as he spotted the remains of the older prisoners in the other cells. *How many prisoners have died here?* He thought, struggling to get rid of the stench. But it never left. There was nothing that could distract him from that until he heard the door of the cellar open and the sound of footsteps made him sit upright, expecting it was Amara. To his disappointment, he sensed the familiar presence of his sister.

Leandra sauntered inside, wearing a long cloak that covered the blood-red gown that she wore. She walked ahead and stooped below to come to Azrael's level.

"The smell is really disgusting, isn't it?" She uttered, scrunching up her face.

"What do you want?" He mumbled coldly.

"Dear brother of mine, aren't you glad to see me? Your sister is here to visit you despite the horrendous surrounding," she replied, looking around and then blowing air from her mouth, cleansing the area on the floor below before she sat there comfortably.

"You're the last person I want to see right now," he told her.

The argument that they had had in the chamber flashed into his mind and he cursed himself for agreeing to her terms. It had been silly of him. He could have done anything else to get himself out of the trap that she had set but instead he had given in like a coward.

"Rael," she began when he hissed at the sound and glanced up at her viciously.

"Don't ever address me by that name again," he whispered grimly; the sound could have chilled Leandra to the core but she composed herself.

"Well then, *prisoner*," she said maliciously. "I'm just here to tell you that the battle is going to strike tomorrow night. It was supposed to be a week away but father decided to attack sooner. It's only good for me though. The faster Lord Lucifer gets defeated, the easier it is for me to get the hell out of here. Anyway, your dearest Amara is not holding up quite good. I heard her pushing Iris away a few hours ago. She was really cold and ruthless. Made my work easier. I don't have to steal her powers now; she'll do it herself by draining everything out." She shrugged.

"Amara isn't that weak. None of her powers are going to drain out. She can fight even better now. Her mind will be focussed on nothing but defeating Lord Mikhail," replied Azrael, with a scoff. Leandra rolled her eyes.

"It's really disturbing as to why you can't call him father," she told him, shaking her head in disapproval.

"He is *not* my father. He is a liar; he is selfish, and an insolent coward. Just like you," he hissed.

"You didn't think of that when you left me, did you?" Leandra shot back with equal malice.

"You know very well why I left!"

"Yes, I do. But did you not think of me for once? I was tortured for days because I protested against him sending you to learn dark magic. I was tortured because I didn't want to learn the same either. I begged you to take me along but you never listened. You left me. You were the reason that I was sent to learn dark magic from all sorts of Conjurers. In the end I went to Noctia Stella. I've been her apprentice since. Did you really expect me to turn into a good person after being trained in dark witchcraft? I became his messenger by choice. I pretended to get acquainted with Lord Lucifer because father asked me to. I entered this coven because he wanted me to be the spy.

And I framed you into being the traitor because he asked me to. But I wouldn't have done that, Rael. I wouldn't, because I loved you that much. I had to do it because had I not, Lord Lucifer's dear apprentice Erasmus would have revealed to everyone that I am the traitor. He had a doubt on me right from the start. Even without framing you into this, I would have been able to destroy this coven. But I had to drag you in because Erasmus had found out. It was fortunate enough for me that he's imprisoned and he remembers nothing since father erased his memory of it. There is but another reason," she smirked. "I did it because you left me at the time that I needed you the most. I want you to feel what it is like to have lost someone you trust. I want you to feel that Amara will never trust you again and she will never love you again. I've seen the way she looks at you and I've seen the way you look at her. At some point I was extremely happy that you had found someone. But my task was to weaken her. I had to let the bond be created between you two and I had to break it.

"Remember this, Rael, however good of heart a witch is, the moment she learns dark witchcraft to an extent that it cannot be undone, she loses herself. I am not the Leandra that you left when we were children. As much as I love you and want you to be with Amara, my identity of being a dark witch does not change. I'm going to destroy this coven bit by bit and then watch you die, because that is what I have been taught. And do you know why I've been taught that?" She hissed threateningly. "It's because you let me enter that arena of darkness. It's because you didn't take me with you when I pleaded you to."

With that, she turned around and strode out of the cellar with her cloak slithering behind. Azrael watched his sister walk away. He cursed himself for having Lord Mikhail as a father. He had not wanted to leave Leandra alone. He had wanted to take her with him but his journey wasn't one that promised her safety. She was a little girl. She did not need to run away like that. But she did not have to stay with the likes of Lord Mikhail either. What choice did he have? Despite everything, he would have taken her. But because their father had threatened him that if he even thought of taking Leandra along, he would kill her. Azrael wanted to save his sister's life.

And for that he had to make some sacrifice. It was obviously extremely shocking when he had found that she was Lord Lucifer's apprentice. It was curious. How could that have happened? Had she escaped when she was old enough to do so? Or was Lord Lucifer doing them both a favour by training them? Those were the questions that had run through his mind when he had met Leandra after twenty long years in the castle. But now it all made sense. It made sense that Leandra was sent by Lord Mikhail. It also made sense that she was the messenger. Azrael's mind went back to the argument where Leandra had so easily and smartly framed him into being the messenger and making Amara believe the same.

It had all started after Amara and Eridanus had left the chambers. Iris and Azrael were sitting beside Leandra, talking about Noctia Stella, when Leandra unknowingly said, "If it weren't for me she wouldn't have been there."

Iris had failed to notice as she was busy mixing some herbs for Leandra as Soter had advised, but Azrael had clearly listened to every word. His head had snapped up to look at her in utter perplexity.

Of course he did have a doubt on Leandra for being the traitor and he had thought of confronting her too, but something always held him back. Her being his sister and the love and adoration that he felt for her made him think otherwise. But his doubt never left.

"If it weren't for you?" He asked her softly.

Iris was still too preoccupied to notice.

"Don't pretend like you didn't have a doubt about me being the traitor," she replied.

Azrael was taken aback. He was not expecting such a straight answer. Yes, he had a doubt but somehow he felt it could not be her.

"Lea-"

"Yes, Rael? You obviously had that doubt, didn't you? And I admire you for that because your doubt was quite accurate," she told him.

Iris had now gotten up and absent-mindedly walked a few feet away to look for water. But Azrael was speechless. What was he supposed to say to her now?

"And before you ask, I *am* the messenger and the traitor that you are looking for," she told him nonchalantly. It was as though it did not matter to her at all. Azrael thought that maybe it was the potions and herbs that were making her mind play strange tricks to have her talk like that. It seemed like a different Leandra to him.

"The reason I'm openly confessing is because I want you to do something for me," she said, leaning forward.

Suddenly Azrael did not seem to like the tone that she was using. He knew that something bad was about to be said and he did not wish to be a part of that. He wanted to run and tell Amara that it was his sister and that Lord Lucifer should take action but before he could do anything, Leandra had grabbed his hand.

"Lea, I'm not doing anything for you. If you really are the traitor then you'll be punished for that," he told her sternly, still not ready to believe that it was her.

"You're so easily manipulated, aren't you? You love me too much to even take action yourself right now. If it were anyone else, I'd have been dragged to Lord Lucifer. But you, you love your little sister. You trust me and that love of yours stops you from being angry with me," she menacingly said.

Azrael did not like the Leandra that he was talking to right now. But she was right. Why was he not reacting? Was it because he was shocked? Or tired after the long journey? Or was it just because he did not want to believe this truth? He failed to understand why he was so calm at this point. He should be rushing out of the chamber to tell Amara. But he was doing nothing of that sort. He noticed Iris walking out of the chamber absently.

"Anyway, not wasting more time, I want you to go and tell Lord Lucifer that you are the traitor," she told him adamantly.

Azrael watched her with a frown. *What?*

"Lea, my love, does it really look like I'm that blinded by this sibling bond?"

His voice suddenly changed, realizing what she was proposing. His own sister was the traitor and had now asked him to do something extremely foolish.

"Why do you think I would agree to do such a thing?" He asked her.

"Because if you don't, I will hand every power to Noctia Stella and the coven would be easily destroyed. Father doesn't know about her strength. If I let him know, Acanthus will be destroyed. Everything will end. Do you want that?" She said with equal intensity.

Azrael let out a sinister laugh.

"And what's to say you won't do it even if I do agree to your terms?"

"I won't. Because with you gone, the strength of the coven will already be diminished. Amara wouldn't be strong enough. Her mind will be boggled. The rest of the coven will become relatively tense and won't trust each other since the one that Lord Lucifer trusts the most turned out to be the traitor. Father's work will be easy. He won't need Noctia Stella then. We could use her later to get the prophecy." She shrugged in the end.

"And you think that the rest of us cannot fight Noctia Stella? I rescued Iris; Amara and I were perfectly capable of battling the *Mortuis*."

"That wasn't even quarter of her power being used. Once she decides to destroy everything, you and your little lover won't be able to fight. Her strength will be tenfold if matched with father's army."

"My answer is no." Azrael remained stern as he stood up to leave.

It did not matter that she was his sister. It did not matter how much he loved her. All that mattered was the truth.

"When I first arrived, I had started to weaken Amara's powers," said Leandra and Azrael stopped in his tracks. "The reason she felt tired a lot of times was because I was deteriorating her powers. I have to admit it wasn't very easy. Every time I tried, she would come out even stronger. You might be strong enough to fight Noctia Stella, but once I ask her to use all her powers to destroy Amara, nobody will be able to save her. Not you, not Lord Lucifer, not this coven and not Amara herself. I was going to escort Iris to Noctia Stella myself while we were at the Sea of Cypress; but those dim-witted spirits that we had carried there – one of them came and fought me. I had already weakened Iris by then. It was easy for Noctia to summon her in the pit. If not for that spirit, I would not have been this injured. Anyway, that is not important. Rael, I am asking you to do something for me. Won't you help your little sister?" She said with a sickly-sweet grin.

Azrael wanted to hex her but he could not make himself do it. He wondered why.

"You are just like him," he told her, shaking his head with a humourless laugh.

"Now, brother of mine, you know what will happen if you refuse to do what I ask of you? Let me tell you. I will break your lover's soul apart, bit by bit until there is nothing left of her. Amara will die. I promise you, Rael, she will die," she replied.

"You will never be strong enough to harm her and I will not agree to this no matter what," Azrael said with rage, turning to face her.

"Yes, you will. You will admit that it was you or I will do it. I can go tell Lord Lucifer that it was you who sent all messages to father. Because apart from Amara you were the only one that knew about the prophecy. I found out because I spied. The sculpted fairy on the topmost tower, it is my medium to send messages. It guards me. It all makes sense, you know; you being the traitor. All the information that father has was known to you and Amara. Since it obviously cannot be Amara, it only makes sense to be you."

The way she threatened him made a chill run down his spine. Suddenly he was worried for Amara. Yes, she was strong and she was powerful but battling Noctia Stella alone when she set out to harm Amara – he wasn't so sure that she could do it. How was he to save her? Worst of all, how was he to deny that he was the messenger when it was him – apart from Amara – who knew about the prophecy? Nobody else was aware. There was no witness.

"No! You cannot make me do this!" He protested.

He shook his head, moisture settling in his eyes. He would think of something. He would find a way. The Lord trusted him more than he did Leandra. He would listen.

"Oh, but I can, sweet brother. I can," she whispered maliciously before her voice became louder for just the two of them in the chamber.

"You will accept it. Accept that it was you who tried to get Erasmus into trouble. Be brave, Rael, tell them that it was you who sent a message to the King's Minister so they could find Lord Zachariah," she said.

Azrael stared at her. She spoke with such intensity that it nearly killed him to think that Amara would be harmed. At that moment, he realized how much he actually loved her. He was so blinded by it that nothing came to his mind. Losing Amara and being the reason of her Death wasn't something he was looking forward to. What could he possibly do?

"You don't mean that, Lea," he told her, taking a step forward trying to reason with her.

What was he doing? Giving in? Acting like he was vulnerable and weak? Maybe then she would stop whatever she was saying. It wasn't possible for him to think of Amara being harmed. But who was to say that she would not be harmed even if he agreed to this? Whether or not he did, Leandra would try to kill Amara.

But before he could begin to manipulate her using his powers, she spoke, "I do. I do mean it. It's only fair to accept that it was you who helped Noctia Stella reach the Sea of Cypress so she could harm Iris. It was you!"

That was when he lost it. What was going on? How was Lea speaking like that so easily instead of convincing him? Why was she openly accusing him of something he had not done? At that moment, his eyes darted towards the door of the chamber, which was slightly open. He hissed a breath. Amara was outside. He wanted to run there and tell her it was all a lie when Leandra stepped forward in his way.

"It was you who let the Lord get into the clutches of Noctia Stella and you tried to deceive them by going with Amara to rescue him! How long will you lie? How long will you act like you are not the messenger of Lord Mikhail? For how long will this betrayal go on?"

There was a malicious smile that she held as she spoke. Azrael was furious. Leandra had framed him so easily that he could not even protest anymore. What could he possibly say that would save him? He shut his eyes for a long moment before opening them and then threateningly said,

"Lea, you need to shut it right now!"

Leandra smiled in triumph, glancing at the door and Azrael made an attempt to rush there once again but she stopped him with what she said next.

"No, I won't! What is your beloved Amara going to say to this? Do you think she'll be happy upon knowing that you're the one threat who is living in the same castle with her and luring her into falling for you? Don't think I don't see the way you're meddling with her feelings. I see it, and I see that she has started to fall for you. You're that brilliant, aren't you? You acted like the one person that she could trust and when she finds out who you really are, what is going to happen?"

She was lying. There was a lie in every single word that she spoke and Azrael – in his rage – did not know how to respond or what to do. All he could think of was Amara who stood outside the door and listened to everything, probably believing it all. He wanted to go and tell her what his sister was doing but he just could not, because Leandra refused to shut up even when he said, "Lea, enough! I won't hear another word-"

She cut him off. "No! I'm going to tell the truth to the Lord. I cannot believe you would do this. I didn't know my brother was a traitor."

And before he could even *try* to stop her, she had opened the door. Then everything had gone numb. He saw the fury, the hurt and the deceit that flashed across Amara's eyes as she stared at him. It was then that he had no control on himself. He could not speak, could not move and answered simply to what was being asked, with a 'sorry'. He had then fallen prey to Leandra's terms when Iris was stood next to her and with her eyes she threatened that if he did not agree, Leandra would harm Iris without anybody even knowing about it.

* * *

Azrael snapped out of his thoughts in the cellar. He blinked, trying to push the tears away. He missed Amara. He wanted her to be there with him and he wanted her to help him recover. He wanted her to understand that he had not done anything that he had been accused of. He wanted her to believe him when he would tell her that it wasn't him. He wanted her to believe him when he would tell her that he loved her. But there was nothing that he could do anymore; nothing at all.

* * *

Amara stared at her fingers. She sat there unmoving, her head resting on the wall beside, eyes expressionless and blank. *What did you do, Azrael?* She wondered. *Why?* There was no sound in her chamber apart from the winds that entered inside as she sat over the window-sill. She was unable to utter a word, unable to move or begin to prepare for the war. There was no time left. Lord Mikhail had decided to attack earlier than necessary, which, Amara thought was because he wished to gain the prophecy as soon as possible. Even though the King had given the time of two more weeks, Amara knew Lord Mikhail wasn't one to follow rules.

Her mind kept going back to the conversation between Leandra and Azrael that she had heard from outside Leandra's chamber. Her heart constricted with pain each time she thought of it and it made her weaker and weaker. She found it hard to believe that Azrael would be the traitor. She was sure, so sure that it could not be him by any chance. She had begun to trust him as much as she trusted Iris. Maybe even *she* would break her trust. *Would she?* Amara wondered. Her mind told her that there was something wrong and that she was having a nightmare. But reality seemed as though it was pinching her inside every now and then, reminding her that whatever had happened was true.

Yet she could not bring herself to believe it. The pain that she felt in her veins was so unbearable that she wanted to crawl into the lake and drown. While her mind was battling with her upon the fact that she actually might have found it in her to love Azrael, reality told her that he wasn't worth the love. Did love really matter? She had loved Leo once, had it mattered to him? Maybe it did not matter to Azrael either. Maybe he had managed to break her trust like Leo had. Leo used her to get to her family, to destroy other witches. In a similar way, Azrael had used her to weaken her powers and send information to Lord Mikhail; information that was extremely confidential and could potentially ruin the entire world of Conjurers, maybe even mortals.

The way that her trust had been broken once again, the numbness inside her began to show. The cold and harsh aura that she had built up to hide all the pain and agony – she felt that it was better she stayed that way. Because whenever she let that guard down, her trust would break. Whenever she opened her mind to trust someone, it was destroyed. She wanted to become the way she had been for the past hundred years. In one year, Iris had managed to help her break that shield. But now Amara wanted it back. At least she was comfortable and she knew no one could hurt her then. The Gods only knew how much Lord Mikhail might have found out if Azrael was the messenger. There would have been so much information shared, it wasn't that hard to decipher anymore. It scared her but that would not stop her from using all her force to protect the prophecy and the treasures, even if her life depended on it.

* * *

Her doubts were all true. Lord Mikhail did know about the prophecy. What he knew, however, was about what the prophecy held and how he had to get to it. Leandra had told him everything by invading Azrael's mind. Since she had the uncontrollable skill of shielding her own mind from any sort of attack, she could venture into anybody's mind and read them. All that she could find out about the prophecy, she had informed her father. What she could not find out, however, were the riddles that needed to be solved to get the treasures. That had been effectively guarded by Azrael in his mind for no one to enter. But whatever she had found was enough for her and Lord Mikhail.

This battle strategy was set in his mind. Nearing the end, he would distract Lord Lucifer by sending a blazing Fire towards the Sea of Cypress which would effectively lead some strong force – preferably Amara or Lord Lucifer himself – to help save Lady Calypsa. Then he would attack with all his might and Lord Lucifer's army would remain in nothing but broken shards. The Fire would swallow whomever that had been sent to the Sea of Cypress, rendering Lord Mikhail as the winner of the battle. He would then go to the Sea of Cypress, defeat Lady Calypsa using the help of Leandra who he was sure would be trusted by the Lady since she had already been there. It would not be hard to get hold of the prophecy then and gaining what the treasures were. All he had to do was understand the prophecy, which no one could help him with. There he was left stranded.

* * *

Her trail of thought was broken when she heard a knock on the door. Amara did not leave her seat. The knock was heard again but she ignored it. Iris stood outside with her eyes watering and her arm raised in the air to knock another time but she stepped back. She had lost Amara once again. She realized that in the beginning she had been right when she worried about Amara being with Azrael. It took a lot of time for her to begin trusting him. When she did, she wished that Amara was happy. She felt that he would keep her happy. But everything had shattered. He was a traitor. He was Lord Mikhail's son. Leandra had been crying all this while, telling Iris how much she hated her brother for doing this and how much she despised being the daughter of someone as evil as Lord Mikhail.

The Lord had questioned Leandra to see if she was helping her brother in any way. Leandra had managed to assure him that she was not at fault. She had left her father as soon as it was possible for her to escape from his clutches. Lord Lucifer had chosen to believe her since Amara was the one that had informed him about Azrael being the traitor. He trusted no one as much as he did Amara. Her word was enough since he knew there could not be any flaw in her verdict. So if Leandra was saying that she was not – in any way – involved in this act and Amara had already agreed upon Azrael being the traitor, Lord Lucifer did not wish to waste time in anything else. They had a war to fight.

"Amara?" Iris dared to call through the door.

Amara did not respond.

"The-the Lord is asking for you," she stuttered.

The tears were blinding her eyes and she wiped them away, clearing her throat. Amara blinked. She pushed herself down from the window-sill and began to walk towards the door of her chamber. She opened it and walked past Iris without acknowledging her. Iris whimpered in hurt. Amara's indifference was something she was unable to live with. But she knew that Amara had a valid reason for that. Iris followed after her. They reached the main hall where Lord Lucifer was seated along with the other coven members and the leaders of the three covens that were supporting them.

"My lords and Lady Nysa, this is Amara, as you might know," said Lord Lucifer, gesturing towards Amara who stood there in silence.

"Of course," Lady Nysa replied with a small grin. "Everyone knows Amara."

Amara did not look up. Lord Lucifer cleared his throat uncomfortably. He sensed that Amara was not in the right frame of mind at the moment. But discussing war strategies was important and she could not be left out. Amara was, after all, his strongest warrior. He could not afford to let her be weak.

"Have a seat, Amara. We are here to discuss the battle strategies," he told her and she obediently took a seat at the end of the hall.

Iris took a few steps back and left the great hall.

"Lord Mikhail's army consists of new Conjurers along with experienced ones. We cannot be sure whether they are strong enough to fight us. They might be trained in physical combat if not in mental. We have to be prepared since newly trained ones can be quite unpredictable," said Lord Theodore.

"But there has to be an obvious disadvantage," Lord Vincent replied. "New Conjureres are mentally weak. They don't have enough meditation power. I think that would prove fruitful to us."

The conversation continued on while Amara's eyes stayed on the floor. Her mind was elsewhere. She was aware that it was important for her to pay attention but the entire battle strategy was in faded whispers in her head. She stared blankly at the floor as the rest of them talked about what had to be done. Amara was lost again.

* * *

Levels below in the dungeon, Azrael was in a similar condition. His eyes were stuck on the floor, unmoving while his mind displayed nothing to him. Another night had passed, another day had dawned and time dragged by. Then as the moonlight streamed in through the bars of the window above, he heard the faint footsteps of the coven heading out the castle. Suddenly he remembered what Leandra had told him the night before about the battle starting the next day.

The war had begun.

CHAPTER THIRTY-NINE

∞∞

A SOПG OF SLAUGHTER

∞∞

A mara watched as the gates of the graveyard closed shut. The creaking sound echoed in her ears and she waved her hands in the air, creating a protective shield around the castle. She wore a black gown that cascaded down the length of her body. A cloak covered the gown with a hood on top of her head. Her sword rested in the case held at her waist in a belt. She carried her miniscule weapons and needles hidden in her armour that was covered by the gown. The rest of the army stood behind her, waiting for her to finish the protection details and join them. She turned around to tell Azrael that he should help her out when her eyes fell on the empty space next to her. He wasn't there.

It was difficult to accept that he was no longer fighting alongside her. But that did not matter. They had a battle to fight, a prophecy to guard and there was no time to dwell over how he had betrayed her trust. It was painful, for all sane reasons it was extremely painful for Amara to have lost someone she had only just started to trust. But now it was insignificant to her. Once again, she had gone back to being the cold and ruthless Amara that she was well-known for. Her mind was focussed on one thing: the battle. There was nothing even remotely more important than the war anymore.

Once again, Amara spoke to no one if not necessary. She kept her distance. Her soul knew how much she missed Azrael, how much she needed him and how it pained to think of what he had done. She had now accepted what reality had to offer. She had admitted to the fact that Azrael was no longer important to her and all she was required to do was fight in the battle with the entirety of her strength. Iris, on the other hand, kept herself busy practicing her skills with Eridanus after the night before when Amara had begun to ignore her again.

She kept herself limited to no one but Eridanus and Leandra who seemed not to have much conversation with her either. How badly she wished to fix everything and tell Amara that it wasn't Azrael but someone entirely different, was killing her. The moment that she had left the great hall for Amara to discuss war strategies with the other leaders, a vision had hit her mind that showed her how miserable Azrael was in the dungeons. She easily invaded his mind – one which had no power to shield itself, and without Azrael knowing what she was doing, Iris had found out that he was innocent. But who the real traitor could be, was still a mystery. She could not find it out because right at that moment, Eridanus had dragged her away to help her practice her combat skills. Iris understood that it was more important for the battle.

Moreover she did not have enough proof of explaining that Azrael was innocent. What she had was Eridanus's support. When she had expressed to him her vision, he had believed her immediately, since he had had a similar feeling. His instincts told him exactly what Iris did. They had even discussed it, but since there wasn't enough proof to show the others, they were unable to do anything about it. Besides, they had still not found out who it was if not Azrael.

Now that the meetings with the other three covens were done and the war strategies discussed, they were all ready to fight. Nobody apart from Lord Lucifer's coven was aware about what had happened with Azrael. Lord Lucifer did not find it important enough to be revealed to the others. It would only show their weakness and at such a crucial point, that was not okay.

Lord Theodore had a coven of almost a hundred Conjurers; all highly trained in physical as well as mental combat. Lord Vincent had about seventy apprentices since his coven was new, but most of them were strong enough to battle. The new ones were sort of intimidated by Lord Lucifer's coven and mostly Amara, for all obvious reasons but she preferred to stay away and did not mingle much which gave her the benefit of not being disturbed.

Lady Nysa, on the other hand, had a coven full of a hundred and ten Conjurers, all experienced and trained in combat. Nearly all of them were old enough to be rehearsed in the same and had also fought a battle years ago, for King Abraham the Third. Along with Lord Lucifer's coven, the army now consisted of about two hundred and seventy warriors. They were all prepared, all skilled and all ready to strike into battle. After Lord Mikhail had sent a message to Lord Lucifer saying that there was no point in waiting anymore and that the King wasn't to be informed about this at all since he was away with his family, the war was to begin sooner than was said.

And now the army stood outside the gates of Lord Lucifer's castle. Amara turned around – pushing the pain that she felt without Azrael away – and proceeded to the front of the crowd. Lord Lucifer had already gone to the battlefield with Lord Vincent, Lord Theodore and Lady Nysa. He had ordered Amara to lead the army there. She stood before them all, looking over to see if everyone had assembled. When she was sure each one was there, she began,

"All of the apprentices from the covens of Lady Nysa, Lord Theodore and Lord Vincent, you have our thanks. Your support for us will be well cherished. We hope to win this battle and will fight for as long as it takes to safeguard us Conjurers as well as humans from the wrath of Lord Mikhail."

Amara felt a chill up her spine recalling the fact that Azrael was Lord Mikhail's son. She ignored it.

"Tonight we strike into battle. All the healers shall be kind enough to be in the healing quarters for the injured at the battlefield. May the righteous triumph!"

She finished and the army responded by repeating the phrase. They all then proceeded to leave for the battlefield. It was not far away so it did not take much time to reach. When they did, Amara spotted the large army of Lord Mikhail standing at the opposite side. She led the army ahead to where Lord Lucifer stood along with the other leaders. The army assembled behind the three leaders with Amara in the front. Lord Lucifer turned around to face them.

"Are we all prepared?" He asked, surveying the army.

They all gave their responses in agreement.

"Well then, may the righteous triumph!"

They all now faced the enemies that stood before them, comparatively higher in number. But it did not mean that their powers were any less. Lady Nysa turned to Lord Lucifer for a moment.

"Do we need the flag of peace?" She asked.

Lord Lucifer looked at her and shook his head.

"I don't reckon it matters anymore. He wants a battle then a battle is what he will get. Under the blessings of mother nature and all the elemental Gods, the righteous will triumph," he told her with a smile.

Lady Nysa retreated. There was a roaring sound from the army of Lord Mikhail. Wasting no time, he announced, "CHARGE!"

The weapon combat began. One by one, the Conjurers from both the armies attacked, crashing into each other in a ferocious symphony. The atmosphere was filled with an array of sounds that echoed throughout the battlefield of Artemisia. Swords clung together, spears clashed and arrows flung in the air, swishing throughout the battlefield, piercing into the skin of warriors. To the far right of the battlefield stood a cluster of Conjurers from both the armies in a fierce swordfight where Lord Lucifer's army seemed to be succeeding.

Eridanus stepped over a few corpses as he slashed his sword furiously amongst the enemy. The land that was once barren and plain was now covered in blood and gore, terrorizing flesh covering the arena. At the East of the battlefield Amara swung forward furiously charging all of her anger and pain into the warriors of Lord Mikhail's army. Her ferocity frightened nearly everyone that was around her. She fought bravely, dodging every attack and battling no less than seven people at a time. None of them were capable of defeating her.

South of the field was being ruled by Sienna and Praxithea who battled three powerful Conjurers from Lord Vane's coven. Two sorcerers swung forward with their spears, ready to plunge into Sienna when she dodged from beneath them swift as a cat, only to have them crash into Praxithea, who fell to the ground amid the pile of corpses, with a spear plunged deep into her chest. Without having the time to pay attention to what had happened, Sienna began attacking the rest of her opponents.

The North was covered with a minimal number of dead because the most powerful warriors were striking forth. Lord Lucifer shot arrow after arrow, aiming at the far end where a sorcerer named Ephialtes was shooting his arrows that crashed into that of Lord Lucifer's, engaging the two into a fierce duel. Varied colours of light flooded the sky as the enchanted arrows struck one another with equal force. Lord Mikhail was at a distance from Ephialtes, battling Ambrosius. Their swords clung together as they dodged one another's attacks swiftly and wistfully, sometimes vanishing out of sight and sometimes appearing all the sudden. Ambrosius was not a weak sorcerer. Lord Mikhail realized that now.

Fabian, Lilienne, Rhea and Coronos fought with the Conjurers of Lord Riordan's coven in the West. There were raging duels of spears and axes swinging and clanging together as the warriors fought with equal malice. Rhea's axe clashed with that of Acastos's and she flung his neck to the far end of the battlefield while a spear plunged into her right arm. Coronos and Fabian battled with Lyros and Megaira as their swords slashes into the flesh of their opponent and Coronus collapsed within the heap of bodies while Fabian dodged another attack.

In the middle of the battlefield, elemental duels had begun. Iris was busy throwing gushes of Wind towards the Conjurers of the enemy and her attacks were being countered by one young witch by the name of Oino from Lord Alistair's coven. Oino sent Fire while Iris sent her Air. Iris pushed all the teachings of Nicholas into force and her Air managed to defeat Oino's Fire, in turn burning Oino to ashes. Iris was then attacked by a sorcerer who used his force of Water, only to have her covered in Water from the waist-down. She began to splutter and gasp for air as the Water began to engulf her completely when she was dragged out by Ourania, a fellow witch who started a wild Fire that the sorcerer tried to counter with more Water. Iris managed to escape while Ourania battled in her place.

Back in the East, Amara's Fire was threatening to swallow up ten Conjurers of Lord Mikhail's coven. Soon enough all that lay in front of Amara was ashes. She turned around and swished her fingers only to have Water flood out of the earth and flow towards the opponents and fifteen other Conjurers had to struggle to counter her attack with Fire. By the time they succeeded, Amara had vanished.

Spells began to shoot everywhere. Colours illuminated the night sky and created patterns of horrific Deaths everywhere around. As Amara shot a curse of paralysis, her mind went straight to Azrael, thinking about how he had the power to paralyze through his eyes and how helpful it would have been if he were there with her.

* * *

"Your name; it means immortal, doesn't it?" Azrael asked.

"I didn't know that," Amara replied, turning away.

Why am I blushing? *She wondered with annoyance. It was not good for her. She needed to get rid of that warm feeling surging inside of her whenever Azrael was around.*

"Have you ever-ever loved . . . someone?" He suddenly asked with hesitation.

Amara snapped her head towards him. She was not expecting such a question. Her heart stopped for the fraction of a second and she blinked. What was she to reply? She could not bring herself to tell him about Leo. Why should she anyway? Azrael was nobody to her. He was just a coven member, or maybe a friend whom she felt comfortable with; but that did not mean that she could tell him everything. It was only Iris; maybe it would only be her and no one else that she would reveal her history to. Amara did not wish to do the same with Azrael. She still did not trust him enough. Iris, on the other hand, she had blind faith on.

"No," she told him, hoping that he would drop the topic before it had even begun.

Azrael looked at the forlorn expression on Amara's face and decided not to talk about it again. It was obviously a sensitive matter and as much as he wanted to find out what had hurt her, he did not wish to spoil the moment. He did not want to leave the woods. He wanted to spend more time with her, if that was even possible.

"Did you know that there are wandering spirits in this forest?" He said to her, looking around in awe.

Amara watched him in amusement. How could she not know about that? Those spirits were her solace. They were her shoulder to cry on before Iris came and joined the coven. Amara chuckled at his question and he looked at her in confusion. Before she knew it, she was laughing unnecessarily.

* * *

Amara forcefully pushed that thought out of her mind and slashed her sword into a throat. Her eyes were blazing fire.

The earth trembled, winds went berserk and the birds vanished in fear. The atmosphere was drenched into a carnivorous rain. The warriors roared and screamed in attack. The skirmish of the two armies created the cry of unrequited horror as bodies were slain. The wind howled and the trees swayed on one side, glaring at the attack that Lord Mikhail threw onto a warrior from Lord Vincent's coven. Lord Mikhail sailed into the air, hovering over the enemy and plunging his spear into body after body.

The earth shivered under Eridanus's spell that disarmed a foe, making her fall to the ground in unbearable pain. His eyes glowed with what seemed like unspeakable fury. He shifted to push off another attacker, throwing him onto the ground and Eridanus shoved his sword into his throat. The combatant fell on the ground.

Iris had joined Sienna and they began mind duels, manipulating and burning their foes down. The armies fought fiercely with one another, slaying almost equal numbers of the enemy. Iris and Eridanus were in two different parts of the battlefield, communicating to each other with their minds. Whenever Iris was faced with a danger that she thought she could not fight, Eridanus would guide her while fighting his own battle. It appalled Iris when she saw the strength that his mind held. Continuing a duel with a powerful sorcerer and at the same time sending her guidelines as to how she should fight back was something that very few of them could do. It took a lot of mental power; and Eridanus seemed to have plenty of it. Iris admired his strength.

Far away out of sight, Leandra trudged from corner to corner, silently disarming Lord Lucifer's army without anyone knowing it. Being in his army, she stealthily fought for Lord Mikhail. He gave her signals as to whom she should end and she succeeded from time to time. But nobody's attention was on her. And nobody found out what she was doing. The chaos was multiplying minute by minute and there was no time for anyone to look at what the other was doing. Leandra found her task to be easier than what she had imagined. Yet she stayed careful so as not to be spotted by anyone since Lord Lucifer's numbers were decreasing faster than they were supposed to, seeing how strong the army was.

There was a sudden flood of Water in waves upon a side of Lord Lucifer's army, which threatened to drown them all. Lord Theodore fought the Water by throwing a gush of immediate Wind in its direction, instantly transferring the Water back to Lord Mikhail's army. A few drowned, others dodged and saved themselves. On the opposite side, Amara ignited a wild Fire that began to spread towards Lord Mikhail's army. In answer,

Lord Mikhail channelled the Water from attacking his army to extinguishing the Fire.

Winds gushed from end to end, throwing the warriors in different directions. Water flooded the area, diverging into other corners. Earth began to crack from underneath them, swallowing a few. Flames burned down the trees along with some warriors. The elements clashed together creating sounds that rang around the battlefield. A distant but faint melody began to hum in their ears as the weapons chimed and curses flew. Cries of pain were heard, attacks witnessed and souls injured. Lord Mikhail's army was defeating person to person, but Lord Lucifer's seemed to be succeeding somehow.

Amara was fighting bravely. She fought faster and better than anyone and everyone. She had defeated a lot of warriors and slain many. There were more injured in Lord Mikhail's army than in Lord Lucifer's. Leandra still clung from tree to tree, hiding herself while muttering spells; a curse here to paralyze, a chant there to kill and disarm Lord Lucifer's army. Yet nobody knew where she was and what she was doing. None were paying much attention either. The ones getting affected kept wondering how they suddenly lost their weapons and got defeated. A few had already been paralyzed and were unable to fight. Leandra's silent attacks were confusing to her victims but hardly anyone was able to pay attention to that.

A highly unusual and perplexing elemental duel was going on between Sienna and two witches from Lord Alistair's coven. They were both channelling their Earthly energy in her direction while Sienna battled using her Spiritual forces. It was a rare fight. Sienna's Spirits were invisibly whirling around in protection while the Earth kept throwing levels of mire into her eyes. The Spirits circled around her, forming an unseen shield that did not let any of the Earth's forces shatter her power. Eventually when their force could not match that of

Sienna's, they dropped on the ground in defeat. Sienna glared at the Earth furiously and it cracked immediately, swallowing the two witches inside.

At Sienna's right, Fabian and Lilienne were battling five Conjurers from Lord Vane's coven. They were throwing elements as well as weapons in their direction, which, neither Lilienne nor Fabian were able to handle. They were starting to fall short of energy as the attacks shunned them effortlessly. It was difficult to battle their enemies that were trained in dark witchcraft. It made their responses weaker. Intense efforts were made from Fabian to counter the attacks but nothing seemed to be working. In the end the two apprentices of Lord Lucifer had to accept defeat as Death began its way to greet them.

The new Conjureres in Lord Mikhail's army were finding it hard to stand before Lord Lucifer and kept looking for an escape. The only ones capable of handling the strength of Lord Lucifer were a handful of learned Conjurers that had training in dark witchcraft. It was quite an amusement for him when he saw the new ones struggling before him before a few of them fell dead. Lord Lucifer felt that he should let them scamper off at times, so he could battle those who were worth his time and strength. The new ones were just too incompetent for him. While he was battling a few feeble sorcerers, Lord Lucifer connected his mind to that of Erasmus's and sent a message to him.

* * *

Erasmus, upon receiving the message while he was meditating in clear concentration, pushed himself up from the floor and glanced at his shackles. They unwound themselves from his limbs, setting him free.

Moments later, there was complete silence in the King's castle. Spending weeks and weeks in the prison, Erasmus had meditated and gotten all his powers back even stronger than ever. Although the dungeons were designed to prohibit the prisoners from exercising their powers, with Lord Lucifer's discreet and extremely planned out help that he received through owls, Erasmus had managed to get his powers back.

He walked out of the cell after he was done putting every guard and every Minister to sleep. The King wasn't present in the court anyway, which made his work easier. When the entire palace was unconscious, Erasmus ventured out of the dungeons and left the King's palace in no time. He gathered a few weapons from the armoury and began to make his way to the Mines of Jestlesine. His hours were numbered. Having no time to spare, he had to reach the Mines of Jestlesine located right at the east edge of the mountains of *Lunaire*, get the desired work done and then head to the battlefield as Lord Lucifer had instructed him to.

When Erasmus reached the Mines of Jestlesine, he gathered what he had been asked to and carefully started to make his way to the battlefield, which was far enough to last a day if he walked. Teleporting seemed like a viable option seeing as how much energy he had accumulated during his time in the prison. He shut his eyes and vanished from the Mines, landing outside the battlefield where from a distance he saw the combat happening in unspeakable ferocity.

* * *

A deafening screech was heard. It silenced the entire arena. The warriors turned to look at the source of the sound and their heads craned upwards watching the vision of wings flapping in the air furiously as a horde of creatures ascended towards them. Iris stood on her tiptoes and frowned, turning to an apprentice of Lord Vincent who stood beside her with his weapons in mid-air since nobody was moving.

"What are those?" Iris asked in awe as the creatures moved closer.

The apprentice blinked once and then spoke, "Dragons."

CHAPTER FORTY

∞∞∞∞∞

SURRENDER

∞∞∞∞∞

There were five of them. They came screeching down towards the battlefield, rushing towards Lord Mikhail's army as Erasmus had instructed them to. The army fled backwards in terror. Dragons were by far the most dangerous creatures to ever exist. The flames fiercely burst out of their throats as they screamed and terrified the entire arena. Lord Lucifer's army stood there watching the destruction take place. The battle was suddenly on their side. They were winning. The dragons had been a marvellous decision. Lord Lucifer proudly acknowledged the fact that his apprentice could communicate with dragons. Then the army of Lord Lucifer stood there with bated breaths. Each one of them looked at the whole battlefield being burnt to ashes as the dragons flew from place to place and spread fire. Nearly half of Lord Mikhail's remaining army had been destroyed.

The few of them that were left had started to teleport; Lord Mikhail included. But for the most part, everyone knew that Lord Lucifer had won this battle. Lord Mikhail was not dead yet, which made things a bit complicated since they did not know where he might have gone. Lord Lucifer turned to Amara who was sitting on top of a rock and aiming her poisonous needles at enemies who were about to teleport.

The needles hit them straight the moment they disappeared. Thus, Amara secured the army from them returning, for they would be dead by the time they reached the desired place. Lord Lucifer signalled to her to go near him and she pushed the remaining needles back in the pouch at her armour, shoved her sword into its case and then walked over to her Lord.

"Go to the Sea of Cypress and see if Lord Mikhail is there," he told her in a whisper.

Amara nodded and grabbed Sienna by the arm before instantly teleporting out of the battlefield. Eridanus stood beside Iris who watched the dragons in awe as they destroyed the enemy's army to bits. They were all in flames. Erasmus had reached the battlefield by now and was heading over to Lord Lucifer when Iris's eyes fell on him. He had only just begun to open his mouth to say something to Lord Lucifer when Iris flung towards him and threw her arms around his neck in a hug. Erasmus took a stumbling step back before noticing who it was and then hugged her back. He smiled to himself.

"You're back," she whispered, pulling away from him.

She had thought that he would be weak and scarred; but his face was glowing with all the meditation in the past few weeks. She had never seen him so radiant after Nicholas's Death.

"Yes, I am, and I've missed you, little one. How have you been?" He asked her, signalling to Lord Lucifer that he would speak to him later and Lord Lucifer nodded in reply.

But the destruction caused by the dragons was now starting to spread towards their army. So before Iris could reply, Erasmus let go of her and turned to the dragons, communicating with them through his eyes. They immediately stopped. The five dragons descended to the ground and began trudging to the far end of the battlefield where they settled themselves silently. The rest of the army then produced Water and began cleansing the whole arena. Then, Erasmus turned to Iris.

"I'm okay. But how are you?" She asked him, grinning.

What she had imagined to be her first and last battle that would supposedly end in her Death, had gotten over so soon that it surprised her. Surely a battle of this intensity could not get over this easily. Yes, she had injuries this time as well but not as bad as the last. Knowing that the battle was already over and that they had won made her feel rather strange inside. An irksome sensation in her mind told her that something really bad was about to happen. She tried to push it away and rejoice about the fact that Erasmus was back and the battle was over, but the sensation refused to leave her.

"As good as I'll ever be." He smiled.

Erasmus's eyes then fell on Eridanus who stood there gliding his hands in the air to conjure Water.

"Iris," Erasmus said.

She turned to him with her eyebrows raised.

"Mind telling me why he's staring at us that way?" He said.

Iris craned her head to look where Erasmus was gesturing.

"Eridanus?" She asked.

"If that's his name. . ." Erasmus trailed off.

"He's umm-" she did not know what to call him.

In the human world they were called 'boyfriends' but in the world of Conjurers, Iris did not think a shallow word of that sort would be used.

"He's a good friend," she uttered after a moment of thought.

Erasmus raised his eyebrows in amusement.

"Really? The way he's looking at you, I can swear on mother nature he's in love," he said to her with a smirk.

Iris's cheeks flushed red.

"Just go and help the Lord, okay?" She told him, playfully pushing him away and he sauntered off with a wink in her direction.

Eridanus immediately left his work and came running to Iris.

"Was that Erasmus?" He asked.

"Yes," she replied. "Can we go and help do the work now? The battlefield looks so gruesome."

She scrunched up her face in disgust and before Eridanus could say anything else, she had limped away with her injured right leg. There were a lot dead in Lord Lucifer's army and many injured. The healers had immediately began working on the gravely injured ones while the rest of the lot who had not been hurt that badly were being healed by Soter as they began gathering the dead. Soter stood atop a huge rock, muttering spells and waving his hands in the air so as to send temporary enchantments to all the less-injured warriors. As the Conjurers cleansed the battlefield, Soter cleansed their wounds.

Eridanus started to go into the direction that Iris was treading in when a vision hit his mind and he abruptly stopped. His eyes rolled upwards and then shut as he was rushed towards the Sea of Cypress where he saw two swords clashing together in fury. Then all the sudden, his eyes opened and he was brought back to the present. Blinking, he sprinted in Lord Lucifer's direction and held his arm to get his attention. Lord Lucifer turned to him with a frown as he was busy speaking to Lady Nysa as they discussed the process of burial of the dead.

"Amara. . ." whispered Eridanus, panting. Lord Lucifer's eyes widened in panic.

"What? What about her?" He asked in a hurry.

"She's in trouble. Lord Mikhail and Amara; they're having a duel at the Sea of Cypress. She's in trouble. . ." Eridanus trailed off, swallowing the lump in his throat.

A moment later, Lord Lucifer had vanished. Noticing this, Iris walked over to Eridanus and asked him what the matter was.

"Amara," he told her. It took not a single moment for her to think of teleporting when Eridanus caught her arm.

"I can't let you go," he said to her.

"Are you mental? I have to go! She might be in trouble," she replied furiously.

"No! The Lord has gone. It's too dangerous for you to go there. The spirits that Sienna took there have turned against them. They're malignant. Something happened to Lady Calypsa. The Lord will save Amara. You can't go. You'll be hurt," he said with his hands on her shoulders as she struggled against him.

"I don't care! I'm going."

She began to push him away when Eridanus looked over at Erasmus and gave him a helpless look. If there was anyone that knew how to contain Iris, it was Erasmus. He walked over to them and Eridanus told him everything. Erasmus took Iris by the arm and pulled her towards him in a protective stance.

"Do you need to go?" He asked Eridanus.

"It would only be helpful," Eridanus replied.

"Then go. I'll take care of her," Erasmus said.

Eridanus did not wait for another word. He knew that Iris was going to be safe. She struggled against Erasmus and watched Eridanus vanish out of sight. She screamed his name but he was already gone.

"Erasmus, let me go! She'll die! Something is going to happen. I know it, I just know. Let me go help her. I have to save her. He'll kill her, he won't let her live. LET ME GO!" Iris continued to scream and throw her arms around as she struggled against his grip.

Erasmus recalled the time when Amara had set the woods on Fire. Iris had fought him in similar ways. The amount of care that Iris had for Amara was astonishing. He had never seen such a strong bond of friendship between two witches. It reminded him of his bond with Nicholas. Ignoring the jab of pain that hit his chest, Erasmus shushed Iris and pulled her away into the caves to calm her down.

* * *

Eridanus landed at the shore of the sea with a thud. He pushed himself up to standing and rushed to where the voices were coming from. There, he saw something that was worse than what he had seen in the vision. Amara and Lord Mikhail were engaged in a deadly duel. Amara's arms had various scratches on them and blood flowed down, mixing with the water of the Sea. Her gown was torn and her head was bleeding. There were all sorts of bruises and cuts on her body. Lord Mikhail, on the other hand, had lesser injuries, but all equally fatal. His abdomen had blood dripping out constantly from the flesh. His leg was bruised and it had been slashed with Amara's sword.

But even with their wounds, the both of them fought with all the power they had. Eridanus looked for Lord Lucifer who was busy trying to rescue Sienna from where she was trapped under a rock. Blood dripped out of her wounds furiously as Lord Lucifer used all his strength to push the rock away. He was weak; weaker than he had ever been. The battle, and the fact that he had to teleport to the Sea of Cypress – which was forbidden – had drained most of his energy. He had to rescue Amara as well. Eridanus rushed to Lord Lucifer's side.

"M'Lord," he said and began helping him push the rock.

Sienna's eyes were threatening to close shut but Lord Lucifer kept telling her to keep them open. She could not afford to lose consciousness at this point. It would be a hazard to her life.

"M'Lord, you need to go and protect Lady Calypsa," Eridanus said to Lord Lucifer.

"The spirits-" he began when Sienna cut him off shaking her head weakly.

"No, m'Lord, the spirits harmed me. They can't differentiate between the enemy and us. It was probably because Lord Mikhail teleported here and we did too. Lady Calypsa must-must have informed them that it is forbidden. They attacked me. I-" she sucked a breath.

Her voice was a distant whisper that Lord Lucifer and Eridanus had to strain their ears to listen. She was considerably weak. The rock was crushing her entire body.

"I battled them to remind them who I was," she croaked. "I managed to send them into the Sea so they can guard the Lady. M'Lord, the spirits won't be enough. They're weak. You have to go."

"But-" Lord Lucifer began to protest when Amara cried out in pain upon Lord Mikhail's attack. They snapped their eyes in her direction.

"M'Lord, you have to go. NOW!" Eridanus bellowed and Lord Lucifer immediately understood the gravity of the situation.

He could afford the loss of a few apprentices but not the prophecy. He immediately entered the Sea and vanished into the roaring waves while Eridanus tried his best to push the rock away from Sienna's body. He used all his might; but he was weak, too. He did not know whether it was going to be possible at all, but he was going to try. Somehow, after having struggled a lot and trying his best not to get distracted by Amara's cries, Eridanus managed to push the rock away and dragged Sienna's body out.

Amara's eyes settled on what Eridanus had done and she heaved a sigh of relief. She could now freely concentrate on battling Lord Mikhail instead of having half of her attention on rescuing Sienna. She began to fight even vigorously. Her groans of pain were echoing around the area as Lord Mikhail threw his sword that slashed away at her skin. But Amara left no stone unturned in harming her opponent either. She struck blows on his injured areas that weakened him more than anything else.

"You need to go back to the battlefield caves," said Eridanus, looking at Sienna's injuries. She shook her head in reply.

"No," she said, her voice breaking.

"Amara. . .she needs help. Do something, I'll take care of myself," she told him.

"I can't leave you like this," Eridanus replied.

"If anything happens to Amara," she croaked, "Lord Mikhail will destroy everything. Go help her, please," she pleaded and Eridanus seemed to hesitate for a while before lifting Sienna and placing her body – away from Lord Mikhail and Amara – on top of the soft, dry sand. She lay there with her hand on her forehead to stop the bleeding. Her eyes were beginning to close.

"Whatever happens, Sienna, do not sleep, no matter what. Please," Eridanus told her sternly and Sienna nodded in response.

Her eyes were getting heavier by the minute and she did not have strength enough to control it. He looked at her for a moment before he heard Amara's cry of pain and turned around to go help her. She was on the ground, holding her leg that had been slashed by Lord Mikhail's sword. Blood furiously dripped out of the wound and Eridanus rushed towards her. Lord Mikhail had now started to walk towards the Sea to dive into it when Amara looked in his direction with bloodshot eyes and he was suddenly thrown back to the ground. She dropped her sword and shut her eyes while Lord Mikhail struggled to get up. Amara wasn't the only weak one.

Eridanus put his hand on Amara's injured knee to stop the blood when a blazing Fire began to rush towards Lord Mikhail. Eridanus helped Amara up so she was sitting and he kept his arm around her shoulder for support. Lord Mikhail glanced at the Fire that was nearing him, his eyes widened and he immediately turned to look at the Sea. The water ascended up in a huge wave and fled towards the Fire before consuming it whole. It then retreated into the Sea. Lord Mikhail stood up, his hand on his abdomen. He staggered towards Amara who was glaring at him ferociously. Eridanus started to pick up Amara's sword to attack Lord Mikhail when she held his hand to stop him. Her eyes were still stuck on Lord Mikhail.

"Let's have a duel of the elements, great witch," he spat, chuckling menacingly in the end. "You give me your Fire and water, I'll reply with my Fire and wind," he finished.

Amara pushed herself up to standing, nudging Eridanus away.

"If you're willing to fight and let the Lord take the prophecy away to safety, I'm willing to keep you at bay," she told him hoarsely.

Her eyes were starting to droop a bit due to the weakness. Eridanus had noticed that she was burning with fever; but he dared not utter a sound.

"Do you think I'm that big a fool? I have an ally down in the Sea that is successfully getting the prophecy to me. All I have to do is kill you. You're a big hindrance, you know that? I sent witch-hunters, you kill them all. I send Conjurers to take away your powers, you defeat them. I try to find out what the prophecy holds; you don't let me. But with you gone, I will get everything I need. So fight with me. Fight until either of us falls dead."

Amara stared at Lord Mikhail as he said those words. If it was really a fight to the Death, she did not care or mind, for it meant protecting the prophecy. She could not lose. And if she did, maybe her Death would be worth it and Lord Lucifer would guard the prophecy even better than she had done. So Amara turned to Eridanus and said, "Go into the Sea, and help the Lord."

Eridanus immediately shook his head. "The Lord is capable enough of handling himself. He isn't injured. I need to stay here with you to help you fight," he said.

"No!" She hissed. "This is a duel. That is the reason the Lord couldn't help me. If a Conjurer has been challenged for a duel, he/she cannot take help from anybody. I can take care of this. You have to go," she told him with austerity.

Of course, Eridanus was aware about the rules of a duel. She was right. There was no point in him staying there. So he left, taking one last glance at Sienna who would take no time in falling unconscious. For a moment, he considered helping Sienna but he knew it would do no good. Without further ado, he reluctantly advanced into the Sea. Amara turned back to Lord Mikhail who stood at a distance for the elemental duel to begin.

Sienna watched as the lights began to dance before her in the night. The moon shone above them in all its glory, the Sea drenched into complete darkness. As the Fire began to ignite from Amara's fingers and rush towards Lord Mikhail, Sienna's eyes threateningly closed shut. Then the duel began. Amara threw the flames in Lord Mikhail's direction; they rushed towards him vigorously. Lord Mikhail responded by his own flame in Amara's direction. The two Fires clashed together creating a horrific song that set the shore aflame. The flames roared like a lion ready to pounce and morphed into one as well. Amara immediately looked at the water before the flames threatened to engulf her. She had only one strategy in mind: *If I die, he dies along.*

With that in mind, she raised her hands in direction of the water and it rose above, drenching both of them into the waves. Amara was thrown back to the shore and so was Lord Mikhail after the Fire had been extinguished. She again made the water rise and morph into the face of a dragon. It scuttled towards Lord Mikhail and was about to pull him in when he used all his force to make the winds whirl around him as a protection. The water dragon could not break the shield and retreated into the sea. Amara then looked at the sand beneath her feet. Even though she was not as strong with the element of Earth, she knew that there was at least something that she could do. After all, she had been taught to handle all the elements. It was only that she was better at Fire and Water.

So she glanced downwards and shut her eyes for a moment in a silent plea for help, before her eyes darted to the tree that was at a distance, following the woods behind the shore of the Sea. With her eyes focussed on the roots of the tree, she struggled with her mind to make it move. Meanwhile, Lord Mikhail watched Amara in silence. He was not sure exactly what she was doing. The problem with someone handling the element of Earth was that the opponent did not know what the attack would be. Earth offered a lot of weapons: mud, sand, trees, rocks . . . everything that had its roots in the surface of the earth. Before he could make up his mind and contemplate what was happening, a tree was throwing itself in his direction and Lord Mikhail panicked. He could not think of a weapon to help him. So he began to run. Amara watched him rush towards the Sea and smiled maliciously at his defeat.

But a moment later it hit her. The elemental duel was supposed to be a fight to the Death; but Lord Mikhail had deliberately tricked her. He had entered the sea; and he was going to get the prophecy. Everyone knew that there was nothing that had enough nerve to attack the dwelling area of

Lady Calypsa. The tree that Amara had used to attack him would not follow Lord Mikhail there. And if he got lost inside the enormous Sea, she would never be able to find him. So when he nearly vanished into the waves, Amara dashed into the Sea and began to swim ahead to look for him. It wasn't easy at all. Her ribs were hurt, her head was bleeding still, and her leg did not give much help due to the wound. She struggled to swim against the strong waves that threatened to drown her any moment. The roaring waves kept pushing her back while she tried to dodge them with all her will. The Gods only knew in what direction Lord Mikhail might have gone.

She pushed the waves back with her arms and shut her eyes, connecting her mind to Lord Mikhail's. It was a risk. If she had to find Lord Mikhail, she needed to locate his mind. However, it was shielded. It had quite a lot of protection around and breaching through it would be a risk, for if anyone did that, they might as well go insane. It was known that attempting to enter a shielded mind was the highest risk ever. There was that little chance of detection. But Amara knew that the shield wasn't as strong at the moment. Lord Mikhail was certainly looking for a way to reach the prophecy. If she connected both their minds, he would not know because his entire concentration lay on the prophecy. Besides, the injuries had made him physically as well as mentally weak.

Amara's mind dashed towards Lord Mikhail's as she swam ahead. She immediately found him hovering around the cave that held the prophecy and the treasures. Pulling her mind back, she began to swim towards the cave with all her might. It was by far the most difficult thing that she had ever done. Swimming through the vast Sea while she had various injuries was something that she never looked forward to. She could not even make a sound. Her throat had constricted and for the life of her, she could not muster up a single sound to utter.

The pain that coasted up her body was blinding her as every moment passed.

She thought of Azrael. He had once accompanied her while they were going to listen to the prophecy for the first time. Had he not informed Lord Mikhail about everything? Being the messenger it was quite acceptable for him to have revealed the entire prophecy – with the riddles – to Lord Mikhail. Then why was Lord Mikhail seeking for the prophecy? Why did he not just aim for the treasures? Was there a chance that Azrael had not informed Lord Mikhail about this?

She continued to swim trying to numb the pain away but as the salty water brushed her wounds, it got even worse. She found it difficult to breathe as she battled against the waves that were engulfing her in. Her weakness made it no better. She was losing strength. Amara neared the cave where she spotted Lord Mikhail lingering over. Before she could dash in his direction, the cave's doors were opened and he swam inside only to vanish once again. Wincing as the water burnt her wounds, she quickly swam towards the cave but her arms seemed to give away. It took much longer than she had imagined for her to reach the door of the cave. The chains were lying on the sea-bed in a cluster along with the locks. Amara slowly began to venture inside.

Mercifully, the water did not follow her in since Lady Calypsa had enchanted the cave in a way that no water entered in through the door. Amara stepped foot on the dry ground of the cave. She shut the door, pulling it forcefully by using all her strength. She cursed herself for being weak enough as she was unable to shut a door easily. But what could she possibly have done? She was no healer; her injuries were fatal and she felt herself starting to fall unconscious even though she knew that she was strong enough to handle it all. But her eyes were heavy and the shattering pain in her body was starting to make her weaker by the minute. It would take no time for her to fall to the floor, unconscious.

Amara settled a hand on the wall and began to push herself ahead, fast as her legs carried her. She limped forward only to drop to the floor, hitting her head on the wall where it was wounded. She groaned in pain, her eyes shut themselves on their own accord. Pushing herself up to standing again, she walked further into the cave, hoping that she would find Lord Lucifer, Eridanus and Lord Mikhail. She wondered who it was that had opened the door of the cave for Lord Mikhail to enter. Azrael was under imprisonment, the rest of Lord Mikhail's army had been destroyed and any of those who were alive, were not exactly equipped enough to even stand in the presence of the Sea of Cypress. With a constant worry as to who it could be, Amara stumbled ahead into the cave.

She heard not a single sound coming from inside. Her vision was getting blurry; her head pounding with unbearable pain and she held the wall for support. It took longer than necessary to reach the opening after the passage in the cave. There she saw Eridanus lying on the floor, unconscious. Lord Lucifer was nowhere to be seen, and Lord Mikhail stood in a corner, Lady Calypsa trapped in ropes on the floor. Amara blinked to adjust her vision. She had to widen her eyes more than necessary to see what was going on. Her entire vision was starting to get foggier by the minute and she struggled to keep it straight as she took small steps ahead.

Amara opened her mouth to tell Lord Mikhail something but no sound came. Her voice was a whisper of syllables that she could not seem to understand. Lord Mikhail had still not noticed her presence. He was looming over Lady Calypsa who seemed unwilling to answer to his questions. Amara strained her ears to listen to what he was saying.

"Tell me where the prophecy is!" He screamed terribly.

His voice was inevitably hoarse and weak, Amara noticed. He looked exhausted and in a lot of pain, but Amara's condition was worse than his. He was not as affected by it. His anger and rage to find what he needed kept him strong enough to keep standing while Amara had descended to the ground, unable to stand anymore. She fought to keep her eyes open. This was not the time to let them engulf her into a sleep; a sleep that she so desired. Her mind began to signal her to let the eyes droop shut but she refused to give in. She had to save Lady Calypsa. She had to save the prophecy. She had to stop Lord Mikhail.

"Where have you hidden it? TELL ME!" He screeched yet again and the sound made Amara's ears cringe in pain.

She wanted him to shut up. But he seemed to be in fury. Lady Calypsa refused to respond to his questions and he was getting impatient by the minute.

"I have sworn to protect it. A sworn guardian will never let an intruder lay hands on what she protects," she told him in her deep-set voice.

Amara let out a sigh of relief. The prophecy was safe. Maybe Lord Mikhail would be unable to get to it. Lady Calypsa would never let that happen. And there was no one known to have ever manipulated the Lady into doing anything. If she had sworn to something, she would never reveal it to someone not entitled for it. But she also knew that apart from Lord Lucifer, only Lord Mikhail was powerful enough to defeat Lady Calypsa. Dreading the outcome, Amara stood up to fight Lord Mikhail one more time but there was no strength left in her. She barely managed to keep standing on her shivering legs. Lady Calypsa turned her head to find Amara standing at a distance behind Lord Mikhail.

"The saviour is here, Lord Mikhail. I don't suppose that she will let you find what you so dearly seek," she told Lord

Mikhail who whipped his head around to find Amara standing there with her body leaning onto the wall beside her.

She pushed herself forward and blinked numerous times to keep her eyes open. Her legs were weakening and she stumbled on her feet. It was hard to keep herself steady.

"She's weak. There is nothing she can do," said Lord Mikhail with a menacing laugh before turning back to Lady Calypsa.

"Do not dream of achieving what you never can. Your strength does not match that of the prophecy's. It is strong enough to destroy you. You have no control over it. Do not attempt to seize that which does not belong to you, m'Lord," Lady Calypsa said.

Lord Mikhail muttered a paralyzing curse, which rendered the Lady unconscious in moments. Although nobody was known to have manipulated her mind, it did not take time for someone like Lord Mikhail to disarm her. He was aware of his power over her.

The spirits were around but they could not fathom enough courage to protect the Lady. Lord Lucifer was gone and there was no strong protection. Amara suddenly feared the worst. Lord Mikhail was closer to the prophecy than he had ever been. Although Lady Calypsa had been rendered unconscious, there was still a chance that she had the treasures and the prophecy protected.

Her instincts, however, suggested otherwise. Something bad was going to happen. Amara could sense it through every nerve in her body. Lord Mikhail now decided to look for the prophecy in the cave. According to what Leandra had told him, the prophecy was supposed to be somewhere in the cave. There was nothing but walls around. Exactly where the prophecy would be hidden, he did not know. Leandra was away battling Lord Lucifer with the help of Noctia Stella, who had now gotten what she needed. Noctia Stella's ardent desire for a tool to practice all sorts of black magic was Lord Lucifer. Choosing a strong sorcerer like him was a challenge to her. Noctia Stella feasted on challenges.

But Lord Mikhail did not care what the *Mortuis* wanted. All he had been told by Leandra was that she could battle Lord Lucifer and destroy him. Lord Mikhail merely had to find the prophecy and listen to what it held. He hoped – for the life of him – he hoped that it was something worth all the effort. He needed those three treasures that the prophecy so spoke of, after what Leandra had informed him. He was yet to know what the treasures actually were. As he looked around the cave to find some source of getting the hidden globe of prophecy, Amara pulled out her poisonous needles to throw them in his direction. But she could not aim properly. The needle bounced off his arm, just managing to pierce his skin. There was no desired effect. Lord Mikhail turned towards her viciously.

He walked over to her and pushed her to the ground by her shoulder and scooted down to hold her throat in his fingers. Amara's mouth flew open to breathe. She gasped for air as Lord Mikhail leaned closer to her.

"Do not attempt to attack me. You're weak. You have no strength to battle me. Let yourself die, because I do not have time to kill you," he told her and let go of her throat, only to stand up and start looking for the prophecy again.

Amara's hands touched the part of her throat that had been held in such a tight grip. The pain began to blind her of all sight and she let out an inaudible cry of pain. There was still no sound that left her lips. A tear fell down her eyes as she battled the pain hard as she could.

It scared her. She lifted her eyes to see what Lord Mikhail was doing. He was lingering around a wall, glaring at it with narrowed eyes. Raising his hand he traced his fingers along its surface. He felt a strange lump over it. The walls of the cave were not smooth; they were quite harsh and had all sorts of lumps. But this one seemed odd. It was smoother than the rest of the surface. Lord Mikhail squinted his eyes and then placed his ear on the wall, for he heard a distant sound. There were whispering noises as he listened. Blinking, Lord Mikhail immediately began to look for something to break the lump. It was obviously a false one. Finding no weapon to help him, he conjured up Fire and let it ignite the wall.

Moments later, the lump shattered and fell to the floor. There was a passage that led inside. Lord Mikhail frowned in confusion and entered the passage. Amara shut her eyes at the pain that went through her body as she tried to sit up. She was unable to stand and settled for crawling instead. She pushed her body in the direction where Lord Mikhail had gone. She could not see him anymore and the Fire was starting to spread everywhere. Amara crawled forward, passing Lady Calypsa that lay paralyzed beside her. Upon reaching the passage, Amara pushed herself inside, wincing as the pain hit her harder and harder as she proceeded.

The passage was a short one. She was unaware of it. The last time she had been in this cave, the prophecy was right outside and there was no passage that she saw. Amara kept pushing her body ahead to where the passage led her. She reached a clearing where three more passages emerged. The passage that stood right before her was illuminated by a faint glow. She heard sounds coming from inside. The entire cave was silent apart from the roaring Fire that was starting to enter through the passage. Amara hoped that it would not burn her to Death before she reached to where Lord Mikhail was. She crawled ahead into the passage and found him staring at the familiar sphere of prophecy that hung in the air, surrounded by coloured wisps of smoke.

She pushed herself ahead and began to slither in Lord Mikhail's direction to save the prophecy when she saw a triumphant grin cover his features. He peered into the sphere only to hear the prophecy echo in his ears. Amara heard the familiar poetry that she had once heard. She kept pushing herself towards Lord Mikhail in a bid to somehow get him away from the prophecy. But it was too late. The Fire had entered into the passage and was now spreading around, shattering a side of the wall, which produced a clinging sound. Amara's head whipped in that direction.

There she spotted the tall vial that had been talked of in the prophecy. Her mind went back to the time that she had sat under a tree with Azrael in the woods – when they had talked all night.

* * *

"Do you know the legend of the Cymmerien Dragon?" He had asked her.

She had replied with a shake of her head. She had not known then.

"Years ago during the time of King Abraham the First, Cymmerien Dragons were endangered since the attacks of witch-hunters had increased," Azrael began. "The blood of Cymmerien Dragons was known to be the deadliest poison there ever was and Conjurers used it to destroy witch-hunters. When powerful witch-hunters realized that Cymmerien Dragons were a threat, they began destroying those creatures. Nearly all of them were killed but one remained. One, strongest and the most sought-after Dragon that was found by Lord Hermys at the Sea of Cypress. He fought the Dragon to extract it's blood and a fierce battle took place.

"Lord Hermys, being the valiant sorcerer that he was, fought bravely and in his injured state, ended up pushing the Dragon

towards the deadly waters of the Sea of Cypress and the droplets of it's blood fell into the water. The blood began to poison the Sea and Lady Calypsa began to suffocate. She realized that the Sea was poisoned. Lady Calypsa's mentor, Goddess Salacia came to her rescue and gathered the blood that had fallen into the Sea, in a vial that she sealed and handed to Lady Calypsa. But during the process of gathering the blood, its smell entered Lady Salacia's senses and she weakened, leading to her death.

"Lady Calypsa, enraged at her mentor being dead, cursed the blood of the Cymmerien Dragon, which is why the prophecy states that a loved one has to be slain."

* * *

Amara watched the tall vial gently sloping across the floor of the cave. She realized how glorious the first treasure really was. It was beautiful to look at. Inside the translucent vial, the breathtaking red poison glittered amidst the flames and Amara stared at it, at a loss of words and movements. When she snapped back into her senses, she realized that the sound of the prophecy had ended and Lord Mikhail's eyes had trailed towards the vial that lay on the floor before him at a distance. Amara began to push herself in the direction of the vial before Lord Mikhail reached it, but he was faster. The sphere of the prophecy dropped from his hands, clattering on the floor and sauntering towards Amara. Lord Mikhail slowly but steadily bent low to reach the vial.

His fingers held the tall vial gently and the cold sensation made him shut his eyes in content. A victorious grin took over his features, even when the Fire was increasing the heat in the cave. He clenched and unclenched his fingers around it, cherishing the feel of it on his skin. The feeling of holding a treasure between his fingers was ecstatic. It filled him with euphoria, and Lord Mikhail never wanted to forget that moment. His eyes shot open as he held the glorious, shimmering vial in his hands and his vicious grin widened more than ever.

Amara's eyes held a foggy vision. She blinked and heard the footsteps of Lord Mikhail leaving the passage. She gasped as pain struck her one more time and she became weaker. For a small moment, her eyes opened wide enough to see Lord Mikhail making his way to exit the passage and then the cave. That was all Amara saw before she dropped to the floor with the sphere beside her waist, and her eyes fluttered shut amidst the flames trembling before her now closed eyes.